HAVERING
CALLPOINT DIRECT

S0-BFC-113

GIDEA PARK

09. FEB	27. OCT 08.	
20. MAR 07.		
	15. NOV 08.	
3. APR 07.	21. FEB 09.	
	02. JUN 09	
08. MAY 07.	23 Jun K	
23. JUL 07.		
16. AUG 07		
10. SEP 07.		
24. SEP 07.		
20. OCT 97.		
25. APR 08.		
17. JUL 08.		
08. 8 AUG 08.		
18. OCT 08		

LIB187

1017877455

Also by Chris Collett

The Worm in the Bud
Blood of the Innocents

Written in Blood

Chris Collett

PIATKUS

ஃ Visit the Piatkus website!

Piatkus publishes a wide range of bestselling fiction and non-fiction, including books on health, mind, body & spirit, sex, self-help, cookery, biography and the paranormal.

If you want to:
- read descriptions of our popular titles
- buy our books over the internet
- take advantage of our special offers
- enter our monthly competition
- learn more about your favourite Piatkus authors

VISIT OUR WEBSITE AT: www.piatkus.co.uk

All the characters in this book are fictitious and any resemblance to real persons, living or dead, is entirely coincidental.

Copyright © Chris Collett 2006

First published in Great Britain in 2006 by
Piatkus Books Ltd of
5 Windmill Street, London W1T 2JA
email: info@piatkus.co.uk

Short extract from A.E. Houseman's *No. 12*, 'Last Poems', is quoted with kind permission by the Society of Authors who are the literary representatives of the Houseman estate.

The moral right of the author has been asserted

A catalogue record for this book is available from the British Library

ISBN 0 7499 3714 9

Set in Times by
Action Publishing Technology Ltd, Gloucester

Printed and bound in Great Britain by
Mackays Ltd, Chatham, Kent

And how am I to face the odds
Of man's bedevilment and God's
I, a stranger and afraid
In a world I never made.

AE Housman, Last Poems (1922) no. 12.

London Borough of Havering	
101 7877456	
Askews	
	£6.99
GIDEA PARK	

Chapter One

Chugging along through the dense, dark early morning, Tim Leavis was counting off the days. It was less than a week now to the winter solstice, when they'd begin to lengthen again. Much as he liked his life, he'd never got used to these early winter starts, and this one was earlier than most, allowing him to feed the animals but still get back for a shower and breakfast before driving across to the village school in time to see Archie perform in the nativity play. The boy had been typecast as a shepherd of course, though Leavis's description of the likely effects on the animal's bodily functions had, at least, dissuaded Mrs Elliot from her romantic idea of having his son carry a live lamb.

Passing a local beauty spot, the powerful beams of the John Deere's headlights picked up a small creature scuttling across the road, before rebounding back at Leavis off something shiny, the radiator grill of a car parked in the lay-by. As far as he could tell, it was a big car, black, though Leavis didn't immediately recognize the make. Someone else making an early start or, more likely, returning very late from some pre-Christmas revelry. The driver's door hung open and Leavis smiled to himself. Not the first motorist to use the woods as a convenient convenience. Better be quick, mate. Cold enough this morning to freeze off your tadger.

But on his return journey twenty minutes later, after

depositing the hay in the sheep field, the vehicle was still there. Coming up behind the car this time, Leavis could see that the boot was also open and that the driver was crouching on the road behind the vehicle, peering underneath. Exhaust problems perhaps. Hoping that it wouldn't take long, Leavis pulled his tractor into the lay-by to offer assistance, and that was when he realised that the figure wasn't so much crouching as lying inanimate on the frozen ground, and suddenly it was not only the air that felt chill.

In the dark, the SOCO almost missed it. The arc lights that had been brought in were trained on the man and woman in the rear passenger seat of the limousine, their posture so natural they could have been calmly waiting for their driver to return so that they could continue their journey. As long as you didn't look at their faces and the identical black holes that had ripped apart each forehead, spraying grey fleshy pebble-dashing across the rear windshield behind them. It was a minimalist job; a high-powered weapon fired at point-blank range, one shot apiece. The victims would have had mere seconds to understand what was happening. And the assassin had, at first examination, left nothing behind; no stray prints, hairs or fibres evident at this stage, though the car would get a comprehensive going over once it was back at the lab. Fortunately, the farmer who'd discovered the gruesome scene had seen enough detective shows to know that he shouldn't touch anything. Colleagues working around the third dead body sprawled on the road beside the gaping trunk were having more luck. Underneath the boot lining in the spare wheel compartment they'd found traces of a white powdery residue.

Edging out of the vehicle the SOCO made one last sweep with his Maglite and caught a momentary glimpse of something, the intense glare of the spotlights partially veiling the semi-transparent letters, which were scribed on the glass of the side passenger window in a reddish brown hue, the author using what raw materials were at hand. Every third

2

one of the twenty-five letters was bolder than the others, the index finger dipped into its bloody inkwell at even intervals until the message was complete.

'Ma'am,' the SOCO ducked his head out and addressed the woman waiting patiently beside the car in the chill air, 'they've left us a message.'

Chief Superintendent Caroline Griffin stepped forward, taking gloved hands from the pockets of her long wool coat. She leaned into the car as the SOCO moved his beam along the communication: *Vengeance is mine. I will repay.*

'Not particularly subtle,' she remarked.

'Or original,' added the SOCO.

But, put together with the rest of the scene, it began to paint a picture.

21st December

There was a first time for everything; Mariner humming along to Slade singing 'Merry Christmas Everybody'. Normally the song made him cringe, but this year apparently signalled a shift in his tolerance levels. Dylan's 'The Times They Are A-Changin'' would have been more appropriate. Christmas shopping wasn't something Mariner did, but here he was doing it, on his own, completely unprovoked and in grave danger of looking like a New Man. It was mostly illusion though. Mariner's underlying motive was rooted in the hope that an hour of exposing his senses to the garishness of Christmas might help him to shake off the image that had stayed with him since early this morning when he'd stood knee deep in an underground sewer, watching a police constable cut open a bound bin liner to reveal the decaying body of a woman.

So far his strategy hadn't been wholly successful, but he had another fifteen minutes before he was due to meet Anna and the others, and another fifteen minutes to distance himself. In Waterstone's the atmosphere was calmer, the background chamber music a notch more sophisticated, but nonetheless contrived, along with the aroma of real coffee,

3

to soothe him into parting with some of his hard-earned, and for a while Colombian medium roast vied with the smell of raw waste that lingered in his nostrils.

Like everywhere else in the Bullring, this afternoon the shop was excessively warm and he sweltered in his overcoat. Another rule broken, overcoats weren't his style, but Anna had persuaded him into one last winter and today it had come into its own; keeping him warm and concealing the uniform underneath. He strolled around scanning the three-for-two bestseller tables, loitering over the latest wave of women's fiction that Anna was so partial to, featuring as it did, feisty, independent, spirited females. This year she'd probably have preferred a volume from the health section, under pregnancy planning and parents-to-be, but somehow Mariner couldn't quite bring himself to move towards that corner of the shop. Instead he picked up a couple of what looked like the most popular of the current chick-lit titles with their ubiquitous fluorescent cartoon covers, and took them over to the counter.

The checkout queue was long, the customers ahead of him apparently starting up their own private libraries, and for some time Mariner found himself standing beside a stack of glossy hardbacks, the early memoirs of former MP Sir Geoffrey Ryland. No prizes for guessing the reason for their prominence today, just a week after Ryland had met a violent end, ambushed and shot dead in his car on a quiet Oxfordshire lane. Mariner absently picked up a copy and skimmed the jacket. *One of the Good Guys*. Not, on the face of it, an attention-grabbing title, even though it might be true. Joe Public didn't want to read about politicians who'd done the job well, they wanted the scandal, like Alan Clark's love affairs. Sales of Bill Clinton's autobiography had gone through the roof; everyone wanting to know the sordid truth about Monica Lewinsky and that dress.

The flyleaf told Mariner little more than he already knew, tracing Ryland's professional life as a human rights lawyer in the 1960s to the natural progression into politics as an MP for an inner city London borough. A specialist in miscarriages of justice at a time when they were rife, he'd given up his parliamentary seat to chair one of the government's most prized flagship institutions, the Judicial Review Commission, the job for which Ryland had received his knighthood. According to the news reports Ryland had died at the age of sixty-eight, no age at all. Only the good die young.

'You taking that one too?' The paperbacks were removed from his grasp and Mariner looked up to see that he'd reached the head of the queue, to be greeted by a sales girl name-tagged Nikki. 'We were all set to send them back to the warehouse,' she told him. 'But they're practically walking off the shelves now. You wouldn't believe what a sudden death can do for a writer.'

'Or a musician,' her friend chipped in from the neighbouring till. 'When John Lennon got shot "Imagine" went straight to number one.'

'Turned James Dean into a legend overnight,' agreed Mariner. They both looked at him blankly. 'The film actor?' he elaborated. '*Rebel Without a Cause*?'

'Oh yeah,' Nikki's friend said vaguely. 'I think I've heard of him.'

'So, are you taking it?' Nikki returned to her hard sell. 'Might be a good present for someone.'

A year ago it would have been perfect. Had his mother still been alive Mariner would have bought it for her. Ryland was one of a group of charismatic social reformers of her generation who, alongside Bruce Kent and Nelson Mandela, she'd idolised. In fact that's just how she'd have described all three: *the good guys*.

'Go on then.' Mariner put the book down on the counter.

'Good for you,' Nikki grinned. 'You won't regret it.'

'I should hope not.'

'You've even got an autographed one.' She flipped open the cover displaying an illegible scrawl. 'He came in for a signing in November and we had some left over.'

'So you met Ryland?' Mariner pulled his credit card from his wallet.

'Yes.'

'And did you think he was?' Mariner asked, as they waited for the transaction to process.

The girl had a great line in vacant expressions. 'Was what?'

'One of the good guys.'

She shrugged. 'He was very nice. And his driver seemed to think a lot of him. He came out back for a fag. Ryland had got him out of prison, so he thought the old man was a hero.'

Mariner considered what he'd read about the recent shooting. Word was that the killings were down to the driver. Not a nice way to repay your hero.

Taking the bulging plastic carrier from the girl called Nikki, and feeling slightly as if he'd been conned, Mariner stepped away from the counter. A tingling sensation crept the length of his spine. Someone walking over his grave, except it was too warm for that. It was a feeling that he was being watched. He'd experienced the same phenomenon several times during the last few weeks, though he'd told no one about it. They'd have suggested therapy. He turned and looked around the shop. The handful of other customers either had their noses buried in books or were studying the shelves intently. He'd caught no one out. He put the feeling down to being tired. It was a long time since he'd had a holiday.

Mariner had arranged to meet Anna, along with DC Tony Knox, at the visiting Frankfurt market, and picked up the tail end of the colourful stalls on New Street. As he progressed deeper into the market the ambience subtly changed, the hard-nosed consumerism of the department stores giving way to a mellower side of Christmas. Under less pressure to buy, shoppers browsed the pastry and pottery stalls exchanging pleasantries, and the easy banter between the vendors created an atmosphere of genuine goodwill. This year there had been a clumsy effort by some local councillors to replace the market with a more patriotic English version but somehow Mariner couldn't imagine hot dogs and burgers creating the same illusion. If he could only forget what he'd been doing all day.

The busiest stands were those grouped below the steps of the museum and art gallery, and offering a range of exotic refreshments. It was here that Mariner spied Tony Knox, beneath one of the food bar parasols, his arms wrapped round a woman; the latest girlfriend they'd heard so much about. Selina, if his recall was accurate. There had been so many now since Knox's wife had left him that Mariner couldn't be sure. The pulling power of the middle-aged divorcé remained one of life's mysteries.

'All right, Boss?' Knox asked as Mariner arrived at his side. The two men shook hands and Knox disentangled himself. 'This is Selina,' he said without ceremony. 'Selina: DI Tom Mariner.'

First impressions were that this girl's model good looks carbon copied her predecessors; Knox continuing his quest for the antithesis to his ex. Slim and leggy in jeans and sheepskin bomber jacket, Selina's hair was pinned up in an explosion of lethal blond spikes, and the total look was straight off a page of the glossies. But the smile, it was pure mischief. 'The boss,' she grinned, one perfectly shaped eyebrow arching. 'I've heard all about *you*.' The stress on that last word implied that it was rather more than Mariner would have liked, but at the same time he couldn't help warming to Selina.

'You too,' he said, automatically. 'Tony said you're an accountant?' As the snippet of information came back to him Mariner struggled momentarily to square the image with the occupation.

'For my sins,' Selina said, reading his face. 'We're not all fat and balding in a suit, you know.'

'So I see.'

'She's also a Blues supporter,' Knox put in. 'So I wouldn't go getting too friendly.'

'Nobody's perfect,' Mariner conceded, with a shrug.

Knox passed him a mug of steaming *Glühwein*. 'Dutch courage,' he said. 'Or should that be German courage? I thought you might need it.' He raised his own mug, slipping an arm around Selina and drawing her closer. '*Prost.*'

'*Prost.*'

'*Prost.*' The mugs clinked together. 'As long as I don't end up slurring my words,' said Mariner. 'Might not look good.' But at the same time he was trying to ignore the growing flutter of butterfly wings in his stomach. Standing up in front of the Chief Constable and other luminaries, along with a hundred or so of his colleagues, wasn't something he was often asked to do, even if tonight he would only be reading from 'The Gospel According to St Luke'.

It said something for the heathens at the Granville Lane OCU that it was Mariner, lifelong agnostic, who was representing them by doing a reading at the force carol service, though his participation came only as a result of having his arm twisted up his back by Jack Coleman. 'It shouldn't even be me who's doing it,' he grumbled, with feeling. 'The job should have gone to a good Catholic boy.'

'Lapsed Catholic,' Knox reminded him. 'And I was never a contender. The Brummie masses wouldn't understand a word I said.' And to demonstrate, he thickened his scouse accent to a series of gutteral spasms.

They heard Anna before they saw her, cheerfully apologising her way through what was becoming a tightly packed crowd. The soft light accentuated the paleness of her skin and brought out the copper tones of her shoulder- length hair. Watching her progress, eliciting smiles and good-natured teasing from those around her, Mariner was reminded what a lucky bugger he was. He'd been feeling pretty virtuous about his purchases, but Anna appeared to have bought out Toys 'R' Us single handed.

'Doing your bit for the national economy?' Knox joked, relieving her of two enormous carrier bags and stacking them out of the way. 'I'll get you a drink.'

'Thanks, Tony.' Stretching up, Anna planted a kiss on Mariner. 'It's just a few bits and pieces.'

'Can't guess who they're for,' Mariner said.

'Tony didn't tell me you had children,' Selina said.

'Anna, this is Selina.' Mariner took his cue.

'Hi.' Anna mirrored the smile. 'We haven't yet, but sometime soon.'

Her words triggered a bubble of anxiety in Mariner's stomach. He wished she wouldn't talk as if it were a done deal, when they'd only just started thinking about the pros and cons. It was a big shift for both of them and he, at least, was still getting used to the idea.

When he'd first met her, kids were the last thing Anna wanted; she had a successful career and a severely autistic brother, a combination guaranteed to dampen the strongest maternal instincts. But during the last year events had conspired to change her mind. Two months ago Jamie had moved into a hostel for independent living, and was doing just that, leaving Anna with time and energy on her hands. Concurrently, Anna's best friend Becky had produced baby daughter Megan, waking Anna to the fact that time might for her be running out, and from then on babies had insidiously crept into everyday conversation. Gradually, without lengthy overt discussion, children had moved from being out of the question, to a possibility and more recently a probability.

For his own part, Mariner had never been so much opposed to children as ignorant of them. His mother, his only close blood relative, had passed away last year, leaving him practically alone in the world, but for a few distant cousins he'd never met. He and Anna had something good together, so in many ways children seemed like the next natural step. It was only after he'd agreed to consider it that the doubts had begun, and Anna had been so euphoric these last few weeks that now he couldn't bear to spoil it for her.

'You're jumping the gun,' he cautioned. 'We haven't had

the appointment through yet.'

Anna caught Selina's expression. 'My brother is autistic,' she explained. 'So we're being referred to a counsellor.' It had been Mariner's suggestion, partly to test out how serious she was. 'There are known genetic links so there's always the chance that our child could have a degree of autism.'

'Better to be safe,' Selina agreed.

'Not that it'll make a scrap of difference,' Mariner said. 'Once Anna's made up her mind about something—'

'We'd need to be prepared for what might happen,' Anna said, dodging the issue. 'Meanwhile the gifts are for my goddaughter, Megan. She's my substitute child, and it's her first Christmas so she has to be spoilt rotten.'

'How old is she?'

'Four months, and I just can't get enough of her.'

'Well, I can't recommend it too highly,' Selina enthused. 'I've got a three-month-old.'

Anna must have been as floored as Mariner, because suddenly they were in the midst of an awkward silence. Knox hadn't mentioned this. His own kids were adults themselves now, and he'd always expressed huge relief that he'd put the nappy-changing and the sleepless nights behind him long ago. And what kind of woman leaves her three-month-old baby at home to go out dating?

Selina laughed, a brilliant peal of uninhibited joy. 'You should see your faces,' she giggled. 'You can relax. My baby's of the canine variety,' she said. 'A chocolate Labrador is something less of a commitment.' So she had a sense of humour, too.

'You must still have your hands full,' said Anna, as Knox returned and passed round fresh drinks.

'I have to admit life will be easier once he's stopped piddling on the floor and chewing my tights.'

'She didn't mean Tony, she meant the puppy,' shot back Mariner.

Selina shook her head sadly. 'I know, but the dog's very

impressionable. It copies everything he does.'

'Hilarious.' Knox didn't share their amusement. 'You two should try a spot at the Glee Club.'

Mariner and Selina exchanged a complicit smile. This was going to be fun. Not since his separation had Tony Knox been out with someone Mariner could so instantly relate to.

After the warming drinks, they queued for burgers with herb-fried potatoes, finding themselves a quiet corner to eat from the flimsy paper plates. The food smelt and tasted delicious but somehow the image – brown, moist and indistinct – deadened Mariner's appetite.

Knox saw the hesitation. 'Brings back memories, does it, Boss?' he asked. 'Charlie Glover told me you'd been knee deep in shit all morning.'

'Thanks,' said Mariner, throwing Selina and Anna an apologetic look. 'One of life's less pleasurable experiences.' Mariner put down his plate untouched.

'You not eating that?' asked Knox, helping himself.

The two women were watching Mariner expectantly.

'You don't want to know,' he said.

'Yes we do.'

'We have to now.'

Mariner sighed, all his earlier efforts undone. 'Workmen found a blockage down one of the main sewers in Stirchley. It turned out to be the body of a woman, wrapped in bin liners and bound with duct tape. We had to go down there to check it out *in situ*.' He saw Anna's grimace. 'There, aren't you glad I told you?'

'I hope you've showered since.'

'Have you got an ID?' Knox asked, garlic wafting Mariner's way.

'Not yet. But we've got a good set of prints from her, so Charlie Glover's trawling through Missing Persons. Otherwise we have to hope she's committed a crime that's put her on CRIMINT. Whoever put her down the drain didn't count on her being found.' In the time Mariner

11

had been speaking Knox had polished off both portions of food.

'We should go, shouldn't we?' said Selina, taking the used plates and depositing them in a nearby bin.

'Yeah, not all of us have the luxury of reserved seats.'

'Not all of us have got to stand up and make pillocks of ourselves,' countered Mariner.

'You'll be wonderful dahling.' To Mariner's surprise Selina grasped his arms, giving him a Hollywood-style peck on each cheek.

'I'm flattered by your confidence,' said Mariner.

Anna was scanning the stalls around them. 'Before we go, I want to get one of those little springy puppets for Megan,' she said.

Mariner glanced at the carrier bags. 'Ah yes, because she hasn't got enough.'

'We'll see you down there, then,' said Selina, and, taking Knox's arm, she steered him down towards the main street. 'See you later,' Knox said, over his shoulder. His arm snaked around Selina, fusing their bodies as one.

'Do you think it's the real thing this time?' Mariner said, watching them go.

'She's lasted longer than any of the others. And Tony can't keep his hands off her.'

'She's a bright girl, too. I don't know how he does it.'

'Confidence,' said Anna. 'Women find it irresistible.'

'Including you?'

Anna shook her head. 'Nah. I just have a weak spot for the underdog.'

'Thanks.'

'We could have waited for them,' said Knox, mildly. 'We've got loads of time, and it won't be a full house.' He and Selina were crossing Corporation Street on their way to St Martin's.

Selina cuddled up closer. 'I wanted you to myself for a bit. I still don't understand why we're spending the evening

12

in a dreary church when we could be at home making our own entertainment.'

'I'm showing a bit of solidarity,' Knox said. He'd explained all this before.

'But he's your boss. Isn't it a bit strange, to be socialising with him?'

'He's been a good mate, too.'

'Was he friends with Theresa?'

'Not friends, exactly. He knew her, that's all.'

'Well, once they've got a family they'll have their hands full.' And seemingly satisfied with her own resolution of whatever the issue was, she squeezed him even tighter.

There was no such intimacy for Mariner and Anna when they followed some time later, bearing the bulky carrier bags. They had to settle for an awkward linking of arms, the baby paraphernalia keeping them apart.

'What the hell have you got in here?' Mariner grumbled, as he apologised yet again for colliding with a passer-by.

'You wouldn't be any the wiser if I told you. It's just toys for Megan. It's not much, but everything's jumbo sized at her age.'

'You're telling me. They'll cost a fortune in postage.'

'I was planning to take them down. I thought I'd go at the weekend.'

'You were only down there a couple of weeks ago.'

Since Becky had left her job as Anna's P.A., she, her GP husband Mark and their small daughter had moved to a country practice in rural Herefordshire. Thus far the geography hadn't proved a deterrent.

'Is that resentment?'

'Of course not.'

'She's my goddaughter. I have to spend time with her. Everything happens so fast at her age, I might miss something. Besides, I've got a lot to learn.'

'It's all right, you don't have to justify yourself.'

'Anyway there's nothing to stop you coming too. You

13

haven't even met Megan yet. I don't know why.'

'It's been busy at work.' It wasn't the whole truth, but he wondered if Anna realised that.

At seven in the evening the main shopping centre was still swarming with people as Anna and Mariner, clumsily arm-in-arm, trundled towards St Martin's Cathedral, past the bronze bull, the armour-plated bulge of Selfridges coming into view like the prow of a slow-moving liner. The church had been retained as a focal point for the massive redevelopment of the Bullring area, and tonight it was stunningly lit by floodlights, the dark spire nestling dramatically between the concrete and glass, and the Burne-Jones stained-glass windows crimson against the twinkling suburban sprawl.

In the distance the West Midlands Police Service brass band could be heard playing the opening bars of the first carol; 'O Little Town of Bethlehem'. Mariner felt contented and at ease and for the first time for as long as he could remember, some excited anticipation of the Christmas season. He turned to Anna to tell her. As he did, there was a flash of white light and the explosion ripped the air between them like a thunderbolt, and a scorching tornado punched him back off his feet, tearing the smile from his face and Anna's arm from his. He heard Anna's scream above the deafening crack of imploding plate glass before he slammed onto his back, his head bouncing hard off the stone slabs.

Opening his eyes, Mariner slowly, painfully, raised his head. The world was unnaturally dark and hushed, and the air tasted of dust. The church that had been so magnificently lit only moments before was hazy, behind a cloud of dense smoke, the dark silhouette of its tower emerging shakily defiant at one end. As Mariner struggled to comprehend, the ringing in his ears subsided and sounds invaded his consciousness. People were screaming and running, alarms were ringing. They were in the middle of a war zone.

14

Mariner fumbled for his phone, his fingers clumsy and unresponsive, and gagging on the dust, it took him three attempts to force out the words. 'DI Mariner, Granville Lane. There's been an explosion in St Martin's. All emergency services needed urgently.' Turning, he saw Anna, prone and still on the ground nearby and a hot wave of panic surged through him 'Anna!' he shouted hoarsely. After what seemed like an eternity she looked round at him and a weak smile split her dirt-caked face. 'I'm okay, really I'm all right. Do what you have to.' She swiped a hand. 'Go.'

Mariner heaved himself unsteadily to his feet, manually locking his knees back into place to support him. 'Wait here for help,' he told Anna unsteadily before crunching through rubble and glass that was ankle deep, towards the ruin of the cathedral and into the jaws of hell.

Chapter Two

The emergency services were there in minutes but Mariner and anyone else who was able had stayed with them inside the crushed citadel clawing at the debris to find the injured and the missing. Hours later they'd sent him out into a blue strobing dawn with dust clogging his airways, his hands chafed and bleeding. Yards from the ruin he had to fight his way through an unruly mob of press photographers ineffectually held back by uniformed PCs.

'Were you inside when it went off? What happened?' Voices assaulted him on all sides.

'I don't know. I was late.'

'What's it like in there?'

'Use your fucking imagination,' Mariner said, coldly, and a flash preserved his dirt-stained face for posterity.

The city was thrown into chaos, with police cordons everywhere. It took Mariner an hour to get to where he'd left his car and to get out. Dozens of injured had been taken to the city's main hospitals, many cut by flying glass. And there was widespread panic that this may just be the first of a number of explosions. He couldn't find out where Anna had been taken and he hardly dared think what had happened to Knox and Selina. People had died. That much he knew, but not how many nor who they were.

16

Finally a text on his mobile from Anna told Mariner that she was at the Queen Elizabeth Hospital. He went in to collect her, still dazed and exhausted, his uniform covered in filth. In the waiting area they held each other tight.

'I called a taxi. I didn't expect to see you for hours. Is it bad?'

'It's bad.'

'Has anybody been—?'

'There have been some fatalities.' He knew of one for certain.

'What about Tony and Selina?'

He shook his head. 'It's still bedlam there.' He wanted so badly to say that they'd be all right, but he couldn't tell her what he didn't know. They'd both been incredibly lucky. Between the shopping centre and the church they'd been shielded by the flight of steps and had escaped serious injury, but it would be different for anyone inside. Mariner went to ask at the reception desk but the staff were inundated with desperate friends and relatives and he would only add to the pandemonium. Instead he and Anna drove home in near silence, the experience beyond articulation.

Helpless to trace Knox, Mariner called Jack Coleman at Granville Lane. But Coleman knew nothing either.

'How many dead?' Mariner asked.

'We don't know yet. It could be up to ten.'

'Christ. I'll get myself cleaned up and come in.'

'No. We've got enough here already. You'll be a liability. Get some rest.' Easier said than done. Half an hour later, Coleman called back. 'Tony Knox is at Heartlands.'

Mariner went straight there. Against the pristine white sheets Knox looked old and grey. He'd suffered cuts, bruising and possible concussion. 'They're letting me out later today. They need the bed.'

Selina hadn't escaped so lightly, her right foot crushed under several tons of masonry. 'They're amputating below the knee,' Knox said, his voice heavy with emotion.

17

'She'll never make centre forward now,' said Mariner.

'No.'

'I'm sorry.'

'She's alive. It's what matters.' Knox was right. By now news had permeated that at least five others, men, a woman, a child, had not been so lucky. 'Is Anna okay?'

'She's fine.'

'They keep asking me what I saw,' Knox said.

'Me too.'

'But one minute I was having a laugh with Colin Fleming, next I was under a pile of crap trying to breathe.'

'I didn't see anything either.'

'You're a star though.' Knox reached for the early edition of the newspaper one of the nurses had left. *Christmas Carnage* cried the headline. He turned to an inside page and Mariner saw himself, or what looked like him, under all the dirt and grime, emerging from the wrecked building just after he'd been accosted by the reporter. 'The lengths people go to, to get in the paper.'

Emergency blood donation clinics had been set up all over the city, including at the hospitals. On his way out Mariner saw the queue. He joined it.

The investigation into the explosion began immediately and in the absence of a rational explanation, rumours were rife, among them the inevitable black jokes about six Irishmen on a train. But this time the witch-hunt took on a different focus. The threat of terrorist activity had loomed large in other major British cities since the war in Iraq and attacks in London by Al Qaeda. The media had already decided that this could be the start.

Although other causes hadn't been ruled out, like a reflex response, security across the city tightened to a level that hadn't been seen since the height of the IRA's mainland campaign during the 1970s. There were police patrol cars everywhere. Bags were routinely searched and vehicles on the main routes into the city were being randomly stopped.

Not that anyone realistically expected to find anything, but the police had to be visibly active. Most of the dead turned out to be civilians. If it had been a terrorist bomb, ironically the main players – the Chief Constable, Mayor and other dignitaries – had escaped relatively unscathed and someone, somewhere would be cursing their own bad luck.

Mariner and Anna tried desperately to carry on as normal but the shock of unspeakable sights and sounds had come between them. Mariner didn't talk about what he'd seen in there. Instead he and Anna spent hours silently holding each other tight, for comfort. TV and radio provided a constant background commentary and nothing, it seemed, could distract Mariner from reliving those hours over and over again. Part of him didn't want distraction and was disgusted at the obscenity of the indifferent world. Sleep became an elusive state and when at night fatigue did finally engulf him his rest was fitful and he would wake with a jolt, sweating and heart pounding, waking Anna too.

They spent whole afternoons and evenings holding hands but saying little. That last conversation before the explosion hung over them, neither willing to revisit it. Guiltily, Mariner hoped that all this might make Anna feel differently about the prospect of bringing a child into the world, but deep down he knew it was for all the wrong reasons.

'My family curse has rubbed off on you,' Anna said. 'Perhaps you've made a mistake taking up with me.'

It seemed a lifetime ago that they'd first met, when Mariner was investigating the murder of Anna's elder brother, Eddie. Before long the case had turned into a triple homicide involving her parents too, so she was no stranger to violent death. But still Mariner couldn't tell her what he'd seen. He kept himself busy by being overattentive to her so that in the end she got irritated with him. It was the letting agent who saved them from a full-blown row.

'Mr Mariner? We've got someone who wants to look at your house.' Roy Shipley sounded as surprised as Mariner was. This was the first show of interest they'd had in the canal-side property. 'He'd like to see it before going up north for Christmas.' Great timing. The last thing Mariner felt like was being sociable.

Shipley picked up on the hesitation. 'If you don't want to trouble yourself I can show him round. I've arranged an appointment for tomorrow afternoon.'

'No, it's okay,' said Mariner. 'I'll be there.' He'd been waiting long enough for this. Back in mid-August it had been clear that Jenny, his previous tenant, wasn't coming back. She'd left university and got a job in the East Midlands. By that time Mariner had pretty well moved in with Anna, along with most of his stuff, so it seemed sensible to try and bring in some extra cash by renting. But it hadn't been that simple mainly because, the agent said, the property was too small for a family and a bit off the beaten track for most people. This was the first nibble, so Mariner couldn't afford to pass it up. And it would get him out from under Anna's feet for a while.

23rd December
Dave Flynn had never been inside a house like this before. After years of turning over grubby flats and bedsits, uncovering all kinds of unsavoury matter, this was how he knew he'd finally made it to the premier league. And it wasn't just him. The whole team was treating the place with the kind of reverence reserved for religious buildings, speaking in hushed tones, their footsteps alternately echoing on the polished hardwood floors, or cushioned by thick Persian rugs. This was only one of the pleasures of promotion to Special Branch. And no one seemed to mind his being here, even though strictly speaking his presence was unnecessary. He wanted to make sure the troops got his first prominent case right. No cock-ups, minor or major.

What he'd seen so far gave him no cause to worry. The lads were doing an efficient, if careful, job; drawers, cupboards, shelves, even the contents of the walk-in fridge.

20

'Anything that might give us a clue about what Sir Geoffrey Ryland was doing on a side road off the M40 at two in the morning of December fourth.'

Not that they were likely to find anything much here, or that Flynn was under any illusion that he was leading this investigation. That was going on elsewhere. After more than a week, his team had only just been allowed access to the house, the lack of urgency matching the lack of expectation. Flynn was well aware that so far everything pointed to Ryland's driver as being the intended victim of the assassination. The Super had told them all as much at the briefing, and from the photos of the scene he'd been shown, and what they knew of the background, Flynn had little reason to doubt that it was true.

The style of the killing was a strong indication that the thirty-eight-year-old reformed heroin runner had slipped back into his nasty little habits and paid the price. The bullets recovered at the scene had been shot from the type of weapon favoured by drugs dealers, and the crude message written in blood an obvious reference. Sir Geoffrey Ryland and his wife had simply got in the way. Until they read the headlines the following day the assassins had probably been totally unaware of the identity of their other, more prominent, victims.

The only contra-indications were the grains of white powder on the ground and inside the boot of the limo. It had seemed a careless, if not wasteful, mistake for professionals to make. But that was a trivial point and in the end it wouldn't be Flynn's call. All he was doing was the wider information-gathering, and ensuring that Sir Geoffrey Ryland's death wouldn't uncover any nasty surprises. Those further up the ladder would make the judgements about what had really happened that night in Cheslyn Wood.

Flynn climbed the stairs to the first-floor landing. 'Anything useful?' he asked.

One of the team emerged from the bathroom. Collins,

Flynn thought he was called. 'A quantity of drugs of any interest to you, sir?'

'What?'

'Diazepam. Prescribed to Lady Ryland.'

'Valium,' said Flynn, taking the bag. He studied the typed label. 'Christ, and a 500 milligram dosage. That's enough to knock out a horse. Depressed or what?'

'She was a politician's wife,' said Collins, as if that was explanation enough.

'Anything else?' Flynn asked.

'We've got a few letters. But it's personal stuff, mostly relating to her. You wanted us to look for anything unusual, unexplained?'

'That's right.'

Collins held up a small key. 'Looks like the key to a bank security box.'

'We've already been into his safety deposit.'

'He must have another one. And this key was taped to the inside of his desk drawer.'

'Meaning it's the one he didn't want anyone else to know about.'

Anna opted out of the meeting with Roy Shipley, so Mariner took wrapping paper and tape to the cottage; might as well do something useful while he was there.

He arrived at his canalside home in time to see a silver Audi estate pulling into the service road. Shipley walked over first, followed by another taller man, broad-shouldered with carroty hair and a dusting of freckles that probably got him relentless teasing as a kid. He extended a hand and a broad smile. 'Bill Dyson,' he said. 'Thanks for agreeing to see me Mr Mariner.'

Mariner was normally good at placing accents but the closest he could get with Dyson's was somewhere north of the border. 'That's no problem,' he said.

'How are you?' Shipley asked. 'I saw your picture in the local rag. That explosion thing. Christ.'

'You were involved in that?' Dyson echoed Shipley's horror. 'It must have been awful.'

'It wasn't much fun.'

'Hideous I would think,' Shipley said. 'But you're here to tell the tale. Thank God, eh?'

Dyson was mortified. 'Look, I had no idea,' he said. 'If this is a bad time—'

Mariner shook his head. 'Not at all. It will be good to see the place occupied. As Mr Shipley's probably explained, I seem to spend most of my time at my partner's house now so it's lying empty much of the time.'

A squall of icy rain blew down. 'Why don't we go inside?' said the agent.

The tour of the three-floor cottage didn't take long but Dyson seemed impressed. He ran his hand over the varnished inlaid wood of the cupboards. 'I love these old places. When was it built?'

Mariner gave him a potted history of the place, as much as he knew. 'The original drawings are even knocking around here somewhere. I'll try and remember to look them out for you.'

'Great, thanks. It looks ideal for me. I'd been looking at flats and bedsits but rooms would suit me much better. All I need is a bolthole to save me from having to retreat back up the motorway every week. I've been living in hotels up to now but that can be pretty soul-destroying after a while and financially it's really not viable.'

'Well some of my stuff is still here and I do come back from time to time, but this is really just a stop-gap arrangement until we decide what to do.'

'And meanwhile I'll find out if I can make a go of it down here.'

'What kind of business is it that you're in?'

'Security.' Dyson dug in an inside pocket and passed Mariner a business card. 'Domestic mainly. I'm pretty well established in the north but would love to make it work down here, too.' He smiled. 'I could start right away. I

23

noticed that you don't have a system. I could do an assessment for you if you like.'

'To be honest I've never felt the need.'

Shipley cleared his throat. 'I should have said. It's *Detective Inspector* Mariner.'

'Ah.' Dyson responded in the way that most people do.

'I hope that won't make a difference,' Mariner said, knowing that sometimes it could.

But Dyson seemed relaxed enough about it. 'I'll just have to make sure and keep my nose clean, won't I?'

They all smiled at what they knew was a well-worn line.

'Where's your main base?' Mariner asked.

'I'm originally from Galloway.'

'That's a beautiful area.'

'Yes, it is. A man's got to earn a living but I'd love to retire back there.' Dyson gestured towards the shelf of battered Wainwright Guides. 'I see you're a walker yourself.'

'It's the best way to get some peace and quiet, I find.'

'You'll have to recommend some local routes for me. Stuck in the car all day visiting clients, exercise is the thing I really miss.'

'I'll do that,' Mariner said, hoping that Dyson wouldn't be looking for company too. For him one of the attractions of a good walk was the solitude. 'When are you thinking of moving in?' he asked.

'Right after the holidays if that's okay. Do you want me to give you a call first?'

'No. The references seem fine. Move in when you're ready.'

'Cheers, I appreciate that. I'll probably dump some of my kit for now and come back from time to time.'

'Whenever you like.'

'Well, we should be going,' Shipley prompted.

'Aye. Back to the bosom of the family and all that. There's snow forecast for later today and I'd like to miss it if I can. What about you? Getting together with the folks for the celebrations?'

24

'Not many of them left,' said Mariner.

'Lucky you.' The remark seemed heartfelt and Dyson was apparently compelled to qualify it. 'Don't misunderstand me. I love my parents, siblings and their offspring dearly but you can have too much of a good thing, if you know what I mean.'

'I wouldn't imagine you're alone.' said Mariner.

'Well. Merry Christmas to you, Tom.'

'Merry Christmas.'

Mariner watched from the doorway as Dyson signalled and then pulled out onto the main road, his rearlights disappearing from view. The house, perched on the edge of the frozen canal was frigid now that the central heating only came on twice a day to stop the system from seizing up. After Dyson had left, huddled in his fleece, Mariner jammed his hands in his pockets and sat and enjoyed the uninterrupted silence for a while, trying once more to exorcise the images that clogged his brain.

The sounds more than anything else were what haunted him. When he'd first ventured into that black hole of choking dust, visibility was non existent and it was the bits of noise that had emerged first; the tormented groans and plaintive cries for help grotesque way-markers in the darkness. At one point he'd been driven on by a faint whimpering. Others came to help and they laboured for an hour, scrabbling in desperation at the rubble and debris until their hands bled, until finally Mariner made contact with soft clothing and flesh. 'Over here!' he'd yelled to newly arrived floodlights.

Through a chink in the debris Mariner could see big blue eyes blinking and unfocused in a ghostly face and he kept talking, compelling those eyes to stay open and engage. But when the lights came on, illuminating the tons of wreckage heaped above, the enormity of the task was evident, and finally with a gasp of breath, the eyes closed and did not reopen. For hours he'd only known his discovery as victim number three. Then when her beaming photograph appeared in the paper he learned that she was ten-year-old Chloe Evans who had come to the service with her retired police officer grandfather. Mariner was tortured by the failure. Never mind that countless others had been helped to safety, they'd failed that little girl.

Mariner wrapped Anna's presents with little enthusiasm. Picking up a takeaway on his way back to the house, he found her curled up in front of the TV watching a Christmas special of some sort.

'What's he like?' she asked. 'The lodger.'

'Seems like a nice guy. He lives up north and wants a base here for business purposes. He's moving in right after Christmas.'

'That's great. How long is the lease?'

'Six months.'

'And then?'

'I don't know. What?'

'I've been thinking.'

Mariner was beginning to take this as a bad sign. 'Oh yes.'

'Now that Jamie's settled we've got a bit more flexibility. It's lovely out where Becky and Mark live. I think we should consider it.'

'What?'

'Moving out of the city. If we sold both of our places we could get somewhere really nice. Somewhere we could do up and make into a proper family home.'

'We haven't got a family yet,' Mariner reminded her.

'I know but—'

Chloe Evans face returned unbidden into his head. 'It's too soon, Anna, leave it will you?'

'But it would be something to concentrate on, to get us through this.'

'We'll get through it anyway,' Mariner snapped. 'We weren't victims. We got away with it.'

26

'I know but—'

'I can't talk about this now. I'm going to bed.' Climbing the stairs he knew he'd reacted badly, but Christ, as if there wasn't already enough going on.

Chapter Three

Christmas Eve
The following day two Detective Constables from Special Branch came to talk to them and take statements. If they noticed that the atmosphere was cooler inside the house than it was outside, it didn't show. It was a frustrating interview. Mariner was still coming to terms with the fact that his only role was as a witness, and in this respect he felt entirely inadequate. He'd been over and over it in his head but on the walk towards the church he'd seen nothing unusual, no one behaving suspiciously, not a thing out of place. Up until the point when the building had erupted it had been a perfectly normal evening. If they'd been there sooner there might have been something, but they hadn't.

'I really don't remember seeing anything,' Mariner reiterated yet again, his annoyance showing through. 'I heard it and felt it, but by then it was too late.'

The interviewing officer was sympathetic. 'You're not alone sir,' he said. 'An event like that, we must have had a hundred expert witnesses in the area, but none of those who survived can remember seeing anything that helps our investigation.'

'Do we know yet what caused the explosion?'

'The investigation is ongoing, sir.'

'But they must have some idea.'

Initially, Mariner had thought he must have missed

28

something. It had been four days since the explosion, normally more than enough time to at least have some idea of the cause, but there seemed a high level of secrecy surrounding it. The team would have been in there examining the forensic evidence and, if it was a bomb, would have drawn some conclusions about the type and amount of explosive used.

'If they do know they're not ready to share it with us yet, sir,' was all the officer would say.

Mariner flatly turned down the counselling that was offered. Resources were stretched and there were others whose need was greater. But he suggested to Anna that she should take it up, using the one lever available to him. 'If we do start a family—'

She stared at him. He'd used the 'if' word.

Jamie had been due to come home for Christmas, but Anna called and arranged for him to stay at the hostel. 'He'll have a better time there than he will with us,' was her reasoning and it couldn't be argued with. Even without the explosion things were strained to say the least. They drove over and took his presents instead to where Jamie had lived since Manor Park, his residential care home, had been swallowed up by a national organisation whose ethos followed the trend towards community-based care. At the time Anna had experienced mixed feelings. Largely indifferent to his role in society, Jamie had been happy where he was, but gradually Anna had been persuaded that getting involved with the community on a daily basis would be of long-term benefit.

Mariner pulled into the drive of the unremarkable semi-detached house to see Louise, the manager, in bright yellow rubber gloves, gathering up rubbish from the front garden and stuffing it into a black bag. It included old nappies and takeaway cartons, more than the wind would have randomly deposited.

'An early Christmas present from the neighbours,' she said, grimly.

'What have you done to deserve that?' Mariner was appalled.

'Oh, nothing specific.' Louise assured him. 'Just the general threat we pose to the neighbourhood. That old confusion between mental illness and learning difficulties lingers on.'

'Not any more, surely.' But the bag of rubbish said otherwise. 'Have you reported it?' Mariner wanted to know.

'I don't want to inflame the situation. They'll get used to us eventually.'

'You've been here nearly six months. How long does it take?'

'Clearly a bit longer than we thought.' Louise smiled. 'Come on in. It's much more festive inside.'

It was. Reflecting the needs of its clientele, Christmas decorations inside the hostel had been kept to a minimum, but the air was rich with the comforting smell of home-baking.

'We're making mince pies,' Louise said. To prove the point, when he appeared Jamie was wearing a floury apron, his hands still spotlessly clean, participation limited to observation only. He came over and rested his forehead on Anna's shoulder, his habitual greeting.

'Hi Jamie,' she said and Mariner could see her fighting the impulse to put her arms round her brother and squeeze him tight, something that would have caused him more distress than reassurance. But in the last days everything and everyone had become more precious and the need to reach out and physically hold on had become more pressing, almost a primeval urge.

Jamie was also adjusting to new circumstances. Along with the move to the hostel, his care worker Simon had also moved on, and Jamie had not entirely taken to his replacement. Today Luke was upbeat. 'He's settling in really well. He likes walking to the shops and going on the bus to the swimming baths and is generally coping better with new experiences.'

'How's the sleeping?' Anna asked. Night times she knew had not been easy.

'We're getting there,' said Luke elusively. 'And how are you?' he asked Anna, in what now always seemed to be a loaded question.

'We're fine,' Anna said, 'better each day.' But she didn't say what a slow process it was proving to be.

From the hostel it was a short walk into Bromsgrove town centre where, by way of an alternative Christmas treat, they took Jamie for a McDonald's. From the outset Mariner was jumpy, Jamie seeming to walk too close to the edge of the pavement to be safe.

'Jamie,' Mariner warned. Jamie moved away from the kerb but within a few paces had drifted back again as traffic raced by just a few inches away. 'Jamie, stay on the path,' Mariner said.

'He is,' said Anna, pointedly. 'He's fine.'

But as they rounded a corner Jamie teetered on the edge of the pavement and unable to stand it any more Mariner lunged towards him and grabbed his arm. Jamie pulled away in alarm and almost into the path of an oncoming HGV that blared its horn. Yards later they reached the safety of the pedestrian area. Anna was incredulous. 'What the hell were you doing?'

'He was too close to the road. I thought he'd get hit.'

'Well thanks to you he nearly did. You know he doesn't like to be touched.'

'I forgot. I don't know why I did it.'

Mariner hated fast-food chains with a vengeance. In his experience they were anything but fast and the food was barely edible. This one proved to be no exception. Excessively bright and filled to capacity with people taking a break from last minute Christmas shopping, the noise and the chaos made his palms sweat and his heart race. The incident with Jamie had shaken them all up too. Mariner couldn't wait to get out, but instead, the tension between them tangible, he and Anna sat in near silence sipping bitter, watery coffee while Jamie, oblivious to the atmosphere, slowly munched his way through a Big Mac, large fries and a chocolate donut, pausing only occasionally to noisily suck coke through a straw. At the adjacent table a mother yelled intermittently at her gaggle of kids, every other word an obscenity. A joyous experience it was not. One of the toddlers, pale-faced with huge grey eyes, fixed an unwavering gaze on Mariner and suddenly he was confronted again with Chloe Evans' beseeching face. He jumped up.

'I'll see you back at the hostel,' he said. And Anna knew him well enough to let him go.

Mariner walked into the centre of Bromsgrove where the statue of A.E. Housman dominated the High Street. *A Shropshire Lad* had been the only book of poetry at Mariner's grandparents' house.

He met Anna back at the hostel but, before they left, Louise asked to speak to them both in the privacy of her tiny office. 'It's a bit awkward,' she said, apologetically. 'We still haven't had any payments through. You owe quite a bit of money.' She passed Anna an invoice. 'I wouldn't mention it now, but I'm under pressure from the finance department.'

Anna was mortified. Since the takeover she'd changed her method of payment to what should have been a simple automatic bank transaction, but for some unknown reason it didn't appear to be working. 'You should have said something sooner,' she told Louise. 'The money is there. I'll write you a cheque now. And after the holidays I'll get onto the bank and sort it out,' she said.

Louise was palpably relieved. 'Thanks, I appreciate it. Have a great Christmas.'

Some hope, thought Mariner.

At home he helped Anna to go through the motions of decorating the tree, wondering if it was as hollow and unsatisfying a gesture for her too. In the evening she insisted that they go to the open air carols on Bournville village green, to try to recapture something of the Christmas mood. In a crowd of thousands, many of them children, carrying glowing lanterns and wearing flashing Santa hats, they stood on the hard frozen ground, the cold spreading up through their feet.

Untouched by the carols, Mariner's attention was snagged by a toddler in a thick snow-suit wandering around in front of them. The crowd was dense and he was roaming further and further from his parents, weaving in and out through the forest of legs. 'He'll get lost,' Mariner thought, irrational panic quickening his pulse. He made to intervene, just as the child turned and made a beeline back to his dad. But minutes later the child made another foray into the crowd, his mum and dad singing enthusiastically and completely oblivious, so when a stranger hoisted the child up and began to move off, Mariner lunged forward and snatched the toddler, causing him to shriek out in fear. A woman screamed and the white-haired man holding the child spun round in alarm. 'What are you doing with my grandson?' And suddenly the situation looked very different.

'I didn't know you—,' Mariner handed back the wailing child. 'It's all right,' he said to the hostile faces. 'I'm a police officer. I thought—' But now he could see exactly how it looked, and explanation was futile. 'I'm sorry.' Turning away he pushed his way back through the crowds and out onto the road, Anna trailing in his wake, unnerved by the outburst.

'What was that all about?' she asked when they were back in the car.

'I don't know. I thought the kid was going to get lost, he was straying too far, and then that man picked him up.'

'He was with his family. They were all his family.'

'I can see that now, but at the time—,' He couldn't explain the panic he'd felt, the overwhelming need to inter- vene that had overtaken him. 'I overreacted, I realise that, but I couldn't help it.'

'Okay,' Anna said, but her tone implied it was anything but.

'I just can't get those five families out of my head,' Mariner said. 'Their Christmas will never be the same again.'

She put a hand over his and squeezed it. 'I know.'

During the night Mariner was woken by a deafening roar. The low-flying aircraft made him cry out in fear. Suddenly there seemed to be danger everywhere, lurking around every corner and he was on a constant adrenalin rush, waiting for the next thing to happen.

25th December

On his own while Selina was in hospital, Tony Knox came over for Christmas lunch the next day and Mariner told him what had happened. 'I lost it,' he said. 'But I don't really know why. It was nothing.'

'I don't like being inside,' Knox admitted. 'It makes me nervous.' So he and Mariner took the puppy for a long walk over Clent and Walton Hills. Early morning frost had given way to a brown and murky day, the cloud low and misty, and the rotting woodland vegetation smelled acrid. Paddy ran huge circles around them, bounding back and forth, dragged by the nose along the scent trails of a hundred other creatures. Selina's baby. Breathing hard from the first steep climb, the men walked in companionable silence for a while.

'Have you seen your two this holiday?' Mariner asked suddenly, kids very much on his mind. He knew he was treading on sensitive ground.

'I took presents over for the grandson,' Knox said, casually. 'Though Siobhan made it pretty clear that she couldn't wait for me to go. Gary's gone up to his mother's for Christmas, but he called in to see me before he went.'

'It's getting better then.'

'They still both blame me for the split.'

34

'That's hardly fair. It was Theresa who left you.'

'She had good reason though, didn't she? I let her down, let them all down. And let's face it, this wasn't the first time.'

There wasn't much room for contradiction.

'Theresa didn't ever want to come here you know. She only had to leave Liverpool because of me.' A direct consequence of Knox shagging the wife of a senior officer, as Mariner recalled. Paddy came lolloping over and Knox picked up a stick and threw it. 'Dogs are much simpler,' he said, 'all the fun of kids, without the emotional stress.'

'Maybe Anna and I should go for a dog.'

'Nah, kids are great really. You'll love being a dad.'

'Yeah.'

After lunch they all went to visit Selina. She'd had the operation the previous day and was still groggy and feeling phantom pains from the missing part of her leg. They kept things light, plenty of jokes about Long John Silver and wooden peg-legs.

'You might have to find yourself another woman,' she told Knox. 'I'll be in with a chance with Paul McCartney now.' Knox stayed on at the hospital and when Anna looked back down the ward for a final wave, she could see Selina clinging to him.

The news continued to be dominated by the explosion, but though speculation in the press was rife, no one appeared to be any nearer to knowing who had been responsible, so the rumours continued to flourish. The longer the silence, the harder it was for Mariner to comprehend. It usually took just a few days to pinpoint the source, which meant that this had to be some kind of public interest cover-up. No political or religious group had claimed responsibility, implying that it related to something bigger and the authorities didn't want to spark a full-blown panic. The less palatable alternative was that there had been some kind of warning and someone, somewhere had cocked up. Not something it would ever be easy to admit to.

*

On the eighth day Mariner brought Anna tea and toast in bed as he had done each morning, but today when he came back to the bedroom she was already in the shower.

'The sales are on. I want to go and snap up some bargains,' she told him when she emerged.

Mariner felt the now familiar flutter of fear. 'I don't think it's a good idea to go into the city, yet,' he said, trying to sound casual.

'I wasn't thinking Birmingham. They're still clearing everything up, and the security checks are a nightmare. I thought I'd go down to Worcester. I can get you another coat.' To replace the one that had been discarded among the devastation of St Martin's.

'I still don't think it's wise.'

'Why not? This is a great time to go. Other people are staying away. More chance of making a killing.' She looked at him. 'Sorry, poor choice of words.'

'Maybe there's a good reason people are staying away,' Mariner said.

'And maybe you're being slightly overprotective? I can't spend another day cooped up in here and neither can you. We have to start getting on with our lives again. Aren't you the one who's always saying we shouldn't let these people win?'

'But we don't know yet if the explosion was the start of a campaign.'

'The press are saying not. But even if it is, I can't imagine Worcester being at the top of the terrorists' list.'

'The press don't know everything. In fact, where this is concerned the press don't know anything. I'll come with you.'

'Are you kidding? You'll be bored stiff within half an hour, and the last thing I need is you pacing up and down outside the changing rooms every time I try something on. Go back to work. It's what you really want to do.'

She was right about that, the inertia was starting to drive him mad, aggravated by the knowledge of what would be awaiting him at the office. 'You'll be all right?'

She tapped her chin, frowning for dramatic effect. 'I don't know, if only someone could have invented some kind of portable communication device that would allow us to talk to each other during the day. Oh, guess what? They have. It's called a mobile phone.'

'Ho ho,' said Mariner, mirthlessly. 'Have you been getting sarcasm coaching from Tony Knox?'

She gave him a hug. 'I'll keep in touch, I promise.'

'Right, I'll just go in and check the post, then.'

'Good idea. Who knows, we might even have something to talk about at the end of the day.' She looked him in the eye. 'Something that we're both willing to talk about, that is.'

Overnight there had been a light fall of snow and the clean purity outside was at odds with Mariner's current perception of the world. At Granville Lane he sat in his car for a few minutes, fascinated, he told himself, by watching the progress of the occasional snowflake, though in reality he was summoning the courage to walk into the building. When he finally did it he was disconcerted to see the tremor in his hand as he swiped his security pass through the pad.

'How are you, sir?' Receptionist Ella's earnest expression lay somewhere between sympathy and wariness, something that Mariner was to see reflected on almost every face he encountered in the weeks that followed, as if he'd been a victim too. A black cloud hung over the station as it did over every OCU in the city. Crime hadn't stopped because of the explosion, although figures later would reveal a significant dip. Even the criminal fraternity had been shocked to the core.

'I'm fine, thanks,' Mariner said.

'Mr Coleman would like to see you.'

Mariner went straight to DCI Jack Coleman's office. As his hand hovered just short of the door, it occurred to him that the nameplate wouldn't be there for much longer.

Coleman was due to retire at the end of January. That was only a month away. It had crept up suddenly. Hearing Coleman's response, he went in.

'Tom.' Coleman got up from behind his desk and the two men shook hands. 'It's good to see you back.'

It occurred to Mariner that Coleman didn't look old enough for retirement. In any other career he could have had another ten years in him.

'Special Branch came to see you?' he asked.

Mariner sat down. 'Mm. Not that there was any point. I can't remember seeing anything.'

'I don't suppose you were meant to.'

'Have you heard much about how the investigation's going?'

'Only what's being released to the press.'

'Bugger all then. What's going on? Usually there's something. They can't not know, they must be sitting on it.'

'If they are I'm sure they have their reasons. How's Anna?' The swift change of subject left Mariner wondering if Coleman was sitting on it too, but he allowed himself to be led down the alternative route.

'She's still in shock. At least I hope she is, because otherwise we've lost the ability to communicate. Half the time we don't seem to know what to say to each other, the rest of the time we're at loggerheads.'

'It'll get better. It will help that you went through it together.'

'Not the worst part. It wasn't so much the explosion. It was afterwards, going in to find people under all that—' He parried the image that flashed through his head.

'Yes, I know.' It was more than polite sympathy.

Mariner could practically see Coleman's mind reaching back thirty years to his first weeks in uniform, and that Thursday night in 1974 when the city had been ripped apart by two IRA bombs. Coleman had been on duty and had helped with the rescue. Mariner knew that the nightmares had gone on to haunt Coleman for years to come and had almost put paid to his marriage. 'It has a certain morbid symmetry to it; an explosive beginning and end to your career,' Mariner said.

Coleman nodded. 'It's a good time to retire.'

'I thought I could understand what happened to you,' Mariner said. 'But really I hadn't a clue.'

'Nobody ever does. Don't underestimate the impact, Tom, on either of you. And be thankful that you have something to help you look forward.'

Mariner looked at him blankly.

Coleman raised his eyebrows. 'I thought you were planning kids.'

'I told you about that?'

'I thought you needed time off for an appointment?'

'Oh yes.' The genetic counsellor. Coleman had done well to remember. It had slipped Mariner's mind altogether. 'It'll be after the new year sometime, I suppose. Though to be honest I'm not so sure about that now. And Anna's gone very quiet about it. I'm glad.'

'You can't let these people dictate how you live your lives. If you do, they've won.' Almost word for word what Anna had said.

'It's not only that,' Mariner admitted. 'The truth is it scares me to death, the idea of having a child. I've got no experience. I keep thinking; how can I be a good dad when I don't know what it's like to even have a dad?'

Coleman smiled. 'That's how I feel about retirement. It's a big life change. Glenys can't wait, but I keep wondering how I'll cope for the first time in my life when there's nothing to do. But I'll do it, and so will you. You're hardly the first to be in your position. Lots of people don't have the experience of typical family life. You're a good man, Tom, that's all it takes to make a good father.'

Mariner wished he could share Coleman's confidence in him. 'Anything happened here that I should know about?' he asked.

'You'll be pleased to know that we're on the way to an ID on your sewer queen. I won't spoil it for Charlie Glover. As acting SIO he'll want to fill you in. But go easy to begin with, don't rush into anything. Take over when you're ready.'

'Yes sir.'

Walking along to his office, Mariner couldn't help flinching from the everyday hubbub of the building; phones ringing, doors banging, talk and laughter. The garish Christmas decorations were an insult to his mood and by the time he reached his desk his pulse raced as if he'd just climbed Caer Caradoc, rather than walked a few yards along a corridor. The temperamental 1950s heating system left his office chill but as he took off his jacket his armpits felt sticky. At least CID was quiet; officers from each OCU had been seconded to help with the leg-work on the investigation into the St Martin's incident, and right now Charlie Glover was nowhere around.

Mark 'Jack' Russell was one of the few men remaining and was immediately attentive to Mariner. 'Is there anything you want sir?'

'Just time to get my bearings again,' said Mariner. Russell closed the door on his way out.

On the top of Mariner's in-tray was Charlie Glover's progress report on the sewer queen. It was as Coleman had said. Glover had run the prints through CRIMINT but as the woman had no record they'd drawn a blank. Missing persons had turned up no likely contenders either. But Charlie Glover had used his brain, and picking up on the unusual labels on the dead woman's clothes had established her nationality as Albanian. The last thing he'd done was to contact the National Immigration Centre in Croydon, to see if the government's crackdown on immigration would be of any help to them. So far it was a competent investigation and, not for the first time, Mariner wondered why Glover, in his late thirties, was still only a DC. He must talk to him about that some time.

Key photographs from the postmortem and notes from the pathologist were included in the file for Mariner. According to the initial findings, there were pressure point bruises to the oesophagus, damage to the thyroid cartilage and cricoid cartilage, and x-rays clearly showed the hyoid bone in the throat to be broken, all consistent with the application of extreme pressure with the thumbs. Conclusion: the woman had been strangled with somebody's bare hands. She was five feet three and slightly built so most men would be physically capable. The facial photograph was not a pretty sight. She had been dead for at least a couple of weeks when she was found, in which time rats had chewed through the bin liner, before attacking her face and torso. They'd need a digital mock-up before they could think of releasing anything to the press. Something else Glover had highlighted: the girl was a mother. She'd given birth around two months earlier.

The likely scenario, Glover concluded, was that she had been strangled, taped into the bin liners and dumped down the sewer, and their strongest lead on a suspect came in the form of the latent prints found on the tape and the bin bags. These were currently being processed by forensics, though, with the holiday, Charlie wasn't sure how long that would take. He'd begun a house to house in the area, though as Glover said in his note, with no photograph and only one spare WPC to help him, it was going to be a slow job. It was probably where he was now.

Mariner looked at the ravaged face. Hard to tell if the girl had been pretty, dead eyes staring up at him. Suddenly they were transposed by another pair of eyes, their life draining away even as he watched. His mouth went dry and he felt a slight queasiness. Pushing the picture away, he went and got some water from the cooler.

Returning to his desk, Mariner switched on his PC to check his email, but his mind wandered and it was hard to concentrate. Everything he did seemed to take longer than usual.

The extensive list of new messages in his in-box mainly originated from people he'd never heard of; an invitation to a New Year's bash in a different department, notification of minor changes in procedures, and forthcoming training opportunities. Each one absurdly banal.

An open air memorial service was to be held for the victims of the explosion, in St Philip's Square in the city centre. A circular gave details of the times and the security arrangements, bordering on the paranoid, and information about the collection for the victims and their families. A memorial book was also available for messages at the museum and art gallery. In other words, it was standard stuff. Only one other message stood out to Mariner as being of any interest. It was addressed to *Walking Man*.

That was the tag inflicted on Mariner by Detective Inspector Dave Flynn when the two of them had been thrown together four years ago at a conference week in Peterborough. Two DIs in a hotel full of Superintendents, they had stuck together, more so on discovering a mutual liking for proper beer in a hotel that specialised in extortionately priced lager. It was when Mariner had first discovered Woodforde's, something that he would forever associate with Dave Flynn. Every evening after the presentations they'd gone out on a quest for real ale, Mariner insisting they walk rather than take taxis, restless for the exercise he was missing during the day; hence the nickname. Flynn had a weird taste in naff music; anything that wasn't cool, but it was only in subsequent years that Mariner had realised that James Taylor featured on his playlist.

Flynn was ambitious. He was probably a Super himself by now. No clue about that in the note, which was characteristically brief and to the point.

In Brum tomorrow (28th). Fancy a pint?
Dave

Mariner wondered idly whether Flynn's visit had anything to do with the explosion. He couldn't see how, but either way it would be good to see him again; a welcome distraction, and the chance for a good piss up. Mariner tapped in a positive reply and sent it on its way.

The contents of his paper in-tray were similarly mundane, and after a while the rhythmic process of opening envelopes began to have a vaguely therapeutic effect, at least creating the illusion of a return to normality. So when he came to the contents of the A4 manila envelope he was quite unprepared. Russell must have been watching him from the bull pen. He was beside him at once. 'You all right, sir?'

Unable to answer him, Mariner handed him the A4 sheet on which a composite of letters cut from a magazine had been glued, in true TV cop-drama cliché. The message was simple: *Next time, don't be late*.

Chapter Four

As a direct result of the letter, Jack Coleman managed to get Mariner access to the team investigating the explosion, which meant going into the city to police headquarters at Lloyd House. Movement around the central area was still restricted, traffic being directed around the ring road and directly past St Martin's. Mariner got stuck behind a silver-grey Transit, identical to a couple more that were parked adjacent to the church. They were unmarked, like mortuary vans, though logically Mariner knew they couldn't be. The bodies had all been recovered days ago.

Bulldozers were clearing some of the rubble and making safe what remained of the tower, but already flowers were piled high on the steps leading up from the church and back towards the city centre, almost knee deep on the pavement, their cellophane glinting in the sunlight of the clear, frosty day. A handful of people shuffled along studying the dedications, in what, since the death of Princess Diana, had become the traditional ostentatious symbol of public grief. It turned Mariner's stomach.

At Lloyd House he was asked to wait in reception, which even on this dazzling day was a dark and oppressive cave, the waves of polished steel that formed the ceiling reflecting only the gloom beneath.

'DI Mariner?' He looked up to see a man approaching, tall with cropped, silver hair. 'I'm Jim Addison,

Special Branch. Would you like to come with me?'
Addison took Mariner upstairs where the anti-terrorist
squad was co-ordinating the investigation and had
commandeered the whole of the second floor. This was
the unit routinely called in to handle any issues relating
to national security, supporting the local force in investigating crimes with wider implications. Their last
previous outing, as far as Mariner could recollect, had
been during the somewhat tamer fuel protests; a far cry
from the current situation. But their presence was indica-
tive of the way the thinking was going – until he'd deftly
lobbed a spanner into the machinery.

In a briefing room Addison showed Mariner, on a plan
of the church, where exactly the explosion had occurred. It
had taken out one whole corner of the building and the five
people killed had all been clustered around seat B5; it was
in the same block that Mariner would have occupied. The
shock must have registered on his face.

'I wouldn't read too much into it,' Addison cautioned.
'The Chief Constable was to have been sitting directly in
front of you.'

Mariner scanned the diagram. 'But he's marked as being
here, on the other side of the aisle,' he pointed out.

'A last-minute change. His wife has a slight hearing loss
in one ear and asked to be positioned on the left-hand side
of the amplifiers.' Addison reached over to another desk
and produced a second plan, pointing to the seat immediately in front of Mariner's initials. 'This plan was
operational until the morning of the service.'

'What do you know about the cause of the explosion?'
Mariner asked.

'The investigation is on-going.' Addison's response was
smooth.

'But you must have some idea, the quantity and type of
explosive used.'

'We're getting there, yes.'

'So?'

'We're not ready to disclose that information yet. We're still exploring the possibilities.'

'Which are?'

A breeze stirred the calm water. 'I can't tell you that either. It's not in the public's interest. We want to be sure, that's all.'

And now Mariner was making them less sure. Because, despite Addison's dismissal, there was now a chance that this might not be an attack on the police force, but an attack on one specific individual. It was another possibility they'd have to consider.

Addison studied the note Mariner had received.

'It came through the usual postal channels?'

Mariner confirmed with a nod. 'The postmark is smudged but still easily recognisable as Birmingham. And it's been tested for prints.'

'I doubt that there will be any.' Addison was confident. 'Anyone you've upset recently?' he asked, giving Mariner the distinct impression that he was being humoured.

'I'm a copper. Where do you want me to start?'

'What about political groups?'

'I had to question members of The Right Way as part of an investigation last summer, nothing since then that I'm aware of.' The enquiry into the disappearance and subsequent murder of Asian teenager Yasmin Akram had, for a while, put several right-wing factions under scrutiny. But not for long, and Mariner had fleetingly considered and, with equal speed, discounted them. 'Do you think this could be them?'

'You want my honest opinion? If someone was getting at you personally there are easier ways of doing it.' Addison handed him back the letter. 'It's far more likely that someone who has a grudge against you has seen an opportunity in the press coverage. Anyone who reads the papers could have seen your picture and cooked this up. Didn't you even make some comment to the effect that you should have been inside the church when the bomb went off?'

He was right. Mariner was being paranoid. Why and how could a disaster of such magnitude have been orchestrated just for him?

28th December

When everything around it was torn down to make way for the International Convention Centre and Symphony Hall, the Prince of Wales, an Edwardian Grade II listed building, had been spared. The pub's clientele had also remained loyal, comprising an eclectic combination of theatricals from the nearby Repertory Theatre and sportsmen from the county cricket ground, making it one of the few haunts in Birmingham where celeb-spotting could be a worthwhile exercise. The reason Mariner chose it as the venue to meet Dave Flynn had more to do with the extraordinarily and consistently good real ale. It was also conveniently across the road from the Hyatt where Flynn was staying.

When Mariner arrived, Flynn, his glass almost drained, was already at the bar, in conversation with a woman. Slim and elegant, a smooth curtain of blond hair hung down her back. She moved her hand along the bar, something concealed beneath her fingers, and at that moment Flynn looked round and caught Mariner's eye. At Flynn's word the woman slipped off her bar-stool perch and walked out, her looks and walk somehow not quite in sync, as if the tight skirt and four-inch heel combo had been a touch overambitious.

Mariner went over. 'You don't hang about,' he observed.

Flynn glanced out onto the street in the direction the young woman had gone. 'Just being friendly,' he said, but Mariner couldn't help noticing that he'd pocketed the card. 'It's good to see you, Walking Man. What are you drinking?'

Tall and muscle-packed, Flynn had put on a bit of weight, Mariner thought, and his dark hair, always unkempt, was beginning to recede, but otherwise he'd hardly changed. 'How are you?'

Mariner shrugged. 'I was one of the lucky ones. I guess it will start to feel like that at some point.'

'It's a tough call. I heard your wife was involved.'

'My partner. She's okay. Still in shock of course, but she's all right.'

'I'm glad.' Flynn glanced around him. 'You haven't lost your touch anyway. This is a terrific pub,' he said, lifting the dregs of his beer. 'I knew I could rely on you.'

'Is that why you're here?' Mariner asked. 'The blast?'

Flynn shook his head. 'Let's go and sit down, eh?' He picked up a battered sports bag from where it squatted at his feet, and led the way to a booth in a corner of the room, where they spent a few minutes catching up on personal lives. Dave's marriage, shaky four years ago, was now over. 'Irreconcilable differences,' he said. 'Stuff we should have resolved before we got married.' The job was the issue as Mariner remembered it, Flynn's wife wanting more of a nine-to-five routine. Fat chance. It brought their train of thought inevitably to work.

'Still a DI then?' Flynn asked.

'That conference was enough to put me off going any further,' said Mariner. 'How about you?'

'I've taken a sideways shunt. I work for the Met Special Branch now.'

Mariner was impressed. It was a bit like staying on the substitutes' bench but moving from St Andrew's to Stamford Bridge. 'That must make for a more interesting life,' he said.

'I'm working on the Geoffrey Ryland case.'

'Christ. Playing with the grown-ups, then.' Mariner looked up at him. 'Is that why you're here? There's a Birmingham connection?'

'You could say that.' Rummaging inside the sports bag, Flynn produced a padded envelope, which he tossed onto the table in front of Mariner. 'And as we used to say in our school playground: "You're it".' He picked up his empty glass. 'I'll get another drink in.'

The envelope had been broken open and left unsealed. Mariner unfolded the flap and tipped out the contents, a pile of assorted snapshots. He picked through them with a growing feeling of disquiet. In all there must have been more than a dozen photographs of varying sizes, some black and white, some in faded colour. Most were curling at the edges with age, and on all but one the backs were annotated with numbers and dates.

Looking up he saw that Flynn had returned to the table and set down a glass of single malt in front of him. 'I thought you might need something a bit stronger,' he said. 'We thought at first that we'd uncovered Sir Geoffrey's penchant for young boys. Then we noticed the pattern.'

The pictures themselves were innocuous enough, but they'd made the hairs on Mariner's neck stand on end. The main subject, the face smiling out at Mariner from all those photographs, in various stages of development, was his. Most of the shots were familiar to him, copies of those he'd seen at home over the years. Only one, of him as a newborn, was unfamiliar. The most recent was dated 1974, when he'd been fifteen and in the fourth year at grammar school. Mariner tried to come up with a logical explanation for the discovery, and could only find the one. He'd always wanted to know. There were times in his life when the desperation had been crippling. But he never expected to find out like this, out of the blue from a guy he hardly knew. His whole body felt wired, as if a few thousand volts were buzzing around his veins. Sensing that some kind of reaction was called for, Mariner somehow found his voice and forced a wry laugh. 'Well, what do you know?'

'You had no idea?'

Mariner took a slug of the whisky in an effort to still himself. 'Not a clue. My mother died suddenly last year and took the secret of his identity to her grave. She'd never felt that the time was right to tell me. Then all of a sudden it was too late.'

'I'm sorry.'

Mariner shrugged, unsure of what Flynn was sorry for.

'It was bloody lucky really.' Flynn was giving him time to try and take it in. 'I happened to be overseeing the search of Ryland's house and was there when one of the plods found the key to a safety deposit nobody knew he had. When it turned up these I recognised them straight away, remembered what you'd told me that night at the Drunken Duck. I can help you to arrange a DNA test, just to make sure. But I'm fucked if I can see any other reason why this guy would keep your life history in photographs hidden away, can you?'

'It's a struggle.'

'And these would seem to pretty well confirm it.' Reaching into the bag again, Flynn passed Mariner half a dozen letters bound by an elastic band. Yellowing slightly, they were written in his mother's sloping italic hand, and among them was a programme for a promenade concert at the Albert Hall.

'The Sibelius,' Mariner said.

'Significant?'

'My mother's got the same programme. I found it among her things last summer.'

'They must have gone together.'

Mariner looked again at the date. 'She would have been pregnant with me at the time.'

'Romantic.'

Tucked inside the programme was a card, half the size of a postcard and decorated with sprigs of holly, advertising the Christmas Special at Pearl's Café: purchase one hot drink and snack and get another free.

'Nothing new under the sun,' observed Flynn. 'BOGOF existed even back then, or in this case POGOF. Pearl's café must have been somewhere they met. Very *Brief Encounter*.'

'Except that Celia Johnson wasn't up the duff.'

The last items, sandwiched between the letters, were a couple of press cuttings. Recent newspaper reports of cases Mariner had worked on, a photograph of him that had accompanied a piece about the death of local doctor Owen Payne a couple of years ago. 'And all this was in a security box?' he asked.

'These are the entire contents. According to the bank, Ryland had accessed it not long ago, too, sometime in November.'

'Christ.' Dazed, Mariner sat back a moment, trying to assimilate what this all meant; his father, a man in the public eye whom he'd known and yet not known at all, a man until recently very much alive and well, successful and wealthy, and apparently aware that he had a young son growing up not so very far away. This area of his life that had been void was suddenly filled with a huge persona, not just anyone, but Sir Geoffrey Ryland, and Mariner was overwhelmed by it. It was too huge to take in right here, right now. He'd deal with that later. In the meantime he steered the conversation back to the questions that came naturally. 'So I finally find out who he was, weeks after he gets shot. Are the press on anywhere near the right track about that?'

'It looks like it,' said Flynn. 'I mean, I'm not party to the main investigation, it's being led by Chief Superintendent Griffin. But she has a good reputation. For a change the media have got a lot of the facts right. Ryland's chauffeur, Joseph O'Connor was a former client. The JRC successfully backed his appeal against a possession-with-intent charge in 1998.'

'Do you know the history?'

'Vaguely. O'Connor was arrested for driving around north London in a van with a large amount of H stashed under the boot. He claimed he had no idea it was there.'

'If his conviction was quashed then doesn't that mean he was right?'

'That part's a bit hazy. As you know, the Commission was created in response to cases like the Guildford Four and the Birmingham Six, to look at wrongful convictions and to root out police corruption. It was one of Sir

51

Geoffrey's bugbears. A lot of people felt that he'd been appointed to the chair for that reason. From what I understand O'Connor's conviction was overturned on a technicality, mainly because his statement had been coerced. I don't think there was much question that rules were broken during the interview. Let's face it, that sort of thing happened more often back then, didn't it? Trouble is that dodgy interview techniques can cloud the issue of whether a suspect is actually guilty or not.'

'Ryland must have believed he was innocent otherwise why would he have taken him on as a chauffeur.'

'Self-justification? Ryland had a point to prove where O'Connor was concerned. There's no doubt that at the time of his conviction O'Connor was spending a lot of time in the company of some major league drug dealers. They split into two factions soon after his arrest, and he may have been innocent of the original crime, but it looks as if he made contact with one of his old acquaintances after the dust had settled.'

'Or they got in touch with him,' Mariner said. 'Why have the press dubbed it a revenge killing?'

'It's not in the public domain yet, but the killers used the victims' blood to write a message to that effect on the window. The two factions are rivals in an ongoing tit-for-tat turf war, as violent and deep seated as the one going on between the Johnsons and the Burger Boys on your patch. The MO is a perfect example of a drug-related hit executed by one of these gangs, identical to the others there have been in the last couple of years. The only deviations are the fact that in this case the innocent bystanders happened to be VIPs and the unusual location.'

'How's that explained?'

'The drugs were in the car being shifted around London until the Rylands' trip to Oxfordshire interrupted the transfer. The assassins must have seen it as a golden opportunity. They were right to. Out in the sticks nobody saw or heard anything.'

'But why would O'Connor get involved in that stuff again and risk what must have been a steady job?'

Flynn clearly hadn't anticipated this interrogation, but he played along. 'Why does anyone get involved with drugs? It's bloody lucrative. Ryland might have employed O'Connor, but it was only as a driver. He wouldn't have been paid much, would he? And it was the perfect cover for moving drugs around. Who's going to stop and search a diplomatic car? He might have only done it the once. Perhaps he was presented with the right offer and was tempted.'

Seemed like a nice guy, the girl in the bookshop had said.

'And are you happy with the theories?'

'Like I said, I don't know all the details, I'm only on the secondary investigation team, but from what I know, it's where all the evidence points. They wouldn't be following that line for nothing.'

'So if it's that straightforward, why involve Special Branch at all?'

'Ryland's position. The Home Office has to make sure we get it right, especially with him.'

Mariner had a feeling that it wasn't quite all, but Flynn's tone implied that he'd no more to say.

'So what else can you tell me about Ryland?' Mariner asked instead.

'Recent history? Probably not much more than you already know.'

Mariner felt a sudden unbearable surge of anger. 'Well at least I know now why he pissed off and left us. He must have been an ambitious son of a bitch.'

'You don't know that. Maybe there was good reason—'

Mariner's glare cut him off. 'Like what?'

Flynn gave an impotent shrug. 'He kept your photographs. You must have meant something—'

'Sure. So much that in over forty years he couldn't be arsed to get in touch or come and see me. Not exactly living at the other end of the planet, was he?'

'You have no memory of him at all?'

'No.' Despite the emphatic reply, something niggled at Mariner; a vague recollection that he could hardly give substance to. At his mother's funeral Maggie, a friend of hers, had mentioned a limousine she'd seen pulling away from their flat shortly after Mariner was born. The two men sat through a long silence.

'Does this mean I've got half-siblings?' Mariner said at last.

Flynn shook his head. 'There are no kids. The people we've dealt with most have been Ryland's mother, Eleanor Ryland, and his staff. Diana doesn't seem to have much family either, apart from a sister who lives abroad. She'll be flying in for the inquest. Oh, and they had a dog; company for Mrs Ryland probably. Judging from the amount of valium we found at the house she was of a somewhat nervous disposition.'

More silence. Flynn would make a great partner in an interview. 'How long are you here for?' Mariner asked.

'Back first thing tomorrow.'

'And if I need to ask more questions?'

'Give me a call any time, though like I said, I'm not completely in the know.'

'Listen. I'd like to tell Anna about this in my own time. It's going to take a bit of getting used to. Is it likely to become public knowledge?'

'No reason why it should.'

'Good, so we can keep this to ourselves for now?'

'Sure.'

'Thanks.' Mariner held up the photos. 'And I can take these with me?'

'I can't imagine how they'd be relevant to our investigation. Happy New Year, mate.'

'Happy New Year.'

Outside the pub they went their separate ways. While Flynn returned to his hotel, Mariner dropped down off the main street into Gas Street basin to walk back along the canal to his own place, hoping that he still had it to himself. He covered the distance in record time, pounding along the towpath, barely noticing anything around him, the thoughts that exploded and ricocheted around his head commanding his attention. Never knowing who his father was, of course he'd been aware that the man might be out there somewhere and simply not interested, but there had, at the same time, been the more acceptable alternatives that he was dead, or had emigrated, or at the very least had never been told about Mariner. But now Dave Flynn had turned all that on its head.

Ryland's possession of those photographs meant that he was far from ignorant of his son's existence, and the only thing really stopping him from making contact was the protection of his reputation and his career. It was possible of course that he'd only recently acquired the photos, but if that was the case, why the entire history? One of the photographs in that little collection was of Mariner at just a couple of weeks old. No, what remained was the inescapable truth that Sir Geoffrey Ryland was fully aware that he had a son, he lived only a hundred miles away, but he didn't want to know him. In the last hour Mariner's lofty opinion of the man had plummeted to the lowest depths.

Arriving at the cottage in what seemed like no time at all, Mariner was grateful to note that his new tenant didn't appear to have yet moved in. The place was so cold inside that he could see his breath on the air. He was going to miss the solitude of this place when he didn't have it to himself.

He'd only intended collecting Ryland's autobiography from where he'd left it, surplus to requirement, but his mind was awash with thoughts and questions and the empty, silent house was just too inviting to resist.

Tonight he'd been given the answer to the biggest question mark hanging over his life, but all that had replaced it were endless other questions. Why hadn't Ryland stood by Rose? The most obvious explanation was that his career came first. He didn't want to be saddled with a wife and a kid before he'd had the chance to make his mark on the world. Funny how, even now, women were condemned for making the same kind of choice, but men had always got away with it. The power of the public image was impressive. Mariner would never have categorised Ryland as that kind of man. But he was a politician, an expert at creating a 'persona' and the single-mindedness needed to go into the profession in the first place would stand him in good stead. Oh yes, Ryland would be used to getting his own way, selfish bastard.

Mariner wondered how his mother had felt about it. Had there been bitter arguments, recriminations? It had been hard for her as a lone parent in the sixties and into the seventies. She'd carried that stigma with her. Growing up Mariner had noticed the way that certain people treated her. Rose had never given the impression that she'd felt abandoned or hard done by, but by the time Mariner was old enough to understand their situation she'd had years to come to terms with it.

On the other hand, Ryland could have simply been scared of the prospect of fatherhood in much the same way as Mariner was now. With a flush of guilt Mariner remembered his reaction six years ago when his then-girlfriend Greta had announced out of the blue that she was pregnant. He'd been shocked and appalled. They'd only known each other a year and had never even discussed the idea of children. Had Rose pulled the same stunt on Ryland? Mariner's reaction to Greta had hardly been supportive. Luckily, if that was the word, he'd got away with it, discovering later that Greta had miscarried their baby. But if he couldn't handle it as a mature adult of forty, how would he have felt at twenty years younger?

The disparity in his situation of course was that Greta's actions had been calculated. Things would have been very different for Rose in 1959. The pill didn't come in until two years later and other forms of contraception were pretty unreliable. Ryland would have known if he was sleeping with Rose that pregnancy was always a risk. The likely scenario, as Mariner had suspected for some time, was that he'd been an accident. But along with that rationale had been the comfortable assumption that his father, whoever he might be, had never been told. What disturbed him now was the revelation that Ryland did know about him and must have done from the start. It was beginning to look as if failing to face up to paternal responsibility could be a hereditary disposition.

Chapter Five

Rose's letters would help to clarify things. First Mariner arranged them in chronological order, starting from when he'd have been about three months old.

There were apologies from her to begin with for not having responded sooner to a letter Ryland must have sent: '... *but you wouldn't believe how much time a new baby takes up. Not much time to sit and write. I know this is hard for all of us but I'm sure that in the fullness of time you'll see that it's for the best. Your parents only want what's right for you and now I can understand what a powerful force that is. Already Thomas and I have our own routine and it wouldn't fit with yours. He likes to cry for most of the evening. It would hardly enhance your studying!'*

Then later: '*As Thomas gets older it will be more difficult for him to understand. I think it might be better if your visits stopped. I know it's difficult for you to spare the time anyway. And it will be more complicated, when he begins to talk.'*

Then when Mariner was aged two and a half: '*The girl you've met sounds lovely, congratulations on your engagement. It was quite a surprise, and I really do hope you'll be happy. Diana sounds good for you, and you're right. She mustn't know about us. After what she's been through we're the last thing that she needs. You must look forward to the future and starting a family of your own together.*

'Thomas and I have a good life. In a few weeks we will be moving away from London and it's best that you don't try to get in touch. Mum and Dad are helping out so we won't need financial support. If you honour this wish I will continue to keep you abreast of Tom's progress but if you don't then communication will cease entirely. We each have our own lives now. We always have had, haven't we?'

The final letter was postmarked Leamington, but there was no address given at the top of the page.

It could hardly have been put more plainly. The decision to go it alone was Rose's, something she'd been cheerful about, even proud of. The letters he'd read offered nothing to dispute it. The thing he'd never learn was exactly how far the young Geoffrey Ryland had gone in guiding her into that way of thinking.

Disappointingly, though not surprisingly, the letters were all from his mother's side and told him little about Ryland. Mariner hoped that the book would reveal more. The pile of leftover Christmas gifts was where he'd left them in the lounge, among them *One of the Good Guys*.

The first thing Mariner turned to was the photo on the dust jacket, which he took over to the mirror. It was in the eyes, he thought. Those in the picture were almost exactly like those reflecting back from the glass. How had he not seen that before? Because he hadn't been looking of course.

But as he probed more deeply, Ryland's autobiography was disappointing. Ryland was obviously planning to milk the book-buying public and this was a first instalment only, covering the time of his childhood and student activism up until the time he became an MP in 1967. And of course it told only what Ryland wanted to tell, painting a story of a charmed life. Suddenly Mariner was learning about his privileged roots. From an upper-middle-class family, his father went to Oundle public school before studying law at University College London. It seemed that Ryland's father's thwarted political ambitions had been mostly responsible for his entry into the political arena.

Mariner was glad he'd read the letters first. Over the next hour he was presented with a different view of Ryland; a rather spoiled only child who somewhere along the line had seduced Rose and then deserted her to pursue a more glamorous life. A war baby, born in 1940, it would have made Ryland only nineteen years old when Mariner was born, his mother slightly older. The book described his time at university when he became politically active. It would have coincided with his meeting Rose but nowhere was she mentioned even in passing. Mariner wondered if Ryland had contacted her about the book, but thought it unlikely.

Every few chapters there was a collection of illustrations; photographs of past Ryland generations and Ryland's childhood, as a toddler through to a teenager, looking startlingly like the snapshot of Mariner at around the same age; then graduation, and finally photographs of Ryland's wedding and early married life.

The wedding photos were from 1965, so Ryland was no longer a student, but he'd still been young when he married. Mariner wondered how Rose had really felt about that. In her letter she'd seemed happy enough, but was she just making it easier for Ryland? In later life Rose had stifled Mariner, becoming increasingly demanding and capricious. But all this reminded him of the side of her, generous and considerate, that he'd known as a kid. Mariner was drawn to the photos of the wedding group. Ryland's espoused, Diana, was the eldest daughter of Lady Elizabeth and successful businessman Sir Reginald Fitzgibbon, who had made his money from pulp products, mainly packaging. Judging by the formality of the photographs it had been a proper society wedding, morning coats and top hats, at what looked like some country pile. Was that the first hint that Rose hadn't been good enough for Ryland? If he'd married her it would have been a very different affair. There could have been something in that because otherwise the newlyweds looked an ill-matched pair.

Ryland cut an attractive, charismatic figure but his wife appeared, to put it mildly, dull. She was slim to the point of emaciation and sporting an auburn bouffant à la Margaret Thatcher that owed more to the 1940s than 1960s. But then, though he knew her name, Mariner had heard little about the woman, so the likelihood was that she possessed the qualities essential to the wife of a politician; quietly supportive, remaining in the background yet loyal to her man. Mariner tried to picture Rose playing that role but it made him smile; she'd have had far too much to say for herself. Ryland couldn't afford that when he was starting out in politics.

Mariner frowned at the picture. Diana Ryland looked oddly familiar, but then he must have seen her picture in the press countless times before, at her husband's side. He studied the rest of the wedding group; proud parents, Charles and Eleanor Ryland alongside the mother of the bride, her father conspicuously absent. The youngest of the bridesmaids, who looked about twelve, was Felicity Fitzgibbon, the sister Flynn had mentioned, or perhaps a cousin? The best man, Norman Balfour, had also featured on the graduation shots earlier in the book. The two men must have been good friends and Mariner wondered if the friendship had endured.

Mariner scanned the final collection of prints for any evidence of children, but the book bore out what Flynn had already said; that there were none. The text covered Ryland's early career as a barrister, but there were no happy family snaps, only photographs of Ryland and Diana, usually at official or large social events and a couple of times on holiday in the Mediterranean, and almost always in the informal shots, with the same breed of dog. Had Diana Ryland ever known about her husband's son? In the letter Rose had advised against telling her and Mariner felt certain that Ryland would have followed that advice. The memoir ended as Ryland was about to enter Parliament at the age of twenty-seven.

For all its detail, the book was strangely unsatisfying. It described only the public face of Sir Geoffrey Ryland, the bits that anyone could access. In the wake of his anger, Mariner felt a sudden plunging sense of loss and regret that this would be the only means of getting to know his father. What he really wanted to know was what the man was like day to day. How did he speak in conversation, what were his mannerisms and facial expressions? Did he see the same things when he looked in the mirror? What were his private views across a whole range of subjects? What made him take the decisions he had? What made him laugh? *Would Mariner have liked his father?*

The only person who might be able to provide him with any of those intimate details was the sole survivor, Ryland's mother, Eleanor. The chances were that she wouldn't know anything about Mariner, let alone be prepared to talk to him. But at least he might get another perspective, albeit a somewhat biased one, on what Sir Geoffrey Ryland was like. In many ways the idea was too tempting to resist. And then there was Norman Balfour who might have remained a close friend. College buddy and best man back in '65 didn't necessarily mean that the bond had lasted but it might be worth trying to find out what had happened to him. There were of course plenty of people publicly associated with Ryland, but that wasn't the same thing at all.

Underpinning it all was the possibility that Flynn, and then he, had jumped to the wrong conclusion about those photographs. Hard to explain them otherwise though, and there was that indisputable physical likeness that even Mariner could see and there were the letters of course. But perhaps he'd take Flynn up on the offer of the DNA test just to make absolutely sure. As exhaustion overtook him, Mariner's thoughts were becoming ever more tangled and confused. He closed his eyes for a few minutes and tried to empty his mind.

The phone's insistent ringing woke Mariner, when his watch said 8am. He must have nodded off, still sitting in the armchair, and his limbs were stiff with cold. For a few seconds he was disorientated, until it hit him afresh like a Tsunami. He went to the phone.

It was Anna. 'I thought you might be there. Haven't got the courage to come home?' Mariner greeted that with baffled silence. 'I assume that you and Dave Flynn went on a bit of a bender.'

Since she'd employed her own logic it seemed foolish to disillusion her. 'Something like that,' he said.

'Well I hope you've got the hangover you deserve.'

'Yes.' There was a degree of truth in it. He was groggy and his head was spinning, but it had little to do with alcohol.

'Are you coming back for breakfast?'

'Couple of things I need to do here first.'

'All right.'

It was true. One of things he wanted was time on his own to think, but first, something else.

Stowed in the cupboard under the stairs were two ancient suitcases redeemed from the house in Leamington before he'd put it on the market, and containing what he'd chosen to salvage of his mother's personal effects. When Rose had died, Mariner was in the middle of a high profile murder enquiry and though he'd spent a little time hurriedly going through them, he'd really had little idea of what might be significant. Now he knew what he was trying to find; anything linking her with Sir Geoffrey Ryland.

The hinges of the door were unyielding through lack of use and the cupboard inside was dusty, the cases naturally right at the back, wedged against the cellar door. Dragging them out, it took Mariner almost an hour to sort through the papers again but, apart from the corresponding programme for the Promenade concert, he failed to turn up even the most oblique reference to Ryland. Old photographs in the collection replicated those Flynn had given him, God, was it only last night? From interest he fetched the padded envelope and laid out its contents in sequence, comparing the pictures with those his mother had kept. Most of them were the annual school photographs. One was missing from Flynn's collection, aged thirteen. Rose must have skipped a year.

Returning the second suitcase to its hidey hole, Mariner came across the old plans to the house and a couple of old books on the canal, one of which featured a photograph of the cottage. He left them out for Dyson, at the same time thinking that he should read them himself one day.

He returned Ryland's memoirs to the small pile of unused gifts, still unable to make up his mind. Was his father a hero or villain? And had he really been killed for something as pointless as a couple of kilos of drugs? He wasn't entirely satisfied with Flynn's explanation of that. Meanwhile, he had a proper job to go back to.

On top of the pile of messages Mariner collected on his way in to Granville Lane, was the record of a phone call from a Mr and Mrs Evans, requesting a meeting. Who the hell were they? With a flurry of unwelcome emotions the name Evans hit its mark. Chloe Evans' parents. He couldn't possibly face them, not yet anyway. What on earth would he say? Commonsense said they weren't to know that he was back at work, so he moved the message to the bottom of the pile. He'd deal with it soon, but not now. There were other matters more pressing, like a body down a sewer.

Tony Knox was still off but, apart from that, CID at Granville Lane was buzzing, the squad at full strength again.

'How come everyone's back?' Mariner asked the nearest DC, Bev Pollack.

'We've been taken off the St Martin's enquiry.'

'Why?'

'Nobody's saying. The continued questioning of minority

groups across the city is no longer necessary. Terrorism isn't suspected.' She was quoting what she'd been told.

So what do they think it is?

'Is that because they've got a suspect or suspects?'

'It's weird. Nobody's saying anything. Only that we were no longer needed on the investigation team.'

It was only yesterday that Mariner had been with Addison at Lloyd House. Had his visit there prompted a new line of enquiry? In any event, he'd be the last to know.

Entering his office Mariner thought at first it was someone's idea of a sick joke; on his desk a ten-by-eight photo of a young girl with big blue eyes. He recoiled from it and was still staring in disbelief when behind him, the door opened. 'Madeleine,' said Charlie Glover.

'Madeleine?' Mariner croaked.

'Better name than "sewer queen". It's the mock-up the tech lads have done. Good job, isn't it?'

Mariner exhaled, the horror subsiding. 'Yes,' he said. 'Yes, it is.' He looked hopefully at Glover. 'And you've identified her?'

But they hadn't. 'I've named her that because she's a ringer for Caravaggio's Mary Magdalen.'

Mariner stared.

'It's one of the wife's favourite paintings. It's only temporary. We'll know who she is soon enough.'

'You've had a breakthrough? Something from the house to house?'

'Better than that, guv. Forensics came back with a lovely set of prints from the bin bag and duct tape that don't belong to the deceased, so must be from who ever gift-wrapped her for us. I sent them through to Croydon and they got a hit. They've faxed through details.' He handed Mariner the printouts, details of one Alecsander Lucca, also an Albanian national. He's applying for British citizenship, so his prints are on file. He's temporarily residing at an address in Stirchley.'

'Close to where Madeleine was found.'

'Surprise, surprise. And while he's waiting for his application to be processed he's working in a local restaurant.'

'That's two strong leads. Well done, Charlie.'

'Yeah, well,' said Glover modestly, 'let's see if they go anywhere first. Want to come?'

Mariner reached for the coat he'd only just removed.

'Good Christmas?' Mariner asked on the drive there, by way of making conversation. Glover, he knew, had a young family.

'Very nice sir. We had everyone over, parents and grandparents.'

'All your parents are still around?'

'Yes sir. Don't know what we'd do without them.'

Wilmott Road was like any number of streets in Stirchley, a kind of rundown no-man's-land that lay somewhere between inner city and suburbia. The population was transient, with many of the terraced properties on short-term lease and residents identifiable by passport and immigration papers, rather than driving licences or National Insurance cards. Mariner and Glover knew this because the street was on the 'sensitive' list as a location likely to be targeted by local racist groups, though so far there had been no serious incidents.

The door of 158 was answered by a lanky man, mid-thirties, with coal black eyes that didn't exactly radiate welcome, especially when Mariner and Glover produced warrant cards. His name, he told them, was Goran Zjalic (he pronounced it 'Yalitch') and he was a Serbian national. He was even less keen on letting them into the house, but Mariner supposed that having been persecuted by his own countrymen, suspicion towards anyone with official status was an understandable reaction. Inside, the accommodation looked temporary, the wooden floors were bare except for a littering of junk mail, and they had to squeeze past boxes of disposable nappies in the hallway to get into an uncarpeted living room that contained only a sagging brown sofa that looked at least secondhand, and a portable TV resting on a vintage 1950s coffee table. Somewhere they could hear a baby crying.

Glover proffered the immigration file picture of Lucca. 'Do you know him?'

Zjalic hesitated, and Mariner imagined a lifetime's habit of weighing up how much information to give. 'He live here,' Zjalic said eventually, pointing upwards.

'You know him well?' Glover asked.

Zjalic tilted a flattened palm. 'We meet in the hallway sometimes.' His voice was thickly accented.

'When did you last see him?'

Zjalic lifted his shoulders. 'Three week, a month. He go home.'

'Home?' It wasn't what they had hoped to hear.

'Tirana. His family there.'

The door opened and a young woman, no more than a teenager, appeared, cradling a very young baby, the one they'd heard, except that now it had a dummy jammed in its mouth. Ignoring Glover and Mariner she spoke insistently to Zjalic, who barked back at her, prompting a hasty exit.

'My sister,' Zjalic apologised. 'Always want something.'

Glover showed him the digitally enhanced picture of Madeleine. 'How about her?'

Zjalic studied the picture for longer, finally, slowly, shaking his head.

'You're certain?' said Glover.

'I don't know her,' said Zjalic. 'Pretty girl.'

'Pretty, dead girl,' said Glover.

Zjalic's eyes widened, with surprise or fear, it was hard to tell.

'And now we badly need to talk to Alecsander Lucca. He may have been the last person to see her alive.'

Suddenly Zjalic was on the defensive. 'I swear. He say he go back home.'

'Do you remember which day? It's important.'

'I don't know. Three, four week.' It was all they were going to get. Glover left his card in the unlikely event that Lucca should reappear.

The manager of the restaurant where Lucca worked could be more specific. Lucca hadn't turned up for work since December 4th. 'A girl came in the restaurant and caused a scene,' he said. 'She's shouting at Lucca in front of all my customers.'

Glover brought out the picture of Madeleine. 'Is this the girl?'

But the manager wasn't sure. 'Could be.' It was possible that their picture wasn't an exact likeness.

'Do you know what the disagreement was about?' Glover asked.

The manager looked surprised. 'Money. Is always about money, no?'

'Was she his wife, or girlfriend?'

The manager shrugged. 'I don't interfere. I just want her out of my restaurant.'

'And did she go?'

'Only with Lucca, He took her home.'

'What time was this?'

'Maybe nine, nine-thirty.'

'And what time did he come back?'

'He didn't. It's the last time I see him.'

'We can check flights on and around December 4th to verify that Lucca has left the country,' Mariner said, when they were back in the car. 'And then it'll be up to Interpol. If he has turned up back home we'll be looking at extradition – with a country that doesn't yet have any formal extradition laws.'

'It should be easier, shouldn't it?' Glover was more optimistic. 'The Albanian authorities won't put up much of a fight. Won't it just be a question of finding him and bringing him in?'

'It's not the Albanians we'll have to worry about,' Mariner said. 'It's the CPS at our end who can make life

68

difficult. Unless we present a watertight case and follow all the correct procedures, if Lucca gets back here and we charge him for murder, we run the risk of him getting off on a technicality. It'll be a diplomatic nightmare. Could take months.'

'Nothing like a positive outlook sir,' said Glover.

'It's called reality. We'll need to get together the evidence for extraditing Lucca, material and circumstantial, and send it off to the International CPS in London. You hadn't got plans for New Year, had you?'

New Year's Eve

Something that had always been lost on Mariner was the human compulsion to celebrate the advent of the New Year, come what may. Tradition had such a lot to answer for. For the sake of conforming, Mariner had agreed they'd go out with Knox and Selina, who was already up and about and determined to get on with her life. Nothing fancy, just a local Chinese restaurant. They all arrived in the car park at the same time. Offers of help declined, Anna and Mariner waited while Knox retrieved Selina's new wheelchair from the boot of his car and wrestled to open it up, all the time trying to make it look as if he'd been doing it for ever.

Several minutes elapsed while Mariner and Anna stood shivering. 'Are you sure there's nothing—?' Mariner offered.

'I'm fine,' came the curt, if slightly breathless, reply. The wheelchair at last unfolded, Knox pushed it round to the passenger door for Selina to get in. Not until they got to the restaurant entrance did they realise there was a step, in itself not a problem, except that the porch arrangement and the angle of the inner door made it impossible for Knox to manoeuvre the wheelchair in. Between them Mariner and Knox grappled with it for a couple of minutes, Selina laughing rather too brightly at their efforts, but in the end Knox had to ask a waiter if there was an alternative way in.

69

It was at the back of the building. 'That's all right, I'll use the tradesman's entrance,' Selina smiled. 'I'm not proud.'

'We'll all go that way then,' said Anna, and Mariner loved her for being so supportive. They trooped down a poorly lit side passage, past waste bins, through the kitchen and past the toilets, only to find once inside, that they'd been allocated a window table and had the task of navigating their way back through the crammed dining area. Progress was hampered while other customers were asked to move, chairs were pushed aside and coats and handbags retrieved. The eagerness of the restaurant staff to help only served to draw more attention to the situation.

'Thanks. Sorry,' Selina smiled, time and time again, until her face seemed to be fixed in a kind of rictus.

'Christ, I'm knackered,' said Knox when finally they were all seated around their table. He grinned as he said it and Selina smiled back, but then the three of them watched in horror as the fragile façade crumbled and she began to sob. Anna was beside her immediately with a comforting arm, as Knox looked on helplessly and Mariner could see the gleam in his eyes too.

'I don't know if I can do this,' Selina wept. Dabbing at her eyes she forced a smile through the tears. 'I can't even get up and storm out of the bloody place!'

Knox closed a hand over hers. 'It won't be like this for ever,' he soothed. 'It'll get better.'

A group at the next table had gone quiet. 'What are you all staring at?' Mariner barked.

Somehow they got through the meal, the forced conversation a stark contrast to the raucousness around them. Mariner had considered telling them all his news, but somehow this didn't seem the right moment. By the time they'd waded through three courses Selina was exhausted and wanted to go home. In the car park they soberly wished each other a happy New Year before Knox and Selina drove off.

Since the millennium celebrations it was *de rigueur* to

launch fireworks at midnight to mark the start of the New Year. Driving up to Rednal, Mariner and Anna parked at the Rose and Crown to walk up Rose Hill on the footpath through the woods, to where the trees opened out on panoramic views across the city. They found a spot away from the crowds and Mariner put his arms round Anna, holding her close to him as they watched the eruption of light and colour.

'Poor Selina,' said Anna. 'A whole new life to get used to. Makes you wonder what the New Year will bring.'

'I think the old one brought more than enough surprises,' said Mariner.

'It's going to be a good year for us,' said Anna, hugging him tight. 'I know it. We've everything to look forward to.'

And so much to look back on, thought Mariner.

2nd January

Mariner had tacked an extra day's leave onto the bank holiday, so that, on the first day it re-opened, he left Anna still sleeping and went to the central library archive. He was the only one there and before long the librarian, a fluttery woman in an ankle-length skirt and jangling ethnic jewellery, that Mariner was certain must contravene the library's rules on quiet, came to help.

'I'm researching Sir Geoffrey Ryland,' Mariner told her.

'A wonderful man,' she enthused, 'and such a sad loss. I'll see what I can find for you.'

It being a slow day, she was back in a matter of minutes with hard-backed albums of newspaper archive material, so much of it she'd had to stack it on a trolley. Minutes later she returned with more and eventually Mariner had to call a halt.

'Well, call me if there's anything else you need,' she smiled.

'This time next year,' Mariner murmured under his breath.

He'd already decided that the simplest thing would be to

work backwards chronologically, so first he looked up the most recent coverage of Sir Geoffrey Ryland's shooting. It had made the front page of all the main nationals so he had plenty of material to choose from. The incontrovertible facts were that Ryland's car had been ambushed in Oxfordshire late at night en route back to London from a regular visit to his mother. It had happened in woodland close to a local daytime beauty spot, and the car had been discovered by local farmer Tim Leavis in the early hours of the morning.

Police arriving at the scene found Ryland and his wife shot dead and still sitting in the back of the car, but more importantly Joseph O'Connor, also shot dead but lying on the road beside the open boot of the limousine. The spare wheel compartment had been prised open, yielding traces of heroin, and ballistics had identified the weapon used for the shootings as a nine-millimetre Browning automatic, the drug dealers' weapon of choice. The police conclusion, that either O'Connor had been knowingly transporting the drugs, or was being used in the way he claimed to have been at the time of his original conviction, was entirely logical. In any event O'Connor was perceived to be the cause of the hold-up, and was, from the outset, the focus of the investigation. A key factor influencing officers on the current investigation was that only days before the shooting O'Connor had been seen in the company of Terry Brady, the suspected owner of the original heroin stash. A witness reported having seen O'Connor and Brady together. Despite the column inches, the hard copy largely regurgitated the same few facts over and over and Mariner had to switch to microfiche to pursue other aspects of the case.

A search on Joseph O'Connor brought up details of his acquittal in May 1998. His original sentence had been eight years for possession of a kilo of heroin with intent to supply. Much as Flynn had said, the conviction was subsequently 'stayed on the grounds of abuse of process'; another way of saying that his confession had been coerced.

72

At first glance it seemed a very humble case to have sparked the interest of the JRC. But then it was a while ago, and was probably one of the first cases reviewed by the Commission and therefore clear cut. They'd have played it safe in the early days.

Because O'Connor's case was a relatively minor one there wasn't much; a short piece in the London *Standard* that included details of where he lived (Mariner made a note of that), and a brief statement of gratitude from O'Connor and his wife Sharon for everything Ryland had done for them, accompanied by a strong denial that he had ever been involved with drugs. All this below a photograph of the newly reunited couple.

O'Connor had been working for Ryland since shortly after his release. What prompted that? Ryland couldn't go giving jobs to everyone he got off. And then O'Connor it seems had let him down. It must have been a good job, not too taxing, and from the newspaper reports it seemed that O'Connor was a family man, married with four kids. So why jeopardise a bloody good job by getting involved in drugs again and why even risk making contact with the man said to have set him up the first time round? Unless, as Flynn had implied, it was for the money.

There were reports on some of the other sentences the JRC had been instrumental in getting overturned, some of them well-known high-profile cases that Mariner had read about previously. The Commission had also been responsible for exposing a number of corrupt special operations squads in different forces across the country. As Dave Flynn had rightly said, the JRC itself was established mainly as a result of the public outcry that had followed the cases of the Birmingham Six and Guildford Four. Ryland might have left the government but he'd continued to play an active part in the politics of justice.

While he was in the library Mariner cast back through the newspapers for any other personal information he could glean about Ryland. In the early seventies he seemed to be

73

often in the headlines, at around the time when he entered parliament. Prior to being an MP he'd been something of an agitator and on joining the government he hadn't entirely given up the cause. Mariner was specifically interested in the time around 1959/1960 when he was born, but he could find nothing much at that time that hadn't featured in Ryland's memoirs.

In 1963 there were a couple of pictures of Ryland with an attractive-looking blonde hanging on his arm and for a heart-stopping moment Mariner thought it was Rose. But it was only momentary self-delusion. The paper described the woman as Ryland's fiancée, socialite Caroline Foster-Young. Interestingly though, Mariner noted, the pictures were taken only a matter of months before Ryland had become engaged to Diana Fitzgibbon. One fiancée to another in a matter of only months; what had expedited that speedy move? There were a couple of news stories about Diana Ryland, along with an entry in *Who's Who*, chiefly as the daughter of Sir Reginald Fitzgibbon who had died shortly before Diana's engagement. She came across as Mariner had surmised, as the archetypal dutiful politician's wife and was involved as trustee of a number of charities, notably helping to launch the birth parents' register for adoptees. That might imply that childlessness hadn't been a conscious decision, although the Rylands themselves hadn't gone on to adopt.

Mariner worked all through the day photocopying and making notes on relevant areas until suddenly he realised how dark it was becoming outside.

'Did you get what you wanted?' The librarian saw him leave.

Had he? 'Yes thanks.'

He'd also reached a decision. From his vehicle in the dark-ened car park, Mariner phoned Dave Flynn on his mobile. Flynn was still working.

'I'd like you to fix up that DNA test.'

'Can you send me a sample?'

'I'll get it in the post to you tomorrow.'

'It'll take a few days.'

'Sure. I'd like an address for Ryland's mother, too.'

'I don't know about that.' Flynn was cagey. 'Meeting you would be a hell of a shock for her and she's still getting over her son's death. She's in her nineties and not in the best of health.'

'She's my grandmother, remember?'

'So she is.' Despite his reluctance, Flynn had been expecting the request and had the details to hand. He recited an address to Mariner over the line.

On his way to Anna's house Mariner went to the cottage where he sterilised a needle and jabbed his finger, squeezing some of the blood out onto the lint of a fresh plaster. He tucked it into an evidence bag with his name and date of birth, sealed it and addressed the envelope to Dave Flynn, marking it 'Confidential'.

Walking to the post box took him past the Boatman, so he stopped in for a quick pint. Three of the old regulars who Mariner knew only by sight needed someone to make up a game of fives and threes. The game was a welcome diversion, and it was closing time before he left the pub.

Chapter Six

On the drive to Anna's house, Mariner felt as if Eleanor
Ryland's address was burning through his pocket. A whole
chapter of his life, both exhilarating and intimidating, was
opening up before him. The house was dark so he crept in
quietly, undressing in the bathroom so that he wouldn't
disturb Anna.

'You've worked late,' she said, as he was halfway across
the bedroom floor.

'I called in at the pub,' he admitted, not correcting her
first assumption.

'Becky phoned. She's invited me to go and stay for a few
days.'

Mariner got into bed and she moved over to snuggle up
against him, her body smooth and warm next to his.

'That sounds a great idea. The peace and quiet will be
good for you,' he said. Ordinarily he might have felt abandoned but this time what he was really thinking was: great,
I'll have some time on my own.

'You don't mind?'

'Of course not, I'll be fine.' He thought of how icy the
roads had been lately and for some inexplicable reason had
a flash of Anna's car skidding off the road and into a ditch.
His heart quickened. 'I should drive you though.'

'There's no need. I can drive myself, unless of course
you want to come too. It might be good for you to get away

for a few days, and I know they'd love to see you. You could meet Megan.'

'There's a lot to do here.' Same old excuse but she didn't push it. Mariner knew he should tell Anna what he'd learned, but for some reason he couldn't. He wanted to find out more about Ryland first and have the chance to work out how he felt about it before others started giving their views. Besides he didn't have absolute proof yet that it was true. What if he told her and then it turned out to be a mistake? He didn't want to risk that. He knew he was behaving strangely but she'd put it down to what they'd just been through.

'Might be just as well that you don't come this time,' Anna said. 'Megan's teething with a vengeance apparently, so they're not getting much in the way of sleep. I wouldn't want it to put you off anything.'

'What about you?'

'Oh I can take it. It'll be good preparation.' The fingers lying on his chest began a downward progression. 'We should start getting in some practice.'

He caught her hand and squeezed it. 'I'm pretty tired.'

'Okay, whenever you're ready.'

But even as she said it, lying in the dark, Anna wondered when that was likely to be. This desire for children had crept up on her suddenly, when she had least expected it, and though she strived to keep it under control and was trying to play it cool with Tom, it was becoming all-consuming. Staying with Becky and Mark would be a mixed blessing. She loved the time with Megan, but the longing for her own child was growing stronger, a feeling that Tom didn't entirely seem to share.

The explosion had been a setback, he'd seemed keener before that, and she couldn't help but think his experiences on the night had simply compounded the doubts that already existed. She could sense him retreating from her again as he sometimes did. She'd just have to be patient and sit it out. Often he was more receptive in the early morning, but when she woke and reached out for him, it was already light and he had gone.

Mariner was with Jack Coleman, watching as the gaffer pored over a list of names. 'The guests for my retirement bash,' he told Mariner. 'God, there's some ancient history here. Why can't they just let me slip out quietly through the back door?'

'You deserve more than that, sir.'

'Even if it's not what I want?' Coleman shook his head sadly. 'Anyway, what can I do for you?'

'To be honest, I'm finding it hard to concentrate, sir.'

'That doesn't surprise me.'

'I wondered if I might take a few more days' leave.'

'Of course, take as long as you need. You and Anna going somewhere?'

'We might, yes.' He wouldn't tell Coleman that it was to opposite sides of the country.

'Charlie Glover's got the Albanian covered?'

'We're waiting for Alecsander Lucca to turn up back home. Interpol have been notified and they're going to let us know. Meanwhile Charlie's putting together the information for the CPS. Until we've found Lucca there's not much else we can do.'

'And then we're into extradition,' Coleman sighed. 'Which could take for ever. Okay. Tell Glover to keep me posted.'

Mariner was home again in time to help Anna to load up her car.

'Look after yourself,' she said.

'You too. And be careful, the roads are icy, don't drive too fast.' He quelled the feeling of rising panic as that same image of Anna's car going into a skid flashed through his mind. 'Are you sure you don't want me to take you?'

'I'm sure. I'll go carefully. Shall I call you when I get there?'

'I'll be out and about. I've got Becky's number. I'll call you.'

The address Flynn had given him for Eleanor Ryland was not so very far away, an hour's run down the M40 and into Oxfordshire, the south Cotswolds. On the motorway Mariner took it at a steady speed but had to work hard to ward off the fear of trucks swerving and slamming into the side of his car. Only when he stopped and felt the tension drain out of his shoulders did he realise how tightly he'd been gripping the steering wheel.

A little way out of the village of Wythinford, The Manse was a Georgian manor house built of the distinctive yellow ashlar stone that characterised the Cotswold area, and set thirty metres back from the lane behind wrought-iron gates and glossy rhododendrons; a blob of mellow warmth in the pallid, frosty landscape. It occurred to Mariner that if things had turned out differently this is where he might have spent his summer holidays, instead of in a caravan at Barmouth. Initially he hadn't the nerve to go in, but the couple of reporters camped outside made it easier for him to loiter inconspicuously for a while.

'Any action?' he asked one of them.

'Not for days. We'll be packing up soon.'

When Mariner did finally get up the courage to approach the gates, his warrant card was enough to get him past the uniformed constable standing sentry duty. The dog he could hear energetically barking on the other side as he rapped the knocker, did nothing more than wag its tail and sniff around his legs once the door was opened. When her son's wedding photographs had been taken Eleanor Ryland was impressively tall, but since then her height had been diminished by the effects of osteoporosis, which had curved her shoulders over like the handle of a walking cane, and her clothes hung loosely from her wasted frame. But she stood unwavering to greet Mariner, sharp eyes peering from a face that was pale and furrowed with age, her thinning silver hair drawn back and fixed with a tortoiseshell clip from which wispy strands escaped.

'Inspector Mariner,' she read from his warrant card, before studying his face. 'Are you new? I don't recall the name.' Despite the physical frailty, her voice was steady and clear; the clipped no-nonsense intonation of the upper classes.

'I've been working with DI Flynn.'

'Ah yes. Mr Flynn. He's a pleasant young man.' She stepped back. 'Nelson. Let the gentleman in!' The dog, a rusty brown wire-haired effort of an animal, similar to those pictured in Ryland's memoirs, shuffled backwards, sniffing the air.

Inside, the house was a museum piece, not so different from those country homes that Mariner's mother had dragged him round as a kid, on the rare occasions when she'd been trying to infuse him with some culture. They passed through a cavernous vestibule into a formal living room where Queen Anne chairs, a sofa and several small card tables were arranged in front of a real log fire. French windows overlooked a terrace and several acres of lawn and shrubs. Eleanor Ryland invited Mariner to sit, before lowering herself carefully into the armchair facing him. 'This is about Geoffrey I imagine,' she said.

'I'm very sorry for your loss, Mrs Ryland.'

'Thank you.' She seemed to be studying him intently. 'I suppose you're of the same view?'

'What view is that?'

'That he was killed because of Joseph, his driver.'

'What do you think?'

'I feel that's what I should believe, because it's what everyone keeps telling me.'

'But you think differently?'

'Joseph seemed so agreeable, and always so genuinely grateful to my son for what he had done.'

'You met him?'

'Many times. He'd been with Geoffrey for several years.

Of course everyone had always warned Geoffrey that he was playing with fire by employing a former client, but he believed strongly that if he wasn't prepared to offer the man a chance, then why should anyone else?'

'He sounds like a man with integrity.'

'Yes, he was.' Her eyes shone with passion. 'Oh, he had his flaws of course, as we all do, but you can be proud of him.'

'I'm sorry?' For several seconds Mariner lost his emotional equilibrium.

She smiled. 'You may be a police officer, but that's not your interest in my son is it? I know who you are. I've only got to look at you. You're my grandson, aren't you? Now, would you join me in a glass of sherry?'

'When did you find out about me?' Mariner asked. He brought across two glasses, poured from a cut-glass decanter, taking the first mouthful, and trying not to grimace at the cloying taste. He'd been tempted to ask about alternatives, but doubted that Eleanor Ryland would recognise real ale if it came out of a hole in the ground. The dog, after his period of excitement, had flopped onto the Chinese rug at their feet.

'Oh, I've known about you right from the beginning, before you were born. Doing the right thing by your mother was something Geoffrey agonised about for weeks, years even, and yes, he confided in me.'

'So he did consider making a go of it with my mother.'

'He wanted to marry her and do what he felt was his duty. It was your mother, along with Charles, my husband, who between them managed to talk him out of it.'

'Charles disapproved?'

'It wasn't so much that. It was more that he had plans for Geoffrey. Charles was a frustrated politician, though he'd never pursued his ambition further than the local council, and when Geoffrey expressed an interest early on Charles seized on it. He wanted Geoffrey to have the best

81

possible chance of success, and having to support a wife and child so young would not have helped.'

'He married six years later.'

'Those years made a world of difference. I know that's probably hard for you to believe, and I'll understand if you choose not to, after all, there's absolutely no reason why you should trust the somewhat biased opinion of a stranger. But that was really the way it was. Your mother was a remarkable young woman and wholly unselfish. She knew that Geoffrey had a promising career ahead of him. Geoffrey was only nineteen and still at university when you were conceived, and while he and your mother had a certain fondness for one another, neither pretended to be in love. I hope that in time you can come to accept it as the truth.'

What she said rang true with what Mariner had read. 'There were some letters, from my mother to Sir Geoffrey,' he said. 'They convey more or less the same thing. And it makes sense of what I know. I never remember Rose being bitter about our situation. I suppose I'd always thought that she'd had time to get used to it, but if she had harboured resentment I'm sure it would have emerged somehow.'

'Your mother was a pragmatist, ahead of her time.'

'You said "was", so you know that she died last year.'

'Geoffrey told me. He saw an announcement in *The Times*.'

So he had seen it. 'I put it there in the hope that he might show up.'

'He almost did. He was devastated by the news. But he and Diana were having problems. Diana was unwell again; the past coming back to haunt them in other ways, so he didn't feel that he could. Did your mother marry?'

'No. She stayed single.'

'These days of course no one would bat an eyelid at your situation, but it must have been hard for both of you.'

Sympathy wasn't what Mariner had been expecting and

he was touched. 'It's had its moments,' he said. 'It got more difficult as I got older. Our relationship became very intense and I left home when I was seventeen because I couldn't stand it any more. There were a lot of years when my mother and I weren't close.' Mariner rarely spoke about any of this to anyone and it surprised him that it surfaced so easily.

'I'm sorry to hear that,' Eleanor Ryland said. She paused. 'I know you must have a poor opinion of your father, but it would be a mistake to think that Geoffrey didn't care for you or think about you,' she said. 'The lack of contact was as much your mother's decision as his. He used to visit you occasionally when you were young, but when he married Diana—'

Mariner nodded. 'One of Rose's letters to him is quite explicit. Diana didn't know about me?'

'No. Geoffrey could never have told her, she wouldn't have coped. But your mother kept him informed for years and sent him pictures. He would bring them to show to me.' Her eyes filled up. 'I would have so much liked to have seen you before, my only grandchild. But the decisions had been made and we had to be strong.'

The good old British stiff upper lip, thought Mariner, realising for the first time that he and Rose weren't the only ones to have missed out for all those years.

'The photographs were what gave it away,' Mariner said. 'DI Flynn came across them, along with some of my mother's letters and some cuttings. Fortunately we're old friends, so for the time being the matter has stayed between us.'

'Strangely enough Geoffrey spoke about you only recently. It was the first time since your mother's death. He was writing his memoirs again, which always stirred up long forgotten feelings. It crossed my mind that he might be planning to contact you.'

'When was this?'

'A few weeks before Christmas.'

'And when was the last time you saw Sir Geoffrey?'
Mariner was still a long way off thinking of Ryland as
bearing any relation to him.

'Two weeks before he died.'

'And how did he seem?'

She smiled. 'Once a detective always a detective, eh?'

'It's a tough habit to break. Was anything troubling him?'

'I keep thinking about that of course. Diana hadn't been
well. She was always emotionally vulnerable. She had one
of those terrible depressive illnesses that comes and goes
and had been going through a bad patch again. And you
would know more than most what a politically sensitive
field Geoffrey worked in. He was always under pressure at
work.'

'It's a difficult job.'

'Yes. Geoffrey knew that creating the Commission was
politically the right thing to do, but once there it was
impossible to keep everyone happy. The great British
public wants to see justice served and overturning wrongful convictions is popular, but not with the Crown
Prosecution Service, nor, would I imagine, you and your
colleagues.'

'Nobody wants to see innocent people convicted.'

'It doesn't make your work any easier though, does it?
Geoffrey was always aware of that tension.'

'Every time there's a high profile miscarriage case, it
undermines public confidence in the whole judicial system.
Was there anyone in particular he'd upset recently?'
Mariner asked.

'That I don't know. He never went into detail. I expect
he thought I wouldn't understand.' She waved a dismissive
hand. 'These are the ravings of a decrepit old woman. You
shouldn't take much notice of me.'

'Did you talk to the police about it?'

'There was nothing specific to tell.' It was too vague.
She was right about that.

Mariner heard the front door slam and moments later a

light knock preceded a young woman with a cloud of permed hair. 'Would you like some tea, Mrs Ryland?' she asked, cheerfully, taking in Mariner's presence.

'That would be lovely, Janet.' As Janet disappeared, Eleanor turned back to Mariner. 'Janet comes in to cook for me every evening, except for the weekends when she leaves something ready prepared.'

Minutes later the woman returned with tea and pastries on a tray, which she placed on the table nearest to Eleanor. 'Would you like to stay for dinner?' Eleanor asked Mariner. 'It will be no trouble and I'd like to get to know my only grandson better. After all, we have a few years to make up for, don't we? It wouldn't be any trouble would it, Janet?'

'Not at all, Mrs Ryland. It'll make a nice change to feed someone with a healthy appetite.' With a parting smile, she closed the door behind her.

'Janet thinks I don't eat enough, but one's appetite does diminish with old age. Can you stay?'

'That would be very nice, thank you.' Mariner reached over and took the bone china cup and saucer from her. 'You're here on your own the rest of the time, then?'

'Well, besides Janet, I have Ralph who does the garden for me and once a week Millie comes to do some cleaning, so I don't do too badly for company. And at the moment I have Nelson, too.' The dog lifted an ear at the mention of his name. 'Geoffrey used to say I was vulnerable out here in the wilds. But he worried too much.'

'I could have a look round before I go,' said Mariner. 'There might be some quite simple things that we could do to make sure that you're safe.'

'Well, if you think it matters.' She was humouring him.

For dinner Mariner had expected something traditional – rack of lamb or roast beef – so when as they sat in the dining room in high backed chairs, the vegetarian moussaka with couscous came as quite a surprise.

'I don't eat out very often so Janet likes to ring the

changes. I much prefer food cooked at home. Your father wasn't a great fan of restaurants either, especially those awful new self-service ones.'

Mariner hadn't heard them called that for a while. 'We have something in common then,' he said. 'What else didn't he like?'

'Liver,' she chuckled, continuing the culinary theme. 'Oh, and avocados. Diana was quite a conventional sort and he got to be quite particular. You don't wear a ring. Are you married, with a family?'

'No.' Mariner hesitated. 'But my partner Anna and I are thinking about it.' It was the truth: they were thinking about it.

'How wonderful! A great-grandchild.'

'Geoffrey and Diana didn't have children?' Mariner hazarded, conscious that he might be on sensitive ground.

'Only Nelson and his predecessors.' At the sound of his name, the dog who had been patiently waiting beside Mariner, staring at the floor and hoping for scraps, immediately scurried round to Eleanor's side. 'I'm taking care of him for the moment but he's really too much for me. I can't give him the exercise he needs. He'll have to be re-homed eventually but I couldn't bring myself to do it just yet. It was one of the cruellest ironies that Geoffrey and Diana were unable to have children, and was something that affected Diana badly her whole life. I think children might have helped her to be less self-absorbed, provided more of a balance in her life. These days of course they could have had some kind of treatment I suppose, but at the time there was nothing that could be done. You must bring Anna to see me.'

'She's staying with friends near Hereford at the moment, but I will. She'd like that too.'

After the meal, Janet brought them coffee. 'I'll just tidy up the kitchen and then I'll be off, Mrs Ryland.'

'Thank you, Janet. Lovely dinner again,' Eleanor said. 'She goes on to her job cooking at the pub,' she told

Mariner when Janet had gone. 'I don't know where she gets the energy.'

'I should go too,' said Mariner. 'You look tired.'

'One of the frustrations of advancing years,' she smiled. 'I'll be out like a light and then awake again at four in the morning.'

'I was going to check your security.'

'Well, if you really think it's necessary.'

'It wouldn't do any harm. Shall I?'

'Yes, you carry on. I'll finish my coffee.'

It didn't take Mariner long to check the front and back doors and the ground floor windows. The frames were old and some of the catches flimsy.

'Is there anything I can help with?' Janet came up behind him as he was testing a window. She looked a little less friendly now.

'I'm just checking how secure the place is,' said Mariner. 'I'm a policeman.' He wasn't sure how much else Janet had overheard but he'd leave it Eleanor to tell her the rest.

'Right.'

But he had the impression that Janet's suspicion wasn't alleviated.

'Have you ever considered having a burglar alarm?' Mariner asked Eleanor as he was leaving.

She was dismissive. 'From time to time I get those people round here trying to sell them, but really it's hardly necessary. There's nothing much to take that's worth anything.'

Thieving wasn't always what intruders had in mind, Mariner thought, but he didn't say it out loud. He didn't want to frighten her.

'I do hope you'll come back to see me again, soon.'

'I'll bring Anna.'

'Something to look forward to.' She put out her bony arms and hugged him.

Freezing fog on the motorway made driving north again

slow and hazardous. From habit Mariner went back to his place where, despite the hour he found Bill Dyson unloading his car. 'I'm sorry,' Mariner said. 'I didn't know you were moving in today. I'll try not to get in the way.'

'No, it's fine. Dyson said, easily. You can give me a hand if you like.' Though there wasn't much to take upstairs.

'How's business?' Mariner asked.

Dyson's mind was elsewhere. 'Eh? Oh, coming on slowly. You Midlanders are uncommonly suspicious of folk from the north, and there's plenty of competition. I may decide it's not worth it after all.'

'Not before the six month let is up, I hope.'

Dyson smiled. 'Don't worry. You'll get your pound of flesh. In fact I really like this place. Even if it doesn't work out here, should you ever think of selling—'

'It might yet happen.' It appeared to be part of Anna's long-term plan. 'Actually I might have a customer for you.'

'Really?'

'I just may need to work on her a bit more. She's an elderly lady who doesn't see the need just yet.'

'I know the type.' Dyson smiled. 'Let me know when she's ready. Oh, and thanks for those drawings you left out. They look interesting.'

'No problem.'

His possessions moved, Dyson retreated to the upstairs rooms and Mariner heard him moving around rearranging things. It was after ten but he phoned Anna's mobile to check that she was okay. It was immediately cut off. He tried again but the same thing happened, then he remembered this from Anna's previous visits. Becky and Mark lived in a low-lying area surrounded by hills and very often couldn't get a signal. He risked ringing the land line hoping that he wouldn't wake the whole household, but he needn't have worried. The cocophony of banging, clattering and wailing wouldn't have been out of place on the Somme.

'It's Megan playing,' Anna said cheerfully.

'She's still awake?'

'She's got teeth coming through so she can't sleep. Becky's a bit low so I've sent her and Mark off to the pub while I babysit. You should see Megan now, she's a little darling. She's sitting up all on her own. How clever is that?'

'It's great.' Mariner hoped she couldn't detect the lack of enthusiasm.

'And it's so lovely out here; green and peaceful. I might start looking at property prices, just to get an idea.' Mariner's stomach clenched involuntarily. 'So what have you been up to?'

'Oh, boring stuff. Trying to catch up on work, all that kind of thing—'

There was a screech in the background. 'Look, I'd better go,' Anna said.

'Shall I call you tomorrow?'

'That'd be great.'

'Talk to you soon, then.'

'Bye.'

When he'd hung up the phone Mariner sat at the computer in the lounge and logged onto the Internet. The article about O'Connor's release had mentioned the street he lived in at the time. Mariner hoped he hadn't moved in the interim. He managed to get a good deal on a London hotel, but paid almost as much for his train ticket down there. Still easier than the prospect of paying congestion charges and finding a parking spot though. Printing off the details he closed down the computer. Then he climbed the two flights of stairs and knocked on Dyson's door. It was shut but Mariner could still hear movement and moments later Dyson appeared.

'I'm going to grab a pint down the way at the Boatman before closing time, fancy joining me?' Mariner asked.

'Ah, I'd like to but I've got a presentation to prepare for and an early start. Some other time?'

'Sure.'

Chapter Seven

On the train to Euston the following morning Mariner was
aware of a strange internal exhilaration and it occurred to
him that for the first time in a long while he had absolute
freedom, with no one keeping tabs on him. It was a sensation reminiscent of the day he'd boarded the rail to
Birmingham at the age of seventeen, leaving home for the
first time. He hadn't often travelled by rail since then, but
it always evoked this childish excitement and a deeper
feeling of absolute contentment, as if this was really his
natural state; independent and answerable to no one. What
did that say for Anna and their plans for the future?

Strictly speaking Mariner shouldn't have been doing this
at all, but this was the first time for several weeks that he'd
felt any kind of buzz and he realised it was because he was
doing what he liked best; following his nose. After weeks
of disinterest he'd at last found something that engaged
him.

By the time the train pulled out there were barely any
spare places, but his early start had secured him a window
seat with a clear view, though his legs would suffer. Rail
transport had changed a bit since 1976; deference to the
golden age of communication with facilities for laptops and
mobile phones. The coach was, he noticed, no longer called
second but 'standard' class and was supposedly a 'quiet'
carriage. In theory only. He'd bought the current edition of

The Great Outdoors from the station bookshop, but it was impossible to concentrate on the written word when the air was pierced by the frequent trilling of mobile phones.

One particular passenger further down the train held a whole series of conversations at ten minute intervals throughout the journey that consisted solely of 'Pete? Can you hear me?' Apparently Pete never did.

Mariner was distracted too, by the view from the window. For several miles the track ran parallel with the sluggishly moving M6 through the vast conurbation of the city, before, finally, the houses dwindled and the scenery opened up into rolling countryside. Watching the dead brown winter landscape skip by, the skeletal silhouettes of the trees bordering rusty furrowed fields, Mariner thought about Anna's idea of moving to the country. In many ways he could understand her thinking. He loved being out in the open air for an afternoon, a day or even weeks at a time. But part of the attraction was the contrast with everyday life. He knew from talking to colleagues that the world of a country copper would be very different, enmeshed as it often was in the politics of a self-absorbed community. He liked the pace, breadth and diversity of his present job, and he'd miss that. There were some aspects of country living that he'd love, but there were plenty of others that he'd hate.

From Euston, Mariner took the tube to West Brompton and the Earls Court hotel that he'd booked; an anonymous, multi-storey concrete tower. It would do very nicely as a base for a couple of days. He checked in and deposited his things in the clean, space-efficient room, then went straight back to the underground where he bought a one-day travel card. He caught the Bakerloo line to South Wembley, riding on the hope that the O'Connors hadn't moved in the last six years.

Joseph O'Connor had lived in a drab council maisonette on the sort of estate that required constant police presence.

Having already gleaned the street name from the newspaper piece, Mariner had got the house number from the electoral register. He rang the bell, a background beat of reggae music bouncing around the stairwell from the flat next door. There was no reply. He was just considering his next move when a woman appeared at the end of the walkway, weighed down by two Netto carrier bags. Certain he recognised her from the press photograph, Mariner moved swiftly away from the door and stepped out of sight to watch her go in, just to make sure. He gave her a few minutes in the house before he went back and tried the doorbell again.

Close to, Sharon O'Connor was a pretty woman, made youthful by black ringlets that fell to her shoulders, and green eyes framed by thick, dark lashes.

'I wonder if I could talk to you about your husband,' Mariner said. He hadn't really thought through what he'd do if she was hostile towards him, he'd have to make it up as he went along. On this unofficial visit he'd hoped to avoid using his warrant card, though doubtless it would have got him in without question, as it had with Eleanor Ryland. Sharon O'Connor must have had a whole procession of police officers ringing her doorbell over the last few weeks. One more wouldn't make much difference. But in the event creativity wasn't called for; only the simplest of white lies.

'Are you a reporter?' Asked more from curiosity than concern. And she could be forgiven that assumption. Today he looked more reporter than copper in khakis and reefer jacket.

'No. My name is Tom Mariner, I'm Sir Geoffrey Ryland's nephew. I'm trying to make sense of what happened that night.'

'Well I'm glad that at last somebody is. I get sick of reading all the bullshit in the papers. Come in.' The Northern Irish accent was still strong.

Compared with the outside environment, the inside of the

O'Connors' flat was immaculate, but then Mariner recalled that O'Connor had been a painter and decorator by trade. Over the fireplace and on the pure white walls of the living room there were photos of O'Connor, Sharon and their children in happier times. The kids must be back at school, the holidays over.

Mariner followed her through to the kitchen where she'd begun unpacking the bags, transferring packets and tubs to the fridge.

'I'm sorry for your loss, Mrs O'Connor. It must be hard.'

'It's not so bad as you might think,' Sharon O'Connor said, candidly. 'Joseph spent quite a lot of time working away over the years, so I had got used to managing on my own. I've got a cleaning job at the offices of an insurance company. Doesn't pay well, but we have a laugh, the girls and me. They've been great since Joseph ... you know. Sometimes for a few seconds I even forget he's dead. The thing I miss most is the car. I never learned to drive.' She stopped what she was doing. 'That's a terrible thing to say, isn't it?'

'You're just being pragmatic.'

'Am I?' She smiled. 'I might if I knew what that meant. She shut the fridge door. 'The rest can wait. Would you like a coffee?'

'Thanks.'

She nodded back towards the living room. 'Why don't you have a seat? I'll be with you in a jiffy.'

Minutes later she brought in two mugs, eyeing Mariner closely as she passed one to him. Maybe she could see the likeness too. 'Were you close to your uncle?'

'Not really. I'm doing this on behalf of my grandmother, Eleanor Ryland. What did you mean about the Press? Doesn't sound as if they're your favourite people.'

She was resigned. 'They write such crap. Joseph was never into drugs in the first place, and if you knew him you'd understand that. They keep saying the shootings were

93

his fault because he'd gone back to his criminal ways, but Joseph never had any criminal ways.'

'What makes you so sure?'

She gave him the kind of hard stare that indicated how tough she could be. 'I'm his wife.' Not 'was' but 'am'. 'The only mistake Joseph made, years ago, was to make friends with the wrong people. He was too trusting.'

'How did he get involved?'

She stared into her mug. 'The simplest way in the world. We'd just moved over here from Ireland. Joseph was keen to get established. Someone gave him the name of a fella that he said might put some work Joseph's way.'

'Who was that?'

'Man called Terry Brady. He owned a few amusement arcades locally and wanted them doing up. Someone had told him that Joseph did a good job, and they were right. He was conscientious and a good worker. After a bit Brady asked him to do his house, too. It's a big place somewhere out in the country, then he started offering Joseph other work, errands and things.'

'Errands?'

'Joseph had an old Transit. Sometimes he helped out with moving machines, that sort of thing. The money was decent for easy work so he'd have been stupid to turn it down. Sometimes he collected cash for them from the arcades. They gave him a big cash box that Joseph gave to the arcade managers. They'd disappear and put in the takings, bring it back to Joseph and he'd drive it over to Brady's for banking. Sometimes it was a lot of money so of course they told him to be careful. When Joseph got stopped by the police it was a real shock. He had no idea.'

'He didn't know that he was carrying fifty thousand pounds' worth of heroin?' Mariner said.

'Of course not. All he did was pick up the box for Brady as usual. He'd no idea that this time there were drugs in it. He hadn't a clue that Brady was involved with that shite.'

Sharon O'Connor was either incredibly naïve or loyal to her late husband. She didn't strike Mariner as being naïve.

'I know that's what he said to begin with, but then he changed his mind and pleaded guilty to possession with intent to supply. What happened there?'

'He was scared. Joseph was skilled with his hands and he was a sweet, kind man, but he wasn't clever, and he sometimes had trouble at the best of times finding the right words. It wouldn't take long for anyone to tie him in knots. And Marvin Jackson had been released without charge, so Joseph was the one left holding the baby.'

'Marvin Jackson?'

'Brady's associate. He was in the van with Joseph. He was arrested but because he wasn't driving he'd told the police he was just along for the ride and they must have swallowed it. They told Joseph that admitting to the charge would be better for him in the long run and he trusted them. I was pregnant with our Kieran at the time. Joseph would have done anything if he thought it would get him out of there quicker. You should have seen the state he was in. Being in police custody was killing him.'

What she said tied in with what Mariner read about the appeal: along comes Sir Geoffrey Ryland and proves that O'Connor had been traumatised by the whole experience and his confession elicited while he was under severe stress. He had been coerced.

'Joseph was set up.' Sharon O'Connor drank the dregs of her coffee. 'Sir Geoffrey promised us that he'd get the bastards who did it, and that they'd get what was coming to them. He said he'd make sure of it. And now it won't happen, will it?'

She was probably right. 'Did Joseph agree to do anything to help, like testify against Jackson?'

'With what? At the time he had no idea what was going on. When Sir Geoffrey got Joseph's conviction overturned he wanted to put all that behind him. Prison terrified him so he steered well clear of trouble. That's why it's so ridiculous to think that Joseph would have got involved in anything this time around.'

'The police have a witness who says he saw Joseph talking to Brady only a few days before the shooting.'

'There was nothing to stop Brady talking to Joseph, was there? The man drinks in the same pub. It doesn't necessarily mean anything.'

'So Joseph couldn't have got involved in anything else?'

'When he got the job as Sir Geoffrey's driver he had too much to lose.'

'How did he get the job?'

'After Joseph was released, Sir Geoffrey phoned him up and asked him if he'd like to do it, as long as he passed all the security checks.'

'And did Joseph like it?'

'He loved it. Sir Geoffrey Ryland saved Joseph's life. He wouldn't have done anything to put him at risk.'

'The papers hinted that you were in financial difficulty. Is that true?'

She glared. 'You've got a bloody nerve. We may have overstretched a bit on the kids' Christmas presents, but doesn't everyone?'

'Where did Joseph first meet Terry Brady?'

'In the Sentinel, at the end of the road. Like I said, we had just moved here and the work wasn't coming in as Joseph would have liked. He needed a job.' Her voice caught and for the first time her vulnerability began to show through. 'Now that was a conversation I wish he'd never had.' There was a box of tissues next to where Mariner sat. He passed it across to her.

1910, the date carved in a brick above the door of the Sentinel, meant that the pub had stood guard over the street through several reincarnations, surviving the Blitz and post-war redevelopment. Fluorescent posters in the windows boasted steak lunches for £3.50 and a quiz night every Tuesday. Inside, the pub had not resisted change so well.

What would originally have been a series of small snugs had been knocked into one cheerless barn of a room with wide screen TV, fruit machines and a dartboard at one end, making it almost identical to thousands of city pubs across the country and a dismal, soulless place. The beer was all keg too, Mariner noted, so he settled on a bottle of Newcastle Brown.

'I was looking for a man called Terry Brady,' Mariner said to the barman, whose occupation flowed over the waistband of his jeans. 'I was told I might find him in here?'

'You're a bit late, chum. He moved out a while back.'

'Where did he go?'

'Spain. He's got a villa out there. He occasionally comes back, but not very often.'

'When was the last time?'

'December time, just before Christmas.' And just before the shootings.

'Are you the landlord?'

'It's my name over the door.'

'Did you know Joseph O'Connor, too?'

'Sure.'

'Have you any idea who it was told the police that Brady and O'Connor were in here shortly before Joseph O'Connor was killed?'

'It was me.' He was proud of it.

'Do you have any idea what they talked about?'

'Oh, they didn't talk. They weren't even in here together for very long; ten minutes tops. They were both in my pub on the same night, that's all.'

'So they didn't actually meet?'

'Not that I saw. O'Connor left shortly after Brady arrived.' Which put an entirely different slant on things.

'And that's what you told the police?'

'Course it is.' Uncertainty kicked in. 'What is this? You a reporter? Why do you want to know?'

'No, I'm not a reporter, I'm just interested, that's all.'

Mariner swallowed the last couple of mouthfuls of his beer and left the pub. From outside he phoned Flynn.

'Can I come and see you?'

'In London?'

'I'm here anyway.'

'Doing what?'

Good question. 'We've got a murder on our patch, possible suspect an Albanian, except he's disappeared back home. We're looking at an extradition.' All perfectly true.

Flynn was wary. 'You couldn't sort it out on the phone?'

'You know, sometimes it's easier to do these things face to face. Anyway, while I'm here I thought I might like to sample life in the fast lane – Special Branch.'

'Oh sure. I'll need to give you the password, though.'

'Password?'

'Yeah. The entrance to HQ is a disguised manhole cover to the left of Trafalgar Square tube station. You'll need to knock four times, two short, two long then give the code word, then you'll be admitted to our underground complex.'

'Ha bloody ha.'

'I'm in an office block on Bramhall Street, Vauxhall, behind the Prudential building.'

'As you can see, this is where the glamour is.' Mariner was sitting across the desk from Flynn in an office remarkably like his own at Granville Lane, only Flynn's was a generation younger, with an outlook over the solid concrete wall of the building next door.

'So how's it going, the Ryland thing?' Mariner asked.

'It's going okay.' Flynn was watching him expectantly. 'How's it going for you – the Ryland thing?'

'How do you mean?'

'You went to see his mother.'

Mariner should have known that on a high-profile case like this it would have been noticed. 'My grandmother, yes I did. I wanted to talk to her.'

'It's not a good idea.'

'She recognised me.' Mariner couldn't keep the satisfaction out of his voice.

'Christ.'

'According to her, Ryland referred to me as recently as a month ago. It's made me wonder why he'd do that. That perhaps he was in trouble or knew something was going to happen.'

'Or maybe it's just a coincidence. He was getting older. He'd just published his memoirs. Perhaps that churned up a few memories. Don't let's get carried away.'

'Anyway, the point is, that neither Sharon O'Connor nor Eleanor Ryland think that the killings were down to Joseph O'Connor.'

'Sharon O'Connor? What do you know about her?'

'Only what she's told me. She claims that he never was involved with anything that he could go back to.'

'And as his wife, her view must be totally objective and unbiased. How the hell did you track her down?'

'Her address was given in early news report from when O'Connor was released. It's there for anyone to see. A quick check with the electoral roll and—'

Flynn's voice tightened. 'You have been busy.'

'Is that a problem?'

'It's just – I'm in a difficult position here. This is my first big case—' Flynn looked as if he was regretting passing on those photos.

'And you don't want me getting in the way. I won't. I just find it interesting. Like it or not, thanks to you, Ryland is part of my life now. But don't worry, Sharon O'Connor doesn't even know I'm a copper.'

'You told her you're Ryland's son?'

'Couldn't quite bring myself to do that. I said nephew.'

'Right.'

'And for the record the O'Connors were not in financial difficulty.'

Flynn shifted uncomfortably.

'You think there's more to this than meets the eye too, don't you?' Mariner said.

'I told you. The chauffeur's being followed up by others. I've just been asked to make sure there are no skeletons in the Ryland closet.'

'Like me.'

'Like you.'

'Are you sure I'm the only one?'

'Haven't found any others yet.'

'So the guy really was squeaky clean. That'll be a first for a politician.'

Flynn stood up. 'Let's go and get some lunch. There's a good little bar just round the corner.'

They went to a Spanish tapas bar that served passable continental lager.

'You've got doubts, haven't you?' Mariner persisted.

'We need to get this clear. I *had* them Tom, that's all. At the start there seemed to be a steer in the direction of the chauffeur. It just seemed a little unusual. But then when I looked, I could see why. There's plenty of evidence from the scene that says O'Connor was the target.'

'And?

'Nothing we've seen yet indicates otherwise.'

'Despite a lifelong history of political agitation and years of confrontation with the government over the JRC, you really don't think Sir Geoffrey Ryland had his enemies?'

'Of course he did, in the same way that all politicians have enemies, but not the kind who'd put a bullet in his head in the dead of night on a quiet country road. There is no grassy knoll in Cheslyn Woods.'

'But you said it yourself, the search of his house was delayed. You don't think that's weird?'

'It was delayed, that's all. We've no reason to think anything had been touched in the interim. Anyway, I'm not paid to think about the whys and wherefores. I've been given a very specific brief. And if you think about it, it all makes perfect political sense.'

100

'In what way?'

'Ryland was the government's champion of fair play. The last thing they want is to have his good name tarnished in any way after his death. And everyone makes mistakes, however good they are.'

Mariner pounced. 'What kind of mistakes?'

'I'm not being specific. You know how it is. After a famous figure dies there's nothing the red tops love more than to dig up some dirt, especially to prove that the deceased wasn't such a shining example after all. Then, half the time, you find out that the muck is being spread by the other side, taking another chance to prove that this government isn't what it claims to be. I'm talking generally here. All I've been asked to do is check what there is and pass on any information.'

'Have you passed me on?'

'I had to.'

'So that if I go public on it they'll be prepared.'

'I hardly think news of your existence is going to threaten the stability of the government, do you?'

'And you really think that's the only reason you're looking into Ryland?'

'Yes I do. So let it drop, will you?'

'You brought me into this, remember? What did you expect? "Thanks for telling me, now I've got a name to put on my marriage certificate, should I ever need to"? All I'm doing is trying to find out more about the old man I didn't know until he was dead. You can't blame me for that.'

'I'm saying, don't go stirring up trouble for the sake of it. What with the explosion, and now this. You're not at your best right now. Don't start reading too much into things.'

Mariner left Special Branch HQ feeling dissatisfied. Flynn may be a friend but he wasn't telling him everything. And he sure as hell wasn't listening.

Chapter Eight

From his hotel room Mariner phoned Maggie Devlin, an old friend of his mother's he'd met for the first and only time at Rose's funeral last year. He was in two minds about contacting her. As a psychologist and trained counsellor she'd be all over him like a rash, but he wanted to find out if she'd known. Mariner recalled her mentioning that as a student she'd been actively involved with human rights organisations like Amnesty International. With her social conscience, the chances were that she and Sir Geoffrey Ryland would at least have had some shared interests. It'd be good to meet Maggie again, just to say hello, but as the only available link with his mother's past he also wanted to pick her brains. He was in luck. She sounded delighted to hear from him and could meet him that evening. Next up he phoned Anna. As before, her mobile was a no go, so he tried the land line. Becky picked up. Mariner had always liked Anna's friend, but she sounded tired and a bit low. 'I'm not supposed to tell you this but babies are hard work,' she said. 'We'd like to keep Anna for a few days, is that okay?'

'Of course.' It bought him a little more time, should he need it.

'It's wonderful having a live-in babysitter, and she's doing some valuable research.'

At that point Anna must have asked for the phone and

there followed some scuffling sound. 'What research?' he asked when she came on.

'Oh, take no notice. It's just Becky being Becky.'

'You haven't put down a deposit on a house.'

'No, nothing like that.' She was keeping something back, but Mariner was too preoccupied to pursue it. They talked about nothing for a couple of minutes and then he rang off. Mariner showered and changed and ordered soup and a sandwich from room service.

He'd arranged to meet Maggie in a Soho bar. He was there ahead of her and beginning to wonder if he'd come to the wrong place when she breezed through the door, her hair wild from the windy evening and dramatic black cloak billowing out behind her. 'Tom! How lovely to see you again.' Mariner caught a whiff of incense as she kissed him on both cheeks, before studying him at arm's length. 'You look tired.'

'I'm fine.'

They had to battle to get through the busy bar, and grabbed a couple of bar stools before ordering drinks from a very camp waiter. 'That bomb that went off. Were you involved in that?' Maggie asked when they were alone.

'They haven't said for sure what caused the explosion, but yes. We were just going into the church. I helped in the rescue operation.'

'That's tough.'

Mariner fought to deflect the recurring mental image. 'It was like Armageddon; blood and glass everywhere.'

Ever the counsellor, Maggie couldn't help asking. 'Have you talked to someone?'

'Others ahead of me in the queue,' Mariner said. 'But I'm used to it. I'm all right.'

'So you said.' She gave him an appraising look. 'And yet you jump every time there's a loud noise. Did you know that?'

Mariner didn't. 'I'm just—'

'—tired. Mm.' Their drinks came. 'You're still with Anna?'

'Yes. We're thinking about having kids.' It just sort of came out.

Most people would have reacted with delight and enthusiasm. Maggie's response was more measured. 'And you're okay with that?' She was a bloody good counsellor.

'Yes,' he said. Then: 'No.' It was a relief to say it.

'Anna's idea.'

'She's just become godmother to her friend's little girl and it seems to have changed everything. She's besotted.'

'It's a pretty normal female response,' said Maggie. 'And how old is she, mid to late thirties? She's at that "now or never" age too,' said Maggie. 'She'll be conscious that the tide's beginning to turn against her.'

'Exactly, so now babies are the hot topic of conversation.'

'And what about you?'

'I've sort of gone along with it, I suppose.' She waited patiently. Good sense of timing. 'Anna's right, now that Rose is dead there's no one else.' No one that Maggie knew about yet, anyway. 'And I can see that it might be nice to create a family of my own. We've got something solid, or at least I thought we had. In many ways it's the natural next step, but actually doing it, that's something else. If I'm really honest, I'm not so sure.'

'Is it to do with the explosion?'

'Partly, it has to be.'

'And?'

'You know the history. I don't know if I'm up to it.'

'Have you told Anna that?'

'No.'

'Keeping it to yourself may not be the best strategy.' It was a more diplomatic line than others would have taken. 'Why do you think you're doing that?'

'Anna's so excited about it. I guess I don't want to spoil it for her. I agreed, because at the time it didn't seem like a bad idea.'

'And now?'

'Now I don't know what to think.'

'So what's changed?'

'Maybe it's finding out who my dad was.' Mariner thought she was going to fall off the high stool. He reached out to steady her.

'You know??'

'You've heard of Sir Geoffrey Ryland?'

Finally, he succeeded in shocking her. 'God in heaven, you're kidding me!'

'So you didn't have any idea?'

'None. When we talked after Rose's funeral I was perfectly honest with you. The only suspicion I had was that black limousine.' She was silent for a moment. 'But now I know, it seems so obvious.' Mariner raised his eyebrows. 'The physical likeness for a start.'

'Yeah, funny what you can see once it's pointed out.'

'And—' She shook her head in disbelief. 'My God, I've been slow on the uptake.'

'What?'

'Ryland was around when we were at college. We hung out with his crowd. A whole group of us met at the first ever CND rally at Aldermaston. After that we used to congregate regularly in a bar not far from here and put the world to rights. That was how I got involved in Amnesty. Students did that then. We really thought we could make a difference. These days kids seem to be too pre-occupied with paying off their loans and getting a foothold on the property ladder to worry about politics.'

'So you knew him too?'

'I was closer to one of his friends, Norman Balfour.'

'His best man.'

'That's right.' She stopped as a thought came to her. 'My God, Norman contacted me about a year ago. I hadn't heard from him in donkey's, and one of the things he asked was about your mother. It was just a throwaway remark: "How's that friend of yours, Rose?" kind of thing. "She had a baby didn't she?" To which I said: "Not so much a

baby now. He's a detective in the West Midlands police."
And we laughed about it. How that's the last thing we'd
have imagined a child of Rose's doing. But then he said I'd
never guess what he was up to either.'

'What was that?'

'He's entered the Catholic priesthood.'

'Not what you'd have expected?'

The eyebrows went up again. 'He was a bit of a lad,
Norman, from what I remember. I wouldn't exactly have
had him down for a life of celibacy.'

'So how well did you know Ryland?'

'Not that well. We were in the same student gang, that's
all. Geoff was out of our league, or so I thought. He was
a pretty charismatic character even then. Back then the
cause was CND and the peace movement. He was very
young, but still got himself in the papers a few times,
speaking at public meetings. I knew that Rose was friendly
with him, but so were a lot of girls.'

Mariner thought back to the press cuttings. 'Like
Caroline Foster-Young?'

'Carrie. Oh God, yes. She came along later, I think. I
remember her at a sit-in we had at around the time of
Kennedy and the Cuban missile crisis. She was American,
so those issues were close to home for her. She was very
glamorous, too. I think she and Geoff went as far as getting
engaged. It was a bit of a surprise when he married Diana
Fitzgibbon.'

'Why?'

'What you might call the ridiculous to the sublime. And
it seemed to happen quite suddenly, unless that's just time
altering my perspective. In many ways Diana didn't really
seem Geoff's type, restrained, where Carrie was wild.'

'He was going into politics. Maybe he needed a different
type.'

'That's true enough. Diana certainly had a dramatic
effect on him. After meeting her he gave up drinking and
smoking; took the pledge.'

'What happened to Carrie?'

'I don't remember seeing her much after that. Perhaps she went back to the States.'

'And not long afterards we moved up to Leamington. Do you know why?'

'No. That was rather sudden too, or seemed like it at the time. But it made sense. Your mother needed some support with childcare and your grandparents were there to provide it. How are you feeling about all this?'

Mariner took a moment. 'I don't know. Elated, confused, betrayed.'

'Those are understandable reactions. You've experienced two earth-shattering events in your life in a relatively short space of time, one literal, one metaphorical. Do you have any idea of how emotionally vulnerable you must be at this moment?' She put a hand on his arm. 'You must consider getting some help.'

'You're helping me.'

'I mean real professional help,' said Maggie. 'It's a miracle that you can get up in the morning, given everything you've been through. A physical explosion followed by an emotional one, on top of other major changes in your life. What does Anna think about your late father?'

'I haven't told her, or anyone else.'

'This is becoming tedious. May I ask why not?'

'I wanted time to get used to it. The only other people who know are the man who told me, Eleanor Ryland and now you.'

'You've met the formidable Eleanor?'

'You know her?'

'I saw her once, and I've heard about her. She's a powerful force.'

'She's been very kind to me. Very accepting.'

'She knew?'

'Oh yes.'

'Well that's a start.'

'She told me about what happened, about why he wasn't

107

around. She painted my mother as some kind of saint. Was it really like that?'

'What are you getting at?'

'Was there ever any question that she wouldn't go through with it? Was she under any pressure?'

'No. There was never any doubt. She wanted her baby.'

'And you think she was okay on her own?'

'Yes, I really think she was. It seemed to me that she had come to terms with the idea that the father of her child wouldn't be part of her life, and she was content with that. In fact I think she quite liked it. It appealed to her sense of adventure. The two of you against the world. Of course, I had no idea why. Knowing who he is – was – she was probably just being realistic.'

'So what do you know of Ryland since then?'

'I've followed his career with interest and our paths have crossed at a distance a few times, because of our mutual interest in world injustice. But whereas I've focused my interest abroad through Amnesty, he's of course been more concerned with domestic policy.'

'Through the Judicial Review Commission.'

'Yes. I have to say I was pleased to see his name appearing on that. I know people who were involved in setting it up, but I don't suppose he'd have remembered me even if he'd seen my name. It must be strange for you, knowing that your father worked on the other side of the fence, so to speak.'

'I've got mixed feelings. I can't help wondering what he thought about my choice of career.' Mariner sipped his sparkling water. 'How much do you know about the work of the Commission?'

'Not much, but I have friends who do.'

'I'm having trouble getting any detail about Joseph O'Connor's case and Ryland's part in it. I'd like to know more. Eleanor also hinted that Ryland was under pressure at work but she couldn't tell me what specifically.' It was pushing the boundaries of their fledgling relationship, but

Mariner just had to ask. 'Do you know anyone who would talk to me?'

'Officially?'

'No, this is just me.' He could see her weighing the argument, and rightly so. What earthly reason did she have to trust him? 'All I really want is to talk to someone who knew him, but I don't know where to start. With the investigation still ongoing, for once it doesn't help that I'm a police officer.'

'I'll see what I can do,' Maggie said finally, but it was a long way from a commitment. 'Listen, you've been through a lot with all this,' she said. 'You must talk to Anna and those close to you, but if you ever need another option I could recommend someone—'

'Thanks.' But they both knew that he wouldn't be taking it up. Maggie had to leave soon after that, something to do with a client, so Mariner took his time strolling back to the hotel. He was, as always, amazed at how different two cities could be. Birmingham was a fraction of the size of London of course and Mariner found himself wondering how anyone could ever become intimate with such a huge conglomeration. New York, it seemed, didn't hold the monopoly on metropolitan insomnia, and the London streets throbbed with activity well into the night. Back in his room he opened the window for some air but was forced to close it again. Even its roar was bigger than Birmingham's roar. He got into a bed that felt big and empty without Anna beside him, and thought about what she was doing now.

Waking early the next morning Mariner regretted making that request of Maggie. It was asking too much. So it was a surprise when she called as he was getting dressed.

'I've called in a favour,' she said. 'A caseworker at the JRC, Helena James, will meet you at twelve thirty in the bistro in Sadler Row, across the road from the Commission.'

His 'thank you' was completely inadequate. And now breakfast was accompanied by the prickle of anticipation.

Mariner was about to meet someone who had worked with his father on a daily basis, and who would know what was really going on. He was so wired he was certain his fellow guests in the huge dining room must be able to see it. From his table by the wall he could observe what an odd assortment they were. Most appeared to be foreign; sharp-suited businessmen, along with several families with young children, seeing the sights, people who would never ordinarily be in the same room together.

The only time Mariner ever ate a cooked breakfast was on the rare occasions when he stayed in hotels, so he always overdid it, and afterwards, stuffed to bursting with bacon, eggs, tomatoes and mushrooms, he was desperately in need of somewhere to walk it off. It was a sharp blustery day, perfect for blowing away the dulling effects of his hermetically sealed hotel room. Returning last night, he felt sure he'd noticed a park across the road, but when he got there it turned out to be Brompton Cemetery. Better still. Graveyards, in his opinion, were highly underrated for their recreational value and invariably empty. This one, a peaceful oasis amid the city clamour, especially on a weekday, was no exception. It had been established, so a sign in the entrance told him, in 1836 and designed by Benjamin Baud, whoever he might be, and was attractively laid out, around an impressive central chapel that seemed to give more than a nod to St Peter's Basilica in Rome.

Wandering the tombs, Mariner scanned the headstones, noting the many varying ages at which those lying beneath had died, some over a hundred years ago. Did anyone ever visit these monuments? Were the descendants close by or had they moved to another part of the world, or had the lineage expired completely in the way that his would if he derailed Anna's plans? Scrutiny of the legends became so absorbing that when he randomly glanced at his watch he got a shock. If he didn't get a move on he'd be late for his lunchtime appointment.

The bistro, down a tiny back street, was marked out by

a pavement blackboard displaying the day's specials. So intent was Mariner on being punctual that he almost collided with a woman approaching from the opposite direction. Apologising, and taking in the rather dull brown coat and stiff demeanour, something made him ask, 'Helena James?'

'Mr Mariner?'

'Yes, shall we?' As Mariner ushered her into the bistro he had time to take in the detail. As dowdy as Maggie was colourful, Helena James wore no rings or other jewellery, her hair was cut savagely short, and the lighting in the café did little for her bare complexion. By the time they'd found a table, Mariner had, probably quite unfairly, consigned her to a single room flat with a cat. The sort of woman he'd once overheard Tony Knox describing as a SINBAD: single income, no boyfriend, absolutely desperate. Not that Mariner was making judgements or anything.

He was glad he'd thought to wear a suit today. It made him look more respectable and the whole enterprise seem more official, and he had an immediate impression that Helena James would be the kind of person who liked to do things by the book. As it was, there was nothing about her that appeared happy to meet with him and Mariner couldn't help speculating on the nature of the favour she owed Maggie. Or perhaps it was simpler than that, and he'd spoiled her plans for lunchtime shopping. Having done his share of basic communication training and handled all kinds of customers professionally, what was clear to Mariner was that he would have to turn on the charm.

As soon as they were seated he took Helena's cool and slightly clammy hand to shake it, closing it in his with his other hand and switching on a big smile. 'I really appreciate your agreeing to see me, Helena. I know your time must be precious. What can I get you?' Knox would be pissing himself laughing at this performance.

She allowed Mariner to order two lattés but to his relief

declined food. Hard to remain charming and smooth when you're chewing your way through a crusty baguette. Sensing that she wouldn't respond to direct questioning, Mariner set off on the scenic route. 'Maggie tells me you're a caseworker at the JRC.'

'That's right, yes.'

'And you worked alongside Sir Geoffrey Ryland.'

A slight incline of the head.

Don't overdo it, thought Mariner, wishing by now that he'd brought his blood-divining kit. 'That must have been interesting. What was he like to work for?'

'He was a lovely man, one of the few remaining people who had real integrity.' The pain in her voice and moistening of her eyes was unexpected. Mariner had assumed buttoned-up emotions. But now he saw the problem; she was mourning her boss.

'Yours must be a fascinating job,' he said, guiding her to safer ground.

She collected herself. 'It's manic, if you must know, an impossible task. We get about fifteen new cases referred every week. It's our job to summarise the main points and present them to the members of the commission. We have to look at whether the conviction was wrongful or the sentencing inappropriate.' So she was passionate about her work, too.

'Do all the cases come through solicitors?'

She nodded. 'The usual route is through the CPS but around one and a half per cent are Home Office referrals.' Very precise.

'Prisoners who have directly approached the home office, or their MP,' Mariner checked.

'—or those who have gone to the press and made a big public noise, giving the Home Office no choice. There are a growing number of pressure groups who are getting very adept at pressing the right buttons.' She didn't approve.

Their coffees came and Mariner made a point of taking the bill. 'Are you sure there's nothing else—'

112

'No, thank you.'

'Yours is quite a task then,' he said, returning to their original conversation.

'It's hard enough without the constant interruptions from lobbyists.'

'Lobbyists?'

'The advocates who think we should take their cases above others. We work through appeals systematically, on a first-come-first-served basis, it's the fairest way, but there are always people putting on the pressure on to consider their client's case first. They seem to think that whoever shouts the loudest will be heard.'

'Does anyone ever take enticements to prioritise?' She wasn't with him, or didn't want to be. 'Members of the Commission, I mean.'

'No.' She was affronted by the suggestion.

'Can you be certain about that?'

'Absolutely. The process is completely objective.'

Mariner found that hard to believe. In his experience any system that involved human beings had some level of subjectivity. But he wouldn't upset her with a contradiction at this stage. Instead he asked. 'How many cases actually go for review?'

'About four per cent.'

'That's all?'

'It's still a substantial number. Of those, about two thirds are upheld, though recently there's been a drop in the number of referrals and a rise in the number of rejected appeals.'

Mariner didn't need to ask why. With the ever-improving forensic techniques, and in particular an increased reliance on DNA evidence, convictions were based on firmer ground. It was much harder to pick an argument with science and juries had confidence in it. If ever DNA evidence was discredited it would bring a whole house of cards tumbling down.

'And how soon are the prisoners cleared of the charges?'

113

'If they're in jail it takes an average of fourteen months, it's more if they're at liberty, usually about nineteen months.'

'Quite a wait, then.' Mariner spoke out loud but the thought had clearly not occurred to her. 'Did Maggie tell you I was interested in knowing more about Joseph O'Connor?'

'Yes. May I ask why?'

'I have a personal interest.'

'I see. Were you a friend of Mr O'Connor?'

'I know his wife.'

'Couldn't she tell you what you want to know?'

'It's a difficult time for her right now. And really I'd like the official take. It's harder to remember detail when you're emotionally involved. Was Joseph O'Connor's case referred to you by his solicitor?'

'It was one of the first we recommended for appeal in 1998. How much do you already know?'

'That the grounds for appeal were that his confession had been made under duress.'

'The transcripts of the police interviews and the medical reports made it clear. Mr O'Connor wasn't the cleverest of men and the questioning, with some of the techniques that were used, tied him in knots.'

'You make it sound very simple.'

'It was, but—' She broke off. 'I'm sorry, but I really don't understand. You're not with Special Branch, so how are you involved?'

This was hopeless. At this rate Mariner wouldn't learn anything new. It was time to take a gamble. 'Can I speak in absolute confidence?' he said.

'Yes.'

'Sir Geoffrey Ryland was my father.'

'What??'

Bugger. She didn't believe him. 'I can't prove it to you unfortunately. Not yet. In fact I only found out myself a week or so ago, but I promise you it's true. That's what my interest is.'

114

'But Sir Geoffrey didn't—' She was studying Mariner's face. The first time she'd properly looked at him. 'My God, he was, wasn't he?'

'Yes.'

It took Helena James several seconds to regain her composure, but when she did her whole demeanour had changed, and Mariner could have kicked himself for not coming out with the revelation right at the beginning.

'It was after Joseph's release that things got difficult,' she said, at last, leaning in slightly.

'How?' he asked.

'The Commission had been set up as a response to apparent widespread police corruption and the first few cases were viewed in some quarters as part of a witch-hunt. I think there was a feeling that despite the way in which his statement was obtained, Joseph O'Connor could still have been guilty.'

Flynn had said the same thing.

'Is that why Sir Geoffrey offered O'Connor a job?'

'Partly, yes, I think so. He didn't say as much but I think he felt he had to demonstrate his belief in Joseph's innocence.'

'It's backfired now though, hasn't it?'

She regarded him coldly. 'That depends on whether you believe what you read in the papers, doesn't it?'

'And O'Connor was released solely on the grounds that his conviction had been unsafe?

'What do you mean?'

'In the course of his appeal, did O'Connor supply the police or CPS with any other helpful information, about Terry Brady or Marvin Jackson, for example?'

'He didn't need to. In that sense his case was straightforward. The appeal court was satisfied with his original statement that he'd known nothing about the drugs.'

'I'm just trying to get a sense of who might want to kill Joseph O'Connor and why they would do it now.'

'I understand that.'

They'd reached a dead end. 'What about the cases you turn down, the ones that don't meet the criteria?' Mariner asked. 'Is there ever any comeback?'

'Naturally. I think we've all had death threats at one time or another. It goes with the territory.'

'Any recently that stand out?'

'Not that I can think of.'

'And these applications for appeal, the information is in the public domain?'

'Some of it is, through the Freedom of Information Act. All you'd need to do is put in an application.' Lowering her voice she leaned in perceptibly nearer to Mariner. 'It's not only the criminals who apply the pressure,' she confided. They were co-conspirators now. 'There are other reasons for the reduction in cases being referred.'

'What do you mean?'

'The government has to protect its own interests. Government ministers, particularly the Home Secretary, can sometimes put one in a difficult position.'

'How?'

'The Home office was concerned about the number of cases being referred for appeal. They were worried about public confidence in the judicial system. It's as if they created the JRC without realising that the floodgates would open. For the last couple of years it's been rumoured that the figures are being manipulated, and that there have been efforts to reduce the number of cases referred.'

'But how could they do that?'

'By imposing stricter criteria that don't necessarily relate to guilt or innocence.'

Someone was bending the rules. 'How did Sir Geoffrey feel about that?' Mariner asked.

'Sir Geoffrey was a fair man. How do you think he felt? He was unhappy about the fact that a government office could force us to be selective.'

'Did he express his unhappiness?'

'He tried. But he knew it would come out eventually

116

anyway. He was writing the next volume of his memoirs.'

'He'd started on that?'

'He'd almost completed the first draft.'

'Did he tell anyone else about this?'

'He may have done, I don't know. After he— After the shooting, security came and removed the hard drive from his computer. It's standard procedure of course, but they turned up the very next day.'

'They were quick off the mark then.'

'The Commission is one of this government's flagship initiatives. I don't suppose they'd be eager to have its flaws exposed, especially as they could be seen as the ones sabotaging it.'

'Helena, do you think Joseph O'Connor was the reason Sir Geoffrey Ryland was killed?'

She treated the question with contempt. 'Sir Geoffrey would never have employed Joseph if he'd thought he was in any way involved in drugs.'

'What if he hadn't known?'

'Sir Geoffrey wasn't stupid. He'd have known.' Just as Sharon O'Connor would have known. Picking up her cup, Helena James drank the remains of her coffee.

'Would you like another?' Mariner asked.

She glanced at her watch. 'Oh God no, I must go. I've got stacks of work to do this afternoon.' She was thoughtful for a moment. 'You never actually knew Sir Geoffrey as your father then?'

'That's right,' said Mariner. 'And now I won't get the chance.'

'That must be strange.'

'It's hard for me to get a feel for the kind of man he was. I'm looking to connect with anything about him. It's why Maggie agreed to arrange this meeting.'

Helena considered for a moment in much the way that Maggie had done. 'Would it help to see where he worked, I mean his office and all that?'

'It would be fantastic.' No need to fake his gratitude

117

now. It was more than Mariner could have hoped for.

'I can't see that it would be a problem. We have visitors all the time. And if it helps you to get closer to him.' It was what Mariner called a result.

'I'm sure that it would,' he said. 'Thank you.' Reaching across the table he took her hand. 'And thanks for talking to me. It means such a lot.' And the colour flooded up through Helena James' pale face.

Chapter Nine

Mariner had to move some to keep up with Helena James on the ten minute walk to JRC offices in Whitehall. It was good of her to go out on a limb like this, and he wondered what she was thinking. That perhaps she was in with a chance? He hoped not. Although occupying one of the grander bleached white Georgian buildings, the offices of the JRC were consigned largely to the less salubrious lower floors, a rabbit warren of corridors and tiny offices with barred and frosted windows level with the pavement. As Helena signed him in at reception, giving him the required visitors pass, Mariner imagined that, even now, his presence was being clocked by Flynn's colleagues in Special Branch.

Once inside, Helena James didn't seem to know what to do with Mariner, until a young woman emerged from a nearby office carrying a bundle of files.

'Sandie,' said Helena, 'I wonder if you could spare a few minutes. This is Detective Inspector Mariner.' He's making enquiries into Sir Geoffrey's death. He'd like to have a look round the Commission, get a feel for the place. Could you give him the guided tour?' Helena James had chosen her words carefully. She hadn't lied, but at the same time had given every indication that Mariner was on this officially.

'Of course, Miss James,' said Sandie. 'I need to take these down to the archive store, but we can see the rest on the way down.'

'That sounds good,' Mariner said.

'Well, I'll leave you in Sandie's capable hands. Thank you for the coffee, Inspector Mariner, and good luck.'

'Thanks again,' Mariner said, but it was to Helena James' retreating back.

Sandie, who looked about twenty, beamed up at him. The badge on her ample chest said 'Clerical Assistant', meaning that he'd been assigned the office junior, but after a while he had a feeling that her selection had been deliberate. Petite and blonde in her tight sweater and short skirt, Sandie was about as far removed from Helena James as was possible. During that brief first exchange Mariner noticed that she had thoroughly appraised him, head to foot, and despite the smile she wasn't particularly impressed. But then, he must be old enough to be her dad. 'So you're a policeman,' she said, with what Mariner thought was a slight hint of disbelief.

'Yes.'

'I went out with a policeman once,' she continued. 'He was really hot.' It explained the disappointment. 'He was always getting into scraps and car chases and stuff.'

'I'm not that kind of policeman any more,' Mariner said.

'No.' She'd already guessed that.

'I do more of the information gathering, building cases, a bit like your job I suppose.'

'Is that what you're doing here, gathering information?'

'Sort of. I just wanted to get a sense of where Sir Geoffrey Ryland worked and what the Commission is like.'

'Okay, well let's make a start, shall we?'

Open and gregarious, Sandie barely seemed to draw breath between sentences, even though most of what she did have to say on the short walk to the main offices was about the weather, the number of tourists there were in London for the time of year and the 'amazing' BLT she'd just consumed for lunch, despite being on a low-carb-high-protein diet, on account of wanting to be able to get into the dress she'd bought for her cousin's wedding in the spring. So, on the other hand, perhaps Helena had chosen Sandie as a kind of punishment.

'This is where it all happens,' she said, with a touch of irony. She stepped back from the doorway to allow Mariner to peer in to a large open plan office, where a dozen or so staff were stationed at desks, on the phone or ploughing through paperwork. On the far side were the closed doors of further personal offices, one of which Mariner guessed would belong to Helena James. And then they were off again, Sandie resuming her running commentary on the world and life in general.

'Did you work very closely with Sir Geoffrey?' Mariner asked in a split second pause that presented itself.

'Oh, all the time. I mean, we have our routine tasks that we do for all the members; answering the phone, filing and photocopying, that kind of thing. I used to do some of that for Sir Geoffrey. He spent a lot of time here so I got to know him quite well and how he liked things done. Would you like to see his office, it's just down here?'

'That would be helpful,' said Mariner, exercising enormous restraint.

A little further along the corridor Sandie turned the knob of an oak-panelled door and Mariner stepped into a high-ceilinged room, dominated by a monster of a solid walnut desk and surrounded on three sides by shelves of leather-bound books. This was the place where his father had spent the last years of his life, sitting at that desk, enjoying the view from the high sash windows that made up the fourth wall of the room. It was the air he had breathed.

This was the closest Mariner would ever get to the man and he'd been unprepared for the emotional impact which left him momentarily speechless. Glancing down he saw that Sandie's eyes were wide, staring unblinkingly at the chair behind the desk.

'It's funny. I still expect to see him sitting there,' she said, uncharacteristically subdued.

'Do you mind if I—?' recovering his voice, Mariner

nodded towards the chair.

'No, it's fine,' said Sandie.

Mariner seated himself in the soft leather, hyper-conscious of the upholstery under him. His only minor disappointment was that, aside from a blotter and a desk tidy, the room had been completely cleared of any personal belongings. But why wouldn't it be? 'What did you think of Sir Geoffrey?' he asked Sandie, who had unconsciously, it seemed, dropped into the chair opposite him.

'He was a lovely man,' she said, immediately, 'always kind and considerate. He always said please and thank you, no matter how rushed he was, and had time to ask how Dominic and me were getting on with the flat. We bought a one-bedroom basement last year and we've been doing it up, it was in a right old state.' Seeing Mariner's face she meandered back to the subject in hand. 'Sir Geoffrey always made sure we got paid extra for late working or for anything that he classed as "above and beyond" as he called it.'

'Such as what?' Mariner sat back, anticipating another list of routine admin tasks.

'Oh you know,' said Sandie, coyly, and for a horrible moment Mariner thought she was implying sexual favours. 'Sir Geoffrey liked a flutter on the horses. In his position he didn't like to broadcast it, so we had this little arrangement.'

Thank God for that. 'What kind of arrangement?'

'I'd take an envelope of cash to this drop-off point, with the name of the horse scribbled on the back, and the bookie's runner collected it and placed the bet for him.'

It wasn't quite what Mariner had anticipated. 'What kind of drop-off point?' he asked.

'A left luggage locker at Euston station.' Sandie's eyes widened. 'Oh. I've still got the key. I should take it back, shouldn't I?'

'Might be an idea.' Mariner was still trying to get to grips with the logic of this activity. 'And did you collect his winnings too?'

Sandie chuckled. 'To be truthful, I think he hardly ever won. It was a little joke between us. When he did, the bookies must have paid the money straight into his bank.'

'How often did Sir Geoffrey place these bets?'

'Not very often, only once a month.'

'Exactly once a month?'

'Yes. Always on the last Wednesday. He used to say it was his end of the month treat to himself. It was what helped him get through the first three weeks.' She giggled. 'Sir Geoffrey had that kind of sense of humour where you never knew if he was joking or not. I mean you couldn't tell from his face at all. He would say these things and I'd think that's awful and then he'd just get this twinkle in his eye—'

'Deadpan,' said Mariner.

'Yes, that's right. That's what Dom said. He said—'

'Did you ever see how much Sir Geoffrey placed?'

She looked shocked. 'Oh no. The envelopes were stuck down and I would never have looked inside.'

'So it could have just been a tenner, or a twenty?'

'Oh no, it was more than that. The envelope always felt as if there was something in it.' She measured with her finger and thumb. 'It was about half an inch thick.'

The flaws in the system were glaringly obvious, but had not apparently occurred to Sandie.

'How long have you been working at the Commission?' Mariner asked.

'Four years this May.'

'And has Sir Geoffrey always placed these bets?'

'I expect so. But he only asked me to start helping with them about, let me see, eighteen months ago.'

'Have you told the police about it?'

Sandie looked horrified. 'Oh no! Sir Geoffrey's wife didn't like him gambling, and I know Miss James wouldn't approve. That's why Sir Geoffrey asked me to do it on the quiet. I'll get into terrible trouble for it. And it can't have anything to do with ... you know ... what happened. You won't tell anyone, will you?'

Mariner didn't necessarily think Helena was ignorant of the scam. He was pretty sure now that it was why he'd been introduced to Sandie in the first place. Ryland had taken advantage of Sandie's loyal innocence and now Helena was doing the same. But betting on horses was a perfectly legal and harmless activity. The Queen Mother indulged for God's sake, so why develop such an elaborate, covert strategy and why the secrecy? Ryland might have wanted to conceal it from his wife, but he could easily have slipped out during the working day to place the bets, without her ever knowing. And if that wasn't convenient there were other, discreet mechanisms. Most white collar gamblers picked up the phone and arranged the transactions electronically.

None of it made sense, unless Ryland got a buzz from the intrigue, the thrill of doing something illicit. No, it had to be something more than that. Either Ryland was telling an outright lie and the packages had nothing to do with horse racing, or it was possible that he was bending the truth and was more deeply involved in something closer to the boundaries of the law. If horse racing was at the root of it then it could be that he belonged to the kind of gambling syndicate that had become increasingly common in recent years.

A group of men, usually businessmen, bought shares in a racehorse, contributed regularly, usually monthly, to the animal's upkeep, and then took a proportion of any winnings. Unless there was race fixing, belonging to such a syndicate was far from illegal, but there were certain seedy connections and it probably wouldn't be the sort of thing a government official should be visibly linked to. Added to which, there was little doubt that heavy involvement in such a venture would not have gone down well with his wife. If she didn't approve of betting she wouldn't have wanted him embroiled in something shadier. 'I doubt that it would bother anyone now, Sandie,' Mariner said. 'So don't worry.'

'It was going to stop anyway,' she said.

'What makes you think that?'

'On the last Wednesday in November Sir Geoffrey went to place the last bet himself.'

'The last bet?'

'Yes. He said he'd reached a decision, and that he wasn't going to do it any more.'

'Why was that?'

Sandie shrugged. 'Perhaps Lady Diana had got wind of it, or maybe he was losing too much money.'

'Was he disappointed do you think, that it was the final flutter?'

'No. He seemed sort of – pleased with himself. "The last one, Sandie," he said. "And then we can get on with the real work."'

'Were you surprised?'

'Only because he had to cancel a meeting so that he could go and do it. Sir Geoffrey hated cancelling meetings. He didn't like to let people down.' She wrinkled her nose. 'Then when he got back he seemed really upset. He'd gone out all pleased with himself but when he came back he seemed really down.'

'You mean deflated, as if he knew the fun was over?'

'It was more than that. He'd brought a bottle of scotch with him because he said it was a cause for celebration.'

'I didn't think he drank.' Maggie said Ryland had taken the pledge when he met Diana.

'That's the thing. He didn't. And he was making out like we were celebrating but all the time he looked as if he was heading for the gallows. Something had really shaken him up. I thought maybe he'd gone for broke and made the last bet a really big one, and that he'd lost a lot of money.'

'Did you ask him?'

'Oh no, I never asked about the money. None of my business, was it? I just had a drink with him and played along.'

'And this was the last Wednesday in November.'

125

'Yes.'

Which would make it only a couple of weeks before he was killed. So why did it fit into that slot in the timeline? Was it just coincidence? Eleanor had said she thought her son was planning to contact Mariner. Was it because he knew his son was a senior police officer and he needed help? Or was it because he knew something terrible was going to happen to him and it would be his last chance?

'Which betting shop did Sir Geoffrey use?' Mariner asked. But Sandie didn't know.

If Ryland was involved in some kind of syndicate it could be as Sandie had described, and that on that final payment day Ryland was planning to pull out. But he'd somehow been thwarted, meaning that other syndicate members may have refused and perhaps even threatened to reveal his secret vice? Or maybe they set a ridiculously high buy-out price that left Ryland significantly out of pocket.

But it was hard to see how either of those scenarios would lead to Ryland's assassination just a couple of weeks later, and even less the murders of his wife and his driver. Mariner had reached the end of speculation alley. Sandie's instinct could be right. The horse racing scam, whatever its exact purpose, was probably completely unrelated to the shooting. He should get back to the task he'd come here to tackle: finding out more about Joseph O'Connor.

Mariner tapped on the pile of files Sandie had deposited on Ryland's desk. 'I'm keeping you from your work. Do you need to do something with these?'

Sandie rolled her eyes. 'I'd forget my head if it wasn't screwed on properly. I've got to take them down to the archives. Do you want to wait in—?'

'No, I'll come with you. Could do with stretching my legs, if that's all right?'

'It's not very exciting.'

'Who wants excitement?'

On the walk down two flights of stairs and along another corridor, past the staff toilets, Sandie was back in full spate, this time concerning the general lack of space for anything and how they were being squeezed out by all the files. The storage area had originally been used as a conference room, but they'd had to put in shelves even though it couldn't be secured, and now there was hardly space to swing a cat, was there? She led the way into a room about 5 metres square that housed with rows of shelves stretching up to the ceiling and packed with alphabetically labelled archive boxes. It took her only seconds to locate the required row, extract the relevant boxes and replace each file, chattering all the time.

'Copies of all the files are kept here?' Mariner tried to get his head round the implications of that in relation to the statistics Helena James had quoted earlier. The amount of storage space needed would be phenomenal.

But Sandie shook her head. 'Oh no. We hold all the records electronically, too, and then once a case is closed the hard copy goes to a special government storage facility.'

'I don't understand. So what are we bringing down here?'

'Sometimes individual members of the Commission ask us to hold a further copy of files they consider significant. Sir Geoffrey did it all the time.'

'Significant how?'

'Sometimes there's a pattern, say the same trial judge, or the same police force.' Or, thought Mariner, the fact that a suspect had been coerced into making a confession; Ryland's witch-hunt against the police.

So somewhere in this mass of paperwork there could be a copy of Joseph O'Connor's file. Mariner knew that asking outright would be a step too far. Helena's introduction had been carefully worded and so far Sandie had quite openly accepted his questioning, assuming that he was here in some sort of general official capacity. Getting too specific would no doubt involve consultation with her seniors, and there was a simpler way of doing this, if not completely above-board. It made him uneasy, but taking the broader view, what he was doing was in the name of justice and if he did uncover something that had been missed by Special Branch it would all come right in the end, wouldn't it? If Dave had been more open and honest with him there wouldn't be any need for all this cloak and dagger stuff.

'I could do with a pee,' he said as they passed the gents on their way back from the archive. 'Shall I catch you up?'

'Oh there's a much nicer one on the upper floor,' Sandie said. 'These aren't really used any more.'

'Oh I'm not fussy,' said Mariner. 'And all those stairs,' he joked. 'I'm not sure if I'll make it.'

'Oh.' Now Sandie was concerned, probably thinking now that the old feller had prostate problems. 'Okay then. You'll be able to find your way upstairs?'

'If I'm not back in an hour send out a search party.'

Sandie, it seemed, had trouble determining when anyone was joking, but she continued on her way, leaving Mariner with full access to the archive and feeling like Michael Caine in *The Ipcress File*. He hoped to God that it was a logical filing system.

Though his watch said only minutes, it seemed to Mariner that it took him hours to locate Joseph O'Connor's file. Contained in the folder were notes on the interview that followed O'Connor's arrest. They looked unobjectionable, but interviews weren't routinely taped until the late eighties, so the accuracy was questionable. On the front page the names of the arresting officers were outlined several times with pink highlighter. Were they the significant aspect of the case? Mariner noted their names in his pocket book: Detectives George Hollis and Stephen Jaeger. O'Connor's confession had been bullied out of him, so the chances were that this wasn't the first or last time these two had indulged in a bit of malpractice.

It brought a new possibility into the equation; that O'Connor was helping Ryland to build a case against Jaeger and Hollis. Sharon O'Connor had denied that her husband

128

was offering any additional help and talked categorically about her husband 'wanting out', but would she necessarily have known? She'd intimated Ryland's promise that he would 'get the men' who'd put Joseph in prison the first time and Mariner had taken that as meaning the men who'd set him up; Brady and his crew. But she could have equally been referring to the police officers who'd secured the wrongful conviction. If that's what she meant then it was a whole new ball game.

If Ryland was planning to initiate disciplinary proceedings against Hollis and Jaeger, citing O'Connor's case in evidence, then the detectives would be keen to keep both men quiet. Offering O'Connor a job could have been Ryland's unsuccessful strategy to protect him. The timing was a puzzle, though. O'Connor had been released years ago. If the officers were taking some kind of revenge, why wait until now? Had it taken this long for Ryland to build the case against them, or had something triggered a decision to act on his findings? Or maybe the policemen in his sights had been tipped off about what was going on.

Knowing what he now knew, it was becoming increasingly difficult for Mariner to understand why Ryland was being overlooked as the victim in the shooting. Potentially there were all kinds of people who were unhappy about what he was up to. The trouble was that none of these revelations would be palatable to the public, especially with a general election coming up and a government that claimed to be tough on crime. It was also exactly the kind of thing the Met would be keen to draw a veil over, preferring instead to divert attention towards O'Connor's so-called previous drugs activity.

Flicking through the other paperwork in the file, Mariner came across a large envelope. He pulled out the contents; a series of eight-by-six black and white surveillance photographs. Two men in conversation beside a car, neither of them Joseph O'Connor; bright sunlight, sunglasses, one of them in a Hawaiian shirt, the other wearing a polo shirt.

Casual, holiday clothes and somewhere warm. Other photographs were almost identical, but with slightly modified poses, so taken in close succession. Mariner could almost hear the shutter clunk and whirr.

Another shot was of the same two men with a third sitting at what looked like a pavement café. Same brilliant sunlight and sharp shadows. The pub landlord had talked about Terry Brady having a villa in Spain, so one of the subjects could be him.

Mariner realised he'd been standing here too long. Sandie would wonder where he'd got to. He should have dropped stronger hints about his prostate. It would have bought him a little more time. Committing as much detail of the photos to memory as possible, including the partial index on the car, he slid the photographs back into the envelope. But they caught on something; a yellow Post It note that had become detached from the pictures. It bore a scribbled message: *Well, what do you know?* **M.B.**

Sadly, M.B. whoever he may be, had chosen not to share any further detail about what he knew, and he provided no clue about the identity of the men or what they might be doing. His frustration mounting, Mariner returned the photos to their envelope and replaced O'Connor's file.

Sandie didn't appear to have missed him at all and had done her own disappearing act upstairs, but in the hushed corridors Mariner tracked the sound of her voice to the open door of an office he hadn't yet been shown. He could see why. The tiny boxroom lacked the order of the main office, the small computer work-station surrounded as it was by piles of cartons, haphazardly stacked on the floor. Sandie was chatting to another young woman of about her age, with dark intense eyes in an oval face.

'Hi,' Sandie smiled, perhaps with relief. 'You found your way back then.' Was it Mariner's imagination or did she just check his trousers for telltale residue? The girl she was talking to looked on curiously. 'This is Trudy, she's new to the team. Detective Mariner is here to look round.'

'Public Information Officer,' Mariner read from Trudy's badge, simultaneously thinking that he really ought to break this habit of staring at the bosom of any young woman he met. 'What exactly does that mean?'

'I'm still finding out,' admitted Trudy, unconcerned by his curiosity. 'I've only been here a few weeks, since the advent of the Freedom of Information Act. Now that the public has a right to access some of the Commission's data, I'm here to process the requests.'

Of course. The legislation that might just work in Mariner's favour. 'Have you seen much action yet?' he asked.

'A bit. At the moment most applications seem to be from organisations concerned with miscarriages of justice, wanting information about referrals that have been turned down. They like to compare the performance of individual members of the Commission.'

'Ah, so you're the very person I need to speak to,' said Mariner, smoothly, as the idea occurred to him. 'Helena James said I'd be able to get a list of the cases rejected by Sir Geoffrey Ryland. Would it be convenient to have that now?' He made a point of checking his watch. 'I have to leave shortly, but—?' It was a technique called bulldozing, not allowing the other party time or opportunity to object.

Trudy looked unsure. 'I should probably check with Miss James. There's paperwork to complete—'

'You should,' Mariner agreed. 'Although she did say she had a lot on this afternoon. All I need are the names and basic details,' Mariner went on, the epitome of the voice of reason. 'I mean, everyone on that list has, rightly or wrongly, been convicted of a crime, so I could easily track them down through police systems, but you'd be saving me a lot of trouble.' It's really no big deal, he was telling her. 'And if the list is being sent out to other groups anyway—'

'All right then, but you won't thank me. It's a long list.'

Long wasn't the word. Nineteen pages of tightly packed data, Helena's fifteen cases a month and 96 per cent

131

rejected over the last eight years, and it took Trudy several minutes to print out a copy for Mariner. As the inkjet clattered and hummed they stood making small talk in the tiny office, and it was while he was idly scanning the notice board above the desk that Mariner spotted the business card for JMB Associates; Professional Investigation Services, an address in High Street, Hammersmith. In other words, a Private Detective Agency. 'I'm sure I've come across JMB Associates before,' he said casually to Trudy. 'Who is it runs that outfit?'

It was Sandie who provided the answer. 'That's up there from when we used this office,' she said. 'It's a guy called Mike Baxter.' M.B.

'Where does he come in?'

'Sometimes the members of the Commission want more background information on a case. Mike helps out.' Good old Mike.

'There you go.' Trudy presented Mariner with the printed and stapled list. 'Some bedtime reading for you.'

'Thanks,' he said, folding it and tucking it into an inside pocket. 'Now I'll leave you in peace.'

Chapter Ten

The sky outside was darkening to a dusky blue as Sandie showed Mariner out. 'Thanks for all your help,' he said. 'And perhaps you could pass on my thanks to Miss James, too. Tell her it's been – enlightening.'

'Okay,' said Sandie. 'Where is it you're staying?' When Mariner told her she described, with great precision, each step of the route he should take back to his hotel.

'If I'm going through Euston I could return that locker key to the left luggage office,' Mariner offered.

'Would you?' She was back in seconds, still chattering. 'I should have returned it straightaway, but you know how it is, one thing led to—'

'I know just what you mean. Thanks again, Sandie. And good luck with the flat.'

Mariner's intention had been to find a pub for a quiet pint, but after Sandie's painfully detailed directions he felt obliged to go back to the hotel first. Maybe he'd have something to eat there before sampling the London nightlife. Already the rush hour was gathering pace and by the last leg of his journey the crowds on the underground were beginning to swell. Though he arrived on an almost deserted platform the bodies were pouring in as if somewhere a sluice gate had been opened, and in only minutes it was jammed solid, bodies on all sides, pressing close, with scant regard for personal space. Instinctively, Mariner checked that his wallet was still safely stowed.

As his discomfort increased, a distant rumble and rush of warm air signalled the arrival of the train, a primeval beast emerging from its lair. The racket grew louder and Mariner's ears popped as they had in the explosion and the bitter taste of adrenalin flooded his mouth, boosting his heart rate.

Headlights appeared from the darkened tunnel, there was a sudden surge from behind and Mariner was violently shoved in the back, making him stagger and lurch towards the open rail-bed as the train thundered towards the platform. For a moment he flailed, toppling forward in slow motion, the pull of gravity sucking him down, until something grabbed at his jacket and he was yanked back onto the platform again, regaining his balance on solid ground, his heart pounding. Almost immediately he was buffeted to one side and a piercing scream faded hideously in his ear, lost in the deafening screech of brakes as the train hurtled by. Murmurs of disgust gave way to a flurry of activity as the crowd, as one, backed away from the platform's edge and several men wearing the uniform of the transport police pushed through from nowhere, making for the front of the train.

'A jumper.' The immaculately–suited African-Caribbean man beside Mariner must have read the shock and bewilderment on his face. 'It happens a lot this time of year. Quite often they come from the back; a last-minute decision.'

'He nearly took me with him,' said Mariner, breathing deeply to control his jangling limbs. He scanned the crowd trying to identify who it was that had saved him, but no one returned his gaze.

'She,' the commuter corrected him. 'Only a kid. They often are. They'll close the station now. Have to find another route home.' And, tutting at the inconvenience of a fellow human being taking her own life, the man turned and began to push his way towards the exit. Weak and slightly nauseous, Mariner allowed himself to be swept along with

134

the herd up to the surface and refreshingly cold evening air. A pub was essential now and the first one he saw was just across the road. He was on his second pint and following it with a restorative chaser when his mobile went. In all the noise and chatter it was difficult to hear, and Flynn's voice sounded hoarse and somehow different. 'Meet me on Damask Street,' he said. He seemed to be whispering. 'It's round the corner from your hotel, quarter of a mile. I'll see you there in twenty minutes.'

'What's going on Dave?'

'I've got something you'll be interested in.'

'Can't you tell me—?' But Mariner found he was talking to himself.

Consulting his *A-Z* Mariner saw that if he left now and made it brisk he was within walking distance of his hotel, and of Damask Street. Either way he had no desire to go back down onto the underground tonight, and if he stepped it up he could easily cover the ground in twenty minutes. With a twinge of regret for the abandoned drinks he ventured into the night air. The London night life was in full swing, but as he followed the route he'd committed to memory, the noise and the light faded away to a quiet dark- ness until Mariner turned into Damask Street, in reality nothing more than a narrow passage that ran between the unseeing rear aspects of high Victorian factories. A row of skeletal fire escapes rose from huddled dustbins, skips and rubbish piled high, the buildings probably defunct and certainly empty at this hour.

It had begun to drizzle and the flat broken cobbles glis- tened under the shining glow of a couple of door lights. A lone rat scurried across the road and rain dripped from an overhanging pipe with tedious regularity. It was bloody cold, too. What the hell did Flynn want to meet him here for?

Then Mariner saw a reassuring human movement, a big- coated figure approaching from the end of the street.

135

Relieved, Mariner began to walk towards him to meet halfway along the alleyway. But ten feet apart something didn't feel right. It wasn't Flynn after all.

Mariner raised his head to nod a cautious greeting at about the same time as the stranger moved his arm, and Mariner glimpsed the faintest glint of something shiny; a blade grasped in a gloved fist. Mariner began to back off but the man matched his movements, and as Mariner turned to run, his foot skidded on the slick cobbles and he stumbled. Taking his chance, the assailant grabbed Mariner's arm, swinging him round, and in his peripheral vision Mariner saw the stiletto blade swing back. Instinctively, he raised an arm to defend himself and cried out as he felt a stinging across the heel of his hand. At that moment a dazzling glare washed over him. A car had turned into the street and was driving straight at them. Instantaneously Mariner's attacker relinquished his grasp and pulled away, running back past the oncoming vehicle in the direction from which he'd appeared. The car slowed beside Mariner and a window slid smoothly down.

'Are you all right my friend?'

His heart thudding and mouth dry Mariner realized that he was. 'I'm fine,' he said. 'You came by at the right time.'

'This is not a good place to be walking at this time of night,' the driver advised, helpfully. 'But if you're sure everything's okay.'

'I'm sure. Thanks.' And Mariner watched as the car, a top of the range Mercedes, glided away from him and rounded the corner at the far end of the street. Thrusting his hands in his pockets, he immediately became aware of a warm stickiness on the right. He took it out again, inspecting it in the dim light. A two-inch gash across the fleshy part of his palm was pouring blood so he mustered what tissues he had stuffed in various pockets and pressed them against it. Following the direction of the sodium glow above the rooftops, Mariner worked his way back to a main, well-lit road and as soon as he was among people again and could relax, he took out his mobile and called Flynn. There was a delay before it was answered and Flynn sounded groggy. 'What's up?'

Hearing his voice now Mariner was pretty certain that the earlier call hadn't been from him. He cursed himself for being so stupid. 'I need to talk to you.'

A pause. 'At this time of night?'

'It's urgent.'

'You'd better come here then.' Flynn gave him the address.

He sounded reluctant and the fear that Flynn may nonetheless be involved in what had just happened to Mariner resurfaced. This was an opportunity to check it out. If Flynn was party to what was going on, surely Mariner would be able to see it in his eyes. He hailed a black cab and relayed the address that Flynn had given him.

At the main entrance to Flynn's apartment block Mariner pressed the buzzer on the intercom and heard Flynn's voice. 'Wait there, I'm coming down.'

'Bring a clean towel or something,' said Mariner, clutching the soggy tissues in his right hand.

'What?'

'You'll see.'

Eventually Flynn appeared. He smelled heavily of perfume and in the light of the lobby his face was oddly defined. He'd been woken from a deep sleep. Mariner was hugely reassured.

'Sorry. I've caught you in the middle of something, or someone.'

'What's that supposed to mean?'

'It's not your perfume, is it?'

'So what??'

'So nothing. You're single. You can see whoever you like.'

'Yes. I can.' Flynn offered the tea towel, a pale checked affair. 'Here. What's this for?'

Mariner showed his blood-soaked palm. 'I had a mishap.'

'Christ. That needs stitches. You should get to A&E.'

'It looks worse than it is,' Mariner lied, feeling the throbbing pain creeping up towards his wrist. He wrapped the tea towel tightly round the wound. 'I could do with a sit down though. Is there somewhere we can go to talk?'

Flynn took him to the end of the street where an all-night greasy spoon was serving twenty-four-hour cholesterol cocktails. From the activity inside it could have been the middle of the day. The tea Flynn got them was the colour of the Severn in full flood. As he sat down Mariner quashed a smile.

'What?'

'You've got a smear of lipstick.'

Flynn wiped it off with the back of his hand, looking so guilty that Mariner was forced to conclude he must be screwing his boss's wife, or at the very least a married woman. 'So what did you want to talk to me about that can't wait until morning, apart from the fact that you've cut your hand open?'

'There's a reason you've been kept away from Ryland.'

'Christ, Tom, why can't you leave this alone?'

'Because he was my father, he was shot dead, and I think there's some kind of cover-up going on here.'

'What are you talking about?'

'Someone doesn't want me getting close to it either.' He held up his hand. 'Before this happened I almost got pushed under a tube train.' Mariner described what had happened at the station, aware that his voice wavered as he spoke.

Flynn gave it short shrift. 'People commit suicide on the tube on a daily basis,' he said. 'Especially post-Christmas. Sometimes others get in the way. Count yourself lucky you didn't go too, but don't take it personally.'

'The phone call wasn't bad luck, and it definitely was personal. Whoever made it knows where I'm staying and they've got my mobile number.'

'What phone call?'

Mariner told him. 'To be honest, I thought it was you.' Flynn looked at him. 'It's all right, I realise now that it can't have been.'

'Maybe it was just a mistake. Someone got the wrong number.'

'Someone who knew that Damask Street was in walking distance of my hotel? And how is it that when I get there a mugger conveniently appears and tries to stab me?'

'Be sensible, Tom. You said this Damask Street was little more than a dark alleyway. You'd have been a prime target; bloke hanging around in a deserted street like that. It was an opportunist.'

The second time in recent weeks Mariner had heard that word. 'I don't think so. I'm being targeted. If that car hadn't come along—'

'The guy in the Mercedes.'

'He could have been the contact,' Mariner said.

'So why didn't he stop?'

'Perhaps the mugger put him off. I don't know. Or maybe the whole thing was staged.'

Flynn sighed. 'You're overwrought, You've been through a lot in the last few weeks—'

'No, I mean it—'

'Be sensible, Tom. Why would anyone want to do this? What could you possibly have uncovered about Sir Geoffrey Ryland that anyone would be so desperate to keep quiet?'

'He was involved in some kind of gambling syndicate.' As expected, this was clearly news to Flynn, but as Mariner began to expound his theory about the betting scam it seemed, even to his own ears, to lose credibility in the telling. 'Ryland was paying out large, regular cash sums as some kind of horse-racing scam. I was told it was a straightforward flutter, but in practical terms that doesn't make sense. If all Ryland was doing was placing bets, he'd do it through a phone account. It would help to check his bank accounts to see how much he was spending.' He threw Flynn a meaningful look.

'Don't be bloody stupid. I can't just wade in and demand that kind of information. There would be questions. And so what if he was into something like that? It's not illegal.'

'So why was his assistant sworn to secrecy, and how come you didn't know about it?'

'Hypocrisy. Ryland was a pretty outspoken critic of the government's recent relaxation of gambling laws, wasn't he? It wouldn't look great if he himself was found to be indulging.'

It hadn't occurred to Mariner, but Flynn was right. Ryland had even opined in the press about it. That's why it had seemed so unlikely. It could even be the reason for Ryland's sudden need to jump ship on the enterprise.

'As far as I know there's nothing else to suggest he was into anything like that,' said Flynn. 'So why don't you leave the real investigators to do their job?'

'Because they're not doing it properly.' Mariner's frustration was growing. 'The theory that Joseph O'Connor was the target for the shooting has more holes in it than a sieve.'

'For instance?'

'Joseph O'Connor's supposed meeting with Brady. Sure, they were in the same pub on the same night but that's as far as it goes. O'Connor left almost as soon as Brady arrived. They never met.'

'Says who?'

'Says the pub landlord, the same pub landlord who gave a witness statement to that effect. Somebody's playing a game of Chinese whispers there.'

'Perhaps it was a misunderstanding. The witness didn't make himself clear, or changed his story. It happens, you know that.'

'Some misunderstanding. The whole thing with O'Connor stinks. Also, Ryland was writing the draft of the second instalment of his memoirs.'

140

'So?'

'I've been told he was using the opportunity to blow the whistle on the government's interference in the JRC. It's supposed to be an independent body, but crippling restrictions have been placed on the cases they can review. The Home Office is virtually running the show. Did you know that?'

'How the hell did you find out? No, no, that's okay, it can wait. What is it you're trying to say?'

'That the JRC is a sham. Don't you think it would be damaging to the government if that truth got out?'

'It wouldn't do them much good,' Flynn conceded.

'So it would be in their interests to keep Ryland quiet, wouldn't it? The day after he died they took the hard drive from his computer at the JRC.'

'I'm sure that's pretty routine procedure. He'd have been handling some sensitive data as a matter of course. No one would want it to get into the wrong hands. So, let me get this straight. What you're implying here is that somehow the government arranged to have Ryland killed and now, because you're onto it, they're after you too?' He made it sound like a cheap melodrama. 'I think your imagination is running away with you, mate. Government officials involved in a sordid back-street mugging? In the real world it doesn't happen.'

'Look at what happened to David Kelly.'

'Oh for Christ's sake, Tom, Kelly committed suicide, as well you know.' Flynn took a weary breath. 'Okay. Supposing you're right. Let's imagine that somebody did set you up and arranged for a mugger to see you off. Isn't it much more likely to be someone related to Joseph O'Connor? His cronies wouldn't want you poking around after the shooting, would they? And the stuff you've described is more their style.'

'They're not the only ones.'

'What does that mean?'

'Remember a George Hollis?'

141

Flynn's eyes narrowed. 'Who's he? No, don't tell me; he's a secret government agent.' But he knew the name, Mariner could tell.

'He got O'Connor wrongfully convicted, and was subsequently indicted in his appeal.'

'We all make mistakes.'

'Must have been a habit with George Hollis. Sir Geoffrey Ryland was taking quite an interest in him. Do you know him?'

'I know *of* him He worked out of Harlesden just before I did, but then, I expect you already know that, don't you?'

'What can you tell me about him?'

'He had a certain reputation as a tough officer who got results.'

'Regardless of the methods?'

'Hollis was from a different era. The way he did things may not always have been universally popular but he had his following.'

Mariner could imagine that following; there were always a few young guys who came into the job planning on being vigilantes and George Hollis sounded just the kind of role model they loved. Jack Coleman was from a different era, too, Mariner thought. It hadn't made him corrupt.

'So now we've gone from government scheming to bent coppers,' Flynn observed. 'You are covering all the bases. Which is it to be?'

'I'm just saying that your colleagues seem to have been quick to jump to conclusions without necessarily considering all the possibilities.'

'You don't know that. *I* don't know that. Who knows what they're considering? Where did you dig Hollis up?' Flynn asked.

'I've spoken to people at the JRC—'

'Yes, let's come back to that. What the fuck were you even doing there?'

'I just stopped by. I was interested to know where my old man used to work. They invited me in.'

'Just like that.'

'And I got talking to people.'

Flynn held his gaze. They both knew what he was saying was nonsense but Flynn wasn't interested in the technicalities right now. 'Who did you "get talking to"?' he asked sceptically.

'A couple of staffers,' Mariner brushed him off. 'It doesn't really matter. I'm just saying that Hollis had a good reason for wanting both Ryland and O'Connor to back off. Is anyone looking into his whereabouts on the night Ryland was killed?'

Flynn sighed. 'I really have no idea.'

'Because it wouldn't be in the interests of the Home Office to have them dragged into this either, would it? Whatever is at the root of this, it looks to me as if it'll all be neatly swept under the carpet.'

Flynn was beginning to get annoyed. 'You should hear yourself. If it's a legitimate line of enquiry someone will be following it up. As I've told you before, it's just not within my remit.'

'But you said it. Right from the start the focus of this investigation is O'Connor, not Ryland.'

'Because that's where the evidence is!' Flynn raised his voice and a couple of people turned their way.

'What evidence?' Mariner countered. 'There's hardly any and what exists is purely circumstantial.'

'Just because we don't have access, doesn't mean it isn't there. My colleagues on the squad are professional coppers like you and me. They'll have good reasons for reaching the conclusions they have.'

'Yes, mainly that it's too uncomfortable to consider anything else. Either that or they're being directed from above.'

This time Flynn was laughing. 'For Christ's sake, get a grip, friend. There is no conspiracy. Isn't that what you told special branch about the St Martin's explosion?'

'How the hell do you know that?'

But Flynn wasn't going to tell him. 'This is not your case, Tom. You're on a hiding to nothing. Leave it and go back to Birmingham.'

'Maybe I will.'

But as they parted company both men knew that the chances of that happening were minimal.

Mariner considered what Flynn had said. He couldn't really deny that he'd been edgy since the explosion, and it was possible that he had over-reacted to the incident in the tube station. But the phone call had been a clear-cut ploy. There was no doubt in his mind that somebody was out to warn him off at the very least. He was certain of it. Had Flynn known Hollis better than he was prepared to admit?

On the way back to the hotel Mariner called in at an all-night pharmacy that stocked basic first aid kits. Back in his hotel room he squirted a liquid plaster over the wound. It hurt like fuck but at least the bleeding had stopped and, when the pain eased off, he bound the hand with gauze and tied it as best he could with his left hand and teeth. Then, downing a couple of paracetomol, he went to bed.

Mariner slept badly, the pain in his hand waking him every time he turned over and making it impossible to lie comfortably. A couple of times he rolled all his weight onto it and yelped out loud. In the morning his whole hand looked swollen and the area around the dressing was an angry red. He took a couple more paracetomol.

After breakfast, Mariner successfully obtained the phone number for JMB Investigation Services from directory enquiries. But, an answering-machine message informed him that the office wouldn't reopen until ten thirty am. On the positive side, it allowed plenty of time to get there, calling in at Euston Station. Back to his unofficial look today, he retrieved the left luggage key from the pocket of his suit jacket.

Of the many aspects of Ryland's covert gambling, the

144

left luggage locker was the biggest puzzle. For one thing Mariner hadn't realised that lockers could be rented long-term, or that duplicate keys could be had. The location also seemed strange, and almost arbitrary. Sandie would have had to make a special journey on the tube to make the drop. The obvious explanation was that whoever collected Ryland's stake, if that's what it was, worked around this area or travelled in from elsewhere. Mariner wondered if any other lockers were connected. Finding number one-four-three, he opened it. It was, as he had expected, clean and completely empty with not a hint of the contents or those who had used it. In other circumstances he'd have been tempted to get it dusted for fingerprints, but if there was no criminal activity going on where would that get him? Suddenly weary, he leaned his forehead against the top of the locker. What was he doing here and what had he expected to find? Perhaps Flynn was right and he was start-ing to lose it. He returned the key to the desk.

The journey out to Hammersmith was a short two-leg tube ride that would still get him there way too early for Mike Baxter, and having overindulged on the fried food again, Mariner's throat was parched and he needed to take more painkillers. The station cafeterias were the kind of fast food operations that he detested, and he wanted a decent cup of tea, so he left the station and gazed along the road in search of somewhere less frenetic. A sign on an opposite street corner caught his eye: Pearl's Café. Christ, was it the same one?

Walking up to the door Mariner could see that, though modernised, it had remained the kind of retro place that Ryland would have liked: tables with checked table cloths, waitress service and a line of stools for customers who preferred to sit at the counter; its original nineteen fifties style. What a find; a place that both Ryland and his mother had known.

Mariner stepped into a humid warmth with the comfort-ing smell of hot toast and took one of the unoccupied tables.

The laminated menu propped between the salt and pepper pots was simple – none of your cappuccino or latté here, just straight tea or coffee, a mug or a pot with scones, teacakes or toast. The waitress, a substantial black woman, came over almost immediately. 'What can I get you darlin'?'

Looking up Mariner was transfixed by the embroidered name on her overall. 'You're Pearl?' he said in astonishment. 'As in; Pearl's Café?'

'Yes,' said Pearl, smiling to expose big white teeth, widely spaced. 'As in; "why wouldn't I be?"'

She looked only about thirty, and as she gazed at him Mariner felt suddenly disorientated. 'This café's named after you?' he asked.

'It's my place,' she shrugged. 'So it seemed like a good name.'

'How long have you been open?'

'Three years next March. Did all the renovations myself.'

'What was it before that?'

Pearl was exercising extraordinary patience. 'Used to be a tobacconist's, but it had been closed for years.'

'I see. I'll have a mug of tea, thanks.'

Replacing the menu, Mariner spotted another small card tucked into the cruet, and advertising New Year lunchtime specials: purchase one snack and get another free. Except for the season, it was exactly like the card that had he and Flynn had found in that packet of photographs, and now Mariner saw how ridiculous he'd been. They had jumped to completely the wrong conclusion. That postcard didn't belong with his mother's letters or the 1958 programme from the Albert Hall. It was a more recent addition. But how and why was it there? It was pretty certainly an indication that Ryland had visited Pearl's Café but he wouldn't normally have any reason to come to this part of London. It wasn't near his house or the JRC. The only thing close by was the left luggage locker, but most of the trips to the locker had been made by Sandie. All except that final one, just before Christmas.

Pearl brought across his tea, a good strong brew in a hefty mug. Mariner showed her the postcard. 'Did you have a similar offer before Christmas?'

'Yeah, and it worked so well that I'm doing it again. Next time you should bring a friend.' She bellowed with laughter. 'If you've got any.'

Sandie had described Ryland's excitement about placing his last bet and his subsequent dejection. It would confirm his notion that Ryland was meeting with someone, perhaps to end the arrangement, or to pull out. But the meeting had gone badly, badly enough that Ryland needed a 'celebratory' drink when he got back to the office. The meeting could have occurred in this very place. A venue close to the left luggage locker would presumably have been convenient to both parties. Ryland loathed fast food joints and this café would be less public than any of those on the station concourse. But how had that postcard got in with the photos? Flynn said that Ryland had accessed his security box in November. It could have been on the same day that he placed his last bet, which begged the next question: were those two events connected?

Ryland was writing his memoirs. Was he sitting looking at the photographs as a way of passing the time while he waited for his fellow gambler to turn up? Or was there more to it? Did Ryland actually bring all the photographs to that meeting as proof that he had a son who was a police officer? Was he countering a threat that was being made against him? Mariner needed to find out exactly when and why Ryland went to his safety deposit box.

Chapter Eleven

JMB Services worked out of an office over a dry cleaner's, the door straight out of fifties noir: discreet, frosted glass with black lettering. Mariner buzzed to gain entry, ascending a narrow staircase that led directly into a cramped two-desk office. Mariner took a guess that the lad behind one of the desks, scruffily dressed in T-shirt and rumpled combats, his hair gelled into a sculptured masterpiece, was too young to be Baxter.

'Jason,' he introduced himself. 'But everyone calls me Jayce. How can I help?'

'I was hoping to speak to Mr Baxter.'

'I'm afraid Mr Baxter's indisposed.'

'How?'

'Came off his motorbike a couple of weeks back.'

Mariner's antennae twitched. 'How?'

Jayce shrugged. 'Taking a bend too fast.'

'Any other vehicles involved?'

'Not that I know of.'

'What's the damage?'

'Broken ribs, bruising. I'm his partner. Can I help?'

There didn't seem to be much choice. 'I'm looking into the death of Sir Geoffrey Ryland,' Mariner said, wondering if Jayce would even know who the man was. Happily he did.

'Mike was gutted about that,' he said. 'They were

friends. Mr Ryland often sent a bit of work our way.'

'Did you know what kind of work?'

'The kind of work we do; investigations. Sometimes Mr Ryland wanted a bit of background on people.'

'Like George Hollis and Steve Jaeger.'

Jayce was suddenly guarded. 'Could be.'

'Any idea what he found out?' Judging by the look on Jayce's face some reassurance was called for. 'I'm not on their side,' Mariner said. 'I'm trying to find out what happened to Sir Geoffrey Ryland.' Mariner eyed the row of steel filing cabinets over Jayce's shoulder. 'You keep files on your—' Mariner hesitated, searching for the correct word '—clients,' he settled on eventually, though that didn't sound right.

'Of course,' said Jayce, a hint of pride in his voice. 'We keep meticulous records. We have to keep track—' Jayce was a bright lad. He saw the next question appear on the horizon. 'And they're confidential,' he said.

'What's the matter? Hollis and Jaeger friends of Mr Baxter, is that it?' Mariner asked. 'I'll bet he's an ex-copper, isn't he?' It was more than a random guess. Most PIs were ex-police or military. 'Were they tight?'

'You know nothing,' Jayce blurted out. 'Mike got out because of the corruption. One thing gets right up Mike's nose, it's bent coppers.'

'Are Hollis and Jaeger bent?'

'They were on the Special Incident Squad.' Jayce spoke as if that said it all, and perhaps it did.

Mariner had been a bit slow. He hadn't made that link with Harlesden, and Flynn hadn't thought to mention it either. The SIS was the equivalent of the West Midlands Serious Crime squad, but had survived longer, theoretically because it didn't have the same inherent problems with corruption. But that was the whole point. Squads like that were snug and people took care of each other. Uncovering any wrongdoing was like trying to prise open an old tin of paint. To expose Hollis and Jaeger for corruption would cause massive fallout, and would give them and their followers a nice fat juicy motive for wanting Ryland and O'Connor dealt with.

Not that Mariner thought for a moment that the two officers would have been directly involved. Their prints wouldn't be on the trigger. According to Flynn, Hollis had a following and it was bound to be the case. Career coppers like Hollis built up contacts, not all of them on the law-abiding side of the fence, and for the right money they were the sort of contacts who could be easily bought. Fitting O'Connor up with the drugs would be simple. Just a question of finding the right person to do it. And *vengeance is mine*? A dramatic, if unnecessary, flourish from the assassin.

In addition, Hollis and Jaeger would have enough friends in the Met to influence the way in which the investigation into the shootings was being conducted. Flynn said that from the outset there had seemed to be a steer away from Ryland and towards the drugs angle. For a horrible moment Mariner thought of the link with Flynn himself. He'd played down any connection with Hollis, but then if he was involved, that's exactly what he'd do. And the attempts on Mariner's life, if that was what they were. Someone had known his movements and had his mobile number. Flynn had access to both. Christ, would he—?

He'd spilled his guts to Flynn and if Flynn was embroiled in this ... He needed to know what Hollis and Jaeger were up to now. 'You sure there's nothing you can tell me?' he asked Jayce.

'That's for Mike to decide. I don't know who you are from Adam.' The lad stood his ground admirably.

Mariner badly wanted to distinguish himself from Adam but somehow he didn't have the same confidence in Jayce's discretion as he'd had in Helena James. And Jayce was unyielding. It was probably the first time he'd been left minding the shop and he was determined to demonstrate his authority. Mariner would have to find out through other means.

Taking a business card out of his wallet he scribbled down the number for the hotel along with his room number, and his number at the cottage. He didn't want Anna on his back yet. He passed it to Jayce. 'Perhaps you could ask Mike Baxter to give me a call when he's feeling up to it. I think I may have something on George Hollis that's considerably bigger than evidence-fixing.'

'Like what?' Now the lad was curious.

Too late, buddy. 'I'll wait and talk to Mr Baxter. As you rightly say, it's his case.'

From the agency, Mariner returned to the hotel, hopeful that Jayce might call Baxter sooner rather than later. With luck Baxter might not live too far away and could be persuaded to meet. But climbing the stairs to his room he decided to clear the messages on his mobile, and that's when he picked up the four from Charlie Glover, all of them asking him to call Granville Lane urgently. Mariner's first thought was that something had happened to Anna. Panic flooded his veins. His mobile battery was low, so he ran the last few yards along the landing to his room, fumbling the key and wasting valuable time, crossed the tiny room in two strides to get to the phone and punched in Glover's direct line. It rang and rang before Glover finally picked up.

'Where the hell are you?' he said, cheerfully. 'I've left dozens of messages on your answering machine. Some woman from Manor Park keeps ringing you at work. Louise. She's been trying to get hold of Anna.'

'So Anna's all right?' Mariner breathed out as anxiety gave way to relief.

'As far as I know. Except that nobody can get her on her mobile.'

'She's out in Herefordshire. There's no signal.'

'Well, one of you needs to phone this Louise asap.'

'Okay. Everything else all right?'

'Sure, you've heard about the bomb?'

151

'What bomb?'

'The explosion at St Martin's, it was a bomb.'

Mariner went cold. 'I thought they'd said it was inconclusive.'

'Not any more. Anyway, call Louise, will you?'

'I'll do it now,' said Mariner, numbly. He couldn't help but think back to that message: *Next time, don't be late*, and the lack of information forthcoming from Addison. Since then Mariner had had two further narrow escapes, which added together made it feel as if he was right about someone being out to get him. Just because he was paranoid, didn't mean ...

Mariner tried Becky and Mark's home number but there was no reply. It was early afternoon so chances were Mark was at work and Anna and Becky had taken themselves off somewhere. Mariner just hoped their outing didn't involve estate agents. The calls from Manor Park, he decided, were probably about the payments. There had been the ongoing problem with the automatic transactions that Louise had mentioned on their last visit. Well, if he couldn't do anything else about it, he could at least reassure them that Anna would be back soon, so he called the hostel.

'Actually we wondered if you could come and collect Jamie for a couple of days,' Louise said.

'Is there a problem?'

'Not really. Well yes, there is, but I'm sure we can sort it out.'

'If it's the payments, I'm sure—'

'No, it's nothing like that.' She was reluctant to disclose over the phone. 'Perhaps if you could come over.'

'Today?'

'As soon as possible really.'

It was the last thing Mariner wanted and now part of him wished he hadn't made the call, but having done so there was no other option. Before checking out of the hotel he called Maggie.

'Thanks for all your help.'

'Did you learn anything useful?'

'I did. Nothing conclusive, but a few things I can follow up.'

'It would have been good for you to get closure on this.'

Mariner grinned to himself. 'Very West Coast. But thanks.'

'Look after yourself, Tom, and keep in touch.'

'I will.'

On the chest of drawers was the database that Trudy had printed off for him. He wondered about its usefulness now and picked it up to drop it in the bin. But something stopped him. She'd gone to some trouble on his behalf. Folding it, he tucked it into the inside pocket of his jacket instead. Mike Baxter wouldn't be able to reach him at the hotel now, but his mobile and home numbers were on the card.

Back in Birmingham Mariner had the taxi drop him off at the cottage to pick up his car. There was evidence from a few additional items, including fresh food in the fridge, that Bill Dyson had fully moved in. But he wasn't there, probably out on the road somewhere trying to flog his merchandise. Sales was never a job Mariner had envied.

At Jamie's hostel Louise met Mariner at the door. They must have been looking out for him.

'What's happened?' he asked.

She was embarrassed. 'It's rather unfortunate. Jamie and some of the other clients were out in the garden. We were tidying up so we left them outside for a while. He must have wanted the toilet but, instead of telling someone, he just did it there and then. Trouble is, the neighbour's grandchildren were out in the garden and saw him through the fence. They're trying to say he did it deliberately and have made a complaint. They're accusing him of indecent exposure. You know how hard we had to work to gain acceptance here so we have to be seen to be acting on the complaint. We wondered if you'd mind taking him home for a few days until the fuss dies down.'

'Then he can come back?'

A pause. 'We'll have to see. We're trying to persuade the neighbours not to go to the press.'

'This isn't great timing, you know,' said Mariner feeling like a selfish shit. 'Anna's away and I have to go back to work.' Not strictly true but it would be soon enough.

'I'm sorry for the inconvenience, but I don't know what else we can do.'

'Couldn't Jamie go back to Manor Park?' The main residential facility was still open.

'Since we've begun moving clients out into community accommodation they've cut down on staffing. There would be nowhere for him to go. You can continue to take him to the day centre though.'

Since moving to Manor Park Jamie had moved to a local day centre on the other side of Bromsgrove. From Anna's house it would mean a round trip of twenty miles each morning and evening. Suddenly they would be restricted all over again. The placement had seemed ideal; a long-term solution that would meet Jamie's needs and allow Anna her freedom. If it broke down it would put a completely new complexion on everything, including their plans for children. So, every cloud—

Jamie was packed and ready to go, but once they were home he wasn't impressed, especially as Anna wasn't there. Anna had moved into her house a couple of years ago, effectively uprooting Jamie from the family home and, although it wasn't completely new, he was less used to coming here. 'Ann-ann,' he kept saying. His way of asking where his sister was. For most of the evening Jamie paced around from room to room, refusing to settle. His edginess rubbed off on Mariner. It didn't help that the place was chilly, having been uninhabited for three days and they seemed to be in perpetual motion, hovering around one another.

Mariner briefly thought about calling Anna, but it would

serve no purpose other than worrying her, and she was due back tomorrow anyway. No point in having her distracted for the entire journey back. Instead he cooked pizza, the only thing he was certain that Jamie would eat, and they sat up watching videos of Jamie's favourite TV quiz shows, until he was falling asleep and Mariner could take him up to bed, prompting him through the routine. He'd never been entirely comfortable with dressing and undressing a grown man, and tonight it seemed to take for ever. Anna had developed numerous strategies for getting Jamie to do things. Mariner was trying to persuade him into his pyjama top when Jamie, in irritation, swatted away his hand, catching his injured palm. 'Oh fuck, Jamie! That hurt!'

'Fuck Jamie,' Jamie repeated cheerfully and Mariner hoped that Anna would be back before her brother's limited vocabulary had been totally corrupted. Despite the late night Jamie woke up well before dawn and it was still dark when Mariner drove him over to the day centre. They were the first to arrive.

Mariner got back to the house to find a message from Anna to say that she was setting off soon and would be back by lunchtime. What to do until then? He booted up Anna's computer. There were just a few news pieces about the Special Incident Squad, mostly about the arrests that had been made, along with a final piece on the disbandment of the unit in 1995. The implication was that it had been shut down as a matter of policy more than anything else, along with others like the West Midlands Serious Crimes whose reputation had spread and tarnished other similar outfits. Neither Hollis nor Jaeger was named in the article and there was no indication of what any of the squad officers had been up to since.

Mariner had just begun another search, when he heard Anna's car pull into the drive and was surprised to feel a stab of irritation that she was back so soon, forcing him to curb his activity. He went down to meet her and they hugged on the cold drive as soon as she was out of the car.

'Missed me?' she asked.

'Of course I have.' Did it only sound insincere to him? But it was she who pulled away first. 'What have you done to your hand?'

'The back door at the cottage is sticking. I forced it and caught it on a nail.' It came out so glibly that she accepted it without question. He was getting a bit too good at this. They unloaded her things, which seemed to be considerably less than she'd taken with her.

'It's freezing in here,' she said, coming into the hallway. 'Haven't you had the heating on?'

'I haven't been here much.' He didn't add that he'd been down to London, but then she didn't seem much interested.

'Get the kettle on,' she said, disappearing upstairs. 'I've got something to show you.'

Climbing the stairs he found her where he'd been, at the computer in the little office plugging in her digital camera. She downloaded dozens of photographs of Megan playing, Megan smiling, Megan crying, Megan with Mark, Becky, Mark and Becky and very often with Anna.

'Look at her. Isn't she gorgeous?' she enthused as the pictures flashed onto the screen.

'She's very pretty,' Mariner conceded, though he was only saying what was obvious from the huge dark eyes and soft black hair beginning to curl at the ends. In truth she looked like almost every other baby he'd ever seen.

'She's fantastic. You've no idea what it feels like just to hold her and cuddle her. When we're out and about Becky says, "She's my daughter" and I can't wait to be able to say that. "That's my daughter" – or son of course. My son. Tom and Anna's son. Don't you love the sound of those words?'

To Mariner they were just words, so he made a non-committal 'Mm.' and tried to imagine it. He really tried.

The pictures that were far more interesting to him were the next ones of rolling green hills and woodland. 'And this is where they live,' Anna announced proudly as if it was her own private estate. 'It's the view from their garden. No pollution or traffic noise or nasty explosions there.'

No, Mariner wanted to say, just an hour's drive to get anywhere, nosy neighbours and forced sociability with people you may not even like. 'Very nice,' he said.

The slideshow ended, Anna decided to have a bath 'to warm up'. 'You can come and join me,' she said, mischievously.

'It's the middle of the afternoon.'

'Call it a special project. We need to get in some practice.'

'Aren't we going to wait and see what the specialist says?'

'It's not going to stop us, is it? All we need to know is what we can realistically do to minimise the risks.'

They ended up in bed, as he'd known they would, but suddenly Mariner found that despite Anna's encouragement his body wouldn't co-operate. This had happened before but never with Anna. The last time was after Greta got pregnant, interpreted by his GP as his body telling him he didn't want babies. He'd have liked to think that this time it was a one-off, because he was tired and distracted, but he couldn't quash a creeping fear that it was starting all over again and for the same reasons.

For Anna it was grist to the mill. 'It's stress,' she said. 'Moving to the country would make such a difference and if we put both our houses on the market we could easily afford it. The house prices out there are amazing. It would be a much better place to raise a child and you could walk to your heart's content. It would help you to relax.'

'I *am* relaxed!' Mariner snapped, making them both crack a smile at the irony of that response.

'Jamie would love it out there, too.'

'Shit! Jamie.' Mariner reached over to his watch and scrambled out of bed. 'We need to go and pick him up.'

'What? Why?'

'There's been a problem at the hostel. I'll tell you on the way over.'

Predictably, Anna was livid. 'It's ludicrous. I bet he hasn't really done anything. It's just political. This would never have happened if Simon was still here.'

'Of course it wouldn't.' Good old Simon.

'I don't believe it. You're still smarting about him?'

For a short time Mariner had been convinced that Anna had fancied Simon, till he'd found out that the man was gay. 'Don't be ridiculous. Look, I'm sure once things calm down—'

But now Anna had found another crusade, and one that wasn't entirely incompatible with the others. 'If it does,' she said. 'And what about the next time? What if he does something else that can be misinterpreted by the locals? His behaviour is like that all the time. That's Jamie. We won't know where we are. We'll have to find him somewhere else.'

She'd reached that decision remarkably quickly. 'Oh that'll be easy,' said Mariner. 'You've been through all this before, remember? There is nowhere else, not in this area. Unless you're talking about Greencote. Do you think they'd have Jamie back?'

'And have him back home permanently again?' Jamie's old day centre was at least close to where they lived, but without the residential facility. 'It would be a retrograde step for all of us.'

What she said was true, and it wasn't good news, but for some strange reason Mariner got the impression that underneath it all she was pleased that this had kicked off. He just didn't understand why. Okay, she'd never really been happy about the idea of the community hostel, but he couldn't see how the breakdown of the placement was going to do any of them any favours.

On the way over to collect Jamie up from the day centre they called at the hostel to pick up a few more of his things, mainly because Anna wanted an opportunity to give Louise a piece of her mind. 'He's being victimised,' she said. But hearing the full story she could see, too, that it wasn't

Louise's fault and that really for the sake of the other residents there was no alternative.

Jamie was at least pleased to see Anna, but the sudden change in routine was disturbing for him and all at once the house seemed too small for the three of them. Tired from the day's travelling and upset that Jamie was at home again, Anna had limited patience.

Mariner had half-planned to tell her about what had been happening to him, but now wasn't a good time. Instead, to give Anna and Jamie some space, he picked up the phone.

Tony Knox was sprawled in front of the TV nursing a can of beer, relaxing for the first time in ... well, he couldn't remember when. When the phone rang he feared the worst, but it was only Mariner. 'Fancy a drink?'

Knox hesitated. Selina wasn't due back from her mother's till about ten, so plenty of time, but he walked through to the hall and examined his face in the mirror. The bruising had about gone. In the dim light of the right pub it was probable that Mariner wouldn't notice it, and if he did? Knox would just have to fabricate something. It wasn't as if he hadn't had the practice just lately. 'All right,' he said. 'Just a quick one. But I've had a drink, so can you pick me up?'

'See you in ten,' Mariner said.

The boss was punctual as always. Knox thought he looked tired, but it hadn't been as easy few weeks for anyone. They went to the Holly Bush out on the Stourbridge Road, a locals' pub that did a roaring trade in food. Tonight the lounge was quiet enough to get seats, busy enough for them to pass unnoticed. Knox was glad. Mariner was telling him about the developments with Jamie. 'I think Anna's more annoyed because it spoils her plans for a family,' he was saying.

'So a week in the company of a four-month-old hasn't put her off?'

Mariner shook his head ruefully. 'She's keener than ever despite having Jamie back. She's talking about moving to the country now, too.'

'She must really want it then.'

'She had me at it this afternoon.' Mariner flashed a weak smile. 'Still I suppose it's like that all the time with you two young lovers.'

Knox almost laughed out loud, the boss was so far from the truth. 'Not just at the moment, no.'

Mariner realised his mistake, or thought he did. 'Shit, I'm sorry, of course, I wasn't thinking—'

'Don't worry about it,' said Knox. Part of him wanted to explain to the boss that he'd misunderstood the reaction, but that would have involved confessing the truth, and right now Knox couldn't summon the energy.

'How did you and Theresa make the decision to have kids?' Mariner asked.

Knox tried to stay calm. 'To be honest I can't really remember.' It seemed like eons ago, and he was fast realising that it was probably the happiest time of his life. If only he'd known. 'It was just something you did; grew up, got married, had kids. It didn't seem to be so much of a conscious decision then. You just got on with it.'

'And how did you feel when they were born?'

Knox felt a stab of pain for what was lost. 'Brilliant,' he said, his voice thick with emotion. 'There's nothing that prepares you for the strength of that feeling. I mean Liverpool winning the championship in 1978 was pretty fantastic, but even that didn't come close. I wasn't allowed in until it was all over, thank God. That was the way it was then. But it was incredible to think that we'd made such a perfect little human being. Amazing.' He tailed off. 'A lot's happened since then.'

'You're still on good terms with them.'

'Only just. And now comes the hard part; introducing them to Selina.'

'It's serious then.'

Oh, it was that all right, whether Knox liked it or not. 'They're part of my life,' he said, stating the bald facts. 'And Selina wants to meet them.' She'd been nagging him about it for weeks now. It would have happened sooner if it hadn't been for the bomb. Knox was just worried about what might happen when they did meet.

'She seems like a great girl. How's she doing?'

'She's getting better all the time. I'm going back to work next week.'

'You're ready for that?'

'I want to get back before the boss leaves.' It was what he'd told Selina. In truth he felt a desperate need to regain some control over his life.

'It'll be weird without the old man,' Mariner said.

'Rumour has it his replacement is going to be a woman.'

'That could be interesting.'

Knox checked his watch again. 'I could do with getting back. Selina's at her mum's but they'll be bringing her back soon.'

'Well, I mustn't keep you from the arms of your beloved,' grinned Mariner. 'She's lucky to have your support.'

'Yeah.' It wasn't the reason Knox needed to get back. The real reason was too embarrassing to admit.

When Mariner got home, Anna and Jamie were already in bed and asleep, and he was relieved to avoid any further discussion about kids, or moving. Knox was right though. It was time he got back to work, too. Coleman's retirement do was tomorrow night and after that he'd only be around for another couple of weeks. Maybe it was time to concentrate his attention on those closest to him. He still hadn't found out much about Hollis and Jaeger, but there were avenues he could explore professionally in his own time.

Chapter Twelve

Next morning Anna took Jamie to the day centre on the understanding that Mariner would do the pick-up that evening. It meant that he got in to Granville Lane nice and early to find that things were moving on Lucca, the Albanian. 'Police over there have picked him up for questioning,' Charlie Glover told him.

'What's he saying?'

'They've shown him Madeleine's photograph, but so far he's denying all knowledge.'

'What about the fingerprints?'

'He says there were bin bags in the communal kitchen. He may have touched them, but so could anyone else living in the house.'

'It's not true with the tape though, is it? Only the person who bound Madeleine would have touched the inside strips.'

'We've got enough material evidence to bring him back, so they're holding him until the extradition is agreed.'

'Where are we on the paperwork?'

'I've got everything together. I was hoping we could go through it before I send it off to the CPS. Talk about pedantic. They virtually want everything in triplicate.'

'We'll be grateful in the long run. It'll ensure that we don't hand the defence a legal loophole on a plate.' With some reluctance Mariner put his own investigating on hold.

'Let's get on with it, shall we?'

They were deep in discussion when Ella from reception called through to Mariner.

'It's Mrs Evans to speak to you.'

'Mrs Evans?'

'She says she's Chloe Evans' mother?' Ella ventured, to help him out.

Mariner sighed heavily, guilty unease stirring in his gut. Glover was gesturing to him, something about taking a break. He ignored it. 'Could you tell her I'll call back, I'm in the middle of something right now.'

'You sure, boss?' Glover said when he'd replaced the phone.

'This is important. We don't want to lose Lucca.'

By late afternoon Mariner was satisfied that they'd put together a strong case and they took it to Coleman for countersigning.

'It's good work,' the gaffer said, looking it over.

'So now we sit back and wait?' said Glover.

'We'll see how it goes. If it seems to be taking too long at the other end we can send someone down to lean on them a bit.'

Glover was doubtful. 'In theory that's a great idea, but I'm all banked up with the stuff that happened over Christmas. It's finding the time.'

'I'll see what I can do,' said Mariner, with half a mind on his own investigation again. A couple more days in London might come in handy. 'If that's all right with you, sir.'

'Whatever gets the job done,' said Coleman.

The day almost over Mariner at last found time for some work of his own. Logging on to the system he did searches on Terry Brady and Marvin Jackson, before trying Hollis and Jaeger. But, limited to the West Midlands database, he came up with nothing. He really needed to get into the system at Harlesden, but to do that he'd also need a bloody good reason. And that he didn't have, at least, not one that he could give without arousing suspicion. He might have to invent something.

Anna had found it impossible to get anyone to look after Jamie that evening, so Mariner went to Jack Coleman's retirement bash alone. In some ways he was relieved. Any time he and Anna spent alone together would inevitably lead to discussion about kids and he couldn't face that tonight. He couldn't find his invitation but that wouldn't matter. It was being held at Tally Ho, the police training centre, across the road from the county cricket ground. Squeezing the Volvo into a space in the already full car park, by the look of it he was one of the last to arrive.

Walking in, Mariner couldn't help noticing that he was one of the youngest, too, in a room scattered with men in late middle age. Their neutral lounge suits disguised which side of the law they were on, and could have so easily have identified them as old lags instead of policemen. Hard to tell the difference sometimes. The crowd from Granville Lane had taken up occupancy of one corner of the room, but Mariner didn't feel much like joining them. Instead he got himself a pint and waited until Jack Coleman, looking less relaxed than normal, was on his own. 'Having fun sir?'

Coleman shot him a look. 'Don't look so smug. You'll have to do this one day.'

'Not if I can help it. I'll sneak out the back door before anyone notices.'

'You'll be lucky. Thanks for coming, I appreciate it.'

'Wouldn't have missed it for the world. Who are all these people anyway?

'Ghosts from the past. They've even wheeled out some of the blokes I trained with. I haven't seen most of them for years.'

'That was back in the days when they used boiling oil instead of tear gas wasn't it?' said Mariner. 'So what will you do when all this is over?'

164

'Oh, Glenys has got it all mapped out. My feet won't touch the ground. First thing is a whistle-stop tour of the grandchildren; Stafford, Preston, Edinburgh.'

'I didn't know you had family in Edinburgh.'

'We honeymooned there. I was trying to get her to hold off until the festival in the summer, but I think she's terrified that I'll get so bored in the first three weeks I'll take up golf or something.'

The Assistant Chief Commissioner cleared his throat into a screeching microphone. Speech time. Mariner shook Coleman's hand. 'Best of luck with it, sir.'

'Thanks. And don't look on this as a chance to desert me. I'll be relying on you to keep me in touch with the real world.'

If I'm still around, thought Mariner. He stayed at the bar and had another drink, beginning to feel melancholy. He was going to miss Jack Coleman. They'd never been what you'd call close, but Coleman was probably the nearest thing to a father figure that Mariner had ever had. After the speeches Mariner found himself next to a group of south-east accents. 'Where are you from?' he asked out of politeness.

'Harlesden.'

At first Mariner thought he'd misheard, his head still running on recent conversations, but he hadn't. 'Really? Home of the Special Incident Squad.' Four pairs of eyes turned on him, curiosity and suspicion shared equally between them. 'I heard it was a very effective unit.'

'It was.' The man who answered stood nearest to him, tall and lean with small, dark eyes in a narrow face.

'Record numbers of convictions,' Mariner continued. He glanced into his drink. 'Still, doesn't look quite so good if you take out the ones that have since been overturned, does it?'

'What are you trying to say?'

'You must know George Hollis,' Mariner scanned the room. 'Is he here?' That would be just too good to be true.

The man looked at him strangely. 'You trying to be funny? Do you know George?'

'Only by reputation.'

'He was a good officer.' The response seemed a touch defensive.

'Was?' Mariner's ears pricked up.

'He retired six months ago.'

'He went early?' Mariner was guessing here.

'Ill health.'

'Really? What happened to his partner, what was his name, Jaeger?'

'He moved on. How was it you said you knew them?'

'Oh, the names just came up in a case I was looking at. Joseph O'Connor. Perhaps you've heard of him.'

'Can't say that I have.' But steel barriers had come down behind the eyes, and Mariner was sure that he saw the other three move nearer, literally closing ranks.

'I was talking to a couple of people at the Judicial Review Commission who worked with Sir Geoffrey Ryland. To be honest they weren't very complimentary about Mr Hollis, but then, everyone has a different perspective, don't they?'

'Who are you?'

'Tom Mariner,' Mariner said, pleasantly. 'One of Jack's DI's at Granville Lane.' He stuck out a hand but no one took it and the temperature in this part of the room seemed to drop a couple of degrees.

'Ryland should have stuck to politics,' muttered one of the other men, short and square with no neck that Mariner could see. 'Fucking Judicial Review Commission has done more damage than good, everyone knows that. It's hard enough trying to get villains put away in the first place. Now every petty criminal who wants to get off the hook blames it on the arresting officers.'

'Is that how George Hollis felt?'

'A lot of us do.'

'Convenient that Ryland got shot then, wasn't it?'

'I don't know what you're trying to say but—'

'All I'm saying is that Ryland was good at exposing

166

coppers who bent the rules, and one of those he had in his sights was George Hollis. Not long after Hollis "retires", your euphemism, not mine, both Ryland and O'Connor get shot in what was apparently a revenge killing. As our American cousins are fond of saying: you do the math.'

'Do you have any idea who you're talking to, son?'

Mariner felt a movement beside him. Jack Coleman was at his elbow. 'Could I have a word, Tom?' He steered Mariner away from the group. 'What the hell do you think you're doing?'

'Just having an open and honest discussion with a couple of your former colleagues.' Mariner realised he was having difficulty getting his tongue around the words.

'And bringing your own career to an end as well as mine? Go home, Tom. I appreciate you coming. I know it's not the best time for you, but you've had your say. Now go home.'

Mariner stopped off at the gents before he left and found himself alongside another man at the urinals. 'You want the truth, Sir Geoffrey Ryland did us all a favour,' the man said, quietly. 'Hollis's time had gone. He was a dinosaur. Most of the squad were glad to be rid of him.'

Mariner didn't like to turn to look. It wasn't something you did. 'I'm having trouble finding out much about Hollis's relationship with Terry Brady, especially their involvement in Joseph O'Connor's arrest,' he said.

'Hollis and Brady had a special relationship.'

'Oh?'

'I've no evidence, but rumour was that in return for being cut into deals Hollis used to let Brady know when and where raids were going to happen.'

Friends on the inside. 'So how—?'

'That's all I can tell you.' And without glancing in Mariner's direction, the man zipped his fly and walked out, the door banging heavily behind him. Now Mariner didn't know what to believe. But it might help to explain why Jackson was released without charge.

Tempted to try and track down the stranger and press him for more, Mariner chose instead to take Coleman's advice and make his way home. Walking down the ramp to the car park he passed a couple of the Harlesden officers standing outside smoking. He was about to get into his car when he thought better of it. He'd had too much to drink, and the Harlesden men were watching him. Wouldn't they just love it if he drove off in his condition? It was still relatively early, the evening just getting going for the Birmingham club scene, so instead he walked back along the service road, their eyes boring into his back, and when he got to the main road he jumped on a number 47 bus.

The Boatman was almost deserted when he got there; another dinosaur taking its last breath. A couple more pints ensured that by the time Mariner left there he was pretty well oiled but managed to stagger back to his house, which was still empty and no car outside. This arrangement with Bill Dyson was going to be perfect.

But Mariner must have slept pretty deeply because when he rose late the following morning, feeling better than he had a right to, Bill Dyson was in the kitchen making toast. He turned a broad smile on Mariner. 'Morning!'

Christ, he was one of those people who was happy first thing.

Dyson was already dressed for the office, suit and tie. 'I hope I didn't disturb you last night. I was back pretty late. Entertaining clients.'

'Not at all. It would have taken a lot to wake me. I'd had a bit of liquid anaesthesia to help me on my way.'

'Dyson grinned. 'Sounds like more fun than I had.'

Was it? Mariner recalled the way the Harlesden men had watched him go.

'You had a phone call,' Dyson was saying, 'about twenty minutes ago, a guy called Baxter? I jotted the number on the pad, just in case.'

'Thanks,' said Mariner, thinking that he hadn't bargained on a social secretary as well as a lodger, but then he realised he was being oversensitive. He went into the lounge and closed the door before calling Baxter back.

'Jayce said you wanted some information about George Hollis.'

'We need to talk. Can you meet me somewhere?'

'I'm out and about today. You're in Brum, right?'

While Baxter was speaking there was a light knock on the door and Dyson leaned in to give Mariner a parting wave.

Mariner halted him with a signal. 'One minute, Mike, please—'

'Sure.'

Covering the handset Mariner asked Dyson: 'Which way are you going?'

'North – spaghetti junction,' Dyson said.

'Any chance of a lift?'

'Sure.'

'I'll just be a minute.'

'No problem.'

Mariner lifted his hand. 'Still there, Mike?'

'Yeah. How about the M40 services at Junction 8, say half eleven?'

'Sounds fine. I'll see you there.'

'Look out for an old Discovery, dark green, personalised plates: JMB.'

'I appreciate this,' Mariner said, climbing into Dyson's car minutes later. 'I'd had one too many so left the car behind last night. It's at Tally Ho just off the Pershore Road.'

'Wise move. Was it some kind of celebration?'

'Of sorts. My DCI's retiring. It was a celebration for him but I'll be sorry to see him go. He's been a pretty solid anchor for me over the years.'

'Oh aye. We could all use one of those.'

'So how are things going for you?' It was the rush hour and the traffic was slow, so it seemed reasonable to make some kind of light conversation.

'Pretty well so far,' Dyson said. 'I already had one or two clients in the area, and I'm finding my way round better. Any news on that job?'

'I haven't had the chance to discuss it yet, but I'll be seeing her again soon. It's down in Oxfordshire, a couple of hours from here. That still your patch?'

Dyson grinned. 'I'm not fussy, I'll go anywhere.'

'She lives out in the sticks and has people going in during the week but she's on her own all weekend.'

'Sounds right up my street. We could put in a link to the nearest police station.'

'That's what I was thinking of.'

'If you want to let me have her address I could go and talk to her.'

'I might need to soften her up first.'

Dyson laughed. 'I get the picture. Well, just give me the nod when you're ready.'

'I will.'

'By the way, not that there's any hurry, but I think there's a problem with one of the taps in the en-suite bathroom. I can't turn it off fully and it seems a shame to waste the water.'

'I'll have a look at it sometime.'

'Sure. Like I said no rush though.'

Dyson signalled and turned off the main road and into the training centre without prompting from Mariner and took him all the way to the empty car park where the lone vehicle stood. A man in navy overalls was gathering litter from around it, the detritus from the previous night.

'Must've been a good night,' remarked Dyson.

'Well, thanks again for the lift,' Mariner said. 'We should go for that pint sometime.'

'That'd be good, though I may not be around for the next few days. I've some work around Carlisle.'

'Hope it pays off.'

'Cheers.'

*

170

As Mariner approached his car the road sweeper was passing it too. 'Looks like you've got a problem there, mate,' he said. He pointed to a wet patch on the ground behind the wheel arch on the driver's side. Probably an oil leak. Mariner dipped in a finger and sniffed. It wasn't oil, it was brake fluid and the puddle was about eight inches in diameter. He'd lost a lot. This would strengthen Anna's view that it might be time to change the nine-year-old Volvo. She'd been saying for ages that it was on borrowed time. Mariner thought back to the conversation with the men from Harlesden. Two of them had been loitering in the car park when he came out to collect his car and had watched him unlock it before changing his mind. He dismissed such scepticism. They were coppers for God's sake. As Dave Flynn would say, he was getting carried away.

That Mariner was on first name terms with the mechanic from his local garage was an indication of the state of his car.

'I can be there in about thirty-five minutes,' Carl said.

It was freezing outside and Mariner was still missing his overcoat, so tucking a note under the windscreen wiper he went and tried the door of the social club. It was open. He went in as a woman with her mop and bucket emerged from the gents.

'My car's broken down. Any chance that I can wait in here, where it's warmer?'

'Suit yourself love.'

In daylight the bar presented a forlorn contrast to the night before, cool and drab, the air stinking of stale beer and smoke. Mariner took a seat by the window where bright sunshine streamed in and he had a full view of the car park. It was a beautiful morning, the sun casting long shadows on the frosted sports field, completely still and lacking activity.

Not relaxed enough to remain inert, Mariner hunted through his pockets for something to occupy him and came

171

across the list of rejected JRC referrals Trudy had given him. Each record on the database was sparse, with few details; just the name, date of referral, the advocate's name and the due release date. But that was all Mariner had asked for. He began idly scanning the names of the appellants that Ryland personally had turned down and crossing out the others. There were dozens of them so he narrowed it down by deleting all except those whose convictions had been for drugs and/or gun related crimes. It was an arbitrary process and didn't necessarily exclude the others, but he had to do something to reduce the dozens of names to a manageable task.

Next he looked at the release dates to see who would have been out in the last year or so, and finally the numbers began to look workable. A glance outside confirmed the car park as deserted, so on the back of an old invoice folded in his wallet he began logging the details of the remaining cases, half convinced that this was a waste of time. He made a note of each person, the case reference number and the name of the advocate who had made the application.

A name leapt off the page; Rupert Foster-Young. It looked familiar. Then Mariner recalled Carrie Foster-Young, the glamorous blonde photographed on Ryland's arm during his student protest days. It wasn't exactly a common name so had to be more than just a coincidence. Foster-Young had applied for leave to appeal four years ago, his offence, aggravated burglary that carried a sentence of eight years. Ryland had turned it down.

Did Carrie have a brother, or even a husband? Despite their relationship Ryland had gone on to marry another woman soon after it ended. Was it because Carrie Foster-Young was already married, or had been married before? Maggie had said nothing, only that the switch from one woman to the other had been sudden. So the likelihood was that it was a brother. The other alternative gave Mariner palpitations, but there was one vital piece of information missing from the datasheet. His mobile battery was low but he risked the call anyway.

'Could I speak to Trudy?' She hadn't been at the Commission long, but Mariner was hoping against the odds that Foster-Young's might be one of the files that had been retained.

'I'm sorry, she's on annual leave today. Can anyone else help?'

Shit. Taking a chance Mariner asked to be put through to Helena James. This time luck was running for him. She remembered the case. 'We all do,' she said. 'He was a persistent character. And it was unusual from the start because he himself kept phoning up from prison in person instead of leaving it to his brief. But then he was relatively articulate. He was on a burglary conviction that looked sound, but he kept insisting that Sir Geoffrey would want to help.'

'Did he give a reason?'

'He claimed that Sir Geoffrey was a personal friend of his mother.'

Mariner's heart thudded. 'His mother? You're sure about that?'

'Yes.'

'And did you refer him to Sir Geoffrey?'

'I had to in the end because the chap was making such a fuss.'

'And what happened?'

'Sir Geoffrey threw the case out, as I knew he would. He said there was nothing to suggest that the conviction was unsafe, whoever he might be.'

'Did he acknowledge knowing Foster-Young?'

'He certainly had no interest in speaking to him. Sir Geoffrey said if he ever had known the man's mother it must have been a long time ago. I wasn't surprised. I know one shouldn't make judgements, but I couldn't imagine Sir Geoffrey associating with anyone like him.'

'Why is that?'

'There was an incident. Foster-Young came to the

173

Commission demanding to see Sir Geoffrey. As it happened Sir Geoffrey was out that afternoon so couldn't see him. But he was like a street person. He was a mess; pale, skinny, sunken eyes. It was the look of an addict. I remember the smell, too. It was quite a warm day and he was filthy dirty and smelled awful. I remember wondering how anyone related to this man could possibly be a friend of Sir Geoffrey.'

'When was this?' Mariner asked.

'Oh, I don't know. About a year ago last spring I suppose.'

'But if he'd already been released what did he want?'

'Justice I suppose. He was angry.'

'How old would you say he was?'

'It was hard to tell. Quite old. About forty or fifty I'd say.'

Thanks, thought Mariner, himself moving from mid to late forties. But her estimate may not be entirely accurate. If Foster-Young was a junkie it wouldn't do much to enhance his youthful appearance. Mariner had seen twenty-year-olds who looked as if they were pushing retirement age.

'How did Foster-Young react when you told him Sir Geoffrey wasn't there?'

'He was verbally abusive, so nothing we're not used to. But he didn't give up. For some time after that he used to phone every couple of weeks asking to speak to Sir Geoffrey. Then suddenly, nothing.'

'He never came back again?'

'No.'

'So Sir Geoffrey never spoke to him?'

'Not to my knowledge, though of course I can't be certain. In the end we just had him down as a harmless head case.'

'Do you still have his details? Is there any chance you could get me his date of birth?'

She hesitated. 'I'm not really sure if I should—'

174

'Helena, were you aware of Sir Geoffrey's betting habit?'

A beat of silence. 'I knew that something was going on.'

'I'm not convinced that it had much to do with horse racing.'

'You think it could relate to this man?'

She was filling in the blanks herself. He wouldn't stop her. 'I've come across the name before. This is important, Helena, otherwise I wouldn't be asking.'

'I'd have to go and look out the file, but I might have time to fax it through later today.'

Mariner didn't want the information coming through to Granville Lane while he wasn't there, so he gave her Anna's fax number.

Ending the call, Mariner saw the flashing bar of Carl's breakdown truck coming along the driveway. He picked up the database and went out to meet the mechanic. It only took a couple of minutes to confirm the problem; a split brake cable. 'But I can't fix it here,' Carl said. 'I'll have to have it in the garage.'

Mariner climbed up into the cab to wait while Carl hooked his car to the towbar. Jumping in beside him minutes later the mechanic passed him something. 'You may want to hang on to this.'

Mariner took from him a black plastic box the size of a personal stereo. It had a heavy duty magnetic strip down one side and looked vaguely like something Mariner had seen before. 'What is it?'

'It's a CPS tracking device.'

'A tracking device?'

'Yeah, people stick them on in case of theft, so that—'

'Yes, I know what it's for.' They used them all the time in the job. He'd seen the techies fitting them. 'I'm just wondering what it's doing on my car.'

'You didn't put it there?' Carl grinned. 'Maybe your missus is keeping tabs on you.'

Preoccupied, Mariner barely cracked a smile. 'Could it

have been the previous owner?' he asked.

'Nah. Too new for that,' said Carl. He started up the truck and they moved off. Mariner pocketed the device, wondering again about the Harlesden officers who'd watched him go and not liking the implications a bit. Carl dropped Mariner off at Granville Lane where he booked out a pool car. Strictly speaking it should only have been used for official business, but the delay already meant that he was pushing it to get to the motorway services as planned, so there wasn't time to wrestle that particular dilemma. Besides he was on police business, Mariner told himself, just not a case that was assigned to him. Fortunately the motorway was quiet, but he drove south into low cloud, the first sleety rain starting to fall as he pulled into the services ahead of his appointment. A quick scan around the car park told him that Baxter hadn't yet arrived.

Chapter Thirteen

Through a sheet of icy rain Mariner watched the green Discovery pull in and park. He allowed Baxter a couple of minutes, then, turning up his collar against the downpour, went and knocked on the passenger window. The door clunked open. Mariner's first impression was that Baxter didn't much look as if he'd been in an accident. Short and bulky, his grey hair cut close to his skull, he filled up most of the driver's side of the car.

'Thanks for agreeing to meet me,' said Mariner, ducking in out of the sleet and slamming the door. 'I didn't expect it to be so soon. Jayce seemed to think you were going to be off for a while.'

Baxter chuckled. 'Wishful thinking on his part. Leave him on his own for too long and chances are I wouldn't have a business to go back to. Also I checked you out with Helena James. She seemed to think it was reasonable that I speak to you.'

Funny, Helena hadn't mentioned that. 'Did Jayce tell you what I wanted to know?'

'George Hollis and Steve Jaeger, right? A charming pair.'

'What more can you tell me about them?'

'Plenty. Hollis has quite a pedigree. You know that he worked out of Harlesden nick during the early eighties,'

'Special Incident Squad, Jayce told me.'

'You know the score on those units. They were completely results driven,' Baxter went on. 'Always a dangerous objective, in my book. Minor considerations like truth and justice tend to get sidelined. Hollis was young and hungry when he joined the squad and presumably impressionable. He would have learned a lot from the more experienced officers on the squad and not all of it good. We know that a number of dubious practices were rife among those élite squads at the time.'

Mariner had grown up with the folklore; unrecorded evidence taken in cars en route to the police station, the 'correction' and fabrication of information recorded in pocket books, the use of intimidation and physical violence during interviews. The bad old days. 'I understand Ryland had linked Hollis to a number of miscarriages, including Joseph O'Connor's,' he said.

'That was classic Hollis, and the first hint we had that there was more going on. O'Connor's was one of the first cases that the JRC handled. His brief was referring the case on the grounds that his client's statement had been coerced. When Geoff looked at the transcripts, this was borne out. He'd talked to Joseph O'Connor and could see that there were words and phrases that he just wouldn't have used. He wasn't the sharpest knife in the drawer.'

'So how did you get involved?'

'Geoff and me go way back when to he was a prosecutor, and bloody good he was too. We'd been involved in a couple of corruption cases before and he knew my views. In the end it's what compelled me to leave. I'd just set up in business, mainly working with the complaints authority to support the drive against police corruption. As part of the investigation into Hollis, Geoff got us to trawl back through transcripts of other cases that he'd had been involved in, some of them going back years.

'Geoff had a nose for a bent copper and he could tell that O'Connor wasn't just a one-off. Naturally, as part of the enquiry we looked deeper into the circumstances surrounding O'Connor's arrest, and that was when we learned that Marvin Jackson had been arrested along with O'Connor but released without so much as an interview. It didn't make any sense, especially when he was the one with the history, so we started to explore the possible reasons for that. The one that leapt out and smacked us in the face was that at about that time Jackson was registered as an informant, with Steve Jaeger as his handler and supervising officer—'

'George Hollis.' Mariner was ahead of him.

'But given the length of time that Jackson was on the books there were surprisingly few results arising from information he'd supplied, in fact the luck seems to have all run the other way.'

'That was a hell of a risk for Hollis to take.'

'He'd been at Harlesden for a while by then and he was a powerful figure. We put him under surveillance and found that there seemed to be something more than a professional relationship between him and Terry Brady. It wasn't hard to figure out. Hollis was taking a cut of Brady's dirty money in return for keeping him out of trouble, giving him information on raids that were going down, that kind of thing. Hollis got complacent, took to holidaying on the Costa del Sol in one particular villa, owned by Terry Brady. He even had the barefaced cheek to meet him out there a couple of times.'

'That's when you took those photographs.'

Baxter smiled. 'This job isn't all about sneaking around in car parks in the pouring rain you know. There is some glamour.'

'It looks to me as if you had a strong case.'

'It took us a while to assemble the evidence and Geoff was thorough. You know what it's like. Corruption amongst police officers, like miscarriages of justice, is a big thing. You have to get it right. There was another complication too. The Home Office was breathing down our necks because they didn't want another corrupt police officer scandal.'

'So what happened?'

'To be honest I don't really know. We were all set to move on it the middle of last year. Hollis was coming up to retirement anyway. He was just over fifty at the time and was planning to go out in a blaze of glory. I think it was that more than anything that rankled with Geoff; that this guy was about to be held up as an exemplary officer when in truth he was anything but. But just as we were due to subpoena Hollis's bank details he slipped out of sight. He got to take early retirement due to so-called "ill health".' Baxter spat out the words with contempt. 'Bastard jumped before he was pushed.'

'Do you think someone tipped him off?'

'He got wind of it somehow. Hollis was popular. There would have been plenty of people watching his back.'

'So that was the end of it?'

'Geoff wanted to go ahead with an indictment anyway but the Home Office had been unhappy from the start and wanted it over. No point in stirring up more bad feeling against the police when they were just beginning to recover their reputation. As far as they were concerned the corruption had ended and Hollis's retirement put a stop to Brady's activities, or so they thought. Shortly after that it was rumoured that he'd moved permanently to Spain. When Hollis left there was a big shake up at Harlesden, a lot of dead wood was cleaned out and Jaeger moved on to pastures new.'

'And you were happy with that?'

'Not much choice. But it rankled with Geoff and I don't think he ever quite let it go. He'd have loved to have got at Hollis somehow.'

'Would he have exposed Hollis in his memoirs?'

'It's possible, though I'm not sure how happy the publishers would have been. If he told the full story, it'd leave a number of people with egg on their faces, including the Home Secretary.'

'You think the Home Office were so desperate to keep it

quiet that *they* tipped off Hollis.'

'It had to be a possibility.'

'Do you know what happened to Hollis?'

'He's decamped abroad himself from what I've heard.'

'And Jaeger?'

'Redemption. He went through internal disciplinary proceedings and appeared to learn from it. He was working as a DI in Cumbria when I last heard. What's all this about?'

Mariner felt slightly foolish now.

'I'm peripherally involved with the investigation into Geoffrey Ryland's death.'

'Well, Brady's fingerprints are all over it, metaphorically speaking. I hear he was back in the country at around that time, and Ryland was pretty well responsible for breaking up his operation. And Brady is that kind of guy. Doesn't like to be messed around.'

'So why is everyone hell bent on blaming Joseph O'Connor?'

'Because it keeps the good names of the police and the Home Office out of it. And if a bad guy is caught in the end, what does it matter?'

'I don't imagine O'Connor's widow would agree with you. And if it's that clear, why hasn't Brady been arrested?'

'I would guess that there's no material evidence yet to connect him to the scene. And with him being out of the country most of the time, it must be hard to even link him to any associates.'

'So that's that. Brady's just being allowed to get away with the murder of a well-known public figure. Doesn't that in itself strike you as being odd?'

'I thought you said you were working on this. Just because there's been no arrest yet doesn't mean anyone's getting away with anything. You should talk to your colleagues.'

Mariner thought of Dave Flynn. 'I have.'

'And?'

'They seem pretty complacent about it too.'

Baxter gave Mariner a curious look. 'Well, I don't begin to get what you're up to, but Geoff was a mate, so if there's anything else I can do to help—'

'Thanks.' Mariner opened the car door and stepped back out into the deluge.

So, despite what he knew, Baxter blamed the unholy triumvirate of Brady, Jackson, O'Connor, too. But it wasn't good enough for Mariner. He thought it far more likely that the trigger for the assassinations were the imminent publication of Ryland's memoirs, which would strip off the gag order placed on him by the Home Office and expose the extent of George Hollis's corruption. Brady may have been a patsy, he may even have been involved, but he sure as hell wasn't behind the shootings. Of the three main parties he was the one who had most to lose.

Leaving the motorway services Mariner realised that he wasn't far from the scene of the shootings so decided to take a detour along the road that ran through Cheslyn Woods. He left the motorway at the next junction, taking him close by the village where Eleanor lived. The road cut through deep deciduous forest on either side, and the only way of determining exactly where the shootings had taken place were a few tattered scraps of crime-scene tape hanging bedraggled from the trees. Mariner parked up, probably at the very same spot the assassins had.

The choice of location was an obvious one, a gravel car park that would yield no clear forensic evidence in the way of tyre tracks or footprints. Even if the car was noticed, which was doubtful under cover of the trees, it wouldn't arouse suspicion and during the night at this time of year, the killers could be pretty much assured their privacy. Then it would just be a question of flagging down the limo, perhaps claiming to be lost, or broken down. Mariner visualised the scene; O'Connor pulling over to be confronted by men, masked perhaps, brandishing deadly weapons.

The gunmen would have needed to be ready for when the car was approaching, which might imply two vehicles, one following Ryland's car, the other lying in wait, though not if some kind of tracking device had been employed, like the one that had been fixed to his own vehicle. It was something else he must ask Flynn about.

From here it was quicker for Mariner to drive north across country and in doing so his attention was distracted by signs to Long Compton; childhood experience tugging at his consciousness. He hadn't visited the Rollright Stones for years and wondered if they were still there, or if he'd remember how to find them. In the end it was simple enough. The site was clearly signposted and as he drew nearer, the landscape took on a familiar shape. Mariner pulled off the road alongside the field. The rain had stopped and even though it was a cold, damp day a group of American tourists was visiting, luckily for him heading back to their minibus to leave the monument deserted. He put his modest admission fee into a collection box at the gate and walked along the winding footpath and into the stone circle, a poor man's miniature and shambolic Stonehenge.

His mother used to bring him here regularly as a child; seventy odd chunks of local limestone, weathered into moth-eaten honeycomb and forming a perfect circle about a hundred feet across. 'How many are there?' his mum used to ask, knowing that it would keep him occupied for hours. Each time he counted, no matter how many times, he'd arrive at a different number. As a child he'd been enthralled by the puzzle and on one memorable summer's day had made Rose sit and wait while he counted them twenty times, determined to come up with a definitive answer. The simple explanation of course was that some of the stones were broken and half buried in the grass, making it difficult to be consistent about which to include. Back then some of them were taller than he was. Now he towered over most.

At one end of the circle, apart from the rest, stood five stones called the Whispering Knights, so named because they all leaned in towards each other, as if plotting some kind of conspiracy. In their place Mariner saw the Harlesden officers, watching him cross the car park and leaning in murmuring to each other. Was it really that complex? If the shootings were a crime of vengeance then there were plenty who had motives.

Terry Brady might want retribution because his activities had been curtailed, but equally Hollis's forced retirement after a lifetime of service would provoke a deep resentment. Or both men could be in league, they'd been pretty tight for years. And was it revenge against Ryland, O'Connor or both? Or was that message just a complete decoy? So much easier to make Brady the public fall guy rather than allow the revelation of two bent coppers and the admission that they were allowed by the Home Office to get away with what they'd done.

For all Mariner knew, Brady could be in on it too, persuaded to return to the UK at around the same time, safe in the knowledge that there would be nothing else to link him to the killings. It was only the middle of the afternoon, but already darkness was beginning to fall and other shadows appeared, increasing the volume of rocks, until Mariner was finding it hard to distinguish between what was real and what was imagined.

Returning to his car he could just about pick out the King's Stone, separate and isolated, on the opposite side of the road, 5,000 years old and weirdly shaped thanks to the nineteenth-century drovers who chipped off pieces to keep as lucky charms and ward off evil spirits. Mariner couldn't escape the feeling that he'd been manipulated out of the loop, being fed only the information that people wanted him to have.

Mike Baxter had been pretty quick to call him back and hadn't questioned their meeting. What if Baxter was part of the whole plan to keep Mariner out in the cold? He and

Flynn, doing just enough to keep Mariner at arm's length from the truth. And then there was Rupert Foster-Young. How close had been the relationship between Ryland and his mother?

Mariner dug his hands deep in his pockets and looked around at the stones. Whatever it was, he wouldn't solve it here. His head buzzing, Mariner drove straight back to the cottage, cold and deserted. Where had Dyson said he was? Carlisle; that was it, and probably snowed in too, if the weather reports were to be believed. It suited Mariner well, and he retrieved the pack of photographs from where he'd stashed them and tipped them out onto the table. Sorting through them he picked out the one he hadn't initially recognised.

Studying it more carefully Mariner could see now that the picture wasn't of him. It was different from the others. Comparing it with the photographs in Rose's collection he saw now that the baby was fuller in the face and with more hair than Mariner had when he was born. It was also the only one without annotation on the back.

No way of telling, of course, if the child in this photograph was also Ryland's offspring, but no other family babies had been mentioned and here was this picture, among the photographs of him, Ryland's other bastard son. If nothing else it was the most logical explanation. The press cutting in the library had shown Ryland in 1963, arm in arm with fiancée Carrie Foster-Young. After that, according to Maggie, it was 'a bit of a shock' when he had suddenly become engaged to Diana Fitzgibbon later that same year, dropping Carrie like a hot brick. Why would Ryland have done that? Was it for the same reason he split with Rose? Then, thirty-five years later, hey presto, a man turns up in prison claiming Ryland as his mother's 'friend', meaning that Rupert Foster-Young was either being deliberately euphemistic, or was genuinely ignorant of the extent of that friendship.

The whole scenario had a certain ring of familiarity to it;

history repeating itself in a pretty short space of time. If Ryland could do the dirty once, on Rose, then he was certainly capable of doing it again, with Carrie-Foster Young. Looking at the snapshot, Mariner suddenly realised that after years of being an only child he had to consider the possibility that he had a half-sibling, and one who had been on the wrong side of the law.

The condition of the photograph itself was different, more handled and worn than the others, but then, it was the only one of its kind so apparently the only one Ryland had. That was interesting in itself, just the one picture and not a whole collection, as there was for him, but back then not everyone owned a camera. Or maybe Carrie Foster-Young hadn't remained on such good terms with the father of her child. And if he did know about his origins, how would Rupert Foster-Young feel about it?

Mariner thought back to the night he'd met Flynn in the Prince of Wales, and his initial reaction. The overriding first emotion was anger. He'd felt angry and resentful towards Ryland, seeing him as an ambitious, irresponsible bastard who'd screwed Rose and then moved on, abandoning both of them. He'd felt angry for himself, but also angry for his mother who'd had to raise him alone.

Since then Mariner had been given good reason to reassess his feelings. For a start he'd been given the consistent message that it wasn't like that, and that actually the young Geoffrey Ryland was a good man caught up in a difficult situation. Okay, so Eleanor Ryland was hardly likely to condemn her son's actions, especially so soon after his death. But Maggie would have seen things more objectively, and there wasn't much room to argue about the content of Rose's letters. Apart from the blip during his teens when it could have all gone horribly wrong, things hadn't turned out badly either for him or for Rose. But how differently he would have felt had his mother been crushed by the abandonment, and he'd spiralled into Rupert Foster-Young's condition.

On top of that Ryland was dead before even Mariner found out, so the anger he felt towards the man was futile. Had Ryland still been alive he certainly would have wanted questions answered, maybe even seeking some kind of redress for the perceived wrong that had been done to him. And what would he have done if he'd known that Ryland was in a position to offer help, but refused to even acknowledge him? Mariner hardly dared imagine how he might have felt about that. And he considered himself to be pretty restrained. Maggie had described Carrie Foster-Young as 'wild' and Foster-Young was a junkie. A drug addict with a hot temper would be unlikely to show the same degree of control, especially with an additional grudge against Ryland. He'd served time too, so would have made contacts and developed a number of different skills inside, and Mariner wasn't so much thinking origami or cake decoration. Working alone a junkie may not have the ability to plan or execute an operation like the one in Cheslyn Woods, but with the right support—

So the motive and means were there all right, but how about opportunity? According to the information Helena had given him Foster-Young wasn't due for release until next year, but he was out, which implied that he'd been released on licence. He'd have had to serve at least half of the seven year sentence which would have let him out in about April the year before last, about eighteen months ago. It would also make it about the time that Ryland had suddenly begun placing his so-called bets on horses.

Suddenly those payments took on a new significance. Foster-Young turning up on the scene as the abandoned child fallen on hard times would hardly do Ryland's reputation any good and Ryland would have been keen to keep him quiet, especially if his wife remained in blissful ignorance. Perhaps Foster-Young was threatening to go to the press and those monthly payments came down to nothing more than blackmail.

At that meeting in Pearl's Café Ryland could have been

planning to end the arrangement, refusing to pay up any more, or making an attempt to pay off Foster-Young completely. It might even explain why Ryland had the photographs with him at the time. But the scheme backfired and Foster-Young wouldn't be fobbed off. Perhaps he even upped the ante, demanding more money, or increasing his threats, enough to disturb Ryland into needing a stiff drink when he returned to the Commission. He wouldn't play ball, so the following week Foster-Young ambushed and killed him, or had him killed. Payback for the way he and his mother had been treated. Mariner had lost count of the number of cases he'd been involved with over the years where what had at first looked like a complex case boiled down to such simple yet powerful motives as resentment and greed.

Mariner shivered. In his eagerness he'd forgotten to put on the heating and he became aware of how cold he was. The prospect of Anna's cosy house was suddenly irresistible. On his way out, he remembered what Dyson had said about the tap in the upstairs ensuite. It might be as well to take a look now, in case it would involve to getting someone in. But reaching the top of the stairs he found the door to Dyson's rooms locked. Although there were keys knocking around it was the first time that Mariner known this to happen. The cottage itself was secure so it seemed a bit overcautious. But the guy was in security so he was bound to be bit neurotic, maybe this was an indirect hint about the burglar alarm. And on the positive side it gave Mariner a good excuse not to be messing about with icy water and he was glad not to have to do the job. He had other things on his mind.

Mariner badly wanted to talk it through with someone. It should be Anna. At some point she would have to know. But this was huge, more than just a five-minute chat, and with Jamie at home it would be impossible for her to give it the attention it needed. Things had hardly been easy between them of late either and he could do without the inquest into why he hadn't told her sooner

Selina was clearly surprised to see Mariner. She was learning to walk on her newly acquired crutches, and when he rang the doorbell was practising walking up and down the hall. Not easy with a four-month-old puppy joining in too. Her upper lip was beaded with perspiration from the effort, and this time her smile seemed forced.

'Come on in. I'd make you a cuppa but I'm just finding out how important hands are. And after all, that's what I keep the manservant for.'

Knox appeared, looking so shattered that Mariner wondered if that last remark had been entirely in jest. 'I'll do it, love,' he said. 'You go and sit down for a bit.'

Mariner followed Knox through to the kitchen. There was only one other occasion when he could remember seeing Tony Knox make a cup of tea before. 'She's doing well,' Mariner said.

'Not as well as she wants to. She gets frustrated.'

'It's early days.'

'I think it's just beginning to sink in though, that this is the way it is. I mean she's lucky with her job, she's pretty well office-based anyway, but she's still got to get there and back. She's going to have a specially adapted car.'

'You all right?' Mariner felt compelled to ask.

'Yeah. You went to Jack Coleman's do?'

'It was a good send-off,' Mariner said, dismissively.

The tea made they joined Selina where she was resting in the lounge. Mariner wanted to get Knox on his own. If he couldn't spill it to Anna yet he didn't want to talk in front of someone he hardly knew, how ever much he liked Selina.

'How's Anna?' she asked.

'Fine.'

'Tony said you've got Jamie back with you. How's that working out?'

'It has its moments, but Anna's taken it surprisingly well,' said Mariner, thinking again that she'd taken it in her

189

stride. 'Once she'd got over the initial disappointment she's all fired up to find him somewhere else. Not that it will be easy.' He turned to Knox. 'Anyway, I came to lead you astray,' Mariner said. 'Fancy a pint at the Boatman?'

Knox looked sheepish. 'I would but I'm cooking tonight.'

Mariner nearly choked on his last mouthful of tea.

'Just shut it, will you?' snapped Knox in anticipation of the response.

'No really, I'm impressed.'

'You're welcome to stay,' said Selina. 'It's *Porc à la moutarde.*'

Mariner cast a sidelong glance at Knox. 'Blimey. You'll be making all your own frocks soon.'

Selina giggled. 'You should see his baby blue chiffon number.'

Suddenly Mariner felt like an impostor in this comfortable domestic scene, and realised how ridiculous it would be to unburden himself here.

Knox saw him out. Standing in the hall, he seemed about to say something, but then Selina called from the lounge. 'Shut the door, love, will you? There's a draught.'

'See you back at the station then,' Mariner said, and heard the door close behind him.

Watching Mariner's blurred form disappearing down the path, Knox went wearily back into the lounge.

'I wish he wouldn't just pop up like that,' Selina said, straightaway. 'Can't you get him to phone first? We could have been doing anything.'

'We weren't though, were we?' said Knox, regretting his irritation immediately. 'We weren't doing anything.'

Her anger flared from nowhere, nought to sixty in two seconds. 'I didn't ask for this,' she screamed. 'I didn't want to be a cripple. If I hadn't gone with you to that stupid fucking church this never would have happened. It's all your fault!' And reaching for the nearest thing to hand she picked up one of the aluminium crutches and viciously swung it at him. This time Knox caught it before it struck, calmly taking it from her grasp and laying it against the sofa. He was straightening up when the mug struck him on the side of the head. 'I'll go and start the dinner.'

Escaping to the kitchen Knox went through the motions of filling the sink to peel the potatoes, his eyes burning and vision blurred, still smarting from the blow. What the hell had he got himself into? He could walk out right now of course, go after Mariner and tell him the truth; that he was being subjected to physical assault on a daily basis. But he'd be so ashamed, because when it came down to it Selina was right. It was his fault she was in this mess.

Exhausted, and feeling somehow let down by Knox, Mariner drove back to Anna's house, which is what he should have done in the first place. For a few minutes he sat in the car on the drive. Hers was a nice place, warm and welcoming, but it was funny how he still thought of it as her house. The truth was that right now he didn't really feel at home anywhere. Perhaps if he told Anna, if they could just get a few minutes to sit down quietly and talk. With renewed purpose, he jumped out of the car and strode up the drive.

Inside he found Jamie in the lounge with the TV turned up way too loud and Anna on her hands and knees in the kitchen, washing the floor, the only thing visible from this angle her bottom, clad in tight jeans.

'That's a sight for sore eyes,' he said, truthfully, his good intentions already thwarted.

'Just don't,' she turned, her face grim, 'unless you want to find yourself cleaning up the mess.'

'What is it?'

'Orange juice. It was in the wrong type of carton. They're not the cartons they have at the hostel.' It needed no further explanation. Jamie would have taken exception to the change and thrown it all over the room. 'We'll be sticking to the floor for weeks.'

'Anything I can do?'

Bit bloody late for that, her glare conveyed.

'You're having a hard time?' he asked.

'I've had better.' She sat back on her haunches. 'A case conference has been arranged for next week to decide what will happen to Jamie. The hostel neighbours have made it clear that they don't want him back living there and Louise is understandably ambivalent. Having him back might put the whole project under threat. I can understand her concern.'

'So what are we going to do?'

'We? That's interesting.' She sighed. 'How about you?'

He didn't know what she meant.

'Jack Coleman's do. Was it a good one?'

'It went well. A good turn-out.' He wouldn't tell her he left in disgrace.

She nodded towards a white NHS envelope on the table. 'We've got an appointment with the genetic counsellor, too.'

'What, already?'

'Christmas must be a quiet time for them. Don't look so surprised. You were the one who thought it was such a good idea, remember?' She turned to get on with the cleaning.

'I'll go and get changed.'

'Oh yeah, and you've had a fax,' she called after him.

Mariner went straight to the office where he saw the fax from Helena James. He sat down at the desk to read it. Rupert Foster-Young's date of birth was 9th October 1963, only months after Ryland broke off the engagement. At the time of his referral to the JRC Foster-Young was serving his time at Chapel Wood prison, where Joseph O'Connor had been a guest of Her Majesty, and at about the same time. If the lobbying started four years ago it would have been about the time when O'Connor's appeal was heard.

This added a further dimension, opening up the possibility

of new resentment when O'Connor succeeded, where Foster-Young had failed, in getting his case appealed. O'Connor subsequently going to work for Ryland presented a golden opportunity to get both of them at the same time, and Foster-Young would already feel antipathy towards Diana Ryland for usurping his mother's place. But would all of that be enough to drive a man to commit violent murder?

Mariner had handled enough cases over the years in which the stakes were lower, and as a long-term drug user, Foster-Young would be prone to paranoia, even schizophrenia. The *modus operandi* also made sense. The assassinations were too clean and neat for a disorganised mind, but while serving time Foster-Young would have mixed with the kinds of people who'd be skilled at the short, sharp hit and could stage it to look like a drugs-related shooting, though it would have hurt to waste those few crumbs of heroin. In the space of a few short hours Mariner had shifted from eliminating Foster-Young as a suspect, to realising that he was looking more like a contender.

A picture was attached to the fax, and the face that stared out at Mariner bore all the signs of substance abuse. Rupert Foster-Young was as Helena had described him: his pale, hollowed-out face was framed by longish, lank hair and half concealed by a straggling beard. All in all, he was in a bit of a state. Maggie had described Carrie Foster-Young as the antithesis of Diana Fitzgibbon, implying that Rupert Foster-Young had lacked stability in his early life. There but for the grace of God, thought Mariner.

The final sheet was a record of the calls Foster-Young had made to the Commission. They ended eighteen months ago, coinciding almost exactly with the start of those mystery payments. Rupert Foster-Young had found a more lucrative way of putting pressure on Sir Geoffrey Ryland.

'Who is he?' Anna had come into the room and was looking over Mariner's shoulder.

'The possible suspect in a murder enquiry.'

'Madeleine?'

'No.' Mariner hesitated. 'Something I'm only partly involved in.'

'He looks old.' She half smiled. 'And now you're going to say he's only twenty-five but he's had a hard life.'

'He's a junkie.'

'Ah.'

Mariner was thinking of the baby photo. 'How does a tiny innocent child get to end up like this?'

'All sorts of reasons. In your line of work, you know that more than anyone.' She put her hands on his shoulders and was gently massaging them. It felt good.

'It's such a huge fucking responsibility though isn't it, bringing a child into the world? So much can happen if you get it wrong as a parent.'

'You just have to do the best you can. Millions of people have kids, but they don't necessarily have them in ideal circumstances. Look at you and me. Neither of us had what you'd call a conventional upbringing but our parents must have done something right.'

'It was touch and go some of the time.'

'But you kept it together. And you come across plenty who have had it all, but still end up like this guy. For all you know he may have had a perfect childhood.' She was right. There were plenty of Rupert Foster-Youngs in the world and they hadn't all had a rough start. It was all too easy to blame it on the parents.

'But even if you do a half-decent job there's the outside world to contend with.'

Anna stopped massaging. 'Chloe Evans,' she said.

'And Yasmin Akhtar, and Ricky Skeet.' The two teenagers who'd been brutally murdered the summer before. 'Their parents are good people but they still ended up going through hell. Why does anyone put themselves through that?'

'Because the bonuses far outweigh the risks. If you spent some time with Becky, Mark and Megan you'd see that.'

She slid her hands inside his shirt and down over his chest, hugging him to her, and making his lower belly begin to tingle. 'I know you're anxious about all this but there's no need. Those other kids, they're the exceptions. Just because you see the worst side of life doesn't mean it's all like that, does it?'

'I just don't know if I'll measure up.'

Leaning over him she reached down further, running her hands over his crotch. 'Oh I think you measure up all right,' she murmured in his ear, swinging the chair round til they faced each other. She knelt down in front of him, her face level with his lap and slid her hands along his thighs, causing him to draw breath. The sound of intermittent applause from the TV floated up the stairs.

'Look there's something I need to tell you,' Mariner said, and that was when there was an ear-splitting crash from downstairs.

Sometimes they just never knew why Jamie did it. Could be something the TV presenter said, could be that the video jumped, but what ever it was, it had upset him enough to pick up the coffee table and throw it at the set. They'd forgotten it could happen. By the time they'd cleared up the mess and Jamie had been dispatched to his room the moment had passed. So Mariner still hadn't told her, but maybe that was for the best. It would be more complete when he'd solved the case.

Lying in bed much later, Mariner realised that he was merely speculating based on what little he knew. He had to find out what had happened to Carrie-Foster Young, and the one person who might be able to help would be Eleanor Ryland.

'Tom?' So Anna was awake too.

'Yes?'

'Is there something going on that I should know about?'

Christ, where do I start? 'Only the usual crap. Nothing for you to concern yourself with.'

'Are you sure?'

'Absolutely.' And he was so wrapped up in his own adventures that it never occurred to him that he should ask her the same question. He rolled over and began nuzzling her neck, pressing himself against her hip. At first she resisted with a sleepy moan, but nonetheless put her arms round him and drew him on top of her. And miraculously this time his body didn't let him down.

Perhaps Anna was right. A move to the country could be good for all of them and maybe he should start thinking about a family, too. Was there ever going to be a right time for that? Whatever their differences might be, he didn't want to lose her.

After making love, Mariner's breathing settled into a rhythmic pattern, but Anna couldn't sleep. Propped on an elbow she studied the contours of his face in the half-light. She could only really see his profile, the detail of his features were masked by the shadows, much the same as he was. Many of his thoughts and ambitions she knew intimately, but there were always parts of his being that remained unreachable and indistinct. She'd thought it was a matter of time, and that eventually those elements would emerge, but lately she felt more than ever that there was so little she understood about him and what he wanted from life.

Once on a family holiday, Dad had taken Eddie and her fishing. After hours of boring inactivity, Anna had finally got a bite and the contest to reel in the fish began. At first the creature came easily, openly, before suddenly jerking back and shrinking away into the murky obscurity of the water, pulling part of the line with it, and each time she had to start again, until finally the fish was near enough for her to land it in the net. She'd never come close to landing Tom. It had been worse since St Martin's, of course it had, but she didn't kid herself that it was anything new. It was something she'd always found attractive; that sense of something deeper and darker lurking beneath the surface. But whatever had happened in the church had affected him.

He'd become increasingly remote over the last few weeks, disappearing for days at a time. It wasn't wilful, this cutting her out of his life, it was simply how he was. Immersing himself in work was his coping strategy. And she'd known for a long time that he didn't take easily to change. But she was beginning to wonder if they had a strong enough foundation on which to build a future. They'd reached a watershed. Soon she would have to decide if she wanted to always be here when he chose to come back, or if she should go her own way.

Chapter Fourteen

Saturday morning was crisp and clear and once more Anna woke to an empty bed. Putting on her robe she went downstairs to the lounge. Tom was talking on the phone, leaving what was obviously an answer-machine message. 'Hi, Maggie, it's Tom Mariner. Just a couple more things I wanted to ask. If you could call me back that would be great.' He left his mobile number and hung up.

'Who's Maggie?'

He seemed unable to meet her eye. 'She's helping on a case.'

'The drug addict?'

'Yes.'

'It's a Saturday,' Anna pointed out, knowing that she was being provocative.

'She's a therapist, works all hours.' Although calm, he hadn't liked the challenge and she knew what was coming next. 'I feel as if I need to stretch my legs today. Is that okay?'

What came out of Anna's mouth was, 'Sure,' though a swell of disappointment coursed through her. Here we go again. Well, two could play at that game. 'Actually, I've got plans too,' she added, coming to a quick decision. 'I think I'll take Jamie over to see Becky and Mark, as he's with us at the moment.'

'Is that wise, Jamie and a baby in the same house?'

She'd surprised him. Good.

'It'll be good for him. And it's a big house. The properties out there are much bigger for the money.' A point well made Anna felt, but she said it with an artful smile to show that she was winding him up. 'It'll only be overnight and Becky and Mark already know Jamie. They'd like Megan to get to know him too.' She was working hard to justify her actions. 'And Becky's been great support, she's a good listener.'

'And I'm not?' He recoiled slightly as if she'd physically slapped him.

'You've been through it too,' she added, regretting the inference. 'Becky's in a position to be more detached.'

She'd only come back a couple of days before and it would have been reasonable for Mariner to object, but he didn't, and the main thing Anna saw in his face was relief. So that's the way it was.

'Okay then,' he said.

'Okay.'

It had been a strange conversation, Mariner thought, setting off on his journey to Wythinford. He'd left Anna packing again, for her and Jamie this time. He couldn't work out why she'd made what was obviously a spur of the moment decision, but by the time he was parking up he'd pushed it to the back of his mind.

Even in chilly January a smattering of tourists were milling the pavements of the Cotswold town, perusing the craft and antique shops, the occasional snatch of an American accent heard. It was still early and there was only one other customer in the Lygon Arms, the kind of guy who'd always be the first in at opening time because he had nowhere else to be. With the absence of anyone serving behind the bar either, Mariner's heart sank.

'Lovely day for it,' said the man, predictably opening the conversation, observing Mariner's walking gear.

'Yes,' Mariner nodded politely, by which time the

barman had thankfully appeared to take his order, but there was a further wait while the beer was drawn.

'Which way are you headed?' the conversationalist persisted.

'I haven't yet decided,' Mariner lied. 'Probably west.' He was being deliberately vague.

'Ah. You're not local, are you?'

'No.'

'Well, may I recommend that if you're out that way—'

'I'm fine, really, thanks,' said Mariner as the barman produced his pint of Old Hooky. With some relief Mariner handed over the right money and could retreat to a corner table to study his map uninterrupted. He'd already noted that there was a public footpath from the village into the next town that went close to Eleanor's house, skirting the side of her property.

It was a beautiful day. Frosty grass crunched under Mariner's boots and low sunlight pierced the hedge branches, casting a giant bar-code shadow onto the footpath. It was the middle of the afternoon as he approached The Manse which was bathed in a buttery sunshine. The track brought him directly to the side of the garden where the fence gave way to a stile. Entering this way he could avoid the journalists, but as he got nearer he saw that they had gone anyway.

He climbed over the stile and walked across the front of the house to the main door. Except for the birdsong it was completely silent. Eleanor seemed pleased to see him, giving him a bony hug, and Nelson welcomed him like a long lost friend. Being greeted by a family member was a warm experience and a rare one that Mariner had long forgotten. He and his mother hadn't been on those terms for years.

'You've lost your vultures then,' Mariner remarked, taking off his boots in the porch before going into the house.

'The reporters?' Eleanor shook her head. 'Oh they'll be

200

back. I think they go to the pub for lunch. The landlord at the Lygon must be doing a roaring trade.'

'Not when I was in there,' Mariner said.

There was no Janet at the weekends, but Eleanor made him tea, waving away his offer to help, and they sat overlooking the terrace at the back of the garden where a large bird table offered refreshment for all kinds of species.

'I love to watch the birds,' she said. 'Except for those wretched magpies that get everywhere, stealing and bullying their way in.'

Speaking of which. 'Do you remember a girl Sir Geoffrey was once engaged to, Carrie Foster-Young?'

Eleanor smiled. 'Oh yes. She was the one who broke Geoffrey's heart. She was a very sweet girl but ...' She paused, searching for the right word. 'Flighty,' she said, at last. 'Yes; flighty, and very energetic.' She arched an eyebrow. 'Had her own room when she stayed here, but we couldn't very well prevent Geoffrey from going to her during the night. She and Geoffrey were what these days you'd call "an item" for nearly two years. I think he might have even married her, but she didn't believe in it, so she said. She was American you know, more for living together. It was all the rage then.'

'So what happened?'

'They had a big falling-out. I never really knew what it was about. It happened quite suddenly and there seemed no question of reconciliation. Geoffrey was seriously considering going into politics at that point so thank God for Diana. She was far more suitable to be an MP's wife and came along just at the right time. She and Geoffrey had so much in common. They were made for each other. I have to admit that Charles and I were somewhat relieved.' Her eyes clouded over. 'Poor, poor Diana.'

'She didn't suffer,' Mariner said, thinking back to what he knew of the crime. 'Death would have been instantaneous for both of them. She probably knew nothing about it.' Although those last few seconds would have been the longest and most terrifying of her life. 'Do you know what happened to Carrie?'

'It was rather sad. Geoffrey told me once, some years later, that he'd bumped into her and she was a drug addict. In some ways I wasn't really very surprised. There was always an unusual smell in the house after she'd been, though at the time I hadn't a clue what it was.'

'Did Carrie ever have any children?'

'I've no idea.' Eleanor shook her head. 'After they went their separate ways Geoffrey only mentioned her on that one occasion and if what he said was true, then I rather hope that she didn't. It's no life to bring a child into.'

'Is there anyone who would know for sure?'

'I suppose Norman might know.'

Of course, Norman Balfour, the university chum who went on to be Ryland's best man.

'He's a lovely boy, full of mischief.'

Mariner smiled. Probably not such a boy now.

'Have you any idea where I might find Norman?'

But she didn't. Hadn't seen him for years, either. But Mariner was hopeful. Maggie hadn't come back to him yet. She may not know anything much about Carrie Foster-Young, but she'd heard from Norman Balfour only a year or two back so would probably know his wherabouts. And hadn't she said he was a Catholic priest? There couldn't be many of those with the same name.

'You'll stay for dinner?' Eleanor said. 'It's only cold cuts that Janet's left me but there's enough for two of us.'

'I ought to be getting back. I've left my car in the village and walked here. I should go before it gets dark.'

It was only half past three but already the light was fading as Mariner set off across the fields. There was still no activity at the gate though he thought he could see at least one vehicle parked in the shadows. Christ, what an excruciatingly boring job. Those reporters had to be dedicated.

*

Mariner spent most of the next day surfing the Net, trying to establish what had become of Carrie Foster-Young. He got plenty of hits on genealogy sites, Foster-Youngs from all over the world trying to trace lost relatives, but none of them the one he wanted. Mid-evening, Maggie phoned him back. 'How can I help?'

'I've been wondering about some of the people my father knew, particularly Carrie Foster-Young.'

'I don't know much I'm afraid, only what I've already told you.'

'Do you know if she had a child?'

'She didn't when I knew her, but the way she put it about, I wouldn't be surprised. When she and Geoff split up she disappeared pretty quickly off the scene, and it was years ago, anything could have happened since then.'

'You said you'd heard from Norman Balfour. Do you know where he is?'

'Yes, he's the diocesan priest at St Dunstan's Church in north London. Why do you want to speak to him?'

'Everybody tells me he was one of my father's closest friends.'

But Maggie wasn't easily fooled. 'This still personal?'

'Pretty much. It may be nothing at all.'

'And how are you doing?'

'I'm fine.'

'You and Anna have talked?'

'We've started to.' Loosely speaking it was the truth.

'Well, keep doing it.'

'We will.' But talking wasn't what he had in mind.

Anna returned with Jamie later that evening, but her embrace was stiff and unyielding. Jamie, worn out by the travelling, crashed out in record time and she came down from the shower a little after that, while Mariner was watching a film on TV. Standing in the doorway she looked tiny and vulnerable in the way that she had when they first met, and Mariner felt a rush of love for her that made his eyes water. He must try harder. When she came and sat beside him, taking his hand in hers and smelling of soap and shampoo, he flicked off the sound on the TV and slid an arm round her drawing her close to him, a tiny fragile bird. 'Good time?' he asked.

'Great. Jamie did really well.' She stopped, uncertain whether to go on. 'There's a residential place not far from where Becky and Mark live. We passed it a couple of times when I was there before. This time we went and had a look round. It's a self-sufficient community. I think it would be really good for Jamie.'

Wow. So that's why Jamie went too.

'I didn't tell you before in case it came to nothing.' Which must mean that it had come to something.

'They have places there for him?' Mariner asked.

'They will have, soon, though we'll have to act quickly to get him in. It's expensive but I think we could do it.'

'It's a long way.'

'Doesn't have to be. Not if we moved out there too.'

'That's a bit drastic.'

'Jamie being evicted from the community home was drastic. I've got to think of him. And why not move? We've talked about it anyway.'

'*You've* talked about it.' Mariner corrected her.

'I don't get it.' She pulled back to look at him. 'I thought you'd want it too. Every chance you get at the moment, you go off walking somewhere.'

'I love the countryside. It's the people who live there.' Like locals who pester you while you're waiting for your pint.

'Not that you're generalising or anything. If you said that about Sparkhill you'd be called a racist.'

'Village life is too claustrophobic. Everyone would know our business.'

'How do you know that? You've never experienced it.'

'I'm just guessing.'

'It doesn't have to be the middle of nowhere. There are

small towns. It should be easy enough for me to get the kind of admin post I'm doing now, and surely you could transfer. I thought it was fairly easy for you to do, if you want to, that is. And it would be a much better place to bring up children.'

Mariner felt as if he was being given an ultimatum.

'I know we haven't had much of a chance to discuss this,' she went on. 'But events have taken over.'

You can say that again.

'It's a big step,' Mariner said, lamely.

'Sometimes life is about big steps. Another word for it is commitment. I thought we both wanted the same.'

'Things change.'

Despite their physical closeness Mariner could feel a gulf opening up between them. He'd had the feeling for some time that he was standing in a boat that drifted further and further from where she stood on the shore. Already the landscape around him had changed significantly and soon he would drift so far away from her that none of it would be the same as hers. What he'd failed to realise that was Anna was in her own boat drifting in the opposite direction, and her landscape was changing too. There were oars in the bottom of the boat and with a bit of effort he could have locked them and rowed back to meet her halfway, but each time he had that chance something stopped him.

There seemed nothing more to say. Turning back to the TV, Mariner turned the sound back on and resumed watching the film. Undeterred, Anna snuggled closer. 'Jamie's crashed out. Why don't you come and join me?'

'I want to watch the end of this.' He must have seen the film at least four times and could practically recite the dialogue, but she didn't point that out. Maybe she recognised his fear.

Next morning, as penance, Mariner left Anna sleeping in and got Jamie up and dressed before driving him to the day

205

centre. From there he went to Granville Lane. Walking in to the building the warmth hit him like a solid wall. 'They've finally got the heating to work properly,' Ella grinned. In CID Tony Knox was behind his desk, a welcome sight. 'It's Coleman's last week. I wanted to be here.' He cast a dazed look over the stack of files. 'I've a mass of paperwork but I can't settle to anything.' He unbuttoned his shirt cuff and rolled up a sleeve. 'And this bloody heat doesn't help. It's like being in a sauna.'

'Give it a chance.' Mariner was staring at a row of deep scratch marks on Knox's arm. 'What happened there?'

Knox blushed, pulling his sleeve down again to cover the marks. 'I was cutting back some stuff in the garden,' he said, which was strange because Mariner had never known him to garden.

As arranged, one of the first things Mariner did from his own work station was to call the garage about his car.

'It's all set,' Carl told him. 'You can collect it whenever you're ready.'

Mariner went back to Tony Knox. 'Want to get out of here for twenty minutes?'

'Sure.'

'You can give me a lift to the garage.'

Knox waited on the forecourt while Mariner went inside to settle up.

'You were right about the brake cable,' Carl said, rooting around under the counter in his shabby little office.

'Time to start looking for a new car?' It was the last thing Mariner wanted to embark on right now.

But, as he finally produced the curved tube he'd been looking for, Carl shook his head. 'It wasn't wear and tear,' he said. 'It looks more like a cut.' And as they both examined the clean straight incision in the toughened plastic, the feeling that Mariner had kept at bay for several days slithered back over him like a chill fog. He emerged from the garage office still clutching the tube and trying to remain calm, but apparently not succeeding.

'What's going on?' Knox demanded.

'Nothing,' he said. 'It's fine.' And for now Knox seemed to have enough on his own mind to let it lie.

But Mariner needed an explanation. The spilled brake fluid was on the car park at Tally Ho, so again the most obvious culprits were the Harlesden plods. But a tracking device was one thing, sabotage was in a different league. Tampering with the brakes might endanger Mariner's life, but it would also put at risk the lives of innocent bystanders. Surely it was too reckless an act for men who would have often seen the resulting mayhem from such pranks.

No, there was someone else who would be much more likely to take that chance without considering the full consequences. Mariner had to face the possibility that Rupert Foster-Young might know about him. When Foster-Young was applying the pressure, either by accident or by design Ryland must have told him about Mariner's existence. He might even have used Mariner's job as a counter-threat, and with enough information Rupert Foster-Young would have had little difficulty in tracking him down. Mariner thought back to that curious feeling he'd had since before Christmas of being followed. Perhaps it hadn't been his imagination after all.

Back at Granville Lane Mariner phoned Chapel Wood prison. 'I'd like some information about a former inmate; Rupert Foster-Young.' Mariner gave the details.

The receptionist at the other end was understandably cautious. 'I'll need to check your credentials and call you back.'

'Of course.' It was routine procedure. Information couldn't be given out to just anyone, but it did nothing to curb Mariner's impatience.

As he waited, Mariner's phone rang. 'Mr and Mrs Evans are here to see you,' said Ella.

This time he had no trouble recalling. 'They're here?' He felt a breathtaking rush of adrenalin.

'They've been having trouble getting you on the phone,' said Ella generously.

'I've been busy.'

Ella's tone was placatory. 'They understand that. They just want to speak to you, sir.'

Mariner had, for a split second, seriously thought about asking Ella to lie for him again. But she was right. This was about them, not him, and it was something he'd eventually have to face. Best to get it over with. He went down to the interview room where Ella had taken them and they stood as he went in. 'Mr and Mrs Evans?' he stepped forward to shake hands. 'Please, sit down.'

'No, we won't keep you.' It was Mr Evans who spoke. 'We know how busy you are. But we just wanted to thank you personally for what you did.'

'I didn't do anything,' Mariner said, wanting to curl up with guilt.

'Oh yes you did,' blurted out Mrs Evans. Looking at her for the first time Mariner could see where their daughter had inherited her big blue eyes. 'We spoke to another of the rescuers, a fireman. He said that you talked to Chloe constantly, all the time you were trying to dig her out. You let her know that someone was there and that she wasn't abandoned. You kept talking to her even after ...' She faltered, took a trembling breath, as tears traced patterns down her face. 'It means so much to us, knowing that she didn't die alone.'

'I only did what anyone else would have done,' said Mariner, swallowing a wave of emotion.

'Have you got children of your own?'

'No.'

'Oh.' She looked genuinely surprised. 'I was so sure that you must have. You knew exactly what to do.'

Without warning she stepped forward, grasped Mariner's arms and pulled him to her. After the clumsy, desperate embrace they thanked him again, and went back to their private hell. The encounter left Mariner feeling weak and

208

sick. What if he and Anna did have children? How could he bear to go through what they had endured? How could anyone?

At Chapel Wood, Mariner's credentials had apparently been deemed up to scratch. There was a message on his desk inviting him to call back.

'Rupert Foster-Young got parole,' the prison administrator told him. 'He was released eighteen months ago, April fourth.' It would have given him plenty of time to approach Ryland in person and set up the blackmail operation.

'Could you give me details of his parole officer?'

'May I ask why sir?'

'I just want to rule out a link with a triple murder.'

Charlie Glover, hovering in the doorway, looked on with interest.

'Just laying it on a bit thick,' Mariner said, for his benefit, as he replaced the phone. 'Follow-up on a case from a while back.'

Glover seemed to swallow it.

'How's it going with our Albanian friend?' Mariner asked.

Glover shook his head. 'It's what I came to say. We've heard nothing yet. The ICPS is taking for ever.'

'I'll talk to Coleman.'

Mariner was in demand. This time when the phone rang, it was Dave Flynn. 'I've got your DNA results. I'm about to put them in the post to you.'

'There's no need,' Mariner said, a plan taking shape. 'I can come and collect them in person if you like. I'll be back in London tomorrow.'

'You're coming down for the inquests?'

Until then it hadn't crossed Mariner's mind, but if the timing was right ... 'Officially I'm chasing up the extradition of our Albanian, but if I get the chance to stop by, I will. When are they?'

'Wednesday, ten thirty, Westminster Coroner's Court, Horseferry Road.'

'Cheers. I'll see you there.' Mariner was about to hang up but Flynn stopped him.

'Tom, wait. The DNA result wasn't the only thing I called about. Eleanor Ryland is dead.'

Chapter Fifteen

'What?' For several seconds Mariner relived the moment he'd been told about his mother's death, that sudden sense of distorted perspective, when everything around him faded to into the background. He and Eleanor had only just been getting to know one another and now she was gone. Mariner felt numb. Someone, it seemed, was scattering poison over every branch of his family and systematically destroying it. A sixth sense told him this wasn't natural causes. 'How?' he wanted to know.

'Someone got into her house and knocked her about a bit. It probably didn't take much.'

He should have insisted on that alarm. 'When did this happen?'

'They think sometime Saturday afternoon or evening. She'd been there a couple of days. The gardener found her when he turned up for work on Monday morning.'

'I was there that afternoon,' said Mariner, dully. If only he'd taken up her invitation and stayed longer.

'You may have been one of the last people to see her alive. Thames Valley police want to talk to you as a significant witness.'

'How do they know I was there?'

'The journalist you spoke to remembered it.'

'I didn't speak to any journalists.'

Mariner went to see Jack Coleman. 'We seem to have

reached a sticking point with the Albanian. How about I go down to the CPS and see where they're up to, apply a little gentle pressure if necessary.'

'Can you do it tactfully?' Coleman was remembering his retirement celebration.

'You know me.'

Coleman gave him a curious look. 'I thought I did.'

Mariner decided to keep the conversation with Flynn to himself for now. It would be news soon enough, but there was no reason for anyone to make the connection with him.

Anna was cooking dinner when he arrived home that evening, but she left what she was doing to come and hug him. 'Good news,' she said. 'I've got Jamie into Manor Park for a night's respite. I thought it would give us time to talk – and anything else we feel like doing.'

'Tonight?'

'Tomorrow.'

Mariner was torn, he really was. 'I've got to go down to London in the morning. Follow up on an extradition. The Albanian.'

She was crestfallen. 'I thought that was Charlie Glover's case.'

'Coleman wants a more senior officer down there.' Extending the truth again. He'd be able to put it on his CV soon.

'How long will it take?'

'Might be a couple of days.'

'Oh great.' Breaking from him, she resumed preparing their meal and Mariner turned to go. 'You'll be back for the appointment I trust?'

For several long seconds Mariner mentally floundered, trying to work out what she was talking about.

'With the genetic counsellor,' she said eventually, exasperated by his ignorance.

'Yes, of course.'

'Only you were the one who wanted it.'

212

'I did. I do. Look I'm sorry about London. It's just bad luck. And Jamie was pretty good last night.'

But tonight was different. Jamie refused to go to sleep and as the night progressed they got more and more irritable with each other. Finally Anna was reduced to her usual tactic of sitting on her brother's bed to persuade him to stay there and Mariner went to bed alone. He woke up at three fifteen. There was a light on downstairs and he could hear movement. Panicking, he got out of bed and crept down the stairs. Anna was filling the kettle.

'What are you doing?' he asked.

'What does it look like? Now Jamie's finally gone off, I'm wide awake.'

'I thought we had intruders.'

Anna dropped her gaze to his boxers and a sly smile crept over her face. She giggled; a magical sound that he hadn't heard for way too long. 'And you were going to ward them off with that?'

'All revved up and no place to go,' said Mariner wryly. 'But since we're both awake now—'

Through her fatigue she managed to be incredulous. 'You had really better be joking!'

'Can't blame a man for trying. Come here.' He held out his arms and she walked into them collapsing, exhausted, against him. Moments later her mouth was locked over his and she was pushing down his shorts. Wrapping her legs around him, Mariner was poised to consummate when, over her shoulder, like a spectre of the night, Jamie appeared in the doorway. 'Fuck!' said Mariner.

'Tom!' Anna slapped him between the shoulder blades.

'Fuck,' repeated Jamie. 'Want a drink now.'

By five in the morning when sleep still wouldn't come and while it was still pitch black outside, Mariner got up.

'What are you doing?'

'I may as well go.'

Feeling like a seasoned commuter Mariner travelled down

to London on the train again and went straight to the International CPS. He was there by mid-morning and caught them out.

'We're snowed under,' the clerk confessed. 'Haven't had a chance to look through all your paperwork yet. Can you call back a little later and I can tell you where we're up to?'

In other circumstances Mariner would have hit the roof, having travelled all that distance, but this time it suited him very nicely. 'Sure. I'll come back in a couple of hours.'

The probation office that Rupert Foster-Young had checked in with was near to his flat, and was part of an old Victorian primary school with separate demarcated entrances for girls and boys. Mariner went into the one marked 'boys'. From the reception desk he was directed along a corridor of class-rooms transformed into open plan offices. He stopped at the door of 3A and approached the woman at the nearest desk. 'I'm here to talk to Brendan Wise.'

From inside the office a young man with black tousled hair looked up from what he was doing. 'Inspector Mariner?' Wise got up and came over extending a hand in friendly greeting.

'It's Tom,' Mariner said.

'You wanted to talk to me about Robert Foster-Young?' The swagger put the streets all over him, but Wise's accent was cultured, and devoid of any regional accent.

'*Rupert* Foster-Young,' Mariner said, hoping there hadn't been some kind of blunder.

'No, you mean Robert,' Wise corrected him. 'That's what he calls himself now, Rob, to be more accurate.'

'He changed his name?'

'Only that part. Think about it. Would you want to be banged up with a name like Rupert?'

Mariner smiled. 'I see what you mean.'

'Before we go any further, do you have some identification?' Wise was unabashed about making the request and Mariner obliged with his warrant card, hoping he wouldn't need to justify the visit. But all Wise said was, 'Let's go for a walk. I need some more fags.'

'Rob was one of my success stories.' Wise went on. They were out on the pavement again, dodging old ladies and mothers with pushchairs. 'He'd got out on license. He'd served four years of his seven year sentence and in most respects he'd stuck to his sentence plan.'

'In most respects?'

'He complied with the educational programme, attended all the courses.'

'What kinds of courses?'

'Computer studies, electronics. Is that relevant?'

'It might be.' If it meant he could fit a tracking device on a car.

'I can look up exactly what he did back in the office.' They'd come to a small corner newsagent's. 'Won't be a tick. Anything I can get you?'

Mariner shook his head and Wise disappeared inside the shop, reappearing minutes later with a pack of Marlboros. He ripped them open with the urgency of an addict, lighting up as they walked, and making Mariner wonder if he'd once been a drug-user, too.

'Rob was meant to have cleaned up his act inside,' Wise said, pulling hard on his cigarette. 'But that didn't quite happen. As I'm sure you're well aware, it's almost easier to get hold of drugs on the inside than it is on the streets.'

Mariner had heard that. 'He was released early,' he said. 'So he wasn't considered a risk.'

'He behaved himself. And he never had been a real danger to anyone else.'

'I thought he was in for aggravated burglary.'

'He was high at the time. He demonstrated remorse for his crime.'

'Surely he could get high again?'

Wise shot him a look. 'The decision wasn't mine, it was down to the parole board, who obviously thought it worth the risk.'

215

'Yeah, sorry, I didn't mean—'

'Sure.' They'd arrived back outside the school and stood side by side on the pavement while Wise finished his cigarette. 'Besides, Rob's mother was ill at the time, too.'

'With what?'

'Cirrhosis of the liver, exacerbated no doubt by long-term drug and alcohol abuse. It's a terrible thing to say but it was the making of Rob.'

'In what way?'

'It was his wake-up call. Made him realise what damage drugs could do. It's what she died of essentially. A couple of weeks after her funeral Rob joined a rehab programme and successfully kicked his habit. His mother left him a flat and some money and the last time I saw him he was determined to make a go of it.' Wise tossed down the dogend of his cigarette and crushed it underfoot, before leading the way back into the building.

'Does he still live in the flat?' Mariner asked.

'He's under no obligation to keep in touch any more, so I've no idea.'

'How did he feel about his spell in prison?'

'Like I said, he expressed remorse.'

'But you know that while he was serving his sentence he made an unsuccessful attempt to appeal his conviction, one that he continued to pursue after his release.'

'I didn't know that, but it doesn't really surprise me. Up until his mother died Rob was your typical junkie mess, irrational, paranoid. After he cleaned up he seemed to genuinely come to terms with what he'd done.'

'Does he still believe that he was wrongly convicted?'

'He never complained to me. Coming off drugs is a big reality check. Puts things back in perspective again.' Wise was speaking from experience. Mariner's instinct had been right.

'So you don't think Rob harbours any resentment that his application for appeal was turned down?'

'As far as I know he accepted that he'd got what was

appropriate. He'd served his sentence and it was time to start again. And like I said, last time I saw him he was very focused on staying clean.'

'Did he ever mention a man called Joseph O'Connor?'

'Not to me, but I know that name. Wasn't he involved with the shooting of Sir Geoffrey Ryland? Christ, is that what you're investigating?' Mariner didn't confirm or deny it. 'What the hell could Rob have had to do with that?'

'Probably nothing,' said Mariner. 'But his name came up as one of a number of unsuccessful appellants to the JRC and he may have known O'Connor. I need to cross him off the list, that's all. Can you give me his last known?'

'Why do you need that?' Suddenly Wise was less forthcoming.

'I just want to talk to him,' Mariner said. 'Nothing heavy, I swear.'

'Well you should know that after he was signed off, he was planning to travel.'

The address Wise gave Mariner wasn't far from the office and the probation officer supplied good directions. It was a second floor apartment in an imposing but rather shabby house. Repeated ringing of the bell for Foster-Young's place brought no response, so in desperation, hovering over the list of names from which he could deduce nothing, and risking a mouthful of abuse, Mariner tried the bell for flat 1B which hopefully would be situated directly below Foster-Young, making the occupant aware of his presence. This time a young woman came to the door carrying a baby on her hip.

'I'm looking for Mr Foster-Young in flat 2B. He's about forty—' Suddenly Mariner realised that he didn't have an up to date description. He didn't need it.

'Rob, yeah, I know, don't we, Lauren?' she addressed the baby, her manner pleasant and in no way troubled by the interruption. 'Uncle Rob looks after you for me sometimes, doesn't he?'

217

'You leave your baby daughter with—?' Mariner checked himself. He'd been about to say 'junkie', but Foster-Young had cleaned up and Lauren's mum may not know anything about his dubious past. No need to alarm her, especially as Lauren appeared none the worse for her experience.

Lauren's mum was looking at him. 'It's just while I pop to the shops and stuff. At least he does when he's here. He comes and goes a lot.'

'He doesn't seem to be here now. Any idea when he'll be back?'

'Sorry.' Lauren was beginning to fidget. 'He's been gone a while, visiting family I think he said.'

'If I leave you a number, would you call me when he gets back?'

'If you like. Shall I tell him—?'

'No. We're old mates and I want to surprise him. If you could just let me know that would be great.' Mariner left his name and mobile number on a scrap of paper.

From the probation offices Mariner got back to the CPS only a few minutes late, to be told by a different clerk that they were awaiting information from colleagues in Tirana. 'How long are you in London for?' he asked Mariner.

'A couple of days.'

'I can do some chasing up again for you this afternoon and see where we stand,' he offered. 'Then I can give you a written summary to take away with you. Can you come back in sometime tomorrow?'

'No problem,' said Mariner.

There was a good chance that Rupert Foster-Young wouldn't appear before Mariner returned home, so the next place on his list, covering all the options, was St Dunstan's Roman Catholic Church. Set in lawned grounds at the end of a residential street, the church was a modern light-bricked building, with a sharply angular asymmetrical tower at one end, and a wall entirely made up of stained-glass depiction of the parable of the loaves and fishes. A handful of individuals were bowed in private prayer in the sleek, pine pews, but a verger directed Mariner to the office-like vestry where Father Balfour was behind his desk. 'None of us escapes the paperwork these days,' he said apologetically, inviting Mariner to sit. Norman Balfour did still look remarkably youthful for his age, with a round shiny face and thick head of hair, liberally streaked with grey. A little fuller in the face, he'd hardly changed since the wedding photos. 'What can I do for you, sir?' he asked.

'I wanted to talk about old times.'

'Did you indeed? And who, may I ask, are you?'

Mariner sensed a straight-talker, so took a chance. 'I'm Sir Geoffrey Ryland's son.'

'Dear God in heaven. Are you sure?' Balfour recovered a little. 'Forgive me. That was not the most tactful thing to say, but you'll know that it's rather a surprise.'

'I understand.' Mariner smiled. 'I haven't had the DNA results yet, but I'm as certain as I can be.'

Balfour was studying him. It was a look Mariner was becoming accustomed to. 'Well, well, the young Thomas. Haven't you turned out to be a strapping lad?'

'So you knew about me, too.'

'Oh yes. It's uncanny. You look so much like him.'

'So I've been told.'

'You're in the police force, aren't you?'

'West Midlands.'

'And is this official business?'

'Not exactly. I'm trying to find out more about my father. I wondered if you could tell me about Carrie Foster-Young.'

'Carrie?' Balfour sighed. 'Poor Carrie. She and Geoff were engaged at one time, but he broke it off when he found out she was pregnant.'

Allelujah. And two strikes against his father.

'She hadn't told him?'

'Of course not, she knew he'd been through it before.' Balfour looked mildly embarrassed. 'With you.'

Mariner's heart had begun to pound. 'But he was the father?'

'No. That was the whole point. Monogamy wasn't Carrie's forte. At the time she was going out with Geoff, Carrie slept around.'

'She was having an affair? Who with?'

'It's not something I'm proud of.' Balfour lowered his gaze to the untidy desk. 'And neither would I dignify a couple of opportunistic leg-overs by calling them an affair.' He glanced up at Mariner. 'Don't look so startled. I'm the original prodigal son. Celibacy may be a requirement of this job, but it wasn't always a requirement for me. Those were hedonistic days. But I don't kid myself that I was the only one. Carrie wasn't choosy, she slept with anyone. I thought it the duty of a good friend to warn Geoffrey about it before he made a commitment.'

'So you told him about her pregnancy?'

'I felt he had a right to know.'

'But how could anyone be sure that the child wasn't his?'

'Geoff and Carrie had never consummated the relationship. Having already got your mother into trouble when he was a student, Geoff was pretty determined not to make that mistake again, especially as he was about to try and get himself elected.'

'And you believed him?'

'What he said made absolute sense. It may have been the first time in history that women had effective contraception, but they also had control over whether they felt like using it. He knew how unreliable Carrie could be, so the only way of being sure was to exercise some restraint until after they were married. She apparently agreed, then got her kicks sleeping around with just about everybody else. It was a shock when Geoff found out.'

'Is that why they split up?'

'Theirs was always a volatile relationship.'

'And Sir Geoffrey married Diana Fitzgibbon.'

'Rebound with a vengeance? Partly I suppose. Diana was

about as far from Carrie as you could imagine. While the rest of us were out enjoying the new permissiveness, Diana was at home doing her flower arranging.'

'One extreme to the other.'

'Not as strange as it might seem, given Geoff's aspirations.'

'Diana was a good career move,' Mariner said.

'You make it sound calculated. There was more to it than that. It's true, Diana was from the right kind of family, but she and Geoff also had a lot in common and there was a genuine connection between them. You only had to see them together. Diana was a very fragile sort. When I introduced her to Geoff she'd been away recuperating from a kind of breakdown. Geoff took her under his wing, as I knew he would. They just seemed to click straightaway. I suppose they each had something that the other needed. Isn't that often how it works?'

Like Knox and Selina, Mariner thought. 'You introduced them?' he asked.

Balfour held up his hands, palms forward. 'Guilty as charged, Officer. Diana's family has been friends with mine for years. I was taking her out to dinner one evening. The thing with Geoff and Carrie had just blown up so I asked Geoff to come along. Diana had been through the mill and needed someone solid and dependable, and Geoff responded to that.'

'Carrie must have been upset.'

'Furious, I'd say. One thing worse than a woman scorned; a pregnant woman scorned.'

'Did you ever find out who the child's father was?'

'Not definitively. Carrie pointed the finger at all of us. She was a manipulative woman, skilled at playing one of us off against the other. At that time of course paternity was impossible to prove and since she was bedding all of us it could have been anyone.'

'Except Ryland. So pregnant Carrie was abandoned?'

'Oh, Carrie did very nicely out of it. Her own family in

the States cut her off without a dime because of her predicament. But she was a parasite. Had money from everyone to put the little bastard through public school. Not that it did him any good.'

'You know Rupert Foster-Young? When was the last time you saw him?'

'About ten years ago, I suppose. His mother had attempted suicide. He couldn't get near to Geoff so came after me for money, accusing me, and all of us, of ruining her, claiming that we had started the drinking and drug abuse. I knew differently though.'

'And did you give him money?'

'I'm a priest. Do you know how much I'm paid? He might not have been sure who his father was but he was his mother's son all right.'

'What do you mean?'

'Drugged to the eyeballs himself. He wanted the cash to feed his habit. Insisted that I owed it to him. He was a nasty little shit.' Colourful language for a priest. Balfour saw what Mariner was thinking. 'Something for the confessional this week,' he smiled. 'I agonised for days about whether I should help him, after all it's my job. But giving him money would have simply speeded his demise, so I prayed for him and trusted in the Lord to find another way.'

'Did Foster-Young claim Sir Geoffrey as his father?'

'Carrie's doing I suppose, but it was more the collective responsibility for his existence that he seemed angry about. He was one of those people who believes that the world owes him a living.'

'He's done a spell in prison since you saw him, you know.'

'Geoff told me. He'd been pestering them at the JRC. Then everything went quiet. He's probably dead himself by now. No great loss to mankind I'm sorry to say.'

'On the contrary, from what I've learned, Rupert Foster-Young has got his life back together again.'

'Well, I'm glad to hear it.' But for someone who might

be expected to have faith in the essential goodness of man, Balfour didn't sound particularly convinced. Even if Foster-Young could play the part of the good neighbour, babysitting a small child when needed, it didn't mean he'd completely changed.

It was Mariner's belief that Foster-Young had equally powerful and not entirely wholesome reasons for cleaning up his act. If he harboured resentment against Ryland and was planning to do something about it he'd need to be thinking straight. And just because he persuaded the professionals he was over it, didn't mean that there wasn't a grudge lurking underneath the surface somewhere. In Mariner's experience resentment like that didn't simply evaporate, and the last person he'd allow to see it would be his parole officer. Wise had described Foster-Young as being focused, but what was it that he was focused on?

'Sir Geoffrey and Lady Ryland didn't have children.' Mariner said.

'They both wanted it that way. It was one of the things that bound them together. Diana was very fragile and prone to depression. Not that it was common knowledge of course. I think most people made the assumption that they had tried to start a family and failed. Back then of course there wasn't much you could do about it. Had to accept your lot and get on with life.'

'Did you know Diana well?'

'We saw less of each other over the years, but she came to mass from time to time.'

'She was Catholic?'

'No, but she was a great support when I entered the priesthood and after a while I think she found comfort in the ritual of it all. Many people do. After the service we would talk.'

For one outlandish moment Mariner considered the possibility that Diana and Balfour could have been having an affair, but he dismissed it instantly.

It brought Mariner to the blackmail. 'Was Sir Geoffrey

Ryland always a gambling man?' he asked, casually.

'Delete always, insert never,' Balfour said. 'I'm the one who used to like a flutter. Geoff was always chastising me for wasting my money.'

'You don't think he could have changed?'

'It's my experience that people are born gamblers.'

It was Mariner's view, too.

'Geoff thought a lot of your mother, you know,' Balfour said. 'He had me contact her old friend Maggie quite recently.'

'She told me that. Was there any special reason?'

'He was writing his memoirs and I think it had stirred up all kinds of thoughts and regrets. I suppose he wondered how you were getting on, his only son. It wasn't the first time I'd fulfilled that role. Our lives had followed very different paths, and politicians have to exercise such discretion in their private lives, but I think I remained a trusted link with the past.' Balfour seemed to hesitate. 'You should know that I counselled Geoff against contacting you directly. I know he considered it from time to time. I warned him that it would do more harm than good. So if you're looking for someone to blame, I'm your man.'

But by now Mariner was beyond blame, and somehow the priest made it sound too simplistic. Leaving the church, Mariner felt he was in the middle of a balloon debate. Who did he believe? The probation officer backing his reformed client, or the Catholic priest who perceived Foster-Young as a 'nasty little shit'. The only way of making up his mind would be to meet Rupert Foster-Young in person. But when he checked his phone there were no messages.

Chapter Sixteen

The following morning Mariner got to the inquest minutes before the proceedings opened. As expected there was a high level of security and a large official representation, for what, as it turned out, was something of a non-event.

Mariner took a seat in the public gallery, nodding an acknowledgement to Sharon O'Connor who seemed to have come with a considerable entourage of family and friends. It saddened Mariner that the one person conspicuous in her absence was Eleanor Ryland, but that aside he felt detached, as if he was here in a professional rather than a personal capacity. Dave Flynn sat below with the police contingent, but the main body of evidence was presented by Chief Superintendent Caroline Griffin, tall imposing and ridiculously young. Several lines of enquiry were being pursued, she informed the court, including the recent past history of Joseph O'Connor. It seemed that the fact that his original sentence had been quashed was being conveniently overlooked. He'd been involved with 'the wrong people' before so it could happen again and Terry Brady had helpfully left the country so was not available to deny it.

There were several points at which Mariner expected Sharon O'Connor to shout out in protest, and if she had he'd have been tempted to join in. But she simply sat quietly, shaking her head in disbelief. Under Section 20 of the Coroner's Act the inquest was adjourned pending further enquiries, but the coroner agreed to release the bodies for burial.

Flynn caught up with Mariner in the lobby melee. 'I've brought you a present.' He passed over a brown envelope. 'Don't say I never give you anything.'

'Thanks.' Mariner felt unnaturally calm. This envelope contained only confirmation of what he now knew was almost certainly true.

'You're not going to open it?' said Flynn.

'Somewhere more private,' said Mariner, pocketing it. 'I'm pretty sure it won't be a surprise.' Part of him wanted to talk to Flynn about the last few days, but he decided against it, considering the reception Flynn had given his other theories. Better to have some concrete evidence first. From the corner of his eye he saw Norman Balfour affectionately greeting a woman. Flynn was watching too. 'Who's that talking to the priest?' Mariner asked.

'Sir Geoffrey's sister-in-law, Felicity Fitzgibbon.'

'The one who lives in Switzerland?'

'That's right. Your aunt I suppose, technically.'

'Technically.'

At first glance Felicity Fitzgibbon was very different from her sister and although approaching her sixties was every inch the exotic continental. Petite and slim with shoulder-length ash-blond hair, she was exquisitely dressed in what looked like beige cashmere.

'A stunner,' Mariner observed. 'She here on her own?' he asked casually.

'She's a single woman so I gather,' said Flynn. 'Rich and divorced.'

'Attractive combination. Got her phone number?' It was flippantly said, but Mariner was rather hoping that Flynn had.

He shook his head sadly. 'Too flash for me. Not to mention a little on the mature side.'

They watched her say her goodbyes to Balfour, and followed her out to where an official black sedan was waiting on the kerb. 'I can't imagine she'd be able to tell you much, either. She's lived abroad for years.' Flynn was warning him off.

But at the start of the inquest, when the clerk had read out Ryland's personal details, Mariner had made a note of the address in Chelsea. Always prudent to have a pocket book handy. Chances were that Felicity Fitzgibbon would turn up there at some point and Mariner was hopeful that it would be today.

She appeared eventually, later that afternoon as Mariner stood freezing in a doorway opposite beginning to think that he'd been sold a dummy. By now she'd eschewed the official vehicle and was driving herself in a soft-top BMW, probably hired, which she squeezed into a vacant parking spot.

The police presence in front of the mews property deterred Mariner from approaching her at that point, so he flagged down a cab, waited until she emerged again and then asked the driver to follow the BMW. Mariner had assumed she'd be going back to her London hotel, but to his dismay she joined the North Circular and then the M40. This was going to be one of the most expensive cab rides ever.

'Where the hell are we going?' the driver demanded, and Mariner had no other choice but to produce his warrant card. 'I'll make it worth your while,' he said. Forty minutes later, as they pulled up in front of Eleanor Ryland's home the meter was on seventy-one quid and rising.

Now that the Manse was designated a crime scene, there was an officer back on the gate and the press pack had doubled. Mariner cast his eyes over them wondering who it was had been making up stuff about him. Probably not a good idea to try and follow Ms Fitzgibbon into the house. He'd have to try and catch her leaving. But she didn't go right in. Instead she engaged in a lengthy conversation with the young constable just inside the gate, which involved consultation with the map she'd brought. Finding out where Eleanor's body had been taken perhaps? Then it was back in the car and off again, but this time across country to the outer edges of Wythinford, and what looked like a garden centre. Then Mariner saw the sign for animal rescue and realised what was going on. She'd come for Nelson.

Paying off the taxi, which almost completely cleaned him out of cash, Mariner walked past the cafeteria and through the Alpines section to the rescue centre, catching up with Felicity Fitzgibbon outside Nelson's pen. The animal was scratching at the gate to be let out, and jumped around wagging its tail as Mariner approached. 'Nice dog,' Mariner observed, pretending to read the information tag, which had a 'Reserved' sticker on it. 'You're having him?'

Her smile was reluctant. Close too her make-up was heavy, her age more apparent. 'He belonged to my sister,' she said. 'She died suddenly. But I have a pretty hectic life with not much room for a pet. I live abroad too, so it would mean quarantine, and it never seems fair to put an animal through all of that.' The dog whined pathetically, its tail wagging with hope. 'It's hard though. He meant the world to my sister and I feel I'd be letting her down if I didn't at least find him a good home. Are you looking for a dog?' For a second her eyes held the same optimistic gaze as the animal's.

'I'm considering it,' Mariner said. And it was true. At the back of his mind for the last couple of weeks he'd been thinking that a dog might be a reasonable alternative to having children. 'My partner would prefer a child though.'

Another half-smile. 'My sister and her husband didn't have children. I'm sure he was a substitute.'

'Previous experience in the role then,' said Mariner.

This time she chuckled, a deep, throaty laugh. 'You could say that.'

A chilly gust of wind rattled the cage door and Mariner saw her shiver. 'Look I realise you don't know me, but while you're thinking it over would you like a coffee? It'll give you a chance to try and talk me into it.'

She was a sophisticated woman and probably got propositioned like this all the time. All the same, her eyes narrowed. 'You're not a reporter are you?'

Mariner feigned astonishment. 'No. I promise you. I'm not a reporter.'

'It's just that my brother-in-law was well known. I have to be careful.' She smiled. 'I'm sorry. That sounded terribly rude. Coffee would be lovely.'

Mariner offered her a hand. 'Tom Mariner.'

Taking his hand, she laughed again. 'There you are, it was meant to be. Who else but a Mariner could take on Nelson?'

'I'm not sure that he's named after that Nelson,' said Mariner, before realising the implication of what he'd said. 'I mean, these days Mr Mandela is a more of a household name.'

She laughed. 'Knowing my brother-in-law, you're probably right.'

On a cold winter weekday the cafeteria was practically empty, but the coffee served in workmanlike mugs was hot and strong. During the course of the conversation Mariner learned that Felicity (but everyone calls me Fliss) lived in Lausanne, where her second husband had been in banking, and that she ran her own fashion boutique, often travelling to Italy to buy stock. 'So you see having a dog just wouldn't be fair.' Her scarlet lipstick glistened over perfectly maintained teeth. 'What do you do Mr Mariner?'

He'd been waiting for this. 'I sell security products, burglar alarms, that kind of thing.'

'And you're having a day off?'

'I've a couple of customers in the area, time between appointments, so I walked out here from the village.'

'You like to walk, too. A dog would be a perfect companion.'

'Your business must be successful,' Mariner said. 'You have an eye for opportunity.'

229

'That's what it's all about, don't you think? Taking life's opportunities.' She'd finished her coffee. 'I should go,' she said.

'What about Nelson?'

'I'm here for a few more days, with luck during that time the kennels can find him a good home. It really would be impossible for me to have him.' She smiled. 'You're sure I can't persuade you?'

'I'll give it some thought,' Mariner said, but they both knew he was being polite. He walked her back to the BMW.

'Can I drop you at your car?'

'No thanks. It's not far, and you were quite right. I like the exercise.' She looked uncertainly at the dark sky, but the rain had held off so hopefully he didn't appear too eccentric.

Mariner watched her go before asking at the garden centre and calling a local cab firm on his mobile. In order to pay, he had to ask the driver to stop at a cash point en route to the nearest train station, where he had to wait an hour and fifteen minutes on a freezing platform for the train back into London. The expenses claim for this little trip was going to look interesting.

Despite the warmth of his hotel room Mariner was shivering uncontrollably and could feel the beginnings of a cold coming on. The comfort of home was a much more attractive prospect. By the time he'd checked out and caught the next train back to Birmingham, it was late evening when he got there, exhausted and aching. Anna was out, having taken Jamie to his activity club at the day centre, but she'd left a note to say that Jack Coleman had been trying to get hold of him, and to contact Coleman at home if necessary.

Glenys Coleman was not pleased to hear Mariner's voice, especially so late. 'I'll go and get Jack,' she said, shortly. In the ensuing delay Mariner heard raised voices in the background, and then Coleman came on. 'Thames

Valley police have been in touch,' he said. 'They want to interview you as a significant witness in the murder, somewhere east of Banbury, of a Mrs Eleanor Ryland, who I understand was the mother of the late Sir Geoffrey Ryland.' Coleman paused. 'What in God's name is going on, Tom?'

Not yet ready for full disclosure, Mariner had prepared his response. 'Just before Christmas I found out that when she was much younger, my mother knew Sir Geoffrey Ryland well. I was told that they were close at one time. I thought that perhaps Eleanor Ryland might have known my mother too. I went to talk to her.'

'Two days before she was found dead?'

'What can I say? It was unfortunate timing. I had nothing to do with her death, I promise you.'

'I'm relieved to hear it.'

'She was alive and well when I left her. She gave me tea, we talked for about an hour, then I left and walked back to my car.'

'Only I would prefer not to have one of my senior officers arrested for murder during my last week,' Coleman said, with feeling.

'Yes sir.'

On the surface, Coleman sounded unworried, but it was a forced cheerfulness. The fact that Mariner was being called as a significant witness meant that his Thames Valley colleagues had nothing incriminating on him. All it meant was that they could place him at the scene before Eleanor died. If they'd had any stronger evidence he would be in custody already. A police officer as a suspect in a murder case would be hung out to dry. All the same, Mariner couldn't help wondering if Coleman knew something that he didn't.

'And what about the CPS?' Coleman was asking.

'Sorry sir?'

'The CPS. Isn't that where you've been for the last two days?'

Shit! In his hurry to get out of London Mariner had

completely forgotten to return to the CPS for the report. 'They're sending something through in the morning,' he lied. 'It wasn't quite ready when I left, but I gave them a kick up the backside. I think my being there in person has moved things along.' He'd have to ring first tomorrow to ensure that it happened.

'Good.'

But Mariner rang off with a sense of foreboding. Unpacking his things he came across the envelope Flynn had given him, the proof in black and white that he was Sir Geoffrey Ryland's son. He opened it and stared at the piece of paper for a long time, so small in substance yet so significant in its content. Also in the envelope was another document. Two sheets of A4 stapled together. It was a summary of the crime scene report from Cheslyn Woods. A peace offering from Flynn, though there was little here that hadn't already been covered by the press; a mention of the message written on the window, and a note at the bottom describing a tracking device that had been found on Ryland's car.

With trepidation Mariner retrieved from his own vehicle the compact piece of hardware that Carl had given him. The name and model number were identical. It increased the odds that whoever had been monitoring Sir Geoffrey Ryland had done the same to Mariner. And he couldn't help but recall who it was who'd studied electronics while in Chapel Wood prison; Rupert Foster-Young. Mariner needed to speak to a friend.

Selina answered the phone sounding less like her bright, usual self and there must have been something in that because Knox declined Mariner's invitation. 'We've got other plans tonight,' he said enigmatically. 'But have a pint of M&B for me, will you?'

'I will, though it'll have to be Banks's,' said Mariner. 'I'm going to the Boatman.' Forty-five minutes later Mariner looked up from his corner seat to see Knox walk into the bar.

*

Tony Knox entered the bar of the Boatman feeling as guilty as if he was bunking off school. Mariner looked rough, and his reaction confirmed what he'd surmised on the phone, that there was more to this than just a drink. The boss looked desperately relieved to see him. The feeling was mutual.

'You changed your mind,' Mariner said.

Knox checked his watch. 'I haven't got long. I've dropped Selina off at her friend's. She's going to call me when she wants picking up, so I'll need to get home.' And he hadn't told her he was meeting Mariner. He hadn't dared.

Mariner picked up on the anxiety straightaway. 'Everything all right?'

'Just a bit tired, that's all.' Knox hoped that would cover it.

It must have because Mariner backed off. 'I'll get you a pint. The Wadsworth's is good tonight.'

'No. I'm not drinking. I'll have a tomato juice.'

'What's this, national abstinence day?'

'I'm not planning on it tomorrow either, or the next day, if I can do it.'

'Christ, what's brought this on?'

'I was getting too used to it, the same way I did when Theresa first left,' Knox said, smoothly.

'You've always kept it under control.'

'No, I just made it look that way. Selina doesn't need that right now.' She'd made that perfectly clear, he'd the bruises on his ribs to prove it. And he wasn't going to take that risk.

'Well it explains the twitching,' Mariner grinned, drawing his own conclusions. 'Tomato juice it is.'

Knox launched in as soon as Mariner returned with the drinks. He hadn't much time. 'So what's all this about?' he asked.

'What do you mean?'

'This isn't just a casual drink, is it? And you look like shit.'

'Thanks,' said Mariner. 'Your copper's intuition eh?'

No, thought Knox grimly, the insight of someone else who's got something to hide. 'You should know,' he said.

'I've found out who my father was.'

Knox thought he'd already guessed what was up: that Anna was pregnant, or worse, that she'd left Mariner. But never in a million years, that. It snatched the breath from him.

'Fucking Nora,' he said, eventually. 'When did this happen?'

'You remember that guy I told you about, Dave Flynn?'

'The one on the Ryland investigation?'

'Yes. Well that's what he came to tell me; that Sir Geoffrey Ryland was my father.'

'Ryland?' This got better and better. The boss was having some kind of a breakdown. Suddenly Knox didn't know how to play it. 'How's that even possible?' he asked calmly.

Mariner gave a sardonic laugh. 'It's all right, I know how it sounds, my father a national icon. It's like the reincarnation nutters who always turn out to have been Marie Antoinette or Florence Nightingale in a previous life. But it all fits. I was aware that back then my mother moved in the same social circles. And I've got the DNA results to substantiate it.'

'Christ Almighty.' Mariner sounded perfectly rational. Knox had no choice but to believe him.

'Anyway, when I found out I couldn't help it. I wanted to know more about why he'd been killed.'

'Even though there are people already doing that job,' he said. 'Why does that not surprise me?'

'And the more I started digging around the less satisfied I was with the explanations being given.'

'But I thought it was clear cut.' Knox had read the newspaper reports. 'The chauffeur was the intended target, Ryland and his wife were unfortunate bystanders.'

'Because that's what you were meant to think. But right from the start there's been something funny going on. Dave practically admitted it to me. The Met just seem to be using

234

the incident as an opportunity to indict one of the biggest drug operators in the area, regardless of who might really have committed the crime. At first I thought it could be the Home Office trying to suppress Ryland's second volume of memoirs. Then I found out that he was building a case against two long-serving Met officers who would have wanted him and O'Connor out of the way. But now I think it's more likely that it's Ryland's other illegitimate son, Rupert Foster-Young, who was behind the killings. He had the motive and the opportunity and he's disappeared off the face of the planet.' Mariner described what had happened when he was in London. 'Someone was after me, I know they were. And now Eleanor Ryland has been killed and the police think I did it. Whoever it is knew that I was there on that Saturday—' Mariner broke off. 'Don't look at me like that.'

'Like what?'

'It's the look you reserve for the care-in-the-community freaks.'

'What do you expect?' Knox defended himself. He could barely take it all in. 'You have been doing well on your own, haven't you?' he said. 'Anna must be going apeshit.'

'Anna doesn't know.'

Just lately Knox considered himself to be a master of discretion, but the boss was something else. 'Which bit doesn't she know?'

'Any of it.'

He was unbelievable. 'Not even about your dad? We've had this conversation before. Why can't you open your mouth and talk to people, like everyone else does?' Present company excepted, of course.

'I had to sort it out in my own head first.'

'Well you're really on track with that, aren't you? Where does Eleanor Ryland come into this?'

'She was my grandmother.'

'That I'd worked out for myself.'

'I went to see her a couple of times, including last

235

weekend. Shortly afterwards she was found dead.'

'It's what most people would call a coincidence.'

'Except that Thames Valley police have got a reporter who says he saw me arrive at the house just before the TOD.'

'But he didn't?'

'I didn't see any journalists that afternoon. In fact I made that very remark to Eleanor.'

'But you were there?'

'Not at the time she died. I think I'm being fitted up.'

'By Sir Geoffrey Ryland's *other* illegitimate son.' Knox had struggled like this at school, with Shakespeare. 'How much have you told the DCI?'

'Thames Valley contacted him, so I had to come clean about knowing Eleanor Ryland. I didn't specify the relationship. Like I said, I wanted to try and make sense of it before telling anyone.'

'And you chose me. I'm flattered.'

'At one point I thought some of Coleman's former colleagues might somehow be involved.'

'What?'

'I'm pretty sure now that they're not, but there's something going on. I just haven't fully worked it out yet.'

Knox watched Mariner rub a hand over his face, making contact with about two days' beard growth. 'You look fucking awful,' he said. 'When's the last time you slept properly?'

'You don't look so great yourself.'

'You can rule out one conspiracy, anyway,' Knox said, wriggling out from under that one.

'Why's that?'

'The St Martin's explosion.' Knox was surprised that the boss hadn't already heard. It had been the hot topic round the station all day. 'You'll never fucking believe who was behind it.'

'Try me.' The tension in Mariner's voice was palpable.

'Adolf Hitler.'

236

'What do you mean?'

'It was a UXB.'

'A what?'

'A World War Two unexploded bomb. All the building work on the new Bullring must have disturbed it. Nothing to do with you, unless Herr Hitler was blessed with tremendous insight.'

'So why all the secrecy?'

Knox had asked the same question when the news had broken. 'They were scared that there might be more,' he said, passing on what he'd been told. 'The building contractors did the mandatory searches of the new sites, but no one took responsibility for the existing public buildings. They waited to release any details until they could categorically state that everywhere else was safe.'

'The grey Transit vans,' said Mariner.

Now what was he on about?

'Haven't you noticed those grey Transit vans all over the city the last few weeks? That must be what—'

Knox's mobile rang and he jumped as if he'd been stung. 'Selina,' he said to Mariner, checking caller identity. Of course it was. Shit! Listening to Mariner rabbitting on he'd completely lost track of time. Now he was going to have some explaining to do. 'I've got to go.' Knocking back the tomato juice, he pushed back his chair.

Mariner was regarding him curiously. 'Don't tell Anna any of this,' he said. ' or Selina.'

'Anna needs to—' Knox began.

'Don't!'

'Okay.' And, his own storm clouds gathering, Knox backed out of the pub.

Left alone in the bar, Mariner felt as if the world was getting smaller and beginning to close in on him. He'd hoped that telling Knox would have been some kind of release, but it wasn't. It didn't help that Knox was so obviously infatuated with Selina. Mariner could understand him feeling some responsibility for her situation, but even so. It was unlike Knox to let a woman get to him that much.

So the explosion was down to the Third Reich. That's why Special Branch treated his letter so casually. They knew full well what had caused the explosion and it had nothing to do with him. He'd been convinced at the time that it was. The feeling of being followed, the composite letter, he was so sure it was all for him. If he could be so very wrong about that, was he wrong about Ryland too? Maybe Dave Flynn wasn't so far off the mark. Maybe it was all in his imagination, his mind fabricating a conspiracy where there was none.

Unable to face Anna, he went back to his place and spent a restless night. He was up early, showered and shaved and dressed in a clean suit. Then he drove down the motorway to be questioned in a murder enquiry.

Chapter Seventeen

The police station was a 1970s cinderblock cube, cheerless and featureless. It felt weird being on the 'wrong' side of the table, though it wasn't the first time in Mariner's life. In his late teens it had been a regular occurrence, though he'd always walked. So far this morning everyone seemed friendly enough. 'Could you tell us what time on January 24th you visited Mrs Eleanor Ryland at her home in Oxfordshire?' His interrogator was an Asian officer, DC Anil Singh. His colleague, young, blond and ruddy-faced sat silently beside him.

'It was about two in the afternoon.'

'You walked there from the Lygon Arms,' Singh consulted his notes.

'That's right. Along the Oxfordshire Way.'

'What time did you leave the pub?'

'About one o'clock.'

'It's a five and a half mile walk. You got there pretty fast.'

'I walk pretty fast.'

'How long did you stay?'

'I'm not sure. About an hour, hour and a half?'

'Not long then,' Singh observed.

'I wanted to get back to my car before it got dark.'

'And what did you talk about with Mrs Ryland?'

'Personal stuff,' said Mariner. 'I was asking her about Sir Geoffrey.'

'Who you recently learned was your father.' Flynn must have told them. 'So you got there at about two and left at around three thirty. You can be certain about that timing?'

'Yes, why?'

'We have one of two witnesses who says you didn't leave the pub until nearly two.'

'What witness?'

'One of the regulars at the Lygon Arms.' The man at the bar. 'Said you had a conversation with him.'

'If you can call it that. And the other witness?'

'A journalist. According to him you called out a greeting as you arrived.' He consulted his notes. 'You were seen to turn and wave and call out "Don't get excited, I'm only family." This was around four.'

'Well, he's mistaken. It wasn't me.'

'He saw you go into the house, but didn't see you come out again. Of course it would have been dark by then, so he could easily have missed you.'

'I told you nobody saw me go in or out. There was no one there. In fact I remarked on that very thing to Eleanor Ryland; the reporters weren't there. She said they were in the pub and that they'd be back later.'

'Really?' Singh's voice dripped cynicism. 'What were you wearing that day?'

It was a standard question and Mariner had searched his memory. 'A dark-blue Berghaus jacket, black gloves, dark-grey trousers, grey walking boots.'

'It was a cold day. Nothing to keep your ears warm?'

'I had a hat with me but it was in my pocket.'

'This is the description we have.' He pushed a piece of paper towards Mariner. It was word for word what he'd said, but for the make of jacket and the hat, which he was meant to have been wearing.

'I didn't even go in through the main gate. I walked to the house from the village along the public footpath. It takes you onto the property from the side, over a stile.'

'At last there's something we're agreed on,' said Singh.

'That's what the journalist says too. And as you walked across in front of the house you turned by the door, waved and called out.'

'I'd have been thirty metres away. How can they be so sure it was me?'

'That's why long lens cameras are helpful.'

'How precise is your TOD?' Mariner queried.

'We'll ask the questions if it's all right with you.'

'I've been told she wasn't found until Monday morning, so it can't be that accurate.'

'But you're the only person known to have visited the house during the weekend.'

'There must have been plenty of time when the house was unobserved.'

'There was no sign of forced entry either, implying that the killer had a key.' Singh raised an eyebrow.

'We only met a couple of weeks ago,' said Mariner.

'Or that it was someone she knew. She let him in.'

But they could still only question him as a significant witness.

'What's my motive?' Mariner asked. 'I've only just found out that Eleanor Ryland was my grandmother. She's the only real family I've got. Why would I kill her?'

The two detectives exchanged a look and DC Singh slid another document across the table, this time packaged in polythene. 'For the tape, I'm showing DI Mariner exhibit 1A.' He gave Mariner a few seconds to look at it. The first thing Mariner caught was the heading: *Last Will and Testament*. His vision blurred. Shit.

'Were you aware that you're named as a significant beneficiary in Eleanor Ryland's will?'

'No.'

'We found this in her safe. You can see how it looks. Diana Ryland was the one with all the wealth, but on her death it went to her husband, then because his mother outlived him, it reverted to her. Did she take much persuading?'

'That's nonsense. I had no knowledge of this will.' They couldn't prove that he did. He was being baited.

'What are your present personal circumstances, Inspector?'

'What do you mean?'

'I understand you and your partner are planning a family. And your partner already has one dependant who needs expensive residential care.'

How the hell? 'I don't see what that's got to do with—'

'Expensive things, babies. I can tell you that for a fact.'

'This is ridiculous. I only found out a few weeks ago that I'm even related to Sir Geoffrey Ryland. How could I possibly know anything about this will? And I don't need the money.'

'You've met with Eleanor Ryland before, on 5th January. What did you talk about on that occasion?'

'Not that, I can assure you.'

'Look at the date on the bottom of the document.'

Mariner did. It had been signed and dated two weeks ago, two days after his first meeting with Eleanor.

'I have to admire your speed,' said Singh. 'But then, she'd have been in a nice vulnerable state, wouldn't she? I'm sorry you've just lost your son, but here I am, a ready-made grandson. Sign on the dotted line.'

Anger and fear boiled up and incensed, Mariner lunged for Singh.

'And I really don't think that's going to help either. Didn't you ask Mrs Ryland on your first visit about when she was alone in the house? The cook overheard a conversation to that effect and later saw you checking how secure the building was. You knew that at that time on a Saturday afternoon there would be nobody else there. Some might view that as preparation.'

'It was conversation, that's all. For Christ's sake. I was concerned about security for precisely this reason. I'm an experienced copper. If I was going to pull a stunt like this, don't you think I might have been a bit more subtle?'

Singh was thoughtful. 'We did wonder about that. But we've talked to a couple of people, friends of yours, who say that you're under a lot of strain at the moment and you're not behaving at all like your usual self.'

'This is making me feel a whole lot better.'

'We can't ignore what was there.' Singh was only doing his job.

Resignation took over. 'No,' said Mariner. He decided to take a chance. 'I'm not the only who thinks he's a son and heir you know.'

They clearly didn't. 'What's that supposed to mean?'

'Back in the sixties Ryland was engaged to a woman called Caroline Foster-Young. She had a child and was convinced that Geoffrey Ryland was the father.' He told them what he knew about Rupert Foster-Young. This was where the ice thinned out, but Mariner was past caring.

'He spread it around, your old man, didn't he?' The two detectives were doubtful.

'Foster-Young has a prison record, for aggravated burglary,' Mariner persisted. 'When he got out he harassed Ryland for money. He turned up at the JRC demanding to see him.'

'Do you know where this man is?'

'That's the other thing. He's disappeared.'

'How convenient for you.' They didn't believe him, but they took down Foster-Young's address anyway. Then they let Mariner go, which made him realise that the only evidence they had was circumstantial. But it was still pretty strong stuff and they wouldn't give up on him yet.

Eleanor Ryland's will, he had noticed, was stamped with the solicitor's name and address. The office was in a nearby town. Mariner had to kick his heels for forty-five waiting to see Peter Donovan but considered it worthwhile.

'You went to Eleanor Ryland's house to witness the change of will. When did she make that appointment?'

'I can't really be sure when she *arranged* it. We don't record that kind of detail.'

243

'Approximately. Was it before Christmas or after?'

'Oh, I'm pretty sure it was before.'

'You're certain about that?'

'As much as I can be.'

'So it was shortly after Sir Geoffrey Ryland was killed.'

'Yes, that was the purpose of the visit. When I saw the news I'd been expecting it.'

And it was also well before Mariner's visit. Singh and his cronies hadn't covered that. It wasn't much but it might count in his favour if things got tight.

Checking his mobile Mariner found a couple of messages. The first was from Dave Flynn. Mariner didn't return it. After all that the Oxfordshire police knew, he couldn't decide whose side Flynn was on any more. The other message was from Rupert Foster-Young's neighbour. It was short and to the point. 'You wanted to know when Rob came home, well he's back now.'

Mariner was weary of driving but he had little choice. He had to try again. Leaving his car at Cockfosters tube station, he travelled back into London. The man who answered the door of Rupert Foster-Young's flat presented a very different picture from the six by eight Mariner had seen and momentarily he thought there must be a roommate. Either that or it crossed his mind that Lauren's mother could have installed a decoy to take the heat off her erstwhile babysitter.

Barefoot, in jeans and a crisp white T-shirt, the man before him glowed with health, the paranoid defensiveness traded, in the flesh, with an open and friendly demeanor.

'Detective Inspector Mariner,' Mariner said. 'I was hoping to talk to Rupert Foster-Young.'

'Rob,' came back the correction 'That's me.' But for all the outward relaxation, suspicion lurked just below the surface, the door closed a couple of inches and the shoulders tensed. It was something that lingered with ex-cons. 'Is there a problem?'

'Not at all.' Mariner remained casual. 'I'm looking into the death of Sir Geoffrey Ryland. I know that he and your mother were friends once. I'm exploring the possibility of any throwback to that time—'

Foster-Young grinned, sheepishly, the tension leaving him. 'Ah. You found out that I'd been harassing him.'

His frankness caught Mariner off guard. 'Someone at the JRC told me about your appeal application, yes.'

Foster-Young stepped back from the door. 'Do you want to come in? I was just making a cuppa.'

'Thanks.' Mariner was thrown by the unexpected hospitality. He followed Foster-Young through a tiny hallway and into a homely, if untidy lounge. A couple of suit-cases lay open on the floor, their contents overflowing. 'Sorry about the mess,' Foster-Young said, without much hint of apology. 'I just got back.' He continued into the kitchen, leaving Mariner in the living room where a pass-port and other travel documentation lay on the table. While Foster-Young was occupied Mariner sneaked a look. It confirmed Foster-Young's identity. Mariner was still staring at the passport when his host returned with two mugs.

'Sorry to be nosey,' Mariner said, putting down the pass-port. 'It's just that the photograph on your prison records— You've changed a lot.'

'For the better I hope,' said Foster-Young, passing over a mug which contained an unusual coloured beverage. 'I was in a bit of a state at that time,' he went on. 'And my mother had been feeding me all kinds of nonsense that Sir Geoffrey Ryland was my father.'

'That's why you went after him when you got out.' Mariner registered a word Foster-Young had used. 'You said "nonsense".' he queried.

'It was total crap apparently. When she died, my mother left me a letter, admitting that she really hadn't a clue who my dad was. It could have been one of several guys but not Ryland. She'd never slept with him. When I pushed Ryland

245

on it he even offered to take a paternity test. I figured that was proof enough.'

'He could have been bluffing.'

'He wasn't. That's when I stopped harassing people and decided to get my life together.'

Mariner was stunned, and more than a little disappointed. The irony of the situation struck him too. Foster-Young had grown up under the misapprehension that Geoffrey Ryland was his father, while he, Mariner, Ryland's real son, had lived in ignorance for all these years.

'My mother was a very mixed-up woman,' Foster-Young went on. 'A living product of the age of free love. She wasn't very good at looking after herself, so my arrival on the scene didn't help much. Responsibility was never her forte.'

'So she picked on Geoffrey Ryland.'

'They were officially dating at that time, so I guess he was the obvious choice. But he wasn't the only one she blamed.'

'Norman Balfour.'

'Poor old Norman. Yes, his name came up too. He's a priest now, you know. I found him and gave him a really hard time over it, thought he'd be a soft touch. I was a mess back then, having inherited my mother's liking for intoxicating substances. I've cleaned up my act a bit since then.'

'So I see. You've been abroad?'

'The US. I've got family there.'

'Of course. You had a good trip?' Mariner asked, regretting the choice of words.

Foster-Young seemed not to notice. 'Fantastic,' he said. 'I met them all. They'd pretty much disowned my mother so I didn't know how they'd take to the bastard son, but they were brilliant. They made me feel very welcome. Times have changed, eh?'

'Did your mother often talk about Sir Geoffrey Ryland?'

'I wouldn't say often. It was usually when she was drunk or high. Half the problem was I think she really loved him. She wanted me to be his son. And as for Diana Ryland—' He held up crossed fingers as if warding off evil.

'She didn't like her?'

'The woman had usurped her position.'

'Did she ever say why that had happened?'

'Not specifically. She used to say that Diana and Geoff deserved each other. I guess because they came from the same "establishment" background and my mother didn't. She always resented the English class system, couldn't stand it. Used to say that Diana wasn't the little miss pathetic everyone made out she was. Mum was more of free spirit. Unconventional. It didn't suit Ryland's political ambitions. Obviously an astute guy. She'd have been a nightmare.' His face creased to a frown. 'Would all this really have impacted now?'

'We're just being thorough.'

Foster-Young drank the last of his tea, noticing Mariner's still untouched. 'Sorry, I forgot that green tea isn't to everyone's taste.' He relieved Mariner of the mug. 'Well, the whole thing's a shame. Ryland seemed like a nice guy. I don't suppose I've been much help.'

'Any background is useful, thanks. We like to build up a full picture.' Mariner was embarrassed about being there now. 'Oh, and you might get a call from the Thames Valley police. Similar kind of background stuff. When did you get back into the country?'

'Yesterday.'

'Then you've got nothing to worry about.' Lucky man.

Mariner left Foster-Young's flat feeling despondent. Foster-Young clearly wasn't involved. Quite apart from anything else, from before the shootings until a couple of days ago he'd been on the other side of the Atlantic. So where did that leave Mariner? The walk back to the tube station was a long one. All the work, all the running back and forth to London and Oxfordshire, the brushes with

247

death, what had it all been for? And what had been achieved? It had become an obsession, but one he found he couldn't give up. What lay behind the killings wasn't just drugs, he was certain of that. Somewhere there had to be something vital he'd overlooked.

Driving back to Birmingham, Mariner tried to work out what it could be that he'd missed. If he tracked it right back to the beginning, it had started before the bombing, that feeling of being watched, except that he'd no hard evidence of that especially now that Robert Foster-Young was out of the picture. The bomb itself could be discounted too, except that someone had taken advantage of it by sending him a threatening note. Was that merely one of his past adversaries making the most of the situation? It wasn't impossible. There were enough of them to choose from.

Then, almost immediately after that, Dave Flynn had shown up. So far, so unremarkable. Things had really begun to get out of hand when he'd first gone to London, digging into Ryland's work at the JRC. Somebody knew he was there, had known where he was staying, and also had access to his mobile number. They must have followed his research as it progressed to Rupert Foster-Young, and witnessed his visits to Eleanor, enough to be able to fit him up. But who could possibly have known all of that? He'd even kept Anna in the dark these past couple of weeks. The tracking device in the car would have helped his pursuer to some extent, but there were times when he'd taken to public transport and the period when his car was off the road all together. Despite all that, someone, somewhere was managing to stalk him. But who the hell could it be?

Dave Flynn was the only one who had been in on this from the start, and also had the resources to follow Mariner. Perhaps that's even why Dave had been brought in to begin with. He'd warned Mariner not to get involved but at the same time knowing that Mariner wouldn't be able to resist a challenge. Maybe Dave was also being used.

Maybe those photographs were a weird coincidence? Mariner still only had Flynn's word for it that they'd been found in Ryland's possession, and it was Flynn who had arranged the DNA test. What if the whole thing was a set up? And if so, what was the point, other than to land Mariner in hot water?

If Ryland was his father then he owed it to the old man to find out exactly what had happened, but suddenly the burden of that responsibility felt overwhelming.

When he reached Anna's house in the late afternoon she was already home.

'Good day?' she asked.

'Fine, thanks.' She would assume that he'd been at the station all day. 'How's Jamie been?'

'He's okay. We need to be at the QE by nine fifteen tomorrow so I've arranged for the centre to collect him on transport.'

The dreaded appointment. Mariner didn't know why they were still going through with this. The urgency of them having children seemed to have diminished and suddenly this seemed to be more about Anna's future than theirs, but then, whose fault was that?

'You still want to go?' he asked.

She looked across at him. 'Why wouldn't we?'

'It's just – things have changed.'

'Like what?' She was challenging him to come out and say it, that what they'd had was gone.

But as usual he ducked it. 'The situation with Jamie for one,' he said. 'What if he's still with us when the baby is born? How will he take to that, and how could we manage Jamie and a baby?'

'That's at least nine months away, even if we got down to it right this minute. And I told you. I'm working on Jamie.' She walked over to him, taking his hands in hers. 'We've been through all this before. Just because you haven't had first-hand experience of fatherhood doesn't

249

mean you can't learn it. And we'd be in it together. You were sure about this once. What's this really about?'

How could he tell her that the weight of the responsibility was too great, that there were so many people he'd already let down, that he couldn't bear the thought of doing it again?

'A lot has happened,' he said, lamely.

'You mean the bomb. I know. The world is a dangerous place. You're up against it every day. We can't let something like that stop us. Is this why you've gone all distant on me?'

'What do you mean?'

'Since Christmas you've hardly been here, and even when you are, you're not. If you don't want to go through with this now would be a good time to say.'

'I just think the timing is all wrong.'

She studied him for a moment. 'Will the timing ever be right?'

'Truthfully? I don't know.'

'We're only going for advice. There's nothing to lose, is there?'

She was right. It was nothing that they hadn't just lost in the last few minutes.

Anna was nervous. As they sat in the plush waiting room at the Queen Elizabeth Hospital, she was too chatty and laughed too easily. Having Jamie back home these last few days had brought the implications into sharp focus and despite her optimism Mariner knew that if the odds of their child having autism were too high she wouldn't take the risk. Secretly, Mariner was glad.

Dr Chang bombarded them with science, then spent more than an hour asking questions about Jamie, his diagnosis and about Anna's extended family, all the while taking extensive notes.

'And what about you Mr Mariner? Is there any history of autism in your family?'

'I don't really know,' Mariner said. 'On my mother's side I'm fairly certain not.'

'And your father's?'

Mariner considered what he'd read about Ryland, what he knew about him. To operate successfully in the world that he had, the man had to have finely honed social skills. 'I don't think so.'

Anna turned sharply. 'But you don't know for sure, do you? Tom's never known his father.'

The consultant glanced at Mariner for clarification.

'That's right, I don't know,' Mariner obliged, convincing himself that technically he was telling the truth. He couldn't possibly know that about Ryland.

Having taken family history details Dr Chang then talked a lot about statistics. Research into autism was still relatively new and there were a lot of unknowns. 'There are, however, clear genetic links, although at present it's not clear exactly how they work. It certainly is not inevitable that any child you have will have autistic spectrum difficulties. In real terms the chances are small, around three per cent, and you're already ahead of the game. The knowledge that your child may have a predisposition is invaluable. There are lots of things you can do with the new baby to minimise the chances of the disorder developing. And of course if you didn't want to take that risk there are other options open to you, such as adoption.'

'So is that good news or bad?' Mariner asked tentatively as they emerged. They were trying to make light of it.

'It's what I expected.' He could hear her disappointment. 'The risk is there all right, isn't it?'

'But it's reduced if we're vigilant after the baby is born. And I suppose we could always go down the adoption route.'

'But he didn't advise against us having a family.'

'That's not his job,' said Mariner, gently. 'All he is meant to do is present the information to us. The decision is ours.'

'So we need to decide.' But over the last weeks, it seemed have evolved into a different decision.

Chapter Eighteen

In the afternoon Mariner went back to work.

'We've had a breakthrough,' Charlie Glover said.

Mariner instantly thought of Ryland, but of course Glover was talking about Alecsander Lucca. 'The CPS have given the go-ahead to apply for extradition. They're starting negotiations with Albanian officials. Your trip down to London must have done the trick.'

'That's great,' said Mariner, absently, his mind very elsewhere. He didn't like to tell Glover that the negotiations could take months. He retreated to his office, but a couple of minutes later Tony Knox put in an appearance.

'How did it go?' he asked.

'What?'

'The appointment.'

'It was interesting.'

'So you're going ahead with it?'

Mariner was feeling sorry for himself. 'It's such a big change. I don't know if I can handle it.'

'Changes happen to everyone whether they like it or not,' said Knox irritably. 'Sometimes you have to just grit your teeth and get on with it.' And he stomped out again.

Even though he'd run out of leads, Mariner couldn't stop thinking about Ryland. Perhaps he'd been wrong about those cash payments and Ryland really had been involved in some kind of gambling racket. But in every other respect it just didn't fit. He'd uncovered no other evidence that related to it, and Norman Balfour had stated categorically that Ryland wasn't a gambler. And if he was involved in some kind of dubious business venture, why involve Sandie? No, Mariner was convinced now that those payments were down to blackmail. But with Rupert Foster-Young out of the picture there were no other candidates.

Nor had Mariner exposed any other Achilles heel that a potential blackmailer could take advantage of. Ryland had no other weak spots, unless he'd committed some kind of impropriety at the Commission. But, according to all those who knew him, the man was overloaded with integrity. He was a brilliant politician but had not fulfilled his potential, turning down a government office for what was largely an administration post at the JRC. The job needed a political heavyweight because there were some difficult waters to navigate, but Ryland could do it with his eyes closed. Starting out in politics his ambitions were such that he'd made a very careful and precise choice of partner, and when things had got tough for her he'd abandoned his career plan to support her through illness.

That illness. Most of what Mariner had learned about Diana Ryland pertained to her frail mental state. It wasn't publicly known and yet everyone he'd spoken to about her had mentioned it. Euphemistically of course – Diana was fragile or delicate, but Mariner couldn't help wondering how that delicacy manifested itself. He'd had taken it to mean that she was easily stressed, highly strung, but what if it were something more? Norman Balfour had cited her poor health as the reason why the Rylands hadn't had children. And it was recurrent problem, from the breakdown in her student days up until the time of Rose's funeral. *'Diana was unwell again, the past coming back to haunt them in other ways,'* Eleanor Ryland had said.

Dave Flynn had talked about the quantity of valium they'd found at the Ryland's house. And valium could be addictive. Was this the skeleton in the Ryland cupboard, that Diana Ryland had a drug dependency problem? Ryland was his wife's guardian, but what lengths would he go to in order to protect her from publicity about her illness. Would he go as far as submitting to blackmail?

Mariner needed to find out more about Diana. Norman Balfour would, he felt, be of little help. He was, by his own admission, a friend and would be more likely to shield her memory from unfavourable publicity. The person who might be more honest was the frank-talking Fliss, and Mariner regretted not finding out where she was staying. Fortunately for him the animal rescue centre had contact details and directed him to a country hotel not far from Eleanor's house. Ringing reception, Mariner was put through to her room. 'Ms Fitzgibbon, this is Tom Mariner. We met at the animal rescue centre.'

'You've decided to take Nelson?' She was delighted.

'No. I'm sorry. Ms Fitzgibbon I didn't just happen on you that day. I'd planned to speak to you.'

'Oh?' She was intrigued, not surprised.

'You're not in any danger. It's just ... I'm Sir Geoffrey Ryland's illegitimate son.'

Silence at the other end of the phone. Mariner was beginning to get used to these many and varied reactions. 'I know it must be a shock. But believe me, it's true. I've DNA proof.'

'Well, well. I knew you existed.'

'You did?'

'You were one of the family's best kept secrets.'

'I'm also a police officer and I've been, unofficially, looking into his death and your sister's. I'm feel certain that something has been overlooked.'

'Like what?'

'I don't know yet, but I'm just trying to cover everything. I wanted to ask you about your sister's health. Is there somewhere we could meet?'

'Why don't you come here for dinner?'

*

254

When they met early that evening in the plush restaurant of the hotel, Mariner could see that Fliss Fitzgibbon was looking at him differently. 'My nephew,' she said, 'by marriage, anyway. How strange to meet you after all this time. 'When did you learn that Geoff was your father?'

'A few weeks ago.'

'Do you hate him?'

Mariner replied carefully. 'It's one of the emotions I've experienced during the last few weeks. I can't deny it. But now I just think he was a victim of his time, manipulated by people he thought were older and wiser.'

'That's one way of looking at it. Shall we eat?'

It was the kind of country hotel specialising in the accommodation of wealthy tourists, where the food was beautifully arranged but left Mariner still hungry. Despite that, the restaurant was doing a brisk business.

'I'm not sure that there's much I can tell you about Diana,' said Fliss Fitzgibbon, when they had ordered. 'At least, nothing that would be relevant to how she and Geoff were killed.'

'I'm just trying to piece things together, and Diana's illness is something that everyone mentions, but no one talks about, if you see what I mean.'

She gave a light laugh. 'You've got that exactly right,' she said. 'But I don't see how—'

'I think Sir Geoffrey was being blackmailed,' Mariner said.

'Blackmail? That's quite an assertion to make.'

'Over a period of eighteen months Sir Geoffrey was making regular cash payments to an unknown person or persons, or rather his assistant was on his behalf. It was done in the guise of a betting scam.'

'Geoff wasn't a gambling man.'

'So I've been told, which is one of the things that makes me believe it was blackmail. The arrangement was causing him some distress, and he tried unsuccessfully to end it just the week before he was killed. It's possible that it was related to Diana's illness, though I'm not yet sure how.'

'Diana would have been so ashamed for people to know about her problems. Mental illness is the last taboo, don't you think? Geoff would have done anything to protect her from that.'

'That's what I thought. I know this may be painful, but what can you tell me about it?'

'Even I don't know all the details. We're going back a long way. Things first came to a head when I was about nine, it would have been the summer of 1962, although Diana hadn't been herself for some time before that. It was university that seemed to do it. Diana did well at school. She wasn't a brilliant scholar but she pushed herself hard and got into Oxford to study law.'

'I didn't know that.'

'Not many people do. My parents, especially my father, were incredibly proud of her. But she didn't stay the course. She came home again before the end of her first term. I don't know if she couldn't keep up academically or if she simply couldn't cope with the rough and tumble of student life. Whatever it was, it had destroyed her confidence. After that she seemed to get very depressed, crying at the slightest thing. I think she felt she had let everyone down.

'I was away at boarding school by then, and whereas on previous holidays I'd had a good time with my big sister, suddenly we were all treading on eggshells around her. Selfish little brat that I was, I merely felt resentful that Dizzy was no fun any more. I remember those particular Christmas and Easter holidays vividly. Easter was especially bad. Then shortly after that she had a complete breakdown. Not that I witnessed anything. I was back at school.' A single tear broke loose and ran down her cheek.

'I'm sorry,' Mariner said. 'If this is too upsetting—'

She took a deep breath. 'No, it's fine. When I got home for the summer Diz wasn't there. She'd been sent away to the country to recuperate. Later I learned that she'd tried to take her own life. It was hushed up of course and never talked about at the time. Any kind of mental illness wasn't something families, especially our kind of family, admitted to. A few months after that my father died of a heart attack. Family lore has it that it was brought on by the stress of what had happened to Dizzy, but either way it was a horrible time for us and, even if it wasn't true, I know she blamed herself. The next time I saw her was at Daddy's funeral and I hardly recognised her. She was wasting away before our eyes, like those anorexic girls you see in the papers. Then in a matter of months she had met Geoffrey and they were planning to get married. Geoff literally saved her life.'

'And did Diana have any further episodes?'

'Yes. She went through a bad patch just before Geoff resigned as an MP. Dizzy was always prone to depression, and she always wore long sleeves.'

That significance was lost on Mariner and his face must have betrayed him.

'When she couldn't cope she used to cut herself,' Fliss said. 'Poor Diana, she was so sweet and gentle. Too good for this world really.'

'Do you remember any recent recurrences?' Mariner asked, thinking that the wine they were drinking seemed exceptionally strong. His head felt slightly detached from the rest of him. It was very warm in here, too. He loosened his tie.

'I think something might have happened last summer, about eighteen months ago. I was planning to come over for a visit, but quite suddenly Geoff called and asked me to postpone.'

'Have you any idea what it was?'

'It sounded serious. Geoff said that Dizzy wasn't up to receiving visitors. It crossed my mind that she may have attempted suicide again, though I don't know why. Not something that Geoff would have wanted broadcast, especially in the position he was in by then. It would have made him politically vulnerable. By the law of statistics there must be hundreds of people in public life who are affected by mental illness in some form or another, but it's rarely talked about, is it? I sometimes wonder if Diana would have been helped if they'd started a family. I'm sure it would have taken her mind off things, and she loved children.' It was a different opinion from Norman Balfour. Mariner wondered who was most accurate.

'Diana took medication for her illness,' he said. 'Is it possible that she could have developed a drug dependency problem, on prescription drugs I mean?'

'She was on medication for a long time, never went anywhere without her little green bag.'

As Mariner had surmised, it would have been easy to exploit Diana's illness for financial gain. Not everyone was thrilled about what Ryland was doing at the Commission. Perhaps someone was hoping to use it as a way of getting him out, too. But who else knew about her condition? Even Diana's own sister's knowledge was sketchy. There would be medical records of any treatment she had received in the past, and Diana would have been treated by a team of medical professionals while she was ill. Had one of them seen an opportunity for extortion, or been got at by someone who did?

'Do you know where Diana went to recuperate when she was first ill?'

'I don't think I was ever told. All I recall is that it was in the country where the clean air would be beneficial to her health. I think it was somehow church related too, like some religious retreat. Our Lady of Lourdes is something that comes back to me but I might be off beam with that. Norman might know of course.' Their main course arrived, but the fleshy slices of duck, swimming in crimson plum sauce made Mariner feel slightly queasy. 'So there you have it, the dirty linen in our closet. Has it helped?'

'Sometimes having the background makes sense of other things.'

258

'You've discussed this with your colleagues?'

'I've only just arrived at it myself,' Mariner said. 'My colleagues also believe that I'm not functioning well at the moment. I should also tell you that as the last person to see her alive, I'm on the list of possibles for Eleanor's murder, but I hope you can believe that I didn't do it. You're the only person who can help me.' As a wave of nausea struck Mariner found himself clutching her wrist.

Smiling uncertainly, Fliss gently removed his hand. 'What would you like me to do?'

'It would help to find out as much as possible about the treatment Diana had, this retreat that she stayed at when she was first ill and anything that's happened since. Could you see if there's anything in her personal papers that makes reference to it?' Mariner squinted at her. Her face seemed to be blurring at the edges and wouldn't keep still.

'It's going back a long time, but I'll try. I'm rather intrigued myself. Where can I contact you?'

Mariner gave her his business card. This wine was potent stuff. The room was moving around him as if he'd stepped onto a merry-go-round. 'I think I need some air,' he said, getting to his feet. But when he tried to walk out of the restaurant his legs seemed to have liquefied.

Mariner's mobile phone ringing close by roused him, and in the semi-darkness he scrambled over the floor trying to locate his jacket. He had a moment of disorientation as he put the phone to his ear. It was Anna. 'Where are you?'

Good question. He was still wearing his shirt but could see his trousers hanging over the back of a chair. He scanned the room and in the half-light something on the bed moved lazily in her sleep and then he remembered. Fliss Fitzgibbon. Afraid to consider what might have happened here, Mariner got up and padded into the bathroom, closing the door softly behind him. His head hurt like hell. 'I called in at a pub and had a few drinks,' he said, keeping his voice low. 'It didn't seem a good idea to drive back so I've

259

stopped overnight at a place. I'll be back soon.'

'Well the case conference starts at eleven, if you're still planning to come?'

'Of course I am, I'll be back well before then.' Even though it was already nine thirty and up until now it had slipped his mind.

When he went back into the bedroom Fliss Fitzgibbon, wrapped in a beige silk robe, was pulling back the curtains. 'Feeling better?' she asked, with a smile. 'Don't look so worried, you only spent the night on the couch. After practically passing out on your way outside, I could hardly let you drive home.'

But this morning there was no choice. Convincing Fliss that he was fit to do so, Mariner drove back slowly, his head aching and his vision blurring intermittently. It was one of the worst hangovers he'd had in a long time, probably not helped by the fact that he'd declined the offer of breakfast. He couldn't imagine his stomach holding onto anything for long anyway.

At Anna's empty house he showered and put on a clean suit, which, though a marginal improvement, also made him late. As he dressed he put a call through to Mike Baxter. It was early, so the office was closed, but he left a message on the answering machine, asking Baxter to find out what he could about a retreat called Our Lady of Lourdes.

Anna had left a curt note on the kitchen table; details of the venue. Next up Mariner couldn't get parking outside the busy social services offices, so the meeting was well under way when he arrived, sweating and breathless, his stomach gurgling ominously. Everyone turned as he went in, there seemed to be dozens of faces. Mariner recognised Jamie's social worker, Louise from the hostel, Jamie's new GP, but there was a man sitting next to Anna he hadn't seen before. He and Anna had their heads together, smiling about a shared joke and looking very friendly.

Murmuring apologies to the room in general Mariner took the seat on the other side of Anna, taking her hand and giving it a squeeze, but all the time under the impression that he was intruding on something.

'This is Gareth,' Anna whispered. 'He's a friend of Mark's. He recommended the Towyn Farm Community. Are you all right?'

'A bit tired, that's all.' In truth Mariner felt terrible. The lights were too bright and the room stifling, but as none of the other men had taken off their jackets, Mariner felt inhibited from doing so too. He could feel the perspiration running down his back.

Jamie's social worker from Manor Park was setting out the options. 'We could do a gradual settling back in at the hostel, but Jamie would need increased supervision.'

'How long would that take?' Anna asked.

'We could perhaps start with Saturdays and then after a few weeks we could try an overnight and slowly build up from there.'

'That could take weeks, months even.'

'We could speed things up if Jamie does well.'

'And if he doesn't?' Anna shot back. 'None of this was his fault in the first place. He's done nothing wrong.'

'Another option would be for you to have additional support for Jamie at home,' the social worker suggested.

Yes, and how long would that last? Wondered Mariner.

'We have a third option,' Anna said, rather too quickly. She introduced Gareth to the group, and he proceeded to give the Towyn Farm Community the hard sell. What he didn't talk about was the cost, but presumably Anna had already worked out the financial implications.

'I'll talk about funding in a moment,' Gareth said, but Mariner hardly heard anything else because suddenly the discussion had faded into nothing more than background noise. Out of nowhere it had come to him, the identity of the person responsible for blackmailing and killing Sir Geoffrey Ryland. The revelation brought with it a rush of

261

adrenalin so powerful that a numbing sensation began to creep up from his neck that he recognised as the precursor to fainting. 'Excuse me,' he gasped before stumbling out of the room.

In the gents he squatted on the floor, ducking his head between his knees until gradually everything began to return to normal. When he could, he stood up and splashed cold water on his face. Anna was waiting for him outside. 'We've taken a break for half an hour. Are you all right?'

'I've felt better.'

'Let's get a coffee and something to eat. Maybe you should see a doctor.'

'Like Doctor Gareth, you mean? You two seem very thick.'

'Oh great, we're going through this again, are we?'

'I suppose you're going to tell me he's gay too.'

'Recently divorced actually. He's been very helpful, and he's good fun.' Everything Mariner was not.

'Well I hope you'll be very happy.'

Anna ignored him. 'Towyn would be very good for Jamie. It's got what the hostel hasn't: open space. That's what he misses. That and people who will make him feel welcome.'

Mariner couldn't argue with that. 'And if he goes there?'

'I'd like to move out there too.' It was what he didn't want to hear. 'I'd like us to do it together, but of course that would be your decision.'

'And if I said no?' Mariner's head was throbbing. He should stop this now, but he couldn't.

'I would go anyway. I've thought a lot about this. If I'm to have any kind of life I need Jamie to be happy and settled. My first duty is to him.'

She'd come a long way. When she and Mariner had first met, Anna was an independent woman who had no intention of taking responsibility for her younger brother.

'You could visit from here,' Mariner suggested weakly.

She shook her head. 'Not in the long term. It's too far.

Besides, it's not only about Jamie. I want to move away from the city. I don't feel safe here any more.'

'You think Hitler's got a few more surprises up his sleeve?'

'It could so easily have been a terrorist bomb, you know that.'

'I thought we had a future together,' Mariner said without conviction.

'So did I, but something's happened to us hasn't it? The bomb has played its part, but it's more than that, isn't it?'

He could have told her then. The timing wasn't brilliant. He was fast learning that it never would be. But again the words stuck in his throat. 'Yes,' he said, lamely. 'It is.'

'Are you coming back in?'

'You seem to be doing all right on your own. I still feel a bit sick.' A good excuse for running away.

'Why don't you get some fresh air? I'll meet you at home later.'

'You sure?'

'I'll be fine.'

What had he done to deserve her? Even when he was behaving like a shit she was nice to him. It just made him feel worse.

Walking back to his car, Mariner remembered what had precipitated his exit from the room. Outside, with a clear head, it was still viable. In his car he put through a call to Dave Flynn, but got only his voicemail. 'Dave, I've another couple of questions, about those photos, and about the crime scene—'

By the time he'd finished his message the positive effects of the adrenalin had kicked in and he was firing on all cylinders. The more he thought about it, the more he realised it was the only answer. There was work to be done, but if he was right he'd cracked it.

The first thing he'd do was to follow Anna's advice. Some outdoor exercise would help him to work out the detail. The more concrete evidence he could take to Flynn, the more seriously Flynn would have to take it. Mariner knew he was only a beat away from proving why Sir Geoffrey Ryland was killed and who had killed him. It had begun with blackmail, Mariner was sure about that, and now he had figured out the motive. The only thing he didn't have was the identity of the blackmailer, but the motive gave him a place to look, and if he could come up with a name then there would be no option other than to re-examine the case. And that was all he wanted.

He'd go home and get his boots, have an hour up at Waseley Country Park, then go back to Anna's. Maybe tonight he'd take her out for dinner and she could tell him what was going on with Jamie, and he could tell her what was going on with him. They could start building a few bridges. Buoyed up by positive feelings, Mariner made it as far as his front door when everything went black.

Chapter Nineteen

Later in the afternoon Anna left the case conference exhilarated. She'd got the outcome she wanted; agreement from the professionals that Towyn would be the best place for Jamie, and an undertaking that Social Care would help to subsidise his placement there. Their contribution wouldn't be a lot but it would help.

'I need to get back,' said Gareth. 'Congratulations.' They were standing on the steps of the social services offices.

'Thanks, and thanks for your help. I'm sure your input helped to sway the decision.'

'Oh, I don't know. You present a pretty good argument. I'll look forward to seeing more of both of you when Jamie makes the move. And I hope Tom's okay.'

'He will be, I'm sure.'

'After what you've told me about his recent behaviour I wouldn't discount post traumatic stress disorder. He sounds like a textbook case. He should think about getting some help, especially if his actions become more extreme.'

'Like what?'

'The mood swings, any aggressive outbursts.'

'I'll talk to him.' But Anna knew that counselling would be out of the question for Tom. He didn't believe in it. Allowing him space and not asking too many questions was the best thing she could do for him right now.

Anna got back home at six in the evening and Jamie was dropped off shortly afterwards. She was disappointed that Tom hadn't yet returned, but his walk had doubtless taken him to a pub, guaranteed to put him in a better frame of mind.

The nausea that she'd been suffering all day had finally subsided. Seeing Tom in that state this morning, she'd wondered if it was something they'd eaten, but now she put it down to nerves. She couldn't wait to tell Tom about the favourable result of the case conference, and about the plans she had, but she'd have to take it slowly. PTSD or not, he had a lot on his mind.

It had been a long and exhausting day for Jamie too and for once he went to bed at a reasonable time. Her head was so full that Anna didn't think she could sleep, but she was away almost as soon as she lay down on the pillow.

When Anna woke at seven the next morning Jamie was still out cold and the bed beside her was empty. Tom would have gone to the cottage, where hopefully he'd be getting some sleep too. He was spending more time there at the moment than she would have liked but he'd once said that often he slept better there, so maybe it was as well. She waited until eight o'clock and then tried his land line. No reply. So the new lodger wasn't around either. Tom had said that he hardly ever was. Money for old rope. She tried Mariner's mobile. He didn't answer and the disquiet which she had so easily rationalised the day before, returned.

Anna managed to get Jamie to the centre and tried phoning Mariner again when she got in to work. She phoned him at home but he wasn't there and he wasn't answering his mobile. Thinking she might have missed him, she tried Granville Lane but, according to the duty sergeant, Mariner hadn't been seen there since Monday.

'Can you put me through to DC Knox please?' Knox came on the line almost immediately. 'Tony have you seen Tom?'

'Not for a few days. Why? I thought he'd gone to the meeting with you.'

'He left on his own yesterday afternoon. We had rather a heated discussion, and he wasn't feeling well. He said he wanted some air, which for him usually means a walk. But he hasn't been in touch since and he's not answering the phones. I'm back at work so I'm stuck. Can you try and track him down for me?'

'Sure.'

Anna realised that she had little idea of what else Tom was working on at the moment. There was Madeleine of course, but she couldn't be the only case. Usually he told her, but she'd been so wrapped up in what was happening to Jamie, and with Megan, that she'd barely noticed what was going on with Tom. And suddenly Gareth's warning made her think. What if yesterday's episode was symptomatic of something more serious? He'd seemed so dazed and out of it when he'd arrived. Suddenly she had an awful premonition and yesterday's queasiness returned with such strength that she had to make a dash for the bathroom.

Knox found Mariner's car parked outside a house that was locked and empty. He let himself in with the key he'd retained from when he'd temporarily lodged with Mariner a couple of years ago, but there was nothing to see. Significantly, Mariner's boots were still in the hall. If the boss had gone for a walk he hadn't bothered putting them on, which was lax considering the weather. The answer machine flashed with six new messages, most from Anna, urging Mariner to get in touch. But there were also calls from Dave Flynn, Mike Baxter and someone called Fliss, whoever she was, all of them asking him to return the call right away. Apart from Flynn, Knox had never heard of these people. It was as if Mariner had a whole other life that he knew nothing about.

As he stood there, Knox heard the muffled sound of a mobile. The only furniture in the narrow hall was a small chest of drawers that Knox knew, from his previous occupancy, was home to phone directories and whose surface was a deposit for post, loose change and other miscellany. He traced the ringing phone to the top drawer, where beside it lay a bunch of keys: those to Mariner's house, what must be Anna's house and the Volvo ignition key, all held together by an old and battered karabiner. What the hell were they doing there? Where could Mariner possibly have gone that he didn't need his keys? The phone's ringing became more insistent. Checking caller identity, the number wasn't familiar to Knox, so out of curiosity, he took the call.

'Tom, it's Mike Baxter,' said the caller.

'Great,' said Knox, hoping that the one word didn't betray his accent.

'Yeah, Our Lady of Lourdes took some tracking down. The building is still there, but it's changed its name to Hollyfield Grange, and has become an upmarket health spa for the rich and famous. It's on the web if you want to have a look,' Baxter quoted a website address. 'Up until thirty years ago it was a women's retreat and adoption agency, run by the Catholic Church. The other branch of the organisation has moved and been scaled down a bit, but it still exists. Does that help at all?'

Knox knew that once he spoke more than a few words, he'd give himself away. Might as well own up now. 'Actually this isn't Tom Mariner,' he confessed. 'I'm DC Tony Knox, a colleague of his. The DI isn't around at the moment but I'll make sure he gets this information. Did he tell you what it was for?'

'People rarely do, I just do the digging. Tell him I hope it helps anyway. And if there's anything else—'

'Sure. Thanks.'

Immediately Knox rang off he phoned Anna, asking her to meet him at Granville Lane.

'What's going on Tony?'

Knox kept his tone light. 'I can't be certain yet. I just want to check out a couple of things.'

Then he went back to the station and, as Charlie Glover wasn't around, knocked on DCI Coleman's door. 'It's Tom Mariner sir. Was he due down at the CPS again today?'

'No, there's no need. Things are finally moving there.'

'Well, this may be nothing at all but I can't find him.'

'It wouldn't be the first time, would it?' said Coleman. 'Since when?'

'Anna last saw him yesterday afternoon, he said he was going back to his place. I've been there and his car is there but there's no sign of him. I found these in a drawer.' He put the keys and the phone on Coleman's desk. 'But there's not much indication that he's even been there. Goes without saying that we've all been a bit concerned about him lately—'

Coleman's PA knocked on the door. 'Anna Barham's here, sir.'

'Show her in.'

Anna Barham looked pale. 'Are you all right?' Coleman asked. 'Would you like tea or coffee?'

She looked as if she was going to throw up. 'No, I'm fine, really.'

'So where are we up to?'

'Tom came to Jamie's case conference yesterday,' Anna said. 'But he wasn't himself. He left early, quite abruptly really, before the end. He didn't feel well,' she said. 'I suggested he should go for a walk.'

'Was he in the car?'

'Yes, he'd found it difficult to park, it made him late.'

'So he must have driven home again, but his boots were still in the hall,' said Knox.

'He left the meeting in suit and work shoes. He wouldn't go for a walk dressed like—' Seeing the items on the desk she broke off. 'Those are his keys and phone. Where did you find them?'

'In the hall cupboard.'

'But that doesn't make any sense. He wouldn't go anywhere without those.'

269

'Maybe he wasn't planning to go far, just along the canal.'

'Locking himself out?'

Knox shared her concern, though he couldn't tell whether Anna had worked out the one obvious reason why Mariner might have gone out without taking his keys. 'I took a call on his mobile while I was there,' he said, keeping things moving for her sake. Picking up the phone he retrieved Baxter's number. 'You know a guy called Mike Baxter. He wanted to talk to Tom about an adoption agency.'

'Have you two been discussing adoption?' Coleman asked.

'It came up when we went to see the genetic counsellor, but I wouldn't say we discussed it in any depth. Right now Tom's rather sensitive about the subject of children. In fact things have been pretty tense between us just lately, what with the uncertainty over Jamie.' She looked guilty. 'I've probably been putting him under pressure too, about moving to the country.'

'Throw another log on the fire,' said Knox. 'On top of the bomb and his dad, he must be reeling.'

'His dad?' Anna was staring at him. 'What do you mean, Tony?' she said uncertainly. 'Tom doesn't know anything about his dad. He doesn't know who he is.'

Knox would have given anything to rewind the last thirty seconds. 'Oh Christ, he hasn't told you.'

'Told me what?'

Knox hesitated.

'Talk to us DC Knox,' ordered Coleman.

Knox shook his head, helplessly. 'This shouldn't be coming from me.' But having opened his big gob, he was left with no choice. 'The DI knows who his father was. It was what his mate Dave Flynn came up there to tell him back in December. Flynn found out by accident while working on an investigation.' Anna and Coleman's wide-eyed reactions couldn't have been better synchronised. It

270

didn't surprise Knox that Coleman didn't know, but he couldn't believe that Mariner still hadn't told Anna. He glanced towards her. 'I know the boss was trying to find the right time to tell you. I assumed that by now he would have—'

'Who is it?' she demanded.

'Not "is" but "was". You'll find this hard to believe.'

'Try me.'

'Tom's father was Geoffrey Ryland.'

'*Sir* Geoffrey Ryland?'

'He told me that his mother and Ryland were friends,' Coleman spoke up.

'They were more than that,' said Knox. 'And since he found out, the DI's been on a mission to find out why Ryland was killed.'

'But they know why Ryland was killed,' Coleman said. 'The papers have been full of it.'

'The DI thinks they've got it wrong. It's why he's kept going off the radar. He's been working his own investigation. He only told me about it a couple of days back.' Knox cast Anna an apologetic look. 'And he made me promise not to say anything. I think this guy Flynn must be involved too. There are messages on Tom's answer machine at the cottage asking him to call Flynn back urgently.'

Anna brightened. 'So that's where Tom could be now,' she said, hopefully. 'Somewhere out there pursuing this investigation.'

'Do we have a number for this Dave Flynn?'

Knox produced his pocketbook. 'Him and a woman called Fliss?' He looked to Anna for clarification, but she pulled a face.

'Never heard of her. Unless she's friend of—' She broke off and flashed a wry smile. 'I've just realised something. I overheard Tom leaving a message for someone called Maggie. He said she was connected to a current case, but last year when his mother died we met one of her old friends; Maggie. I'd bet anything it's the same one.'

271

'Let's start with Flynn, see what he has to say.' Coleman dialled the number, switching to speaker phone, to allow them all to listen in. Flynn picked up on the third ring. Coleman introduced himself and the others present. 'We're concerned about where DI Mariner might be. We need to know what you know, DI Flynn.'

Flynn recounted his meetings with Mariner since December. 'Tom was obsessed with the investigation and was sure that the team had got it wrong. He's been convinced that O'Connor wasn't behind the shootings, and that Ryland was the intended target. He'd got it into his head that there was some kind of conspiracy going on. He thought there was somebody after him too.'

'The bomb has been explained. It—'

'No,' Flynn cut in. 'When he was down in London there were a couple of incidents.' Flynn relayed what Mariner had told him. 'But the last time I spoke to him was at the inquest and he seemed to be over it.'

'He had a problem with his car, too,' Knox said. 'The brake cable had been cut, and he found a tracking device attached.'

'Jesus,' said Flynn. 'There was a tracking device on Sir Geoffrey Ryland's car, too. Maybe Tom was right.'

'But I thought Special Branch had someone in the frame for the shootings,' Coleman said.

'They have, in that they know who it was based on motive and circumstances, but I spoke to a couple of the guys yesterday and they admitted that to date they still have no material evidence to back it up.'

'So it's altogether possible that they could be wrong and DI Mariner could be right.'

Flynn was reluctant to admit it. 'As far-fetched as it sounds, yes.'

'And now Mariner's disappeared.'

'When he was interviewed by Thames Valley police he told them that he thought Ryland might have another illegitimate child, who Ryland had refused to help through the

JRC, but they've spoken to him and he's as clean as a whistle. Turns out he'd been brought up to believe that he was Ryland's son, but his mother had lied about it. Sir Geoffrey offered to take a paternity test, so the guy gave up on it.'

'So who does it leave us with?'

'I don't know.'

Ella on reception buzzed up to Coleman. 'There's a lady here who wants to talk to DI Mariner, but I can't locate him. She insists that it's urgent she speak to him. Do you want me to pass her on to someone else?'

'What's her name?'

'Felicity Fitzgibbon.'

'Fliss,' said Knox and Anna as one.

When Mariner opened his eyes it was to darkness so absolute that there seemed little discernible difference from having them closed. He blinked a bit to try and clear his vision, straining to distinguish some kind of form or shadow but there was nothing, only black obscurity. He was lying face down on hard ground, so cold that it stung his cheek. He must have fallen. He remembered lifting his key to put in the door and then nothing. But where was the street light, and where was his house?

Disorientated now, he wondered if he was back in the Cathedral. If the last few weeks had been an elaborate hallucination and that he'd been in the church when the bomb went off after all. Maybe he was already dead. Maybe this was what death was like and he'd be like this for an eternity. Slowly he became aware of his body. Though his limbs were stiff he found that he could move them and the oppressive black blanket that pressed down on him was only empty space. Dead air.

He tried twisting his head to look around him, but shooting pains stabbed the backs of his eyes and the vice that seemed to grip his skull tightened, as if it was squeezing out his brain bit by bit. The slightest movement made him want

273

to retch. A pounding like a drumbeat in his head came and went at intervals; the blood pumping through his ears. The back of his head tingled and he lifted a hand to touch something tacky, his hair matted. Blood. He must have hit his head when he fell. But where was he, and how had he got here?

Something pricked at his senses, reminding him of childhood; of winter Sunday teatimes sitting with his mother by the fire. At last he identified it. It was the coalscuttle. He could smell the coalscuttle. But that was impossible. It was in the house in Leamington, except it wasn't even there any more. After his mother died, the house had been sold, the contents cleared. The thoughts were making his head hurt more. He let them go.

Mariner's mouth was parched, but perversely he needed to pee. God he needed to pee, so much that he was hard and aching. A bit of him was inclined to just let it happen, put up with the discomfort. Too much effort to do anything else. But something stopped him. He raised his head, resurrecting the agonising hammering on his skull. Pausing to let it settle, he tried again, and bit by bit managed to inch himself to a sitting position. As he moved his legs, something rattled on his right ankle; he reached down to feel a cold steel band a couple of inches wide clamped round it, and attached by a thick bolt to a heavy-duty chain. He felt along it as far as he could reach, but every link was smooth and sound. In the absence of any tools it was indestructible. He was being held prisoner, but who was his captor?

He returned to his original aim. Each time he moved was like shaking up one of those snow storms in his head. Putting out his hands to push himself up to his knees, he retched again, a violent spasm that came deep from his gut. But he hadn't eaten for hours, maybe even days, and only sour gastric juices burned in his throat. Eventually he was on his feet. White lights flashed behind his eyes and he almost blacked out again with the effort. Something crunched underfoot as pushing off from the icy wall he *shuffled to the limits of his bonds, unzipped his fly and emptied his bladder with painful relief.*

He moved back towards the wall, weakness overtaking him, and sank down again onto the ground. In a rush, he remembered Anna. This was his fault of course. He'd made it happen. Forty-odd years of not being on the receiving end and now he'd screwed up his chance of being a father. It was like one of those dreams he used to have as a kid, stepping out to play at Villa Park only to find that he'd forgotten his football boots so spent the duration of the match, and the dream, fruitlessly searching for them, the opportunity for glory cruelly stolen. This was his punishment for walking out on Anna at the meeting. They'd planned it but he still wasn't sure, couldn't embrace the idea. He was afraid of it and now he'd pushed it away.

Something that Anna had said kept coming back to him: 'I'd love to be able to say that. That's my daughter – or son. My son. Tom and Anna's son.' It had seemed important at the time but he couldn't identify why. Then the fog rolled in immersing him again.

Jack Coleman's office was becoming cramped now that Felicity Fitzgibbon had joined the party.

'I've been trying to get Tom on his mobile since early this morning,' she said. 'When I couldn't get through I thought the best thing was just to come straight here. I've found something among my sister's papers that I think he needs to know about.'

'And your sister is—?'

'Was, Diana Ryland. Tom thought that Geoff was being blackmailed, and that the blackmailer had tried to up the stakes. Geoff wouldn't play, which is why he was ambushed and shot dead.'

'Did he think the blackmailer was Ryland's other illegitimate son?' Knox was finding it hard to keep up.

'No, he'd given that up. He came to ask me about my sister's mental illness. He thought that perhaps someone

275

who knew her history of attempted suicide and drug dependency might have access to records that, if they were made public, would humiliate Diana and damage Geoff.'

'Did he have any idea who the blackmailer might be?' Coleman asked.

'No, but he asked me to go through Diana's papers, to look for anything that alluded to the treatment she'd had, or anyone who had helped her or had access to her medical records.'

'And you found something?'

'It wasn't at all what I expected.' From her handbag Fliss produced a letter. 'I don't think Diana even posted it.' The letter was written on the headed notepaper of Our Lady of Lourdes Retreat, and was dated July 1963. Knox, who was sitting nearest to her, took it and read it first.

Dearest Mummy,

It's all over now and the baby boy is born. I was in labour for twenty-one hours and I thought the pain would never stop. I've called him David and loved him instantly, even though the nurses have warned us not to get too attached. They took a photograph that I will be able to keep. He is feeding well and putting on weight. The nurses take good care of us but, they make it clear that they disapprove of us. There are eight other girls here and I'm one of the eldest. The youngest is only thirteen and three of the girls have travelled from Ireland. We have little in common so we don't talk to each other very much, all keeping ourselves to ourselves, though one or two of the other girls seem to have struck up friendships ...

'I thought my sister's mental health problems stemmed from her failure to cope academically at university,' said Fliss, as the letter circulated the room. 'Diana never told me the truth, but when I found this I contacted her friend Norman Balfour. He knew all about it. It seems that shortly after she started at university Diana went out with a man who raped her. The resulting pregnancy came as a terrible shock for my parents. My father died not long afterwards. Diana always said it was her fault, and now I understand why.'

'So the baby was adopted?' Knox said.

'In the circumstances, giving up her baby must have seemed the only option. Norman helped to arrange it all. It must have been terrible for Diana. She travelled up to the retreat all on her own and was alone when she gave birth. She got to take care of her baby for six weeks, but at the end of that time she just had to hand him over and never see him again. No wonder she never got over it.'

They'd forgotten that Flynn was listening in. 'Tom had asked me to find out the location of the photographs we found,' he said, his voice crackling from the phone. 'While most of them were in Sir Geoffrey Ryland's safety deposit box, one of them was found at the house. He must have known it was different.'

Fliss Fitzgibbon's voice trembled. 'It would have been the only picture Diana had of her baby.'

'There's something else,' said Flynn. 'It didn't seem significant at the time. The message: *vengeance is mine*, it was written in Diana Ryland's blood. Forensics thought it was convenience, her body was next to the closed window, but perhaps it was a conscious decision by the killer.'

'*Vengeance is mine*,' repeated Coleman. 'This man took revenge on the mother who gave him up at birth. You said someone told you about this?' he asked Fliss.

'Norman Balfour. He's an old family friend.'

'Does he know what happened to Diana's child? Did he ever contact her?'

'Norman didn't think so. They wouldn't have wanted that. I think it would have killed Diana.'

'That's what made Sir Geoffrey so vulnerable to blackmail,' said Coleman. 'He wasn't protecting himself, he was protecting his wife.'

'It's exactly what Geoff would have done,' Fliss agreed.

277

'He'd have gone to the ends of the earth to keep her safe.'

'This child would be in his early forties now. Do we know anything about him?'

'Nothing.'

The letter had worked its way back to Coleman's desk. Knox picked it up and re-read the heading. 'But this retreat, Our Lady of Lourdes, arranged the adoption, so they might have records, or know where they are. It's what the boss was trying to find out. He knew it would lead him to the identity of the killer.'

'And if our man knows that Tom is on to him—'

'He'll be after Tom, too.'

'If he hasn't found him already.' Anna's voice trembled as she put into words what they'd all been avoiding.

'And we don't have a fucking clue who he is, or what he looks like,' said Knox.

'Where was this retreat place?' asked Coleman.

'A place called Wicktown,' Fliss Fitzgibbon said. 'I looked it up. It's about fifteen miles north of Glasgow.'

'You want me to get hold of the local force, Boss?' Knox asked.

'That will take time, and if it's a remote area, they'll be low on manpower.' Coleman was weighing up the options. He reached a decision. 'We'll achieve more by going up there ourselves. We know what we're looking for, so will pick up on anything more loosely connected. See how quickly we can book flights.'

Knox was unenthusiastic. 'Me too, sir?' It was the last thing he wanted.

'Is that a problem?'

'No,' said Knox, his reluctance unmistakable. 'I'll get on to it.'

As he left the room, Knox overheard Anna enlightening his baffled boss. 'Tony doesn't like flying,' she said.

Chapter Twenty

Mariner woke, disturbed by a movement, something or someone was there. Terror tightened his chest, and he tried to slither back, pressing himself against the wall. 'Who's there?'

'I've come to say goodbye, Tom.' It was a man's voice, a few feet away to his left, hoarse, husky and unrecognisable, like the voice that had phoned him in London.

'Why am I here? What do you want?'

'I want what's owing to me.'

'What's that?'

'I want a life. The kind of life you've had. Swaps are very fashionable these days, aren't they? There are house swaps and wife swaps so why not a life swap too? You can have my shitty one and I'll have yours. I want you to share my experiences, but don't worry, not all of them. I'll spare you the beatings, and you won't be forced to scrub the floors and walls until your hands bleed. But I will leave you in this dark, freezing cellar and starve you, to death eventually, so that when the time comes, I can take what's rightfully mine.' The lilting accent was beginning to show through.

'You killed the Rylands.'

'You're good at your job, I'll say that for you. When did you work it out?'

'After I'd spoken to Fliss. I realised what her sister's

279

breakdown was all about. It was nothing to do with academic failure. It was you, wasn't it?'

'I've never been described as an illness before, though I've been called a few nasty things, most of them by my loving parents, when they could be arsed to speak to me at all.'

'Your adoptive parents. Is this what it's all about? Revenge on the person who landed you with them?'

'I should have had a different life. I should have had a privileged life, with wealth and education, or at the very least love and affection. I could have been successful. Instead I grew up in a house where beatings, starvation and filth were the norm, where I was treated the same as the pigs in the sty. It's no start in life, you know.'

'Things didn't work out perfectly for me, either.'

The bitter peal of laughter made Mariner shudder.

'You have no fucking idea. Look at you, a good job, nice house, a lovely woman. I bet she's a great shag. You've got everything you could possibly want. Except that now I want it. I've had my revenge on the woman who put me there. Sadly not so satisfying as I had hoped it would be. I had to get the job done quickly so I barely had time to introduce myself to my mother before blasting her brains out. But now the recompense; a comfortable life, the life that's rightfully mine.'

'But you have a good life, a successful business—'

A sardonic laugh. 'What business? I packed that in years ago, working my arse off being nice to people. Earning a pittance from a boss who thrived on humiliation? The best thing about it was trying to try and sell a security system to Hollyfield Grange, when suddenly my life took a turn for the better.'

'You found out about your mother.'

'It didn't take much to chat up the girl on reception. She was an easy lay, and first time I shagged her in one of the empty guest rooms, she told me. 'You'd better wear a condom, I don't want get pregnant. Though I'm in the right place, aren't I?' I didn't know what the little cow was on about, until she told me that Hollyfield was a home for unmarried mothers. She'd seen all the old records in the basement. I knew it then. Mam was always threatening to send me back to "the home" and I just knew this was the place.'

'You knew you were adopted.'

'I was never allowed to forget it, that I was a bastard-child, I was worthless and I deserved everything I got.'

'So the girl found your records?'

Another laugh. 'You think I'd trust her? A couple of weeks later I demonstrated how weak their security was, broke in and found it myself. All things come to those who wait. I'd given up ever knowing by then. I'd tried for years to discover who the bitch was who had dumped me with those evil people, but each time I just hit a brick wall.'

'It must have taken you a while to track your mother down.'

'Her address was on the record card. It might have been harder if she was nobody, but when you live like she did it's easy to find out. That's what really hurt, seeing the kind of life she'd had and knowing that I could have been part of it.'

'Giving you up destroyed your mother. She suffered every bit as much as you did.'

'Who the hell fucking cares? It was her choice and her decision. She didn't have to give me up. She could have afforded to keep me. But she couldn't stand the stigma. Abortion would have been better than being raised in that hell-hole.'

'It wasn't her fault. She was forced into a bad decision.'

The voice rose in anger. 'She could have kept me if she'd really wanted to. Your mother did. What's more important, your child or your reputation?'

'You can't just take over my life,' Mariner croaked.

'I can recreate it though, given the right resources, and with you out of the way it can be done.'

281

'You're planning to contest the will?'

'I have DNA proof that Diana Ryland was my mother. That I'm her flesh and blood.'

'It's not that simple, surely.'

'Ah, it won't be easy, I know, but it can be done. It has to be. I didn't want it this way. It would have been much better for everyone if Sir Geoffrey had continued to play ball. Those regular little payments would have helped me to start my new life.'

'So it was blackmail.' Knowing he was right brought Mariner no comfort.

'It was gratifying to know how easily I could get at them. He was desperate to keep me away. He said that seeing me again after all those years, and learning what had happened to me, would kill her. Ryland paid me to keep my distance, and everything would have been fine if he'd continued to co-operate. But then he let me down in the small matter of my inheritance. I wasn't being unreasonable. I was prepared to wait. But I was meant to get everything; enough to keep me in luxury for the rest of my days. Then Ryland let slip that there wasn't just me. He taunted me with you. You'd made something of yourself, and what's more you could get me into a lot of trouble. I thought he was bluffing, so next time we met he brought proof.'

'At Pearl's Café.'

'Hah! A bunch of fucking useless photos and press cuttings. For an intelligent man he was pretty stupid. He told me you were the polis. Ooh, that really scared me. But he'd ruined it. At the time you didn't even know he was your dad, but he was going to tell you. And then he would write you into the will, too. That way he said it would be fair. Fair! As if anything in life is fair. I couldn't have that. I had to do something, rather sooner than planned.

'I'd read all about Joseph O'Connor and the controversy surrounding his release. All I had to do was set him up. It all went brilliantly at first. Special Branch completely bought it, as I knew they would. It was simple. But then you came along and started interfering with that too. The others were happy to accept O'Connor as the fall guy. Seemed like justice was finally being done. But you couldn't let it go, could you?

'Not that it's mattered, at the end of the day. Ryland had given me enough information to find you. Pompous bastard didn't even realise what he'd done. I hope you appreciate the effort I went to with the name, by the way. Weren't quite the Poirot with that one, were you?'

Mariner managed a half-laugh. 'All the time it was staring me in the face.'

'After that, everything fell neatly into place as if it was meant to be. Even Adolf Hitler played his part. From then on it was just a question of when and how.'

'You tried to kill me before.'

'I didn't try very hard, not at first. An untimely accident, wrong place at the wrong time, it seemed like a good idea. If that bastard in the Merc hadn't come along it might have happened, but I wasn't too worried that it didn't work out because now it's given us this opportunity to talk. And it only delayed the inevitable.'

'But why do you need to kill me too?' Mariner said. 'I don't need anything. I could sign over my claim on the estate.'

'Easy to say that now, but I was brought up on broken promises. People never mean what they say. They change their minds all the time. Let you down. And I've come this far, I'm not sure that one more death will make any difference. This way it's tidier.'

'But the Rylands were worth a fortune. There would be more than enough for both of us.'

'Share it? Oh no. I never was any good at sharing anything. And why should I? The money belongs to my family. It was my mother's. Your father just married into it.'

'Why have another death on your hands? You'll have killed four people.'

'Five, but hey, who's counting?'

The penny dropped. 'You killed Eleanor, too.'

'Only from necessity. While she was still around everything would revert to her. I hadn't planned it. After all, she was not long for this world anyway. All I'd intended to do was check that there was nothing nasty in her will, to make sure that there wasn't anything detrimental to me. But then I thought, why wait? Why not save time and finish her off too.'

Mariner felt sick. 'I led you to her, didn't I?'

'Don't flatter yourself. I'd been tracking Ryland for months, and he was a regular visitor there. But it was helpful to know when she'd be on her own. I'd been trying to work that out.'

'So what's it all for?' Mariner asked wearily, his concentration beginning to flag.

'I want my villa by the sea, where it's warm and sunny, with my own swimming pool and a BMW convertible. Cyprus probably. I did a tour there while I was in the army. There are some lovely places out there. The army taught me a lot, but I don't intend taking orders from anyone again.' There was more movement, scuffling. 'Well, it's been great talking to you, but I have to go now. Enjoy having my life, but don't worry, in this temperature and without food and water, it won't last long.' The voice was receding.

'Where am I?' Mariner called out in desperation.

'Just think of it as coming home.' There was a brief flash of light, followed by a clunk, and darkness and silence again prevailed.

Mariner knew he should make some effort to move towards that light, to try to get out of here, but he had no energy. He was exhausted. All he wanted to do was sleep. Rolling onto his side, he closed his eyes.

Chapter Twenty-One

Armed with a warrant to obtain the relevant information, Jack Coleman accompanied Knox up to Scotland himself. 'I'd no idea my last week on the job would be so exciting,' he said, grimly.

'No sir,' but Knox wasn't really listening. He was staring out of the tiny cabin widow at the precariously wobbling wing, his hands gripping the arm rests until his knuckles were white. Even Coleman's concession of a pre-fight drink had failed to calm his nerves. It didn't help of course that the aircraft was a small fifteen-seater shuttle that creaked and rattled its path through the sky, and he couldn't decide if this was a fair trade for a couple of nights away from home. Selina hadn't taken it well, and if he hadn't dodged at the right moment, he would have found himself explaining something else to the DCI.

'Not long now,' said Coleman.

'When we find him, I'll make bloody sure the DI knows what he's put me through,' Knox retorted. But he didn't express what he knew must have crossed Coleman's mind, too; that it might be 'if' and not 'when'.

Knox's discomfort came to an end just over an hour later as they touched down at a grey, cloudy Glasgow airport in the early afternoon. Picking up a hire car they took the M8 to north of Glasgow and into the open country through rolling hills to Wicktown, a bleak and functional collection of buildings strung out along a narrow main street that was more the size of a large village.

Their first stop was a courtesy call to the nearest local police station, where Coleman had expressed hope for a man of his own generation, who would remember something about Our Lady of Lourdes. They were to be unlucky. DC Tyrell was in his mid-thirties and had recently transferred from Dunfermline. But he was able to direct them to Hollyfield Grange.

The retreat-turned-health-club was a solid granite manor house some way out of the town, whose long drive cut through an avenue of stunted trees. An expansive, gravel car park was littered with luxury vehicles, from 4x4s to sports coupés. Duncan, the manager, was older than Knox expected, around fifty, with immaculately groomed hair, so flawlessly black that it could only be from a bottle, ditto the tan. He'd already checked that they had permission to access the files.

Inside, the building had been gutted and completely refurbished in ultra-modern glass and stainless steel, and the atmosphere was hushed as he took them through thick-carpeted corridors away from the main reception area, past tanning rooms and therapy suites. Everyone they met, whether dressed in shiny designer sports wear or the white uniforms of the staff, seemed to glow with unnatural good health. It was just the sort of place Mariner hated, thought Knox.

'How long are you gentlemen in bonnie Scotland?' Duncan turned a dazzling white smile on Knox, his gaze lingering just a little too long.

'Until the job's done,' said Knox, stonily.

'Well if you would care to avail yourselves of our facilities here, we'd love to have you. We're always happy to accommodate officers of the law.'

'Thanks,' said Knox. 'But I don't do health clubs.' He was sure he saw Coleman smirk.

They'd come to a storeroom, its steel reinforced door

securely locked. 'We had a break-in a couple of years ago,' Duncan told them, isolating a key from the bunch and unlocking the door. 'We agreed to retain the archive here but it only if it was secured. The records are confidential after all.' Pushing open the door, he flicked on overhead strip lighting to reveal a long, narrow room, each side lined with steel filing cabinets, 'Good luck,' he said. 'Hope you find what you're looking for.'

A quick glance revealed that the files were in alphabetical order, and armed with Diana's maiden name, theoretically it should have taken only a matter of minutes to find her records. But when they got to 'F' the file wasn't there.

'Who ever broke in two years ago, must have taken it,' said Coleman. 'Our man was doing his research. Shit!' He slammed the drawer shut from frustration.

Something on top of the cabinet fluttered, catching Knox's eye. 'No he didn't,' he said, grabbing the thin sheet of card. 'He just wrote down the details and didn't replace it.'

The record was in the form of an index card, and stated Diana Fitzgibbon's name, age and address, along with the names and address of the couple who had adopted the 7lb 4oz boy born on 3rd July 1963. The baby hadn't gone far. The couple who'd adopted him, Fiona and Angus McCrae, lived at Keepers Cottage, Wicktown.

But without local knowledge Keepers Cottage proved too vague an address to locate and after an hour's of driving around country lanes they were forced back to the police station. 'We have names and an address,' Coleman told Tyrell. 'Fiona and Angus McCrae, at Keepers Lodge.'

'Well, you'll not find either of them there,' the Sergeant shook his head. 'Keepers Cottage hasn't been inhabited for years. The only reason we get called out there is if there are kids vandalising the place, and even that's not happened for months.'

'Is there anyone who might know what's happened to the McCraes?'

'Give me a minute, will you?' Tyrell lifted the phone. 'Hello, Jim, I need your help with something.' Explaining the situation to the person at the other end, he ended with the traditional pleasantries before hanging up. 'Jim Paterson will talk to you,' he told Coleman and Knox. 'He was the Sergeant here until a couple of years ago. He remembers them. His house is just up the main street there, number fourteen.'

Jim Paterson's neat bungalow was on the edge of the village. He was awaiting them and already had the kettle on. 'Angus McCrae died back in 1978, and Fiona passed away from St Hilda's rest home last spring,' he told them, as they sipped tea around a tiny kitchen table. 'She hadn't lived at Keepers Cottage for years. It wasn't fit for human habitation anyway, the place was an anachronism.'

'We're actually looking for their son,' Coleman said.

'Which one?'

Good question. Knox looked over at the gaffer. They hadn't considered that there might be more than one, and had absolutely nothing to offer in the way of description.

'We don't know,' said Coleman lamely. 'He was adopted.'

'They both were, but I'd guess it's Kenneth you're after. Clive still lives over in Dunnoch, but I've no idea what happened to Kenneth. He was a troubled boy, but then they were a very unusual family.'

'In what way?'

'Angus and Fiona were devout Calvinist Christians. The family kept to themselves and the children were educated at home and expected to help their father on the land. The father was a gamekeeper on the estate, when it still was an estate. Ten years ago the land was sold to the Forestry Commission and the big house converted to a country hotel and golf course. The boys' education seemed to consist of pest control, trapping vermin and repairing damage to fences and dry-stone walls. They didn't attend the local school and you never saw them riding bikes or hanging around like the other kids. On the rare occasions when they did come into the town it was always with their parents and they never looked happy. Often they were poorly clothed for the weather up here, and my wife used to say the whole family looked in need of a good dinner.'

'You think the children were neglected?'

'By modern standards, I'm pretty sure they were. These days Social Services would have been in and taken them away. I've an idea their mother was subjected to regular beatings too, but we'd no proof, and no one could ever get near enough to talk to her. People knew what was going on, but back then nobody discussed that kind of thing. Angus died in a shooting accident when Kenneth was about fifteen.'

'What happened?'

'The two of them were out on the moors and Angus was shot in the thigh. Kenneth came to get help but he got lost and it was almost dark before he got back to the village. Then we had to go out and find Angus. By the time we got there he'd bled to death. He must have died in agony.'

'It was definitely an accident?' Knox asked, thinking about the man they were pursuing.

'The coroner recorded a verdict of accidental death. The gun could have backfired. Who was to say that it didn't?' But his words lacked a certain conviction.

'Have you any idea where Kenneth is now?'

Paterson shook his head. 'He signed up for the army as soon as he was old enough and I haven't seen him since, though I heard rumour a few years ago that he was back in the area. His brother might know.'

Clive McCrae still worked the land. His wife Moira took them through the spotless kitchen of their grey, pebble-dashed council semi and into the long garden, where, in the drizzle, McCrae was doing the winter work on an immaculately laid out vegetable patch, breaking up the hard frozen soil with a fork. He didn't give them an ecstatic welcome, but stopped what he was doing to speak to them.

Knox let Coleman do the talking.

Of his relationship with Kenneth, Clive McCrae had little to say except, 'We were never close.'

'We know that you and Kenneth were adopted.' Coleman gave him a quizzical look.

'I came after him. I don't think he ever forgave me for that.'

'Did he resent the fact that he was adopted?'

'We both did, to differing degrees. Everyone assumes that adopted kids are lucky, adopted into warm loving families who desperately want them. It wasn't like that with us. We were taken in for slave labour. Kenny found it harder to deal with, but then he had a tougher time. He was older and he hated the outdoor life. He seemed to know that what we had wasn't normal. I didn't really understand that until I met Moira.'

'Did Kenneth ever express any interest in knowing who his birth mother was?'

'I know he blamed her for everything, but since he knew nothing about her it was convenient to do that. He used to say that he hoped she was dead too, that she'd died a painful death giving birth to him, because that's what she deserved. There was a lot of hate and anger in him.'

'About his adoption?'

'About everything. He was hard. But my father made him that way. Like me, Kenny hated killing animals, but we were made to set traps and then our dad would watch while we took out the dead creatures and if we ever balked, he would rub our faces in the blood. Everything was done in the name of God, even the thrashings.'

'You were beaten?'

'Several times a week with whatever was to hand, to make us better servants of the Lord.'

'Weren't you angry?'

'Anger didn't change anything. I survived. The experience has certainly helped me to appreciate the life I have now, so perhaps my father would say it was justified, part of His plan for me.' As he spoke McCrae raised his eyes skywards. Despite everything, he had kept his faith.

'We could use any photographs of Kenneth,' Coleman said.

'I've only the one, and it's hardly recent.' Resting his fork against the fence, McCrae led them back into the house, removing his boots on the mat outside and washing his hands in the kitchen along the way. Coleman and Knox trailed him into the lounge. They remained standing as he went to the drawer of an old-fashioned oak sideboard, riffling through papers until he came up with a curled monochrome snapshot of two young boys, the taller one, lighter haired, staring expressionless into the camera. It would be no help at all. 'I can't even remember who took it,' McCrae said. 'We didn't have a camera. We weren't that sort of family.'

'Which regiment did Kenneth join in the army?' Coleman asked.

'The Guards.'

'And when would that have been?'

'He joined at sixteen, as soon as he could get away from here. It would have been what, some time in '79.'

'Have you any idea where Kenneth is now?'

'I heard he came back here for a while after he left the army. He'd married a German girl, and brought her back here to a caravan on Loch Cree. He was working in the security business. Then much later someone told me his marriage had broken down and his wife had gone back home. Like I said. We've never been close.'

Showing them out, McCrae said: 'Our parents were cruel people and we didn't have an easy childhood. It should have brought Kenny and me closer together, but it didn't.'

Regimental HQ and archives for the Scots guards were at Wellington Barracks in London. Knox and Coleman retraced their steps to Wicktown police station and met Andy Tyrell.

'Can I use your phone?' Coleman asked.

291

'Be my guest.'

Having verified Coleman's identity, the archivist at Wellington Barracks agreed to fax through details of McCrae's army record, including a more up-to-date photograph. He also gave them details of McCrae's then commanding officer along with his telephone number.

'Ever seen him before?' Coleman handed the picture to Knox. Knox hadn't.

Captain Ron Allgood (retired) remembered McCrae as a good soldier; 'An excellent marksman and good at undercover work. He had a great practical aptitude and was disciplined. He could put up with more hardship than most.'

'He'd had the experience,' Knox murmured, under his breath.

'Where would he have served?' Coleman asked.

'All over. We did regular tours in Northern Ireland, Germany and of course we're the Queen's ceremonial regiment.'

'So he'd know London well.'

'Oh yes.'

'Why did he leave?'

'I don't recall a specific reason. A lot left after Tumbledown.'

'He was in the Falklands?'

'Oh yes. McCrae could have made a career of the army, but he got out after eight years. He'd served his time. Possibly in the end he was frustrated that promotion didn't come soon enough.'

'And why was that?'

'There was a question mark over his literacy and numeracy skills. But to be brutally frank, the men didn't much like him either, so he wasn't what you'd call leadership material. He was a loner and I think his colleagues found it hard to completely trust him. Outwardly he could be very charming, but he had an unholy temper, and there was something unpredictable about him, verging on the schizophrenic, although he passed all his psych tests. There were never any explicit disciplinary issues but I always had an impression that he didn't like taking orders. And he had a massive chip on his shoulder about the fact that he was adopted. He was convinced that it put him at a disadvantage.'

So Kenneth McCrae was finding more reasons to be angry with the world.

Coleman faxed through the photograph to Granville Lane with instructions that it should be released to the press immediately in the hope that somebody, somewhere would recognise it. But he was well aware of how much time that would take, when time was a commodity in short supply. It was now more than forty-eight hours since Mariner had disappeared. A picture meant that they could put out a TV appeal for both Mariner and McCrae, but it wasn't hopeful.

Andy Tyrell offered to drive them up to the caravan Clive McCrae had mentioned. Loch Cree was a bleak place, the van parked on its shingle shore alongside the oily water and partly concealed by woodland. Green streaks of mildew down the white panelling helped the caravan to blend into the landscape and looking in through the grimy window revealed no sign of recent habitation. The door was fixed with a rusting, heavy-duty padlock and moss sprouted around the rubber seal. It hadn't been disturbed in a long time. There was nothing more they could do here.

They were cutting it fine for the flight back so, thanking Tyrell, Coleman and Knox headed back to the airport. In his haste Knox took a wrong turning, driving several miles before realising his mistake. Consulting the map they were making their way back to the main road when Coleman, in the passenger seat, shouted 'Stop!' and Knox screeched to a halt in front of a splintered wooden sign. They'd found Keepers Cottage.

'You sure we've got time for this, Boss?' Knox asked.

'We'll make time.'

The building itself lay at the end of a half-mile track,

making Knox wish they'd hired a four-wheel-drive. When the track became impassable, fifty yards short, he killed the engine and they got out to have a closer look. The dwelling was derelict, as Tyrell had said, with four ground-floor rooms beneath a rotting roof, mottled with gaping holes. No electricity, bathroom or running water, just a stone sink in the kitchen, a galvanised metal bath hanging up and a stand-pipe in the yard. A foul-smelling outhouse had a broad wooden bench along one side with holes cut in it that had served as the toilet. Rusty animal traps lay lethally around.

'Christ Almighty,' said Knox. 'They lived here in the sixties and seventies, but this is what you'd expect of a third world country.'

'What's that noise?' Coleman said. They were standing in the yard Knox listened. 'I can't hear anything.'

'It came from that shed, like a moaning sound.'

But the door to the hut was firmly locked, withstanding Knox's efforts to open it.

'Anyone there?' he shouted, but got only silence in return.

'Break it down,' said Coleman, hope beginning to rise. Knox heaved his shoulder against the door and it gave way almost immediately, splintering in several places. It opened onto a dark stone cave, completely empty. At that moment the wind gusted, the timbers of the low roof emitting the keening sound that Coleman had heard before.

'Fuck,' he said, under his breath.

Knox shivered. 'Let's get out of here.'

'It's hopeless,' said Coleman. He was knocking back complimentary peanuts on the flight back to Birmingham, while Knox sat rigid beside him. 'McCrae could be anywhere and we still don't even know who we're looking for.'

'We've got the photo,' Knox said, forcing himself to engage. 'The DI had a feeling that someone was after him. Someone must have seen McCrae.'

'If he hasn't drastically changed his appearance,' Coleman said. 'His CO said that McCrae was good at undercover work. He'll have had good training. He's someone who stays in the shadows. And he could have just gone to ground. If he's already taken care of Tom—' Coleman broke off, with a humourless laugh. 'Strange, isn't it, how we always use such soft euphemistic phrases? If he has and Tom's . . . well . . . then McCrae could just drop out of sight and we'll never find him.'

'But I still don't get it,' Knox said, jerked by a spasm of fear as the plane juddered through a patch of turbulence. 'Why the DI?'

'McCrae must see him as a rival. They're both the illegitimate sons of a Ryland. Clive told us how much Kenneth resented him, that hatred has simply been transferred to Tom. If Tom is right about McCrae, he murdered his birth mother in cold blood. And I'd lay odds that Angus McCrae's death wasn't an accident, either. We're not dealing with a rational individual here. Clive McCrae spoke about his brother's bitterness and anger. Who else is left for him to vent that rage on? And if Mariner has already figured out what we now know, he poses a direct threat to McCrae. It's not looking good.' It was the understatement of the century.

Chapter Twenty-Two

From Birmingham Airport, Coleman returned to Granville Lane to co-ordinate the search while Knox went straight to see Anna.

'I've been throwing up,' she admitted. But Knox could say nothing to reassure her. He showed her the photograph. 'Have you seen this man hanging around at all?'

'No.'

'Has Tom talked about meeting anyone new recently? He might not even know who it is.'

'I can't think of anyone.'

'Anything out of the ordinary happened?' Anna pulled a face, as they both instantly thought of St Martin's. 'Sorry, stupid question.'

'Tom has rented rooms at the cottage,' she said suddenly. 'You know, the ones you and Jenny had.'

In a different age, thought Knox. 'Who's his lodger?'

'A guy called Bill Dyson.'

'When did he move in?'

'Just before Christmas. But according to Tom he's never there.'

Knox reined in a ripple of anticipation, remaining outwardly calm. 'What do you know about him?'

'Not much. He's from up north somewhere, and he sells burglar alarms.'

He was working in security, Clive McCrae had said.

Knox had assumed as a security guard, but Christ, it could be him. 'You've never met him?' Knox asked.

'No, but the letting agent has.'

As it was, they didn't have to find Roy Shipley to show him the photograph. He'd already seen the appeal on the local news and had contacted Granville Lane. 'The man you're looking for with Mr Mariner is the one who's renting rooms in his house.'

'Kenneth McCrae?'

'He doesn't call himself that, I know him as Bill Dyson, and his hair is longer than in your picture, but it's him all right.'

'Could you come in to the station?'

When he arrived, Shipley was shown up to Coleman's office, where Knox waited impatiently.

'I don't understand,' Shipley said. 'Dyson gave me references, showed me pictures of his family—'

'He made it up,' Coleman said, simply. 'Is there anything else you can tell us about him?'

'His car. He drives an Audi estate, silver grey, and he ran a burglar alarm business called Apex Security. I have his card.' Shipley produced the business card from his wallet. 'I rang the number before I came here, just to make sure I wasn't making some terrible mistake. Mr McCrae hasn't worked there for years. And he didn't own the business, he was a sales rep. According to them, not even a particularly good one.'

'Thank you, Mr Shipley,' Coleman said, reassuringly. 'You've been a great help.'

They were just in time to get out an appeal for the silver Audi on the local early evening news, and meanwhile Knox joined the team that was searching Mariner's house, the last place they could be certain that he'd been.

'We've found some blood spatters,' a SOCO showed him the dark brown stains on the step by the front door.

'He'd cut his hand,' Knox said, at the same time knowing that the cut had long healed.

297

Other forensics officers were going over every inch of the house, every nook and cranny brightly lit with spotlights and Knox had to step around them. Apart from that, the place looked perfectly normal, the post even neatly arranged on the hall table. Breaking into the second floor flat they'd found it empty, the only thing Dyson had left were drawings and a couple of books about the canal. 'It's as if he's never been here,' said Knox, but he arranged for SOCO to sweep it anyway.

The drum beats were going in Mariner's head again, the death knell. He'd no idea how much time had passed since Dyson had been here. His body had been still for so long that it was easier now not to move at all, though occasionally he was seized by attacks of uncontrollable shaking. He had a raging thirst, his mouth so dry that every so often he had to peel his tongue from the roof of his mouth. He couldn't see her, but at one point he was convinced that Anna was there beside him, telling him how stupid he'd been, as if he needed that pointing out. Just lately he'd been coming and going so much that no one would miss him for days. And now he was going to die of exposure, starvation or both before anyone even knew he was missing. And he hadn't a clue where he was. He had no idea for how long he'd initially been unconscious or how far Dyson had brought him, even if he was still in the UK. He could already be in Cyprus, except that he didn't think it would be this cold. Did they have a winter in Cyprus? He thought of warm beaches and sunshine and was overcome by a sudden drowsiness . . .

The call came in shortly after the news item, a sighting of Dyson's car parked only streets away from Mariner's home. Coleman spoke to the caller, a resident living nearby. 'Is it still there?' he asked.

'I can see it from where I'm standing, under the street light,' the man told him.

'You're sure it's the same vehicle?'

'I noted the registration the first time I saw it, in case I was going to have to report it as abandoned, but then it went. A couple of days later it came back again.'

Knox met Jack Coleman and a couple of uniformed officers down there. The car was parked within walking distance of Mariner's house. 'Meaning that there were times when Dyson could have been there without wanting anyone to know,' Coleman said. 'Stalking Mariner from there would be a piece of cake, and Mariner would have had no idea it was happening.'

Breaking into the vehicle they found a folder in the glove compartment and examination in the beam of the powerful torch revealed printouts of an Earls Court hotel, a list of numbers; Mariner's mobile, Anna's number and the invitation to Jack Coleman's retirement. There was a sheaf of newspaper cuttings about the Rylands and the press photo of Mariner emerging from the bombing, along with features from previous years, including the arrest of the teacher Brian Goodway for the murders of Ricky Skeet and Yasmin Akhtar. It was the information McCrae had used to find Mariner in the first place.

'But where the hell is McCrae now?' Knox demanded, looking around him as if the man might suddenly emerge from the shadows.

'He must have another vehicle, or he's hired something,' Coleman surmised.

'He's taking a hell of a risk.'

'Maybe that doesn't matter, because he's long gone by now. And he has no idea that we're onto him. Get uniform to take his photograph around local car hire firms. Get people at home if needed.'

'And what about DI Mariner?'

It was the question they'd both been avoiding. If McCrae had made his escape, he'd be unlikely to encumber himself with a prisoner.

'He needs Mariner silenced,' said Coleman, calmly. 'He has no reason to keep him alive.'

'But if he's not in the house, or here in the car, where is he?'

'We know that Mariner came back to the house yesterday afternoon. If McCrae was lying in wait, where would be the easiest place to dispose of a body in the immediate vicinity?' Like clockwork they both turned in the direction of the canal. 'We need to get some divers down here. And make sure Anna stays away. She mustn't know.'

Tony Knox was becoming a liability, Coleman realised. It was close to midnight and they were both on the freezing canalside under a dome of floodlights, watching and waiting as the small team of divers began their gruesome task. Periodically, Knox leaned over, yelling orders, even though he wasn't in charge. Only a matter of time before either he fell into the icy water, or got punched in the face by an exasperated diver.

Coleman walked over to him. 'Why don't you go inside and check on forensics. Phone the labs and see if they've come up with anything. You're not helping here.'

For a moment Coleman thought Knox was going to put up a fight, but after a moment's hesitation the constable did as instructed.

Inside Mariner's house, Knox used his mobile to put a call through to the labs. He tried the vehicle workshop first, but it was too soon for any fingerprints.

'We've found something of interest though.'

'What?'

'Two dog hairs from a Border terrier.'

Eleanor Ryland had a dog, Fliss Fitzgibbon had said so, which would mean that McCrae might have been to see Eleanor Ryland, too. What were the chances that he had murdered her as well? The possibility did nothing to reassure Knox. Ringing off he next tried the central lab who had taken numerous samples from the house. 'Have you found anything?'

'Nothing conclusive,' was the frustrating reply. 'But we found something odd. I took some residue from a footprint on the rug in the hall. You can probably see it if you look.' Knox went back to the hall. Sure enough there was a faded print on the beige runner, halfway along. 'It's going out of the house,' Knox observed. Coleman appeared, giving a brief shake of the head to indicate that nothing had been found, waiting while Knox finished the call.

'Yes, strange in itself,' the SOCO was saying. 'And what I assumed to be soil turns out to be coal dust.'

'He's got a woodburner,' Knox said.

'That's the point. It burns wood, not coal. May be nothing of course, but I just found it puzzling.' He rang off and Knox relayed the conversation to Coleman.

'Coal dust?' he said. 'So where the hell would it come from?'

'This cottage used to service barges,' said Knox. 'I remember Mariner telling me that once. The barges would have burned coal on their stoves.'

'So there must be a coal store somewhere. But where?'

'McCrae had the plans to the cottage in his flat.' Knox ran up the stairs, two at a time, grabbed the plans and was back, breathless in less than a minute. Spreading the papers out on the table it took a few seconds to make sense of the drawings, but then Knox saw it.

'It's right under our feet,' he said, calmly. 'There's a cellar.'

Coleman mustered all those remaining in the house. 'Check inside and out. We're looking for the entrance to a cellar.'

It wasn't easy. A circuit of the exterior revealed nothing that would lead them underground, and all the interior doors opened onto storage space, including the deep cupboard under the stairs, which was piled high with boxes of papers and miscellaneous junk. But it was while flashing

301

a torch around it that Knox noticed the drag of fingerprints in the light layer of dust covering one of the boxes. Pulling out some of the cartons into the hall allowed him to get a better view of the cupboard's interior walls, and there he saw the hinges and bar-catch of a door.

'It's here! Help me clear this junk out!' he yelled, and was immediately inundated.

On the edges of Mariner's consciousness the pounding had become a constant, loud and insistent, Mariner's pulse racing and signalling the end. It was to be the last thing he heard. Was this how Chloe Evans' last minutes had been? There was a deafening crack, and a blinding glare burned his eyes as he strained to focus on the dazzling shaft of light that had appeared, leading him away to the other place. Funny though, he never expected St Peter to have a scouse accent, nor that the guardian angel's first words, with a catch in his voice, would be, 'Fuckin' hell. Look at the state of you.'

After so long in a vacuum, the activity that followed over-whelmed Mariner's senses, so that he wanted to bellow for them to go away and leave him alone. But his mouth was so dry that he could hardly speak. Tony Knox brought him some water, which he gulped down greedily and promptly threw back up all over Knox's trousers.

It took half an hour for the fire crew to sever the chain that bound him to the wall, and more time to cut off the ankle-cuff, exposing his raw skin. During that time para-medics stretchered him and attached a drip. As it all went on around him Mariner drifted in and out of consciousness, hardly able to distinguish what was real and what was in his throbbing head. Knox was talking to him, his face close by. 'McCrae's gone,' he said. 'Did he tell you where?'

'McCrae?' Mariner murmured, his tongue flopping clumsily in his mouth.

'Dyson's real name. It was Bill Dyson who did this to you.'

'Mm.' It was easier to nod.

'Dyson seems to have been an arbitrary choice.'

Mariner shook his head. '... Diana's son,' he slurred. '... obvious.' Drifting off again, he rallied himself. 'Cyprus,' he said.

'That's where he's going?'

Mariner blinked a negative. '... not yet. He's waiting ... to contest the will ... lying low.'

'Loch Cree,' said Knox enigmatically, and then he was gone.

Later Mariner learned that, taken by surprise, Bill Dyson had come quietly. Shortly before dawn local police officers including an armed response unit, had surrounded the caravan on the loch. Inside they'd found, among other things, a laptop with the necessary program to manage the tracking devices on Ryland's car and on the Volvo.

Day 1

Mariner opened his eyes onto a white world, everything transformed from dark to light, but as his eyes focused he could distinguish a face looking into his. Anna.

She smiled and squeezed his hand. 'Hello, you.'

With effort, Mariner smiled back, but, then, from nowhere, his chest heaved and great wracking sobs convulsed his body. Wrapping him in her arms, Anna held him tight to her. 'It's all right. You can let it out. You're safe now.'

'I should have told you,' Mariner said, when the storm had passed.

'And when did this profundity occur?'

'The first time I woke up in the cellar.'

'Bit late then, really.'

'You could say that.'

Before she went she helped him shave.

'If I had a mirror I could do it myself.'

'You're too scary for a mirror. We've put it away.'

303

Tony Knox came to see him, bringing copies of *The Great Outdoors* and a couple of bottles of Sam Smith's. 'They're bound to let me drink that in here,' Mariner said. 'But thanks.'

'So when did you know it was Dyson?'

'I'm not sure. I remembered Dyson talking about his "chosen family". It seemed an odd phrase to use. And then he came, while I was in the cellar. He came to tell me he was going and of course I recognised his voice. He confessed it all. Is there enough to charge him?'

'Plenty. He was stupid enough to hang on to the murder weapon. The barrel markings match the casings on the bullets recovered at Cheslyn Woods. They found dog hairs in his car, too.'

'It could be cross contamination,' said Mariner. 'He gave me a lift once.'

'Maybe, but we've got a sighting of his car near Eleanor's house on that Saturday afternoon, someone sitting in it. A neighbour saw it but thought he was just another reporter. She came forward after the TV appeal.'

'So I'm off the hook.'

'You were never really on it, Boss.'

'I don't know why it took me so long to work it out. Diana's "illness" came up time after time, and all along people were telling me how much Geoffrey and Diana Ryland had in common, but I couldn't see what it was. I couldn't link those two things together; him dealing with the guilt of having abandoned me, while his wife grieved for the loss of her child.'

'You got there in the end.'

'Only just. And if you and Coleman hadn't realised what was going on—'

'It was a joint effort. Would have helped if you'd told someone the full story of course, but we were lucky to be able to piece it together, with help from Anna, Dave Flynn and Fliss Fitzgibbon.' Knox reached into his pocket and produced a letter. 'She left you this, by the way.'

'She's gone back to Switzerland?'

'Couple of days ago. Oh, and bad news on Alecsander Lucca.'

'The extradition's been turned down?'

'Worse that that. Lucca was shot dead by a sniper while they were moving him from one jail to another.'

'Is Charlie Glover any closer to identifying Madeleine?'

Knox shook his head. 'And now we might never know. Some you win, some you lose eh?'

'How's Selina doing?' Mariner asked.

Knox shifted uncomfortably. 'She's moved in with her mother for a while. Things were going too fast. It was getting a bit,' he groped for the right word, settling on, 'intense.' He seemed about to say more, but stopped. 'Anyway, I'd best get back. The new boss is in, so got to make a good impression.'

'What's she like?'

'Haven't had the pleasure yet.'

'Let me know when you do.'

'Sure. You're looking better now anyway.'

'Thanks.'

But as Knox left, Mariner couldn't help wondering what it was about the way he looked. It couldn't be that bad. There had to be a mirror somewhere, maybe in the bedside cupboard. He was reaching down, conscious, but unconcerned that his hospital gown gaped, exposing his bare backside to the fresh air. With the blinds pulled shut in his private side-ward there was no one to see.

'Inspector Mariner?' The unfamiliar woman's voice was low and husky, with an understandable trace of amusement. Mariner shot back up, hastily covering himself, and came face to face with a tall, slender woman, olive skinned with thick dark hair. She was impeccably dressed, and barely suppressing a smile.

'Sexy,' thought Mariner.

She offered him a hand. 'I'm Davina Sharp, your new DCI. I wanted to come and introduce myself, see how you're doing.'

'Bollocks!' thought Mariner, but recovering, he shook hands with her. 'You saw my most attractive feature first,' he said, brazening it out. 'Since everyone keeps telling me how rough I look.'

'And how are you feeling?'

'Better.'

'You've been through a major ordeal.'

Mariner allowed himself a modest shrug.

'You're quite the caped crusader,' she went on, 'and lucky to get away with it, from what I hear. My view is that maverick detectives should stay where they belong – on TV.' She smiled, warmly. So this wasn't so much a social call as an early warning. 'Crimes are most effectively solved through teamwork, and officers who decide to go it alone, in my experience, put themselves and their colleagues at risk. I do hope this is a conversation we won't have to repeat.' She smiled again.

'Ma'am.'

'Well, I'm glad that you're on the mend, and look forward to having you back at Granville Lane. I expect you can't wait.'

'Specially now, thought Mariner. 'Yes Ma'am,' he said.

Anna thought it hilarious when he told her about it that evening.

'Great start,' she said, 'flashing your arse at the new boss. Will it cramp your style, this teamwork stuff?' she asked.

'What do you think?' Mariner said. 'Some people are team players, and some are not.'

'No guesses which camp you fall into. It might not be as bad as you think.'

'It's serious enough for her to come here and lecture me on my sick bed. Maybe it's time to stop getting so hung up on work.'

Anna brightened. 'Really?'

'And what would you think about adopting?'

'Adopting?'

'I'd like to take on Nelson.'

'We'd need plenty of space to walk him.'

'I know. And I'm not discounting kids,' he said quickly.

'I'm glad to hear it.'

'But one thing at a time, eh?'

'One thing at a time.'

Worm in the Bud
Chris Collett

In Birmingham a local journalist is found dead in his home. A puncture wound in his arm a testimony to his death by lethal injection, the cryptic note by his side: 'no more', seems at first to suggest suicide but Detective Inspector Tom Mariner has learned to take nothing at face value. There is something a little too staged about events, especially as just that evening Mariner had witnessed Edward Barham pick up a prostitute in a bar he was frequenting. As the police investigate the house further they discover there is another witness to events at 34 Clarendon Avenue. Barham's younger brother, Jamie, is found in a cupboard under the stairs. It seems likely that Jamie Barham had witnessed his brother's killing but his severe autism has left him without the means to communicate what he has seen ...

Mariner is determined to build enough of a relationship with Jamie to get to the truth. And the fact that this means spending time with Anna Barham, Jamie's new – and reluctant – guardian, is no great hardship. But is Edward's death related to his recent investigations into a local crimelord? Or is there something else, something that only Jamie can tell them – if he so chooses ...

Praise for *The Worm in the Bud*:

'This first novel comes from a writer with twenty years experience of working with adults with learning disabilities and her depiction of Jamie and his effect on those who care for him rings true ... While lonely Mariner is immediately engaging and his sexual vulnerability and lack of confidence adds both humour and poignancy. Collett sustains the intrigue – we want to know who done what and why – and is a writer with promise.' Cath Staincliffe, author and series creator of TV's *Blue Murder*

Blood of the Innocents
Chris Collett

When two teenagers go missing on the same day on Mariner's patch, it seems to be nothing more than a co-incidence. Leaving aside their age and disappearance, the two have little in common. Yasmin Akram is the talented grammar school educated daughter of devout Muslim professionals. Ricky Skeet disappears after storming out of his council house after a row with his mother's latest boyfriend.

Mariner knows Ricky's mother from his days in uniform, so he is less than happy when his superiors – bowing to media pressure – take him off the Skeet case and reassign him to the more politically sensitive investigation. The press – and his bosses – seem convinced that Yasmin's disappearance is a racially motivated abduction, especially since the Akrams have found themselves the target of the far right and a prominent white supremacist group. Working with Asian liaison officer Jamilla Begum on the more high profile case, Mariner soon discovers that the picture of Yasmin her school-friends paint is far cry from her parents' claim that she is a total innocent ...

Killing for England
Iain McDowall

Chief Inspector Jacobson and DS Kerr had been on leave
when the body of a young black man, Darren McGee, had
been fished out of the River Crow. The autopsy had pointed
to suicide by drowning. But now Darren's cousin, Paul
Shaw, is in town: a top-notch investigative journalist with
an axe to grind and a claim that Darren had really been the
victim of a racially-motivated murder.

Jacobson isn't convinced. But when Paul Shaw turns up
as dead and as terminally-wet as his cousin, Jacobson and
Kerr are faced with a baffling double-murder to investigate.
And a dangerous confrontation lies ahead with the murky
world of the Far Right.

Praise for Iain McDowall:
'has a vivid sense of place ... Crowby becomes more than
a fictional town: it's almost a state of mind. Moreover its
inhabitants are wonderfully characterised' ANDREW
TAYLOR
'a lean, impressive debut ... Kerr and Jacobson are a pleasure to meet and who offer hoped for more rich reading in
future additions to the series' WASHINGTON POST

A Cursed Inheritance
Kate Ellis

The brutal massacre of the Harford family at Potwoolstan Hall in Devon in 1985 shocked the country and passed into local folklore. And when a journalist researching the case is murdered twenty years later, the horror is reawakened. Sixteenth century Potwoolstan Hall, now a New Age healing centre, is reputed to be cursed because of the crimes of its builder, and it seems that inheritance of evil lives on as DI Wesley Peterson is faced with his most disturbing case yet.

As more people die violently, Wesley needs to discover why a young woman has transformed a dolls house into a miniature reconstruction of the massacre scene. And could the solution to his case lie across the Atlantic Ocean, in the ruined remains of an early English settlement in Virginia USA?

When the truth is finally revealed, it turns out to be as horrifying as it is dangerous.

Praise for Kate Ellis:
'a beguiling author who interweaves past and present. Like its predecessor ... the book works well on both levels'
The Times

How to Seduce a Ghost
Hope McIntyre

Although she loves her boyfriend Tommy, Lee is suffering from commitment phobia because, as a ghost-writer, she values her privacy above all else ... and she can't bear his mess. At the same time, though, she doesn't really like living alone in her big, creaky old house in Notting Hill. But whilst Lee tries to remain in denial about the state of her crumbling home, a neighbour is suddenly killed in a fire, and it looks like arson.

Lee's latest commission, ghosting the autobiography of a soap opera star, seems to offer her an escape from her problems at home. Until she meets her subject's smoulderingly sexy manager, and finds herself compulsively attracted to him. But then Lee is drawn into a murder investigation as there is a second fire and another murder closer to home. As her home deteriorates further and her precious privacy comes under increasing pressure from all sides, could it be that Lee herself is in danger?

Praise for *How to Seduce a Ghost*:

'Smart and hugely enjoyable' Elizabeth Buchan